LONG LIVE THE QUEEN

# LONG
# LIVE
## THE QUEEN

ELLEN EMERSON WHITE

Feiwel and Friends   New York

For my editor, Jean Feiwel, who has always been swell.

A FEIWEL AND FRIENDS BOOK
An Imprint of Macmillan

LONG LIVE THE QUEEN. Copyright © 2008 by Ellen Emerson White. All rights reserved.
Printed in the United States of America. For information, address Feiwel and Friends,
175 Fifth Avenue, New York, N.Y. 10010.

Library of Congress Cataloging-in-Publication Data

White, Ellen Emerson.
    Long live the queen / Ellen Emerson White.—1st Feiwel and Friends ed.
        p.    cm
    Summary: The President's daughter is the victim of kidnapping by terrorists.
    ISBN-13: 978-0-312-37490-7
    ISBN-10: 0-312-37490-9
    [1. Kidnapping—Fiction. 2. Terrorism—Fiction.] I. Title.
    PZ7.W58274Lo 2008
    [Fic]—dc22
    2008007124

Originally published in the United States by Scholastic Press.

Feiwel and Friends logo designed by Filomena Tuosto

First Feiwel and Friends Edition: August 2008

10  9  8  7  6  5  4  3  2  1

www.feiwelandfriends.com

# LONG LIVE THE QUEEN

# 1

IT WAS ALMOST dark, but Meg kept her sunglasses on because they reminded her of skiing. Despite the fact that it was May, and she was holding a tennis racquet. Her theory had always been—when in doubt, delude oneself.

She lowered her racquet, having served the last in another series of ten balls. A gardener near the fence lifted seven fingers, and she nodded her thanks. One nice thing about living in the White House was that there was always someone around to call lines. She picked up the jug of water she kept on the baseline and drank some, studying the other side of the court. Seven out of ten. Not bad. Then again, *eight* would be even better. She put the jug down and reached into her ball basket.

Leaning back to serve, she noticed that everyone around the court—her Secret Service agents, National Park Service people, a couple of reporters—was standing much straighter, indicating that the President was somewhere nearby.

Meg grinned. "Is it my imagination, or is there like, a head of state behind me?" she asked without turning around.

Her mother laughed. "The serve looks good."

"I don't know, I'm trying to get more on it." Meg walked back to where her mother was standing, the number of agents—and general onlookers—having swelled considerably. "Do you feel like hitting a few?" she asked, already pretty sure of the answer.

Her mother looked down at her dress and high heels. "It would lack elegance, Meg."

Meg nodded. It had been quite a while since her mother had had enough energy to play. People were actually only supposed to wear white soled shoes on the court—but, she had a sneaking suspicion that no one would have the nerve to call the President out on that one. Then, she checked the bottom of her sneakers, suddenly noticing that the soles were white, grey and black—and no one had bugged *her* about it, either.

"Besides," her mother said, "I expect your father and brothers are waiting for us."

Meg looked up at the sky to try and guess what time it was—not that she was exactly Nature Girl—then remembered that she had on a watch. She hated watches, but apparently hers was some kind of security thing, because the Secret Service had requested that she keep it on at all times. She had never wanted to pursue the issue further, and even though she'd been wearing it for well over a year now, she still wasn't used to it.

"High time for dinner," her mother said.

Past seven. "Yeah," Meg said, and leaned down to pick up some of her tennis balls.

Her mother bent gracefully for one as Meg scooped up six or seven, using her sweatshirt front as a sort of pouch. "Is this quality time we have going here?" she asked, dropping her balls into the yellow metal basket.

Her mother picked up another one, holding it with her index finger and thumb. "That appears to be the case, yes."

"Madam President?" one of her aides said, standing near the entrance to the courts.

Her mother sighed, handing Meg the ball. "Excuse me."

Meg watched her stride over and confer with the aide—as well as Winnie, the deputy chief of staff, who had just shown up, recognizing the Presidential expression of interested concern even from behind. Her mother sure knew how to walk. It was too dignified to be a sweep, but too fast to be stately. The influence of too damned many Katharine Hepburn movies, Meg's father had always said.

"Statuesque" was the word the mainstream media was inclined to use. Meg just liked to sing "Twentieth Century Fox" at her.

Her brother Steven—who was almost fourteen—either swaggered or slouched; her brother Neal—who was nine—bounced, mostly. Her father—well, he just walked. Occasionally, he hurried. Meg, personally, would either slink or slog. Sometimes, to drive her parents crazy, she and Steven would shuffle. They were big on scuffing, too.

"Pretty cool," her mother said, unexpectedly next to her again.

Meg stopped in the middle of her tennis racquet guitar solo. Morrison and the guys would have to wait. "Um, just singing."

"So I heard," her mother said.

Meg flushed and took off her sunglasses, going over to pick up the rest of her tennis balls.

When she was finished, they walked towards the White House— with the Secret Service in tow, of course—along the cement oval leading to the South Portico, passing commemorative trees like the Jimmy Carter Cedar of Lebanon and the Lyndon B. Johnson Willow Oak. Their dog, Kirby, invariably used the George W. Bush Cutleaf Silver Maple. Steven had encouraged this.

In June, there was supposed to be a ceremony during which her mother was going to plant a Japanese Tree Lilac, and Meg was hoping that it would be scheduled after school was out—mostly, so that she could have the fun of watching the President incompetently wield a shovel during the ground-breaking.

It felt as though they were walking unusually slowly, and Meg glanced over at her mother. "You look tired."

Her mother shrugged. "Busy day, that's all."

Maybe. Meg kept looking at her, noticing the slight hunch to her left side. Since—well, Meg tried to think of it as "the accident," because the phrase "assassination attempt" made her sick—anyway, even though it had been over seven months, her mother was often in obvious pain, and almost always exhausted. "Um, how do you feel?" Meg asked.

Her mother's posture changed, the hunch disappearing. "Fine."

Meg nodded—although she didn't buy it for a second.

"So," her mother said, gesturing back towards the tennis court. "You're certainly practicing non-stop these days."

"I don't know." Meg grinned. "Did you read *Save Me the Waltz?*"

Her mother smiled, too. "It's my assumption that you're hoping to play at school this fall?"

She was hoping, actually, to start signing up for a few USTA/Mid-Atlantic junior tournaments and see if she could build a decent ranking. Yeah, she'd have to go to lower-level open tournaments first, but there seemed to be several L5 tournaments within easy driving distance every weekend, and if she won a couple of them, she could move up to—"Um, yeah," she said. "Sort of." Although her parents had been very strongly pushing her to go to Harvard, with Yale and Princeton as fallback choices—getting *in* to college wasn't exactly an issue for the President's daughter, even if she were a verifiable cretin—she had decided on Williams, instead. Small, very academic, surrounded by Berkshire ski resorts. Her kind of place.

The skiing, anyway.

"Did you know," her mother said conversationally, "that professional tennis players change their clothes *right* in the *middle* of the locker room?" She paused. "In front of *everyone?*"

As arguments went, that one wasn't bad. "Oh, you're just trying to scare me," Meg said.

Her mother shrugged. "I have it on excellent authority."

"I wouldn't worry," Meg said. "It's not like I'm good enough." She carefully didn't add a "yet," but her mother's look at her was so penetrating that she must have heard it, anyway.

"Well," her mother said, and nodded hello to the Marine guards on duty, as they went through the South Entrance.

For that matter, Meg nodded, too—but they were so busy being alert that they probably didn't notice.

She followed her mother through the Diplomatic Reception Room to the Ground Floor Corridor, which was red-carpeted, with an impressive series of arches forming the ceiling, and portraits of First Ladies on the walls. It was going to be pretty funny to have her father—who always looked uncomfortable in pictures under the best of circumstances—hanging there someday.

Her father's press secretary, Preston, was coming down the hall with a couple aides, heading towards the East Wing, and he stopped short, giving her mother a crisp salute.

Her mother smiled, and returned it. "At ease, Mr. Fielding."

"Thank you, Madam Prez." He winked at Meg. "Get that serve percentage over eighty?"

Here and there. "Almost," Meg said.

"Good going." He touched his own throat, where a green silk tie was knotted, indicating the white towel around her neck. "Sort of a fashion risk."

"*Everyone* in Milan is wearing these," Meg said. And most of the haute couture houses were thinking of coming on board with the style, too.

Preston laughed, continuing on his way with his assistants.

Meg watched him go. Official job aside, what he really was, was her whole family's best friend—and about as cool as it was possible to be. He and her father made an incongruous pair—Preston, the sleek, suave young black guy; her father, very traditional and WASPy. "Is he like, your favorite person in the world who isn't related to you?" she asked.

"Yes," her mother said, and stepped into the private elevator. "Going up?"

"Oh." If she were alone, Meg would definitely have taken the stairs—in lieu of more interesting enemies, she had always made a practice of fighting calories—but, with her mother being tired and all—"I mean, yeah," she said.

They rode up to the third floor—her family spent a lot of time hanging out in the solarium, which had its own small kitchenette, the biggest television in the Residence, an extensive library of music and movies out in the main corridor, and some extremely spectacular views.

Steven and Neal were on one of the couches, watching an old *Simpsons* episode, since they were both entirely addicted to the show—and, as it happened, Meg was pretty fond of it herself. In fact, she and her brothers wasted so much time slouching in front of reruns—and Red Sox games—that her parents found it rather unnerving, and often tried to limit their viewing time, with absolutely no success. And her father was not terribly convincing on the subject, since he was such a big Boston fan, that he had been known to do things like leave Kennedy Center events early, in order to catch the last few innings.

As a rule, Meg was more inclined to watch particular *networks* than specific shows—Comedy Central, The E! Network, ESPN—but, she was also secretly quite fond of the internal White House feed, which showed live speeches, press briefings, Rose Garden ceremonies, and the like, and often watched it for hours on the sly.

Her father was sitting at the big glass table where, once in a very great while, they would do unexpectedly ordinary things like play Monopoly, or have low-key meals, although her parents disapproved of eating in a room that had a television in it. But, they *did* make exceptions for the Academy Awards, and playoff games, and such.

"Good day at school?" her father asked.

Meg glanced up. "I'm sorry, what?"

He smiled, putting down his Sam Adams. When he wasn't being the First Gentleman, he always drank straight from the bottle. "Did you have a nice day at school?"

"Oh. Yeah. Did you?" Meg shook her head. She really had to make more of an effort to pay attention. "Have a nice day, I mean."

"Very nice," he said, smiling more.

Having said hello to Steven and Neal, her mother was standing behind her father now, her hands on his shoulders.

"Long day?" her father asked.

"*Very* long," her mother said. "And not over yet."

He nodded, reaching up to cover her right hand with his, and sensing that there was a hug or a kiss or something coming from that, Meg went over to sit on the couch.

"Don't you guys ever get tired of this?" she asked, indicating the television.

"Nope." Steven yawned. "Josh called and said for us to give you a big"—he made a smacking sound with his lips—"from him."

Neal laughed, making his own kissing sound.

Since she and Josh had officially been "just friends" for over a month now—and were still pretty self-conscious about the whole thing, that exact message was unlikely. "What did he really say?" Meg asked.

Steven shrugged. "Hi."

Neal made another smacking noise.

Meg looked at them, then at herself. What a motley little set of children. Three pairs of sweatpants, three pairs of irregularly tied sneakers—theirs high-top Nikes, hers Adidas Barricades, and three sweatshirts—one that said Williams, a New England Patriots one, and Neal wearing an outgrown green hoodie of Steven's. And it wouldn't kill any of them to go do a little hair-brushing.

Her mother might have been worn out, but she looked predictably elegant in her tan dress, and her hair and make-up were perfect. Her father was distinguished—but dull—in a grey suit, white Oxford shirt, and striped tie. She and Steven took after her mother: dark hair, blue eyes, very high cheekbones. Neal, like her father, had lighter brown hair, and always looked as though he was about to smile. She and her mother and Steven were grinners—she and Steven, somewhat more raffishly.

"Thank you," her mother was saying into the telephone. "We'll be down directly." She hung up. "Do the three of you want to go get washed up for dinner?"

"No," Neal said, and giggled.

"Hell, no," Steven said.

Their father frowned at them. "Go get washed up."

"So, wait." Meg looked from her parents to her brothers. "Am I like, the swing vote here?"

Her parents shook their heads.

When it was just the five of them, they almost always ate in the private Presidential Dining Room on the second floor. The furnishings were, so Meg was told, American Federal—which seemed to mean mahogany—and the room had the usual dramatic White House chandelier. The antique wallpaper was blue, with scenes from the American Revolution painted on it, and none of them liked it much.

"So. How was practice, Steven?" their mother asked, coming back into the room after her third low-voiced conference with aides out in the West Sitting Hall.

"Okay," he said, through a mouthful of roast beef. "I was mostly shagging, because Coach wants me to pitch on Friday."

Their father narrowed his eyes. "You went six innings yesterday."

Steven shrugged. "So, he had me taking it easy today. Can you pass me the carrots, Meg?"

Meg helped herself, then handed the dish across the table to him. The White House butlers preferred to do all of the serving themselves, but had figured out, early on, that her family was much more relaxed whenever they got the chance to be at least a *little* bit normal. The butlers had become extremely skilled at replenishing their food and drinks so discreetly that, most of the time, Meg almost forgot they were there.

Although no one really talked about it, her parents weren't very happy about Steven playing—the Secret Service had advised against it. After her mother had been shot, all of their security had gotten much tighter, and because tennis courts were so exposed, Meg had had to drop off the team at school. For the same reason, the Secret Service hadn't wanted Steven to play baseball—either at school, or in his league, but he had gotten so upset that her parents had finally had to allow it. Much to Meg's relief, their security in general had relaxed a little in the last few months, going back to its pre-shooting level. Which, God knows, was intense enough. She had no intention of permanently giving up competitive tennis, but she wasn't looking forward to the discussion about it with her parents. They were beginning to drop not-so-subtle hints, but so far, she had mostly managed to avoid the subject—and predictable confrontation.

"Your mother asked you a question," her father said, sounding amused.

"She did?" Meg looked at her mother. "You did?"

Her mother grinned. "I did."

"Oh." Meg shook her head. "I'm sorry, I'm just—I mean, lately—I don't know."

"It's called senioritis," her father said.

Or post-AP-exams exhaustion. No doubt, the *DSM* would soon recognize PAEE as a legitimate phenomenon—and high-strung students everywhere would be overmedicated accordingly.

"No way," Steven said. "She's always been like this."

Neal laughed. "*Always.*"

"Yeah, well," Meg served herself quite a large baked potato, "wait until I go away to school. You guys'll be like, crying all the time, because you miss me so much."

"No way," Steven said. "We'll have parties every day."

"Wakes, more likely." Her cat, Vanessa, had come in to sit behind her chair, and Meg slipped her a piece of roast beef, her father lifting his eyebrows at her. "I mean," she straightened up, "you won't have anyone to tell you swell jokes, or help keep the country running smoothly, or explain words you don't understand—"

Her parents laughed.

"Yeah," Steven said. "And all the flies and bugs that follow you around'll leave."

Meg nodded. "Well, *of course* they're coming with me. I wouldn't go anywhere without—"

"One bad thing," Steven said, grabbing the salt shaker out from underneath Neal's hand. "We won't be able to get any good drugs anymore."

"Told you you'd miss me," Meg said.

"Well, goodness knows I'll miss the dinner repartee." Their mother nodded her thanks as Felix, one of the butlers, poured fresh coffee into her cup. "Meg, have you gotten any further in your thoughts about what to wear to the Prom?"

To which, yeah, she and Josh were still going. As—pals. Chums. Compatriots. "I'm going to make something out of my curtains," Meg said, managing—just barely—not to laugh at her own humor. The clothes-making scenes in *Gone with the Wind* and *The Sound of Music* were probably her two favorite movie jokes ever. And the time Carol Burnett wore the curtain dress with the rod still in it.

"Is that a no?" her mother asked.

Oh, the President was quick. Very quick. "Yeah," Meg said. "It's a no."

# 2

SHE SAT IN her Secret Service car the next morning, trying to finish her English homework, typing wildly about conscience and conflict—and just generally being so god-damn thematic and ponderous that she was boring the hell out of herself.

"Try and hit red lights," she said to her agents.

Chet, who was driving, laughed; Dennis didn't. Par for the course. She had her regular detail of agents, including two who served as fairly traditional bodyguards, and several others who rode in the lead or follow cars, manned the command centers and holding rooms, and did advance work and logistics—and whatever else happened to come up during a given eight-hour period. They were assigned the same group of agents for six weeks at a time— and then, the agents would usually go off to do two weeks of various training cycles before resuming their assignments. She was on her third detail since her mother had taken office, because every six months or so, the Secret Service would rotate in a new group. Steven and Neal were both actually on their *fifth* details, because apparently, the Secret Service was convinced that younger protectees were inclined to get too attached to their agents. Since Neal mostly just ambled around pleasantly in his own little world, and Steven *hated* being guarded so much that he didn't always cooperate, she didn't think it was an issue for either of them.

For her part, she was looking forward to her next detail, because while Chet was fun, and most of the others were friendly and tried not to be intrusive, Dennis was too damn intense—so attentive that he made her nervous.

"Sorry, Meg," Chet said, slowing to make the turn onto the

school grounds. They always varied the entrances and exits, and to-day was apparently a parking garage day. "Did my best."

Meg saved the document to her flash-drive, and then closed her laptop—which her parents had paid for in full, but had been issued by the NSA or DIA or something, because it was extra-light and secure and high-tech, and *very* cool. "I can probably finish up during homeroom." She opened her knapsack to put the computer away. "In the end, we are all alone. Each, our own judge." She looked at Chet. "What do you think?"

He laughed.

"The most frightening demons may, in fact, be within ourselves," she said.

He shook his head, pulling in behind the lead car. "Your poor teacher."

Who had given them the damn essay assignment in the first place and was, therefore, ineligible for sympathy. "Exploring the hidden darkness can be—" Meg unbuckled her seatbelt and got out of the car, not sure what it could be. She swung her knapsack over her shoulder. "Revealing." She frowned. Illuminating? No, too obvious.

Her agents didn't like her to stand around when she didn't have to, so she headed directly into the school—Dennis, as always, a little too close behind her. She walked more slowly, hoping that he would back off, although he almost never did.

Seeing Josh on his way down one of the side halls, she stopped to wait for him. Sometimes, to give him grief, she called him Mr. Shetland, and today was no exception.

"Nice sweater," she said.

He smiled back. "Thought you'd like it." Before, he would have put his arm around her, or taken her knapsack for her or something, but now, he just stood there, looking uncomfortable.

Feeling pretty ill-at-ease herself—although it had been her idea to "de-escalate" things in the first place, Meg coughed. "Well," she said.

"Yeah." He straightened his glasses. "Anything new?"

She shook her head. "Not really. I talked to Beth last night." Beth was her best friend back in Massachusetts, where her family *really* lived. Or had, anyway. Either way, she and Beth talked a lot—and emailed and texted each other constantly, too.

"What's going on with her?" Josh asked.

That was a perfectly ordinary question, but somehow, it felt stilted. "Not much," Meg said. "She's going to the Prom with that Harvard guy." Beth was nothing, if not a social success.

"Are they getting serious?" he asked.

"No, I don't get that feeling," Meg said. In fact, mostly, the guy sounded like a putz. A *college* putz, but still, a putz.

Behind her, Dennis had moved closer again, and she folded her arms, not wanting to turn around and yell at him.

Josh noticed and put his hand on her waist, steering her ahead more quickly.

"Thanks," she said.

He hesitated, then dropped his hand, putting it in his jeans pocket. "Why don't you talk to him about it?"

Which both he and Beth had suggested more than once. Meg sighed. "He's just doing his job."

"Yeah," Josh said, "but he's not supposed to bother you."

Having agents *at all* was bothersome, so it was really just a question of degree. "I'm probably overreacting," she said, her arms still folded.

Josh glanced over his shoulder. "Tell your father, or Preston. I'm sure it wouldn't be a big deal for you to get someone else."

Mr. Gabler, who was the Special Agent in Charge of the Presidential Protective Detail, would probably be able to come up with a plausible reason to send Dennis off for some form of specialized training, but she didn't want the guy to suspect that the President's daughter had been complaining bitterly about him, since it would hurt his feelings. "I guess so." She sighed again. "I don't know. This rotation's almost over, anyway."

"In other words," he said.

Yeah. She nodded, and stopped as they got to her locker. "Did you do your English yet?"

"The demons of darkness are potent, but elusive," he said.

Meg laughed. "Yeah. I did it, too."

JOSH CAME OVER after dinner that night—romance or not, he was still her closest friend in Washington—and they ended up in the West Sitting Hall, which was considered the First Family Living Room, and had furniture from their house in Chestnut Hill and everything. Having a *familiar* non-museum quality couch around, as well as two easy chairs from their old den, was very comforting.

He was wearing another Shetland crewneck, this one sort of deep-sea blue, and she touched his sleeve. "Gosh, this is *so* nice," she said.

Josh looked sheepish. "It's kind of cold out tonight."

In Washington, in May. Right. Jorge, who was one of the butlers, had brought out Cokes and some homemade, still-hot potato chips for them, and she leaned forward to take a sip from her glass. "How was practice?"

Josh shrugged. "Okay. Nathan hit so damn many home-runs that the rest of us got stuck chasing them around half the time."

Meg grinned. Their friend Nathan, who was about as big as the average NFL linebacker, left nothing to understatement when it came to sports. He played first base and hit clean-up on their school's team, Josh played second, and another good friend of theirs, Zachary, was the center fielder. Because of this, Steven approved of all of them.

"Did you find anyone to hit with?" Josh asked.

Meg nodded. "Mr. Carlton, from CBS." A cameraman, who was a pretty damn good player. One great thing about the White House was that she never had any trouble finding singles partners.

"Did you beat him?" Josh asked.

She allowed herself a small grin. It was important to be a good sport. "Yeah."

He grinned, too. "Badly?"

"No. Two out of three," she said.

Which didn't mean that the guy hadn't been upset about it. Threw his racquet, even, when he thought—mistakenly—that he was safely out of view.

"Hey," she said. "Want to go look at dresses?"

"Mmm, boy," he said, with no enthusiasm whatsoever.

"I meant, my *mother's* dresses. You know, for the Prom. You can help me figure out what to wear—I'm sure she'll let me borrow one." Well, sort of sure. Meg stood up. "Come on."

He hesitated. "I don't know. I kind of don't think I should go into your parents' room."

"They won't mind," she said. "Besides, they're not going to be home until pretty late."

He looked worried, but followed her into the Presidential Bedroom Suite.

Actually, her parents had very strict rules about the two of them hanging out in bedrooms together. Not that she and Josh had ever done—much—that was particularly controversial. Even by nervous parents' standards. Since her social life outside the White House was completely in the public domain, and the odds of *really* being alone in the Residence were pretty slim, neither of them had ever really been able to relax enough to get too carried away. As time wore on, Josh had gotten more and more frustrated about this, while she—in many ways—had been kind of relieved. It had made life significantly less complicated.

"What," Josh said, smiling at her.

"I'm sorry." She shook her head. "I was just—"

"Thinking," he said.

Yeah.

Her mother had so many clothes that they were kept all over the place, including the storage area right between her room and Steven's, as well as up on the third floor, but the closets opening off the master bedroom and dressing room were a good place to start. When he saw the neat rows of suits and dresses, and skirts and blouses and gowns—and *shoes*, his mouth literally fell open.

"Jesus," he said.

"Want me to do my Daisy Buchanan impression?" Meg asked.

He laughed.

"Is that a no?" she asked.

"Big no," he said, then pointed at the large tags on all of the hangers. "What are those?"

Visible evidence of White House OCD. Meg shrugged. "They always write down when and where she's worn the outfit so, I don't know, she doesn't repeat."

"Hunh." He leaned forward to study one of the tags. "Who are 'they'?"

"I don't know," she said. "The Cast of Thousands." Although, in this case, it was probably the social secretaries. She and Steven always called the White House staff the Cast of Thousands—for obvious reasons. She held out one of her favorite gowns, a dark sapphire-blue, very simply cut. "What do you think?"

"I don't know," he said. "When was it worn last?"

She grinned. Josh was pretty cute, when he wanted to be. Sometimes even when he *didn't* want to be. "Well, hell, I don't know, either," she said, and checked the tag. "Right after Labor Day. At a thing for NASA."

"It's nice," he said.

An extreme understatement.

He pulled out a strapless black dress. "This one's pretty."

"No *way* would she let me borrow that," Meg said.

"Why?" He looked at it again. What there *was* of it. "Oh."

"Yeah." Meg put the black dress back—which had only been

worn at her mother's birthday party up at Camp David almost a year earlier, with just a few of her parents' very closest friends in attendance—and took down a white one, with a scoop neck and three-quarter sleeves. "This, she'd let me wear."

"Kind of bridal," he said.

"Yeah." She hung it up, taking out a shimmery golden dress. "How about this?"

He shook his head.

"She looks—monarchial—in it," Meg said.

"Is that a word?" he asked doubtfully.

She frowned. "I think so."

"I *don't* think so," he said.

She made a mental note to look the word up later, although she almost never remembered to do things like that. "She looks—queenly."

He laughed. "Got it."

"In fact, she—" Meg stopped, suddenly hearing her parents out in the bedroom.

"I thought they weren't home," Josh whispered.

"I guess they're back," Meg said, and raised her voice, since she could hear her mother approaching the closet. "Hi, Mom."

"Oh, hi." Her mother paused in the act of taking her hair down when she saw Josh. "Hello, Josh."

"Um, hello, ma'am," he said, looking embarrassed. "We were just—"

"He wanted to try on some of your clothes," Meg said, helpfully.

"Oh." Her mother smiled. "Are there any you'd like to take along with you?"

Josh blinked a few times, now looking mortified. "Uh—they're all very nice."

"Well, just help yourself," she said.

They followed her out to the bedroom, where Meg's father had just turned on the Red Sox game.

17

And, damn it, Detroit was winning 6 to 3 in the top of the seventh. "So, *that's* why you're home early," Meg said.

Her mother nodded. "It was, perhaps, a factor."

"I don't suppose I'll ask what you all were doing in the closet," her father said, concentrating on the television.

"The key question is, what were we all doing coming *out*," Meg said, quite amused—as was generally the case—by herself. A serious character flaw, no doubt.

"Actually," Josh said, "we were just about to go upstairs and watch a movie."

Meg nodded. "That's right, we sure were. Do you guys want to, too?"

"No, thanks," her father said, hanging his dinner jacket over the back of a chair and sitting down to watch the game.

Her mother shook her head, too, indicating her desk, and the piles of papers and reports and briefing books. "No, thank you. If your brothers are up there, though, please tell them we're home."

Predictably, her brothers *were* in the solarium, and Steven was in a foul mood, because during the time it had taken them to walk upstairs, Detroit had scored two more runs. Meg kind of wanted to watch the rest of the game, but when—in short order—Boston fell behind 11-3, she and Josh went down to the Washington Sitting Room, instead. It was part of a third-floor bedroom suite, but not an *actual* bedroom, so she was still technically adhering to the letter of her parents' law.

Which didn't change the fact that they were having trouble making eye contact. The fact that they had fooled around pretty intensely, more than once, in the adjoining bedroom made everything seem just that much more awkward.

Meg broke the silence. "Want me to sing, 'I'm Coming Out'?"

Josh laughed. "Not really."

"I do it really nicely," she said. "Dulcet tones, people say."

He laughed again.

"No one takes me seriously," she said.

"Gee, wonder why," he said, and sat down on the red-and-white upholstered couch.

After a minute, she sat next to—but, not *right* next to—him, and they didn't speak for a while.

"This is pretty hard, Meg," he said.

She nodded. "Would you, um," she didn't look at him, "feel better not seeing me at *all*?"

"No," he said. Instantly.

Good. "I don't want that, either," she said.

It was quiet again.

"Why can't we just wait until September?" he asked. "And then, you know, go away to school."

They had already had this conversation about thirty times, without making much progress. Maybe she should have allowed it to happen that way—just let them drift apart, never initiating any sort of discussion about it, taking advantage of the fact that he was going all the way out to Stanford, and that they wouldn't have to worry about running into each other. But, she'd felt him getting more and more involved, while she—it hadn't seemed fair. She still wondered whether breaking up had been such a great idea, but it wouldn't have been right to pretend that—she sighed.

"I need you as a friend," she said. "I need you *more* as a friend."

He nodded. Unhappily.

And now, they had reached the usual impasse.

"I need you as a friend, too," he said. "I'm just—it's hard."

Yeah. She wanted to touch his hair, or hold his hand, or something, but wasn't sure if she should.

"Is it okay if I put my arm around you?" he asked.

"I'd like that," she said. "I'd like that a lot."

# 3

ON TUESDAY AFTERNOON, she played tennis with the Associate Deputy Secretary of the Department of the Interior, Mr. Kirkland. His reputation had preceded him—he had won a couple of government employee tournaments, *and* he was only thirty-four—and apparently, her reputation had, too, because when he won service, he smashed the first ball in for a very intimidating ace. And the second one.

By the third serve, she had adjusted to the speed, and managed to chip it back, but he won the game in four straight points.

"Do you want to switch sides on odd games?" he asked, at the net.

She looked at him, seeing a not-very-well masked patronizing smile. If there was anything in life that she hated, it was being patronized.

"Sure," she said, and switched sides.

The work on her serve for the past several weeks had made a difference, and she won her game, too, although he passed her once at the net. They stayed on serve right up until the ninth game, which she lost, and he took the set, 6-40.

"You're quite a fine player," he said. Smiling.

What she wasn't—although she was careful never to advertise it in public—was a good loser. "Thank you," she said, and got ready to serve the first game of the second set, noticing that there were quite a few people—including Preston—watching from the sidelines, mostly over by the two round tables and the little changing house in the corner, or through the fences.

An audience to her probable defeat. Swell.

She bounced the ball three times, pulled in a deep breath, and then pounded it into the service court. Ace. Only her second one of the match. She spun the next one in to his backhand, and he was caught off-guard, Meg easily putting away the return.

She pulled out the game in five points, and they switched sides again.

"That's a tricky little serve you have there," he said.

Little. "Thank you," she said.

She won the set—mainly by slashing cross-courts and making him run, then waited on the baseline for him to start the first game of the third and final set. He was taking his time—toweling off, drinking some water, straightening the strings on his racquet—so, she decided that her main strategy would be to lob over his head if he came to the net, and to drop-shot short if he stayed back. *Remind* him that he was in his mid-thirties, and maybe not as fast as he used to be.

*His* strategy, it seemed, was to hit the ball as hard as he could—which meant that if it went in, she lost the point, more often than not; if it went out, she won. They were tied four-all, her serve, when she started double-faulting. Three times, to be exact, and suddenly, he was serving for the match.

She gritted her teeth. Damn it, damn it, damn it. Talk about the worst possible time to choke. She bent down to tie her shoe, finding it a real battle to keep from swearing aloud, so pumped up that she wanted to kick this guy from here to Bethesda. She took a deep breath. Okay, okay, she had to work harder, that's all. Work *a lot* harder.

His first serve came slamming in, and she hit the return right past him as he ran up to the net. Almost right *through* him. Love-fifteen. She went down the line with the next two, and won the final point with a little drop-shot he couldn't quite get.

Okay, okay, five-all. Time to make her move. She put everything she had left into her serve, and two aces—tricky little serve, indeed—and several hard rallies later won her service game. Six-five, her favor.

They switched sides again, Mr. Kirkland not saying anything this time, and she was aware that it had gotten very quiet around the court. She kept her eyes down, concentrating on not paying attention to anything except the next game.

The first serve came in hard, but she blocked it back. They hit forehand to forehand once, twice, three times, and then his shot ticked the net-cord, falling over onto—her side. Fifteen-love. Hell.

She smashed his next serve right back to him and he adjusted late, hitting it out. Fifteen-all. He doubled-faulted, and it was fifteen-thirty. She missed with a cross-court backhand, and it was thirty-all. The next point was another tough rally—forehand to forehand, backhand to backhand, down the line, cross-court, back down the line—and he finally hit one into the net. Thirty-forty. Match point.

She bent to wait for the serve, ignoring all of the people around them, blocking out everything except for the ball. The point. The victory so close that she could—again, they had a long rally, *so* long that she felt her arms starting to shake from nervousness. He followed a hard backhand up to the net; she waited, timed her swing, and then lobbed it over his head, just inside the baseline.

Game, set, and match.

Mr. Kirkland looked disappointed, but smiled as they shook hands. "You're an excellent player," he said.

She flushed. The fever to win at all costs almost always left as abruptly as it would arrive. "Um, thank you. So are you."

"Rematch sometime?" he asked.

"Sure," she said.

Feeling shy, she spent some extra time gathering up her gear, hoping that the people who had been watching would leave. Most of them did—more than one coming over to tell her what a good match she had played—and she thanked them politely before going to sit at one of the tables in the far corner, next to Preston. He was drinking sweet tea—someone in the kitchen made a very strong, authentic version, to which half of the staff was completely addicted—and she nodded when he raised the pitcher.

"Well, no one'll ever accuse *you* of not having the killer instinct," he said, pouring her a glassful.

She looked at him uneasily. "It *shows*?"

He laughed. "I'd say so."

Great. "Is it unattractive?" she asked.

"Your mother seems to be doing okay with it," he said.

Meg automatically looked towards the West Wing, even though she couldn't see it from where they were sitting. "Yeah, but—she's different."

He also glanced in that direction. "Old Cal Wilson thinks you're a determined little lady."

Meg grinned. Cal Wilson was an economic advisor, and *very* Southern. "End quote."

"Afraid so," Preston said.

Mr. Wilson was a nice man, albeit extremely old-fashioned. She wasn't crazy about tea, but she was thirsty as hell—and it was there. She picked up her glass, drinking half of it as she checked out Preston's outfit. A linen suit, so grey that it was almost blue, with a lighter blue shirt, and a teal silk tie. To her amusement—and her brothers' great glee—Preston had shown up on more than one Ten Most Eligible Bachelors' list. Mostly notably, *Cosmopolitan*.

"What," he said, smiling.

She reached for a sugar cookie, from the plate in the middle of the table. "I was thinking about you and *Cosmo*."

He rolled his eyes.

"You know what Beth says?" she asked.

"I can guess what Beth says," he said.

Meg just grinned. She and Beth held the theory that despite the fact that Preston lived with a woman who worked for the State

Department, what he was *really* waiting for was for one of them—they could never agree upon *which* one—to be old enough, before venturing into marriage. They had agreed, however, that this notion might best be kept to themselves.

"So." Preston indicated the court. "What's the story?"

The man was nothing, if not up-front. She helped herself to a second cookie. "How good do you think I am?"

"Out of *my* league," he said.

She shook her head. "I'm serious. Do you think I'm getting good?"

He shrugged, and refilled both of their glasses. "Jed Kirkland doesn't exactly lose all the time."

She thought about that, then folded her arms.

"What," he said.

"Do you think Mom and Dad would let me play a few tournaments this summer?" she asked. "I mean, you know, USTA stuff?"

"Pretty high profile," he said.

Unfortunately, yeah. But, hell, the publicity and other junk didn't interest her at all; she just wanted to *play*.

He sighed. "I don't know. Can't see them being thrilled about the idea."

"Well—" She decided to try the only halfway decent argument she had. "Steven gets to play baseball." Although he hadn't convinced them to let him join a travel team.

Yet.

"Steven *lives* to play baseball," he said.

"Yeah, but—" She stopped. She would rather die, than whine in front of Preston. "I guess everyone's used to him being really intense, and me just screwing around."

He nodded.

"Is there any way I could go to tournaments, and not attract attention?" she asked.

"Lose," he said.

Yeah, that'd do it, all right. "I, um, I might lose a lot, anyway," she said.

There was only one cookie left on the plate, and he broke it in half, taking one piece for himself and handing her the other. "If you thought *that*, you probably wouldn't be quite as interested in doing it."

She had to grin. "Well—maybe." Or even, definitely.

"How about I talk to Gabler"—who was the SAIC of the PPD, and so, was ultimately in charge of their security—"and find out some logistics," he said. "Then, you can present the idea a little better."

She nodded gratefully. He knew her parents about as well as she did. But, since they hadn't even let her finish out her high school season, she wasn't very optimistic about them allowing her to play in an even *more* public, and difficult to secure, arena.

Which completely and totally sucked, as far as she was concerned.

"You might be able to talk them into it," he said. "You never know."

And, as all New Englanders could personally attest, October 2004 was proof that strange things actually *could* happen. "I don't think I'll hold my breath," she said.

He nodded. "I'm afraid that's a wise choice," he said.

"SO," BETH SAID on the phone, when Meg called her after supper that night. "How's it going with Josh?"

Meg shrugged. "I don't know. I guess it's better. I still feel like a snake, though."

"But, you're going to go on Friday," Beth said, "right?"

The Prom. "Yeah," Meg said. "It seems like mostly everyone's going with friends, so maybe it won't feel as weird."

"What are you going to wear?" Beth asked. "The blue one?"

Her mother had, after a few "don't you think we could come up

with something a little more appropriate?" remarks, finally agreed.
"Yeah," Meg said. "What are you wearing?"

"Black," Beth said.

Naturally. "Is it like, completely sultry?" Meg asked.

Beth laughed. "Yeah. Is yours?"

Hmmm. "Slightly," Meg said.

"Not everyone can carry it off," Beth said in a kindly one-day-when-you're-as-cool-as-I-am voice.

Right. Besides, it was probably better for her *not* to look sultry, since she and Josh were trying so damn hard to be entirely platonic—although she had a sneaking suspicion that they might backslide a bit during the post-Prom parties.

Beth let out her breath. "Stuart wants to get a room at the Sheraton downtown."

Meg laughed. "What, he won't spring for the Four Seasons?"

"I'm serious," Beth said.

Oh. *Whoa.* "Wow," Meg said.

"Yeah," Beth said.

Double wow. "Are you, um—what do you think?" Meg asked.

Beth sighed. "I don't know. I mean, it might be—it seems like a way to—I don't know."

It was quiet for a minute.

"And don't ask me if I love him," Beth said, "okay?"

There was no need to do so, since she had just answered the question. And, actually, she'd never had any sense that Beth really *liked* the guy, although she seemed to find him mildly entertaining—and enjoyed the fact that, because Stuart had a mustache, her stepfather openly and vehemently disapproved of him.

"Besides, it might work out," Beth said, sounding very defensive. "And maybe he'll come down and visit me in New York—" because she had decided to go to Columbia—"and I'll go up and see him in Cambridge, and—well, what the hell, you know?"

It was quiet again, and Meg knew that if she didn't say something, Beth would take silence as condemnation.

She paused for a couple of extra seconds to think of the right words. "If you care about him, and you're sure he's going to be nice to you, then, yeah, maybe it's a good idea."

Which must not have been the right words, because they just kind of—hung there.

"But," Beth said.

It was impossible to dissemble around Beth. "But, it kind of sounds like you just want to get it over with more than anything else," Meg said.

"What's wrong with that?" Beth asked. Defensively.

An excellent question. "Nothing's *wrong* with it," Meg said. "In fact, sometimes I wish I'd gone that way with Josh." And it was—very, very faintly—within the realm of possibility that she still *might*, if the post-Prom parties were as rowdy and devil-may-care as she suspected they were going to be.

"I don't get why you didn't," Beth said. "He's a really sweet guy, he's *crazy* about you, and he would have made sure that it was romantic and all."

Yes. All three of those things were true. Meg sighed. "And I was still going to break up with him, no matter what, so it wouldn't have been fair."

It was silent for what seemed like a very long time.

"So, you think you'd have been using him, and I'd be using Stuart," Beth said.

Maybe. Meg frowned. "Well, it's not exactly cruel and unusual punishment." She *hoped*. "But—yeah. Potentially."

There was yet another pause.

"You know," Beth said, finally. "I kind of wish our mothers knew that we're actually taking this stuff *seriously*."

Oh, yeah, that sounded like a great idea. "What, are you

kidding?" Meg asked. "My mother and I talk openly, and comfortably, about sex all the time."

Beth laughed. "Thanks, Meg. Now I'm going to have major nightmares tonight."

Yes, she probably was, too.

After they hung up, she was lying on her bed, reading *As I Lay Dying*, when her mother knocked lightly on the open door, and then came in.

If there was a God, the President had no plans to discuss any form of sex in any way whatsoever.

"What are you reading?" her mother asked.

Meg held up the book.

"Are you enjoying it?" her mother asked.

Meg shook her head.

Her mother smiled, sitting down on the end of the bed. "You know, you can occasionally take a *break*, Meg."

This, from the woman who averaged less than four hours of sleep a night?

"How's Beth?" her mother asked. "Have you talked to her lately?"

Was that a friendly question—or a pointed, probing one? Not that she thought White House flunkies were quite capable of listening in on people's private conversations, and then running straight to the President and telling her everything, in a—futile—attempt to curry favor. "Fine," she said, cautiously. "Waiting for graduation, mostly."

Her mother nodded. "Well, I hope you'll get to spend some time with her this summer."

Okay, so it had been a random query, without any apparent ulterior motives. "Are we going to go up there at all," Meg asked, "or just to Camp David?"

"I don't know," her mother said. "I thought we might try for a week or two in August. And, among other things, we'll have that trip to Geneva in July."

Meg grinned. "You make it sound like a vacation."

"The glass is half full," her mother said.

"Wait," Meg pretended to reach for a pen, "let me write that down."

Her mother smiled.

Speaking of which. "What are you going to say in your speech?" Meg asked. Her mother had been invited to give the main address at her graduation—about which, Meg was both embarrassed and pleased.

"You mean, at the school," her mother said.

Meg nodded.

"Oh, I don't know," her mother said. "About how you all have only just begun, and can choose many paths on the highway of life, I suppose."

Meg looked at her uncertainly. "That's a joke, right?"

Her mother shrugged. "Shouldering adult responsibilities, seeing graduation as both an ending and a new beginning—"

"Now I *know* you're kidding," Meg said, almost positive.

"Well, what would you expect me to say?" her mother asked.

"I don't know." Meg frowned. "I was kind of hoping you'd tell some jokes."

"Jokes." Her mother frowned, too. "I see."

"We could get Jon Talbot's father to come," Meg said. Who was an extremely conservative Senator from Alabama, and not one of her mother's favorites.

"I'll think of some jokes," her mother said.

Good. Not that her mother didn't always tell jokes—too many, her advisors worried—in her speeches. "You won't say stuff about *me*, right?" Meg asked.

"I expect I'll have to *mention* you," her mother said.

Talk about embarrassing. If there had been a cool cloth handy, she would have put it on her forehead. "You won't say you're proud of me or anything, will you?"

Her mother laughed. "If you think about it, there would be a lot more commotion if I went, and *didn't* speak."

Meg nodded. Either way, though, it was going to be something of a circus.

"I think it will be more low-key than you expect," her mother said, apparently reading her mind.

One could only hope. "Do you really think so?" Meg asked.

Her mother hesitated. "Well—"

"Neither do I," Meg said.

# 4

IT WAS THURSDAY, and Meg woke up in a very good mood. A *hell* of a mood. The switchboard, which she used as an alarm clock, only had to call once, even. And, it was sunny.

"Yes," she said to Vanessa, who stretched and purred. "We *do* need to put on 'I Love Rock and Roll.'" She clicked on to one of her favorite playlists, and "I Love Rock and Roll" came on. Loudly.

She decided to wear her Williams sweatshirt—half because she liked it; half because it would annoy her parents a little. And this wasn't a day to wear an *un*ripped pair of jeans.

The playlist was a rowdy one, full of songs like "Respect" and "Brick House" and "We've Gotta Get Out of This Place"— including the hilarious Partridge Family version, and as she got ready for school, she sang them to Vanessa.

Who didn't seem to be overly impressed.

At the Presidential Dining Room, she stopped in the doorway, seeing that the rest of her family was already at the table.

"Good morning, my little subjects," she said.

"Oh, Christ," Steven said. "Not that again."

Neal shook his head. "Not *that*."

"Good morning," her parents said, her father frowning at Steven for swearing.

Meg stayed in the doorway. "The proper greeting is, 'Good morning, dear Queen.'"

Her family continued eating breakfast.

"*Well*," she said, and swept to her seat.

"What are the odds of Her Majesty returning to her chambers and putting on something more presentable?" her father asked.

Meg pushed up one sweatshirt sleeve, amused. "The Queen is content, as is." She picked up her orange juice, then stopped, looking around the table. "No kippers? I *say*, you Americans are a savage lot."

Both of her parents laughed.

"What *are* the odds of your going and changing, Meg?" her mother asked.

"I like to think I change and grow every day," Meg said, and very solemnly sipped some juice.

Steven pretended to throw up, Neal giggling and imitating him.

"Anyway," Meg said, sipping, "this particular queen feels that comfy is as comfy does." She glanced up at Pete, the butler who was waiting by her place. "Just a mimosa, please."

Her father's eyebrows went up.

"Remember the time difference," she said. "I'm *accustomed* to a cocktail right about now."

Her mother sighed, pushing away her morning news summary. "Don't you have homework or something that needs finishing?"

Meg shook her head sadly.

"What your mother means," her father said, "is that maybe she's trying to concentrate."

"No news is good news," Meg said, and reached across the table to grab the Lucky Charms box away from Neal, the two of them scuffling slightly.

"Neal, give your sister the box," their father said, sounding tired.

"She should ask!" Neal said.

Her mother frowned at her. "She *should* ask."

Meg sat back, folding her hands in her lap. "I guess the colonies have had a bad effect on me." She smiled at Neal. A—monarchial—smile. "Will you please pass me the cereal, sweetpea?"

"What a jerk." Steven pushed away from the table, putting on his Red Sox cap—their father wouldn't let him wear it when they were eating—and grabbing his knapsack. "Later."

"No royal kiss?" Meg asked.

"No way," he said.

How disrespectful. "No *presidential* kiss?" she said.

"Right," he said, and grinned sheepishly at their mother. They weren't big on hugging—at least, she and Steven weren't—but, since her mother had been shot, they were all a little more careful about trying to say pleasant good-byes. "Um, see ya."

"Savage." Meg checked her watch—and saw that it *was* kind of on the late side. "I'd better get going, too." She grabbed a handful of Lucky Charms from the box. "Mmm, can't tell you how happy I am about the extra marshmallows they added."

"Charming," her father said, watching her.

Meg grinned. "Want to see *charming*?"

"No," her mother said quickly.

"Your loss," Meg said, and took another handful for the road. For the car, anyway. "Um, let's be careful out there," she said, which was her good-luck-charm good-bye. Courtesy of *Hill Street Blues*, which she watched with her father sometimes, when he was feeling nostalgic.

"No presidential kiss?" her mother asked.

Oh, please. "Elected officials kiss *queens*," Meg said. "Not the other way around."

Her mother stood up, her expression amused.

"That's okay," Meg said. "You can owe me."

"Are you staying after today?" her father asked.

Meg nodded. "For a while, maybe. Then, I thought I'd come home and—"

"Tennis," her mother said.

Meg shrugged. "Kind of tough to find a cricket game around here." She picked up her knapsack. "See you later."

Her regular classes had pretty much wound down, since they

were all supposed to be spending most of their time working on their big senior projects—she had elected to do a four-week immersion course in Chinese, because—well—the school offered it, and she had always been too busy taking French classes to give it a try, and—not that she liked politics, or had any career ambitions in that direction, or anything—but, learning a little Chinese seemed like a good idea. A guy from the State Department had been coming over to the White House for a couple of hours twice a week to tutor her, but she was also sitting in on first-year classes full of wide-eyed—or irredeemably smart-ass—ninth and tenth graders, and spending a lot of time in the language lab.

Of course, she wasted a good chunk of the day hanging out, aimlessly, in the senior lounge, too.

Josh was writing a piano concerto for *his* project, and since she'd promised to wait for him while he met with his advisor after school, she sat in an auditorium in the Arts Center for a while, watching a rehearsal of the original play her friends Alison, Gail and Phyllis were doing for *their* senior project. Then, she went back over to the main building, since she was going to meet Josh by her locker.

The halls had pretty much cleared out, and she sat down on the floor. She was going to do a couple of pages in her Chinese workbook—oddly, even though her normal handwriting was disgraceful, she had been told that her Chinese script was quite deft—but, she sent Beth a quick *"I hear the Copley Plaza is nice"* text, instead.

Aware of Dennis lurking nearby, she looked up.

"I told Josh I'd wait until he was finished," she said. "Then, I'll be ready to go."

He nodded.

"Twenty minutes, maybe," she said.

He nodded, withdrawing slightly.

Beth had already sent back a snide, but cheerful, response, and they were still texting back and forth when Dennis came back over, frowning.

"Let me have that for a minute," he said, indicating her watch. "There's some kind of signal problem."

She glanced at it automatically. "What do you mean?"

He shrugged, holding his hand out. "I don't know—maybe you banged it when you were in the gym."

Instead of going to lunch, she had played some basketball with Josh and Nathan and Zachary, and a few other senior guys—and it had been a fairly rough and clumsy game, during which she had landed on the floor more than once. So, yeah, she'd probably mangled the damn thing. With luck, it wouldn't be too expensive to replace.

She handed the watch to him, her arm feeling strange without it. *Looking* strange, too, with the watch-shaped mark on her wrist. She grinned, pushing her sleeve back down. "You want me to be like, extra careful?"

He didn't really respond, adjusting his earpiece.

So what else was new. She went back to texting.

"Hi," Josh said, jogging down towards her, wearing his cleats and carrying his glove. The baseball season had ended, but the guys were scrimmaging pretty regularly, anyway, because they were very gung-ho—and still disappointed to have come in second in the MAC Tournament.

She wrote "*Off to the Hay-Adams! Details to follow*", and then signed off.

"Feel like watching us play for a while?" he asked.

It was tempting, but she shook her head. "No, I'm going to go home and work on my serve." She reached over to snap the elastic strap he used to keep his glasses on when he played sports. "What's next—clip-on sunglasses?"

"Yeah," he said. "Don't tell anyone."

She laughed, and as he put out his hand to help her up, she took it. Briefly.

Today was a side exit day, and he walked her down towards the driveway below the tennis courts, where her car would be waiting, Dennis behind them, Chet just ahead of them.

"You want to come over tonight?" she asked. "Hang out for a while?"

"Sure," he said. "Eight okay?"

He was carelessly forgetting a very crucial detail. "If you come at seven," she said, "we can watch the beginning of the Red Sox game."

"Ooh, yay," he said, and took his time—obviously just to annoy her—putting his Nationals cap on. "Hit lots of aces."

"Hit lots of home-runs," she said.

He adjusted the cap. At length. "You *know* who's going to be hitting home-runs."

As always, Nathan. She grinned. "Well, have fun chasing them."

As she walked outside, she glanced back to see if he was still there—which he was.

"Tie your shoes," Dennis said.

"What?" She looked down, so used to wearing them loose—except when she was actually *playing* tennis—that tying them never occurred to her. "Okay." She bent down.

"Wait until you get to the car," Chet said, without turning.

She shook her head. "It'll only take a—"

Now, he turned. "Wait until you—" He stared at her left arm. "Meg, where the hell's your—"

Out of nowhere, there was an explosion up ahead of them, followed by a second one, and then a third, as two cars and a van came speeding through the smoke, veering right up over the sidewalk at them.

"Get her inside!" Chet said, his gun already out, blocking her.

Meg stared, too stunned to react as men in masks burst out of the cars and fired automatic weapons. The smoke was worse, but she saw Chet stumbling back, blood spurting from his chest and neck, and horrified, she turned to try and find Dennis, who was face-down on the pavement, blood spreading out underneath him. There was more shooting—the agents from her lead car?—and then, another explosion.

The school door was opening—Josh!—and she had just enough time to yell "Get down!" before she felt herself being lifted right up off the ground and thrown into the van, the impact of the metal flooring jarring up through her hands and knees. Men piled in after her, still shooting as the van skidded away.

The door slammed, the light dimming, and the van was loud with mask-muffled shouting, the air so thick with the smell of nervous perspiration and halitosis that she couldn't breathe. Her arms were being wrenched up behind her, tight metal digging into her wrists, and then, she was on her back, a man straddling her, aiming what looked like a machine gun at her face.

"Where else you bugged?" he shouted.

She just stared, breathing hard, too scared to move.

He hit her across the face with the gun. "Tell me!"

She felt bright, sickening pain first; then, blood rolling down the side of her face. He hit her again, harder, and she felt tears—it couldn't be blood from her *eye*—joining the trickle of blood.

"Answer me!" he yelled.

"I—" her vision was blurred by warm liquid— "I—"

She felt rough hands everywhere—and *fists*—and then one of the hands dug in, viciously, between her neck and shoulder, and she groaned, her heart beating so hard that she couldn't really hear anything else.

"Tell me!" he yelled again.

"Okay," another, much calmer, voice said. "She doesn't know. Just get to it."

A light flashed into her eyes and hands pried her mouth open, something metal touching her teeth, Meg struggling away in complete terror.

"Put her out first," the calm voice said.

"Fuck that!" one of the others yelled. "She—"

"Put her out," the man said.

# 5

DARK. HOT. PAIN. Most of the pain was in her mouth, along with thick liquid, and she choked a little, her lips too numb to spit it out right. Everything felt heavy, like she'd been in an accident, or was sick, or—Jesus Christ.

There was something metal on her left wrist, then chain links, then another cuff around what felt like a bed frame—oh, Christ. Shooting, Chet and Dennis lying on the—oh, Christ, oh, Christ, oh, Christ. Panicking, she yanked at the handcuffs through the dizziness, trying to sit up, to run away—except she couldn't, she— oh, God. She yanked harder, fighting to sit, to stand, to—but, the cuffs were tighter, and it was darker, and—the door slammed open.

Oh, Jesus. She sat very still, very stiff. The man came in, his face misshapen by a stocking mask, and she gulped down a moan of fear, moving back away from him, finding herself in the corner of a wall.

He came closer, not speaking, and she held her breath, shaking so hard that the bed seemed to vibrate.

The man just stood there, looking at her, then laughed, very quietly.

Her voice wouldn't work and she swallowed, feeling nausea up in her throat. Her tongue hit a deep hole and she realized, the nausea much worse, that she was missing *teeth*. That half the side of her mouth was—oh, Christ. Oh, Christ, oh, Christ, oh—control. She had to find some control, couldn't let him—

"W-what's going on?" she asked, her voice higher and shakier than she'd ever remembered hearing it.

He didn't say anything.

She swallowed. "Are you like—Shiites?"

This time, his laugh was more genuine.

"Are you someone *like* that?" she asked.

He didn't answer, reaching up to turn on an overhead bare lightbulb. The sudden light hurt her eyes, but she kept them open, getting her first good look at him. He was tall—at least as big as her father—with dark hair bunched up under the mask. He was wearing a blue t-shirt, jeans, and leather high-tops. The familiarity of seeing New Balance basketball sneakers was surprisingly comforting.

"Are we in *America*, at least?" she asked.

His hand came towards her face and she flinched away, not sure what he was going to do. It closed around her jaw, his thumb pressing in right where the teeth were gone and she winced, trying to pull free.

His fingers tightened. "If I hit you there, it's *really* going to hurt," he said, in the very calm voice she'd heard in the van.

She stopped pulling, her muscles tensed against the pain, back to being terrified.

"Right," he said, and turned her face towards him, studying the right side of her forehead. "Your head hurt?"

Her *mouth* hurt. She sat as still as she could, her heart pounding so hard that she couldn't get her breath.

He released her and she sank back against the wall, bringing her right hand up to hold her jaw, shutting her eyes so she wouldn't cry.

"Didn't expect us to leave that transmitter in, did you?" he asked.

She opened her eyes, confused enough to forget the pain.

"They probably told you it was a filling," he said.

A filling. She flashed on going to the dentist right after her mother had been elected, and yeah, she had had a cavity—only the second one ever, and—Steven and Neal had had cavities, too. Steven and Neal—oh, God. What if these people had—

40

"Lucky you have good teeth," he said. "I would have taken them *all* out."

Meg didn't even really hear that, terrified for her brothers. "Am I the only—" She didn't want to give them ideas. Didn't want to say anything that might—how the hell had they known about her teeth, when *she* hadn't even—"Give me your watch," Dennis had said, "there's a problem with the signal." "Tie your shoes," he'd said, even though she was never, ever supposed to stop unnecessarily when she was in transit—oh, Christ. She looked up, aware that the man was watching her. "That bastard sold me out," she said.

His smile was especially scary through the mask. "Looks that way."

"Well, is he—" She stiffened, realizing for the first time that she wasn't wearing her jeans, or her Williams sweatshirt, or—Jesus *Christ*. She looked down—which hurt her head—and saw an unfamiliar grey sweatshirt, grey sweatpants, and white socks. Feeling very exposed, after the fact, she brought her knees up close to the rest of her body, covering her chest with her free arm.

The man's smile widened. "Was beginning to wonder if you'd notice." He paused. "You have some interesting tan lines."

"I don't—" She swallowed, feeling sick to her stomach. "I mean, why—"

"Wild guess," he said.

Because they couldn't take chances. Because she might have been bugged. She probably *had* been. She swallowed again, remembering how many men had been in the van, not wanting to imagine them all—she would be able to tell if they had done anything *really* awful—right?—but, the thought of them all looking, and touching—"Did you—do anything?" she asked, trying to block out any thoughts.

He didn't answer.

Christ. "You can't tell me *that*?" she asked.

He moved his jaw. "Time was a factor," he said finally.

She decided to take that as a no, letting some of the tension out of her muscles, but keeping her arm across her chest. "It's not like they go pawing through my dresser, putting bugs on everything," she said stiffly, although now that she thought about it, they probably *did*. Why the *hell* hadn't her parents warned—because, of course, they wouldn't want her to worry. Because—she couldn't think about her parents, or her brothers, or—Josh. Jesus Christ. The school door opening, all of the shooting, and explosions, and smoke—what if he—she shut her eyes, moving her hand up to cover them.

"Need to use the bathroom?" he asked.

Definitely. But, it could wait. "Can you just—" She took a deep breath. "Were people hurt?"

"No kidding," he said.

Oh, Jesus. "People—my age?" she asked.

He smiled. "What, worried about your *boy*friend or something?"

She looked up uneasily, afraid to say yes, but really wanting—needing—to know.

The man smiled more. "He's in the hospital—I don't know if he died or not."

Which was terrifying, but there was something so glib about the way he said it, that she tried to see his expression through the mask. The smile was all that showed. "Are you lying?" she asked, feeling her voice shake.

"Maybe," he said.

"*Are* you?" she asked.

"Got shot about five times," he said.

"I know you're lying," she said, shakily.

He bent down, the mask looming close to her face. "If he isn't dead yet, I can send someone to finish the job."

That made her cry, and she lowered her head, not wanting to give him the satisfaction of seeing.

42

He nodded. "Figured you for a crier."

She couldn't stop, and had to lower her head more, blocking her face with her hand.

"Doing the President proud," he said.

"Doing *your* parents proud, too," she said, trying to stop.

He laughed. "You need to use the bathroom, or not?"

She nodded, not lifting her head.

"Okay." He took an extra pair of handcuffs out of his back pocket, snapping one end around her already cuffed hand, then bringing her right hand over to cuff it.

When he unlocked the cuff that was attached to the bed frame, her left arm fell, and it was so numb that she had to use her right hand to lift it off the mattress. She tried to move her fingers, wincing as some of the blood came stinging back in.

"Must hurt," he said.

There was no sympathy in his voice, and she didn't bother looking up, gently massaging her left hand with her right, hampered by the handcuffs.

"Let's go," he said.

She slowly flexed her hand. "Did you throw away my shoes, too?"

He bent down, picking up a pair of cheap blue sneakers and dropping them on the bed.

Her legs felt very tired and heavy, and she maneuvered them over to the sneakers, slipping them on. They were only a little too big, and she tried to tie them, but couldn't with the handcuffs.

"Come on," he said impatiently. "Let's go."

She swung her legs over the edge of the mattress, uneasily, holding her wrists just above them. "Do I have to wear these?"

"You should thank me for letting you wear *anything*," he said.

Instead of feeling embarrassed this time, she was only angry. "Yeah," she said. "Thanks for the dental work, too."

He just looked at her, and she stood up, her legs unsteady. Standing made her so dizzy that she sagged back down towards the bed, realizing for the first time how much her head hurt, how much she—aware of how irritated he was getting, she slid her right foot forward one step on what felt like a concrete floor, then lifted her left one for another. Only—what if he was lying? What if he was *pretending* to take her to the bathroom, but was really going to kill her, or—she felt a wave of fear worse than the dizziness and stopped where she was, afraid to move.

He made an annoyed sound and grabbed her arm, yanking her forward. Then, they were out in a dark, empty corridor, with a wall to her left, a door straight across from her, and a hall that went about ten or fifteen feet to her right before turning a corner. A storage building? Or a factory? Something industrial, anyway.

"In there," he said, indicating the door.

She turned the knob and saw that it was, indeed, a bathroom. There was a light switch on the wall and she pushed it up, going in and closing the metal door behind her. She leaned against it briefly, feeling for—and not finding—a lock. Not that she had expected one.

Okay, okay, she had to stay calm. Couldn't panic. Couldn't lose it. She forced herself to look around the room. Small, windowless, the sink rust-stained. Like a gas station, sort of.

"Don't take all night," he said through the door.

Night. Did that mean that it was night? Yeah, he would have said "day," otherwise. Was it still today? Or had she been unconscious for a long time? Or—he probably wasn't kidding about her hurrying up.

She saw that they had—at least—put underwear on her. Men's underwear, apparently new. She was very careful not to touch anything—especially in a place like this—but stayed at the sink as long as she could, washing her hands, her face, her neck, and then her face again. Her mouth really hurt, but what if they were in a place where the water was contaminated? She couldn't risk—

The man opened the door. "Let's go already."

"Is this water safe to drink?" she asked.

"No kidding." He grabbed her elbow, pulling her roughly into the hall.

"I can't rinse my damn mouth, at least?" she asked, knocked off-balance.

"Try *shutting* your damn mouth," he said.

What she tried to do, was get back into the bathroom, and he slammed her up against the wall, keeping her there with one forearm pressed into her throat, yanking a gun out of the back of his jeans and pointing it at her face.

"You want me to kill you?" he asked. "You want me to kill you right now?"

She stared at the gun—a *real* gun—a gun that he might—that he was about to—that—

He jabbed the gun into her cheekbone. "Answer me!"

She shook her head, too scared to open her mouth.

"*Answer* me," he said.

"No," she said, her voice so small that *she* could barely hear it.

He looked at her for a long minute, then nodded, stepping away so suddenly that she fell, landing hard on her right elbow.

"Come on, get up," he said, kicking her, and she groaned. He kicked her again, so hard that it felt as though her entire ribcage was caving in. "Hurry up."

With an effort, she pushed herself to a sitting position, then all the way to her feet, hunching over her side.

"Get in there," he said, gesturing with the gun.

She nodded, walking quickly into the room, not protesting as he used the extra pair of handcuffs to chain her to the bed frame before uncuffing her right hand from the other pair, testing the lock with one hard jerk.

"Are you coming back?" she asked.

He didn't answer, turning to leave.

Okay, at least he was wearing a mask. That meant that they weren't going to kill her. As long as she couldn't identify them, she would be safe.

"I won't try and look at you," she said, as he reached up to turn the light off.

He turned it back on. "What?"

"I just meant—" She blinked from looking at the bulb. "I mean, I'm not *stupid*."

"Only wore it to scare you," he said.

She frowned. "I don't—"

Very slowly, he pulled the stocking mask off. "Maybe this'll scare you more," he said, and smiled.

She stared at him, at his face—a surprisingly normal face—and her stomach both twisted and fell. His face. Jesus Christ, that meant—Jesus Christ—"I thought—" She gulped. "Y-you aren't going to let me go?"

"No." He smiled again. "I'm not."

# 6

AFTER HE LEFT, slamming the door, it was very, very quiet. Very, very *dark*.

Okay, okay. She wasn't going to cry. She *really* wasn't. No way. She pressed her sweatshirt sleeve across her eyes, fist clenched, concentrating on swallowing—over and over—to keep control. Okay, okay, she had to try and be calm. To figure out what she was going to do. If there even *was* anything she could do.

They would find her. Every damn security agency in the country would be working on this, and they would have to—except, they already would have. She could be anywhere in the world, and there was no way that they could—calm. She had to be calm. Her mother was the *President*—and would be able to do something. All she had to do was wait. And try to be calm. Cool. *Brave*.

Her mother would be brave. Her mother would be completely, totally, *amazingly*—oh, Christ, what if something had happened to her brothers, too? And what if Josh really was—she couldn't think about it. If she thought about it, she would start—wait, she was *already* crying. Oh, hell.

She forced herself to lean back against the bed frame. To take a few deep breaths. She closed her eyes, tears still pushing out and down her face. Oh, God, her mouth hurt. Her mouth, and her jaw, and her head, and her side—her mother would be brave. Her father would be brave. *Preston* would be brave. She, at least, had to try.

Jesus.

Tentative in the darkness, she pushed down against the mattress with her free hand, moving herself into a more comfortable position. Her handcuffed hand was already falling asleep, and she moved her fingers a few times. Handcuffed. Jesus Christ, she was actually—she had to be calm. The only way to—very, very calm.

The inside of her mouth was really aching and, very cautious, she touched the hole with her tongue. It was still bleeding—although not as much—and seemed very deep. Two molars, probably. Maybe even three. She shivered, remembering the light in her eyes, the cold metal on her teeth—thank God he had had them knock her out. It would have been—thank God.

Maybe he was lying about killing her. Trying to keep her off-balance. Scared. Easy to handle. They'd have to be *crazy* to kill the President's daughter. Kidnapping was bad enough. Even with Dennis's help—Jesus, was he out there with them? Or, with all the blood she'd seen, was he—it was still hard to believe they had pulled it off. And they must have. If it was night, hours had passed, and she should have been located by now. But, how had they managed—he was smart. Extremely smart, with the same aura of professionalism she associated with Secret Service and FBI agents and soldiers. Detached, clear, unemotional—what if he was an insider, too? What if—he didn't seem like a terrorist. This guy was American; this guy was obviously well-educated. And there didn't seem to be anything fanatical about him. Neat, dark hair; lighter, expressionless eyes; straight nose. Christ, he could be any one of the youngish ambitious men that overpopulated Washington, wearing well-cut suits and carrying briefcases.

Actually, with a suit and a pair of Oakleys—had she seen him before? Had he maybe been around the school, or at one of her tennis matches, or—she had probably seen him before. He hadn't planned the thing overnight.

Her mouth hurt so much that she decided to concentrate on *that* for a while, resting her head against the wall. It was throbbing, like the beginning of a terrible earache, and the whole side of her face felt hot. He could have let her rinse it out, at least. Although that might have made it hurt even more. But, this way, it was sure to get infected.

Not that she didn't have worse things to worry about.

There hadn't been a mirror in the bathroom, and she reached up to touch her forehead, finding a huge bump. There seemed to be a split in her right eyebrow, and thick moisture, which had to be blood. The water from washing her face had been brownish-red, and the cut—which felt *huge*—must have opened up again. She let her hand drop, wiping the blood on her sleeve.

Not *even* her sleeve. Or her sweatpants, or her underwear, or— time to think about something else.

There was a tiny crack of dim light at the bottom of the door and she focused on it, afraid of the darkness. The light chain was somewhere in the middle of the room. If she could reach it, maybe—but, he wouldn't like it, and he might come in and hurt her. *Kill* her.

Kill her. Christ, this couldn't really be happening. One minute, she was talking to Josh; the next—no. If she thought about it, or him, or—it just couldn't be happening.

And crying sure as hell wasn't going to get her anywhere.

Of course, it wouldn't *hurt*, either. He might come in and laugh at her, but—to hell with him. There'd be something wrong with her if she *weren't* crying in this situation.

Only—would her mother be crying? No. Her mother would be *plotting*. Okay. She would try plotting. Do something constructive. Something to stay in control.

Maybe the handcuffs weren't fastened right. It was highly unlikely, but she pulled at them, anyway, the metal edges hurting her skin. First, she tried a slow, gradual pull; then a few quick yanks, the metal digging deeper. She traced the cuffs with her right hand, searching for the locks, tugging on the chain to see if anything was loose. Defective. But, predictably, nothing was.

Okay. What about the bed? She felt the frame, shook the bars. Thick, solid metal. Iron, probably. What about weight? Maybe if she lifted the bed with her handcuffed hand, the weight would make them pop open. It was worth a try, anyway. She moved her legs over the edge of the mattress, not wanting to stand up in the dark and leave the security of the bed.

Which proved that everything was pretty god-damn relative.

She stood up carefully, letting the dizziness ebb away before turning her attention to the bed frame. She pulled on the cuffs— no result. Maybe, if she pulled *really* hard, she could—she tried it, using both hands on the chain. The bed scraped over a foot and she stopped instantly, afraid that someone might have heard the noise.

She waited, holding her breath, but the hall was quiet. Would it be safe to risk lifting the bed? And if she could get over to the light, and turn it on for a second, she would feel a lot safer. Less scared. She reached out as far as she could, letting her arm swing in the darkness.

Oh, Christ, what if there were spiders, and rats, and—she would have seen them before, when the light was on. This was just a room. A small, empty room. A room in God-only-knew-what, God-only-knew-where, that she would be in until these people decided that it was time to—she yanked on the bed to distract herself, dragging it over another foot or two, towards the middle of the room. She swung her arm again, and the light pull brushed over her wrist. She felt around, the darkness seeming more dense than normal air, until she was holding it tightly in her hand. Even doing that much made her feel better and she gripped the little chain, deciding whether or not to risk turning the light on.

The hall was still very, very quiet.

Okay. She turned the light on. It *was* just a room. Maybe ten-by-ten, no windows, the walls closer to grey than white. There was no furniture, except for an old wooden chair near the door, and the bed frame—black cast iron—was even more solid than she'd been afraid it was. The mattress was covered by a white sheet, and she elected not to look underneath it. The sheet looked brand-new and was perfectly clean, except for the blood-stains where her face had been.

Her clothes smelled new, too, and it was strange to think of him, or someone, going out to shop for all of this unisex stuff. Strangely civilized. Smart, too, since a cashier would be likely to remember a man buying woman's clothes. Not that this guy struck her as someone who would slip up on a detail like that. Not, apparently, a guy who had screwed up anywhere. So far. When he got in touch with her parents, though, *that's* when they'd trace him. He had to have demands, or a motive, or something. And that was how they would get him.

Should she turn the light off? Not take chances? Or take a minute and check out the damned handcuffs a little more closely? That was an easy choice, and she crouched next to the bed, studying the shiny metal. Nothing she could break, nothing she could bend, nothing she could do. Where, for Christ's sakes, had he gotten *handcuffs?* They didn't sell them in stores, did they?

Jesus, was she tired.

Slowly, she straightened up, not sure what to do next. The smart thing, would be to turn the light off, move the bed back, and wait. If he didn't know that she could turn the light on, that was an advantage. Of some kind, anyway.

Okay. Even if the darkness was scary, she'd do it. As she reached out for the light chain, the door smashed open and he stood there, looking at her.

Part of her wanted to burst into tears, wet her pants, cringe; the other part of her just looked right back at him. The same part was also, out of nowhere, mad as hell. "Got a *prob*lem?" she asked, and consciously turned her back, giving the bed an awkward kick towards the wall.

He came over behind her, so close that they were almost touching. "Maybe you ought to think about being a little more scared," he said quietly.

She pushed the bed to get further away from him. "Maybe *you* ought to go to hell."

She saw his fist go back, then found herself crumpled on the floor, handcuffed arm twisted awkwardly, blood gushing from her nose and over her upper lip. She stayed there for a minute or two, disoriented, then lifted her free hand towards her nose, touching the blood. Then, she tried to get up, but was so dizzy that she had to sink back down.

He smiled. "Need a hand?"

"Fuck you," she said, and blinked, surprised by the reaction— and that she was crying.

He shook his head. "Mom and Dad wouldn't like that much."

She kicked at him with her left leg and he stepped out of the way.

"Getting angry?" he asked.

"No!" she said.

He grinned. "Not even a little?"

Bastard. She wiped her sleeve across her face, an alarming amount of blood soaking into the cloth. "What, is that the part you get off on? Or just the beating me up?"

"I'm getting off on just about all of this," he said, his voice managing to be both vicious and pleasant.

She slouched down, covering her face with her arm, still stunned by the fact that someone had just *hit* her. With his *fist*.

"Crying?" he asked.

She lifted her head just enough to look at him. "They have agencies you don't even know about working on this. Agencies *I* don't even know about."

He nodded seriously, folding his arms and leaning against the wall. "Consider yourself pretty important, do you?"

"No, I—" Frowning hurt, so she stopped. "I mean, *I* don't have anything to do with it."

He nodded. "Yeah. Good thing 'family' is such a big priority for your mother."

"No, she—" Meg stopped again. "It doesn't work that way."

"If she were a good mother, you wouldn't be here right now," he said.

Well—yeah. There was some truth to that. "It could have happened, anyway," she said, hearing the uncertainty in her voice. "I mean, they're pretty rich."

"Maybe, but *that* would just be ransom. You'd get out of it all right. But now," he shook his head, "because she doesn't love you—"

"It's not her fault," Meg said defensively, almost forgetting the blood and pain. "I mean, just because she's—"

He nodded again. "Worries about you kids first and foremost. Always there for you."

These were old arguments, old accusations. Things her family had worked to put to rest. To understand. Things that were none of his god-damn business. "I think you're just trying to upset me," she said.

He shrugged. "Seems to be working."

Since she *was* upset, she changed the subject. "You know, you'll never get anything. There's no *way* they'll negotiate with terrorists."

"Hmmm," he said, and made a point of tightening his fist. "Wonder what it would take to convince them?"

It was a good question—with far too many terrifying possibilities to explore. "Doesn't matter," she said. "They still won't ever negotiate."

"Tough price to pay," he said.

Jesus, there were so many things he could do to her. So many things she assumed that he, ultimately, *would* do to her. She swallowed. "*Especially* because it's her family, they can't. You should be smart, and let me go."

He nodded. "That'd be smart, all right."

Her nose was hurting more and she ducked her head, despite the blood still streaming out, to try and ease the pain.

"Tip your head back," he said.

Feeling dizzy, she lowered it more.

"Come on, tip your head back," he said, sounding impatient. "You want to bleed for the next week?"

She looked up slightly. "What's it to you?"

He frowned, moving away from her. "Hey, if you *enjoy* it."

"Not as much as you enjoyed *doing* it." But, she tipped her head back, feeling the blood run down somewhere inside her head. Afraid that she was going to cry some more, she closed her eyes, taking a deep breath to distract herself. Talking was a hell of a lot *better* distraction, though. "Don't I have to have my picture taken, or have you film me begging and kneeling, so you can put it on the Internet and everything?" While he and the others presumably stood nearby in hoods and masks, brandishing their weapons.

"Watch a lot of television?" he asked.

"Well—yeah," she said.

He nodded. "Thought so."

"Well—" She frowned, forgetting how much it was going to hurt. "I wouldn't do it, anyway."

He raised his eyebrows. "Oh, yeah?"

"Yeah," she said, trying to sound defiant. Fearless, even.

He took a quick step towards her, his right fist up, grinning when she flinched. He lowered the fist. "Okay. If you say so."

"Yeah, well—I wouldn't." Actually, if they hurt her badly enough, she probably *would*. Which was a humiliating thought. "You, um, you must want *some*thing. I mean, otherwise, what's the point?"

"Thought you said I wouldn't get anything *anyway*," he said.

"Well, yeah, but—" None of this was making much sense. She tilted her head to look up at him. "I mean, it seems like sort of a waste."

He shrugged. "Doesn't affect me."

"I don't—" How the hell could it *not*? Unless—she thought for a second. "You mean, you're working for someone?"

He grinned, firing his hand at her as though it were a gun, the gesture frightening—and also mildly amusing.

"You were supposed to say 'Bingo,' " she said.

His grin broadened.

"Well—who are you working for?" she asked.

He didn't answer, taking out a Swiss Army knife and cutting the light pull so that it would be out of her reach. He saw her watching and hefted the knife ominously, before grinning again, and putting it away.

A knife. There were a lot of terrible things he could do to her with a *knife*. She forced herself *not* to gulp. "Do they know how totally stupid this is?"

He shook his head, looking very amused.

"Well—" Christ, he could, at least, *talk*—"who are they?" she asked.

"Right," he said.

"Are we like, in their headquarters or something?" she asked, mentally crossing her fingers.

"Hmmm," he said. "Now, where's the first place you think they'd look?"

That gave her some hope, but she was careful not to show it. "You mean, they're letting people know who they are?"

He shrugged affirmatively. "The only thing they can *get* out of this is publicity."

That meant that someone would find her. The FBI, the CIA, a counter-terrorism unit, *someone*, would find her. All they had to do—

"Before you get all excited, my"—he gave the word extra irony— " 'employers' don't know who, or where, I am."

Hell. Naturally. "Going to be tough to send you that W-2 form," she said.

He started to laugh, but stopped himself.

"How did they hire you, if they don't know who you are?" she asked.

He shrugged. "Word gets around."

Looking at him, she could believe it. *She'd* hire him, if she wanted a really difficult crime committed. "Did they pay you a lot?"

He nodded.

"How much?" she asked.

"Right," he said, and shook his head.

She studied him, wondering if money were the only motivation. Surely, it had to be more complicated than that. "It must be a hell of *a lot* of money. Or do you like, hate the government or something?"

"Hard to resist the challenge," he said.

And, clearly, he had risen to the occasion. What a waste of ability. "You know, if you were nice," she said, "you could really accomplish a lot."

He laughed. "Oh, undoubtedly."

"You could really *help* people," she said.

He nodded. "Unh-hunh."

Undoubtedly. He sure didn't *sound* like a terrorist. At least, not her image of one. She narrowed her eyes. "Did you go to a good school?"

He laughed again. "Want to see my class ring?"

Automatically, she looked at his hands. No rings, of course. An expensive, but plain, Rolex. Nothing distinctive. She tried to read the time, and he immediately took the watch off, tucking it into his pocket.

Damn. "Well—how do you communicate with them?" she asked. "I mean, how are you going to know what to do to me, or anything?"

He smiled, very slowly looking her over. "Oh, I have a few ideas of what I'd like to do to you."

She couldn't help shuddering, moving her arm to try and cover herself.

"*More* than a few," he said.

Yeah, fine, whatever. She nodded stiffly. "I get the point."

"The *point*," he said, "is that once I have you, it's my show. They can do or say whatever they want, but the deal was autonomy."

Meg frowned. "So, they take all the credit, yank everyone around thinking they have me, but *really* don't have anything to do with it?"

"Bingo," he said.

# 7

WHEN HE WAS gone, with a mocking "Sleep well," she couldn't stop shivering. It seemed even colder and darker sitting on the floor and, with a lot of effort, she managed to pull herself up onto the bed. Spots of color seemed to be bouncing against her eyes, and she closed them, the throbbing in her nose joining her jaw and her head. Moving around had started a fresh rivulet of blood, and she tilted her head back against the wall. Her whole face felt sticky, and she wondered—for the first time—if her nose was actually *broken*. Jesus Christ.

She closed her eyes more tightly, praying that the pain would fade. People got beaten up all the time and still managed to— Christ, Steven had come home with so many black eyes and bloody noses over the years that they—Steven. Was her family safe? And Josh? She was almost sure that he had been lying about Josh being— but, what if he *wasn't*? What if—thinking wasn't going to help much. And, if she started crying, it wasn't going to help at *all*. The important thing was to stay cool, and—why the hell hadn't they ever briefed her about something like this? All of that god-damn security—and here she was, lying in some *place*, and—weakest link, they were probably saying to her mother. Human error. Lack of precedent. We're really sorry. One thing for sure—all hell must be breaking loose.

The blood seemed to be stopping and cautiously, she brushed at it with her sleeve. Talk about gross. Her eyes seemed to be swelling shut, which was going to make it even harder to stay awake. But, she couldn't *sleep*—she had to be ready. He—or someone else— might come in, and—and—it was hard to decide which would be worse: them coming in to kill her, or coming in to do something—obscene. Something—her stomach literally seemed to turn over and she made herself swallow, not wanting to throw up. Not that there was much of anything inside. Jesus, what a day to decide to skip lunch.

Not that she was hungry. Exactly. But, she was definitely *thirsty*. All she could taste was blood, and everything *hurt*, and—okay, okay, she had to focus. He'd said "Sleep well," so he probably wasn't coming back until the morning to bring her food or whatever. Which meant that maybe he was lying about not negotiating. Otherwise, it would have made a lot more sense just to execute her—Christ—or—the only thing she could tell for sure, was that he seemed to be feeling pretty safe. Seemed, to a degree, to be playing this by ear. So, all she could really do was wait. He was cocky as hell, but that didn't mean that she wasn't about to be rescued. Except that the longer this went on—unless it stretched into *days*, and they could get intelligence—*weeks?*—the less likely it was that they would be able to find her.

Unless he was stupid enough to have her right in downtown Washington. Yeah. Sure.

The smart thing, was not to do anything to make him mad. Turning on that light was the stupidest thing she'd done since—well, since not telling her parents that Dennis made her nervous, and asking if she could have a different agent put on the detail. Christ, if only she'd—but, it was too late to be worrying about *that*. What she had to do, was get this guy to *like* her. If he liked her, then he wouldn't want to hurt her, or kill her, or—just thinking that word made her stomach twist again. But, if she could make him like her—the Stockholm Syndrome, that's what they called it. On—well—television, they were always talking about the Stockholm Syndrome. Which had happened in some bank—in Stockholm, no doubt—where the hostages had started identifying with the robbers, and—oh, yeah, like she was going to end up *liking* this guy. It would be a long, cold day in hell before—Patty Hearst. Jesus Christ, this was going to be even bigger than the Patty Hearst—maybe that's why he wasn't killing her yet, maybe he was going to try and terrorize her into—aware that she was sitting rigidly, muscles tensed, waiting for him to come bursting in again, she made herself relax.

But, as news events went, this one must be *really* big. The 24-hour cable stations would be going crazy over the whole thing. Hell, by now, they had probably composed *theme music.* And had experts filling air-time speculating about whether she was still alive, or if the government was engaged in clandestine negotiations, and if there was any chance that such a sheltered, coddled, delicate young woman like the President's exclusive-private-school-attending daughter would be able to withstand the various forms of pressure and terror she was almost certainly facing. With luck, none of them would actually *say* anything like, "So, do you think she's being raped, or what?" on the air.

And she had no control over any of that. Over much of anything at all, actually. She maybe didn't *want* to sit alone in a dark room and wait, but she didn't have much choice. All she could do was try to keep her cool—and try even harder to god-damn well withstand absolutely *everything* that happened to her, no matter how unspeakable it was.

She closed her eyes, trying to think some soothing thoughts. Things could be worse. She could be dead already. She could have been shot and in even *worse* pain. She could be lying here *without* the unfamiliar sweatshirt and sweatpants. The concept of which was too horrible to pursue. Both arms and legs could be chained, she could be gagged, or blindfolded, or—she could have her period. *That,* would be a nightmare. And she had just gotten over it, so as long as they didn't keep her for several weeks—these were not comforting thoughts.

She pulled in a deep breath, slowly letting it out. The air hurt the hole where her teeth had been, but using her nose to breathe hurt even more. Still, she had to relax. Stay calm. Think productively. Continue taking slow, measured breaths. Sleep was a very tempting idea. But, the door might open when she least expected it, and realistically—she must be getting under control, she was thinking about this calmly—if they were going to kill her soon, it would be stupid to sleep the rest of her life away. She shouldn't waste it like that.

Which, unexpectedly, struck her funny. What was she going to do—sit here and compose poetry? Make peace with Her God? Although, if she was *in* this situation, Her God was obviously on vacation. Probably still not back from the one he took the day her mother got shot—although that was pretty blasphemous, and she found herself glancing up at the ceiling. That'd *really* make her day, if she saw a lightning bolt right around now.

She should probably be praying. Seemed like an appropriate time for it. But—well, that kind of foxhole stuff always seemed stupid to her. Like, when her mother had been shot, she didn't pray, because she *never* did. If she were God, people who only prayed when they wanted something would really bug her. To be able to justify praying in a situation like this, she should pray *every* day. Thank God for sunshine, and whiskers on kittens, and all. And, as for the old "if you get me out of this, I'll never yell at Steven and Neal again, or be cranky, or selfish, or—" Yeah, right. She'll probably make it about six hours.

So, she wouldn't pray.

On the other hand, maybe it was worth a try.

She had to grin, amused by the convenient little mind reversal there. When in doubt, rationalize. Not that she was going to turn around and suddenly embrace religion—but, it was funny that part of her *wanted* to.

Damned if she wasn't calm. Calm*er*, anyway. God's work, perhaps? The thought of which almost made her laugh. Be pretty amusing if she came out of this a born-again Christian or something.

"When God closes a door, somewhere he opens a window," she said solemnly, being the Mother Superior in *The Sound of Music*, and this time, she *did* laugh.

There was a movement out in the hall, and she sat up straight. Was he out there, listening to her? Or, if not him, someone who was guarding her? She could imagine the guy reporting in: "I don't know, boss, she's just sitting in there, laughing her head off."

The movement stopped, but she stayed alert, waiting for whatever might happen. Not that she should be surprised that someone would be out there. If—when?—the place got raided, the guy would want to be in position to use her immediately as a hostage.

Her left arm was numb again, and she clenched and unclenched her hand, trying to get the blood circulating. Which reminded her how much her jaw and nose and head hurt, and how cold it was—and how much calmer she had felt before. Any *second* now, they might come in here, and—oh, Christ. Oh, Christ, oh, Christ, oh, Christ. He was going to kill her, in some horrible, violent, scary way, and there wasn't anything she could—oh, Christ. What was he going to do? Just like, open the door, take out his gun, point it at her, and—or, Jesus, what if they were planning to *behead* her, the way so many other—oh, God, God, no.

She wanted to cry—to *whimper*—but, they might hear her. Of *course* he was going to kill her—he wasn't wearing a mask. And no one was going to show up and rescue her. That was movie stuff. This was—the panic faded into slight amusement. Real life, she'd been going to think. Speaking of movie clichés.

She slouched back against the iron frame—he could have given her a damned pillow, at least—and let her eyes close.

Time for some more deep breaths.

SHE MUST HAVE fallen asleep at some point, because when the key turned in the door lock, she had to wake herself up. Everything hurt more than ever, and she groaned, trying to find a less excruciating position. Her eyes wouldn't open quite right and she squinted in the direction of the door, seeing the same man.

"It's *Prom* Day," he said, with a Jack Nicholson grin.

Josh. Tears instantly in her eyes, she looked away.

"What's the matter?" He came over to the bed, prodding her shoulder. "Got a—*problem*?"

She turned away as far as she could, blocking the exposed side of her head with her arm, in case he decided to hit her again.

"Giving me the silent treatment?" he asked.

She didn't answer. The idea of making him like her worked a lot better in the abstract.

"I see," he said, and folded his arms. It was quiet for a minute, then he spoke again. "The President gave a *brave* angry speech last night."

Meg looked up.

"*Thought* that might interest you," he said.

Meg swallowed, her throat so dry that she wasn't sure she would be able to speak. "What did she say?"

"Oh, I don't know." He bent down so that his face was at a level with hers. "That your life is a sacrifice someone in her position has to make. That it's too bad, but"—he snapped his fingers— "those are the breaks."

Even the President wasn't *that* tough. Meg shook her head.

The man grinned. "She said to hell with it, and to hell with *you*."

Meg just shook her head, staring at his eyes to try and read the lie.

"Okay." He straightened up. "How about 'can not, have not, and *will* not negotiate with terrorists'?"

*That*, she probably said. "Probably just because they've already figured out where you are, and they're going to get you," she said.

"Unh-hunh." He sat on the bed, Meg moving away from him as far as possible. "She's got balls, your mother," he said conversationally. "After she told the country that she didn't care what happened to you, she said that what terrorists wanted more than anything was publicity, so she was requesting a complete news blackout."

Jesus. Serious grist for the Beltway mill. "Did they go for it?" Meg asked.

"Fuck, no," he said. "Are you kidding me? They're already out there falling all over each other."

So much for patriotism. Although some of the more reputable outfits were—she hoped—being more responsible. Her head was really aching, and she rubbed her temples with her free hand. "That just means that everyone in the media is looking for you now, too, and you're going to be that much easier to catch."

He nodded. "I know. Hell, I'm already booked on CNN tonight."

He *had* to be kidding, but it was kind of shocking that, for a few seconds, she almost believed it.

Then, to her horror, he reached out and ran his hand across her stomach. *Underneath* her sweatshirt. "No one really seems to be upset about *you,* but a lot of them sure are torn up about what happened to your boyfriend."

She tried to jerk away from him, but was caught short by the handcuffs, and the wall—and the idea that Josh really might not be okay.

"Saw an interview at your school, and they were all crying and wailing," he said. "Turns out, he got shot about ten times."

Oh, Jesus. "Before, you said five," she said, hearing her voice tremble.

He shrugged. "Doesn't make him any less dead."

Oh, God. He was lying. He *had* to be lying. Josh was so sweet, so—so *nice.* Not someone who deserved—not that anyone deserved—there was no way that he was telling the truth. In fact, he was probably lying about *everything,* just to try and keep her from being able to think clearly, or fight back, or—

"So, the Prom," he said, and patted her stomach, very cheerful. "Tonight the night you were *finally* going to sleep with him?"

She hunched down, not looking at him.

"Now, you must *really* regret waiting," he said pleasantly, sliding his fingers down towards her hips. "Being a good little girl."

Bastard. She knocked his hand away. "For all *you* know, I've slept with half of Washington."

"Really?" He pretended to look shocked. "Men *and* women?"

Whatever else he was, he was smart. Smarter than just about anyone she had ever met. "And *pets*," she said, spitting the words out.

He looked away, but she saw a little grin. "I'll leave you to your memories," he said, and got up.

"Aren't you going to bring me some food?" she asked.

He paused, halfway to the door. "Why?"

"Well—I mean—" Why, when she was going to be dead, anyway. She swallowed. "Y-you aren't?"

"Would you *trust* it?" he asked.

No. "No," she said.

He nodded. "Smart girl."

Jesus Christ, they weren't even going to *feed* her? "Well, wait," she said, as he opened the door. "Could I at least have a book or something? Or a radio? Or—"

"No," he said.

For some reason, the flatness in his voice brought tears to her eyes, and she had to blink a couple of times to keep them back. "Well—what about a pillow? I mean, I really—"

He shook his head.

"Could I have a *blanket,* at least?" she asked, feeling panicky. "It's so cold in here, I—"

The door slammed, and she was alone again.

# 8

HOURS PASSED. AND it *was* cold. And she was tired, and hungry, and *thirsty*. She slept on and off, but mostly just sat in the darkness, her brain feeling both numbed and as if it were on fast-forward. She didn't want to think—especially about the future. Especially about the *present*. Which just left—everything else she didn't want to think about.

Her head felt so thick and dull, that she couldn't seem to put any logical thoughts together, anyway. Just flashes, really. Their house in Massachusetts. How quiet it was, how safe. The smell of the Vicks VapoRub their housekeeper—and adopted grandmother—Trudy had always put on her late at night, when she had nightmares. She'd had a hell of a lot of bad dreams when she was little. Mostly, not being able to find her parents, not being able to go somewhere with her mother, and—ironically enough—being grabbed and taken away. Although, in the dreams, it was always monsters.

Which was also ironic. Like, just because this guy was civil, he wasn't a *monster*? Yeah, right.

Her handcuffed arm felt completely dead, and she squeezed it with her other hand, trying to get the circulation back in. It didn't matter what position she sat in—it still fell asleep after a few minutes. Not that it really mattered, since she'd be lucky if she ever got a chance to *use* it again. If he wasn't going to feed her, he obviously wasn't planning on keeping her around too long.

But, she wasn't going to think about that. There was no point in—unless it was going to be something horrible. Something *barbaric*, something—it wasn't fair, this shouldn't be happening to her. He was right—if her god-damned mother loved her, this *never* would have—no, damn it. She wasn't going to think that way. It wouldn't solve anything. Christ, worrying about the pain in her head and face—and, increasingly, her stomach—would accomplish more.

She huddled against the wall, shivering in the thin sweatshirt. It wasn't that she was *cold*, so much as—she just couldn't stop shivering.

Okay, she needed to concentrate on something else. *Anything* else. Except, all she kept coming back to now was her mother. The way their lives had always revolved around whether she was home or not. When she was coming back, what they would do when she got there. It was always so strange, sitting—for example—in Beth's kitchen, and watching Mrs. Shulman make dinner or whatever. After the divorce, Mrs. Shulman had dated a lot of significantly younger men, and then married a much older man—but, at least she was always *there*. There for meals, there for holidays, sometimes even there after school.

"Yeah, well, your mother may not be around," Beth had always said, "but at least, when she is, she has a clue."

"If she had a clue, she'd *be* around," Meg would say, and they would agree to disagree.

She thought about her father teaching her how to ride a bicycle, Trudy taking pictures so that her mother would be able to see them later. About all of the plays and tennis matches and assemblies and teachers' conferences her mother had never been able to come to—big vote on an appropriations bill, or something otherwise stupid—and how it was sometimes even worse if she *did* come, because the press would almost always show up, too, and waste a lot of time asking The Congresswoman, or The Senator, or The Candidate, or whatever the hell she was that particular year—*damn* her.

And damn that bastard out there for making her feel this way. Her family had spent a lot of time trying to work through these very things. Accepting them, in fact. Her mother was a difficult person, she was a complicated person, but she *was* a good person.

And she *did* love them; she always had. So, Meg was god-damned if she was going to let this son-of-a-bitch change any of that.

She had to concentrate on good memories. About Christmases they'd had, or times they'd gone skiing, or even how much closer they had all gotten since moving into the White House. Suddenly, her mother *was* there for meals, and birthdays, and just plain old conversations. She worked harder than she ever had, but then again, she worked right downstairs. Obviously, she still had to travel constantly, but as a rule, especially when the trip was overseas, the family went with her. All in all, things had gotten much better since she'd been inaugurated, and during the past year, it was the *outside* world that had been making things terrible. First, her mother's shooting, and now—but, she was *not* going to think about it. She wasn't. Period.

Only, that naturally made her think about something else she was avoiding. Some*one* else. Josh. The guy couldn't have been telling the truth—but, what if he was? What if—she'd seen poor Chet, and god-damn Dennis, and all the blood—and Josh could easily have—good things. "Think good thoughts," her father had often said, "life is short." He certainly had *that* one right.

She slouched lower, very close to crying. Josh was so nice. So nice to *her*. If only she'd broken up with him *completely*, so that there was no chance that he would have been anywhere near her, and no chance that he—or not broken up with him at all. Not done anything to make him unhappy. If, yeah, she'd slept with him. She should have—oh, Christ. She knew she had Secret Service agents, and she *knew* she had them for a reason—letting Josh be a target was at least as bad as her mother letting *her* be one. If anything had happened to him—now, she was crying again, and she pressed her face—nose be damned—into her arm.

She was still crying when she heard the key in the lock, and quickly sat up, wiping her face off with her sleeve so he wouldn't be able to tell.

The man came in, cocky as ever. "Keeping yourself amused?" he asked.

She didn't say anything, blinking as the light came on, and he smiled when he saw her face.

"Now, did I have you pegged as a crier, or *what*," he said.

"Fuck you," she said, and whisked her sleeve across her eyes again.

He shook his head. "Those manners sure are going downhill."

She hated him. She hated this arrogant son-of-a-bitch. Smelling food suddenly, she realized that he was holding what was left of a hamburger. A Big Mac. A delicious, beautiful Big Mac. Without meaning to, she licked her lips, which—judging from his grin—he found very funny.

He sat down in the wooden chair. "Give me a minute to finish this, and you can go to the bathroom."

The hamburger smelled so good that she couldn't look at him, her stomach hurting so much that she had to resist the urge to hold it with her uncuffed hand.

"All of this excitement makes me hungry," he said.

Bastard. The smell was almost dizzying, and she hunched over, not wanting to give him the satisfaction of watching.

He took his own sweet time, but just before finishing the last bite, he stopped. "I'm sorry—did you want some of this?"

She shook her head, to his obvious amusement.

"I mean, if I thought you were *hungry*, I would have brought you something." He came over to the bed, going through the handcuff routine until she was free of the bed frame, her hands cuffed in front of her. "Okay, let's go."

Her legs were stiff and weak, and each step was an effort.

"Come on, *move* already," he said, and shoved her so hard that she fell into the wall.

Which hurt. A lot.

She took as much time in the bathroom as she could, enjoying the change of scene. Rinsing her nose and mouth set off jagged shocks of pain, but she didn't stop, drinking from her cupped hands, and washing her face over and over again.

He threw the door open. "I say you could stay in here this long?"

She gave him an "*ask* me if I care" look, and kept drinking.

"Get out of there." He yanked her into the hall, Meg too tired to fight him, water splashing all over her sweatshirt.

"What's your hurry?" she asked, as he pushed her back into the room. "The boys putting together a stir-fry?"

He grinned—almost laughed. "We're making our own sundaes."

She came very close to laughing, too—much to her own disgust.

"How's the news blackout going?" she asked, as he cuffed her back to the bed.

He gave her wrist a sharp tug, checking the locks. "As far as I can tell, your loving mother got up this morning—and went right back to work."

She was almost sure that most of the things he had told her so far weren't true, so that probably wasn't, either. At least, not the way he was making it sound.

"Didn't even look like she lost any sleep," he said.

Not likely. She moved her jaw, wondering if she could trick him. "Your employers must be all upset, and yelling at you and everything."

He put the handcuff keys in his pocket. "They don't know where I am, Meg," he said, pleasantly.

*Meg?* She scowled at him. "You can't call me that."

He smiled. "I can do whatever I want."

"Yeah, well, you *can't* call me that," she said.

"Right." He paused. "Meg. Anything you say." Then, he snapped off the light, and walked over to the door.

"When are you coming back?" she asked, hating herself for it. The door closed.

IT WAS A long night. The longest night she could ever remember. Longer than Election Night ever *thought* of being. The only smart thing to do would be sleep, but she was too tired. Too *hungry*.

She curled uncomfortably on her side, bringing her knees up as high as she could for warmth, trying to use her shoulder as a pillow. It wasn't like her arm wasn't *already* dead. Lying in the dark and thinking would be a disaster, so she tried to remember the title of every book she'd ever read. Every movie and television show she'd ever seen. Every single song in her music collection. The *words* to the songs.

It was so boring, that she managed to doze off for a few minutes here and there, but it wouldn't last, and she'd be staring into the darkness again.

The only thing she was sure of, was that the next time he came in, she would have to make her move. He was going to kill her, anyway, so she might as well try. Also, she hadn't actually *seen* anyone else, so if she could elude him, she might be able to get away. That corridor had to go *somewhere*.

It was so quiet that when he came down the hall, endless hours later, the sound woke her up. By the time the key was in the lock, she was ready, slumping into an exhausted, defeated position. He opened the door, grinning when he saw her.

"Tough night?" he asked.

She didn't answer, not even raising her head, wanting to make it obvious that she had given up completely.

"*Knew* you wouldn't be able to hold out much longer." He cuffed her wrists together and uncuffed her from the bed. "Bathroom?"

She shrugged dully.

"You expect me to carry you, or something?" he asked.

She shook her head.

"Then, get moving," he said.

She took her time pushing herself up, using the wall for support, giving her legs a chance to get some strength back. She took a couple of steps, then sagged down so he would think she could barely walk.

"For Christ's sakes," he said, sounding impatient.

"I'm trying," she said weakly, all of her weight against the wall.

She waited until she was sure he was too annoyed to be paying close attention, then shoved past him and out into the hall. Running with handcuffs was awkward, but he'd reacted late and she was already around the corner, well ahead of him, when two men with stocking masks and machine guns snapped into position in front of her. She skidded to such a fast stop that she fell, landing hard on her hands. At first, she was stunned, then she looked up at them, still too surprised to be scared. The situation seemed unexpectedly ridiculous, and she laughed.

"Yeah," she said to them, out of breath, gesturing with the handcuffs. "I'd be scared of me, too."

Neither of them reacted, and she turned over onto her back to find the other man standing there with his gun leveled at her, his eyes colder than usual, his hand quivering slightly.

"Oh, come on," she said, moving to a less vulnerable position, sitting against the wall. "Would you respect me if I *hadn't* tried?"

He didn't answer, the gun pointed at—almost touching—her face, his arm visibly shaking.

Jesus Christ, he was going to shoot her. This wasn't like the other time, he was actually going to— "Hey, come on," she said, her voice trembling as much as his hand was. "It's not like I—"

"Shut up," he said, quietly. Viciously.

She nodded. "I know, but—"

"Shut up!" he said.

She did, too scared to breathe, watching his left hand come over to steady his right. He was deciding whether or not to kill her, he was about to—she sat absolutely still, terrified that even the tiniest movement might set him off, watching a gun that was pointed at her *face,* a real, loaded—she looked at his eyes, seeing nothing rational, or even human, in them.

They stared at each other for what might have been hours, unwanted perspiration blurring her eyes; then, slowly, he let out his breath and lowered his still-shaking arm, shoving the gun back into his jeans.

She collapsed against the wall, the last minute or two having been the most exhausting of her entire life. She sat there, dazed, not quite believing that she was still alive. That he hadn't pulled the trigger, that—the other two men were right behind him, gripping their guns, but she knew they wouldn't fire unless he told them to.

He was moving closer, and she lifted her head to see what was going to happen.

"Look, I won't do it again," she said, almost not recognizing her own voice. "I just—"

He didn't answer, suddenly kicking the outside edge of her kneecap, Meg both feeling and hearing a scream tear out as the top and bottom halves of her left leg twisted in different directions. He kicked again, even harder, then stepped back as she crumpled over what looked—and felt—like a severe dislocation.

He stood there, watching her for a second, then crouched down, resting his hand on it. "Next time," he said, very softly, "I use a bullet. Understand?"

She didn't say anything, breathing hard, covering her face with both cuffed hands so he wouldn't see her crying.

He increased the pressure, Meg trying—unsuccessfully—to keep from moaning.

"Understand?" he asked.

She nodded, the crying closer to whimpering.

"Okay." He straightened up, indicating for the others to return to their posts. "Now, get back to that room," he said to her.

She looked down what now seemed like a *very* long hallway.

"If you don't," he said, "I'll kick out the other one."

And he would. She knew perfectly god-damn well that he would. And if she *still* didn't move, he would probably do the same thing to her arms, and then—she swallowed, pretty close to losing control.

"*Now*," he said.

She swallowed again, the pain fading in and out of nausea, worse than anything she could ever remember. "C-can you at least uncuff me?"

He shook his head, very slightly smiling.

"Yeah, well, fuck you," she said, and pushed against the floor with her good leg, struggling not to scream as her bad one stretched and jarred with the effort.

It took a long time, using her right leg to propel herself inch by inch, and she kept her hands over her face, having to cry the whole way. She was too weak to get onto the bed, but he didn't help her, just grabbing her wrists to recuff her to the frame.

As he finished, she managed to look up, away from what had been her knee. "I *ski*, you bastard," she said, hearing her voice shake with hatred.

"Past tense," he said, gave her leg another kick, and left the room.

# 9

IT HURT SO much that she couldn't stop crying, every muscle stiff, her teeth digging into her lower lip. If he was going to kill her—and the reality of *that* was more and more obvious—then, why didn't he—they—just *do* it? Instead, he left her lying here, hour after hour, her leg ripped to—she cried harder, making small animal noises she didn't even know had existed inside of her.

The floor was cold and hard, and she tried to drag herself onto the bed, the pain so intense that she almost fainted. But, she tried again, using her elbow for leverage, almost biting through her lip as her leg flopped in an impossible direction, her whole body reacting with a convulsive shudder. Arms trembling, she pulled herself the rest of the way up, tasting blood by the time she was on the mattress. She lay there, crying, praying for this to be *over*. For him to hurry up and kill her.

It was a long time before he came back, and when she heard the key, she turned her head towards the wall, pretending to be asleep.

He came over, stood by the bed briefly, then walked away. Thank God. She heard the door close again and relaxed a little, waiting for the key to turn. When it didn't, she lifted her head slightly, wondering if he could still be—

"*Knew* you were faking," he said, from somewhere near the door. She slumped back down.

"Took all the fight out of you, I guess," he said, turning the light on.

She covered her eyes with her sleeve, the crook of her elbow at her nose so it wouldn't hurt more than it already did.

"Okay, fine," he said, and she heard the chair scrape across the floor to somewhere near the bed, and he sat down. There was the sound of a cork, then liquid pouring into a glass.

She stiffened, not sure if he had something sadistic in mind, but then, he put the bottle on the floor. From the smell, scotch. Christ, was he just going to sit there and drink? And *then* what would he do? Oh, Jesus.

"Want a drink?" he asked, his voice sounding a little thick.

She pulled in a few shaky breaths, not wanting to cry in front of him. Again.

He laughed. "Hurts, hunh?"

"*Please* go away," she said through her teeth.

"I don't feel like it," he said, and laughed again. "Sure you don't want one?"

She tried to turn further in the other direction, but moved her leg in doing so and had to groan. Oh, Christ, it hurt. It really, really hurt. Oh, Jesus. Jesus God, did it hurt.

"You'd feel better if you had a drink," he said.

Her breath was coming out in short gasps, a small high note of hysteria somewhere behind them, and her heart had started beating much harder, too.

"Fine," he said, and she heard more liquid pouring. "It's your own fucking choice."

He didn't say anything else and slowly, she got herself under more control, concentrating so intently that she almost forgot he was there.

Almost.

The steady throbbing in her knee was echoing inside her head—along with all of the other throbbing, underscored by a constant, searing pain, worse than anything she could—the tears wouldn't stop either, rolling down her face in what must be *grooves* by now, making her head hurt worse than ever.

"It would help you sleep, you know," he said.

That made a certain amount of sense, and she opened her eyes, considering the idea. If she could sleep, it would be a lot better than lying here, hour after hour, crying and in pain. At this point, she could sleep away every last second of her life and not give a damn. Just so this whole thing would be *over* already.

"It's—medicinal," he said.

A drink wasn't going to make things *worse*. She didn't think. And it couldn't be poisoned, not with him sitting there drinking it. So she nodded, rubbing some of the tears away with her hand.

"O-*kay*," he said, pouring some in another glass, then topping off his own.

"What is it?" she asked, and he turned the label so she could read it. Laphroaig. Jesus. Her *parents* drank that, sometimes. Lagavulin. Talisker. Stuff like that. In fact, even though her mother usually went out of her way to avoid "one of the boys" activities, she had been known to attend—and even throw—single malt tasting get-togethers. Beth had always described this as being inescapably—if not *indefensibly*—preppy. And the Speaker of the House, who was conservative as hell, but still one of her parents' closest friends, had once told her that when her mother first got to Washington, her occasional proclivity to organize such events was one of the only reasons any of them could stand her initially. But, at least, she never smoked cigars—although, once in a very great while, Meg would catch her father with one.

And, thinking about her parents was a really bad idea. She swallowed a hard jolt of homesickness, wishing that she hadn't asked. "K-kind of expensive," she said.

He shrugged, holding out her glass. She reached over, her hand trembling so much—from pain? Shock? Exhaustion?—that she had trouble taking it.

"Can you undo my other hand?" she asked. "So I can hold it better?"

He shook his head.

Naturally. She sniffed the pale gold liquid, not sure if she had ever even tasted scotch.

"Cheers," he said, his voice mocking.

Instinctively—too many White House dinners—she lifted her glass towards him, then to her mouth. Medicinal. Christ, as long as she didn't choke on it—he would be sure to make fun of her. She tipped the glass up, letting the liquid moisten her lips. It tasted awful. Like really intense cough syrup or something.

He made an amused sound, but didn't say anything, and she took an actual sip. The taste made her shudder, but the warmth going down felt very good. Soothing. Gaining confidence, she tried a bigger sip, then looked over at him.

"Come here often?" she asked.

His laugh was the most genuine she'd heard it and, smiling a little herself, she drank some more, only recoiling slightly from the taste. The warmth was giving her courage, and she looked back over.

"Hello," she said—using the proper soft accent. "My name is Inigo Montoya. You killed my father. Prepare to die."

This time, he really did laugh. "Golly. Can you do *Caddyshack*, too?"

As a matter of fact, she *could*. Extensively. She took an even bigger sip. Not bad. In fact, this stuff could grow on her. "Distinctly peaty, with a full-bodied, yet subtle, finish," she said.

He gave her such a sharp glance that she realized she had just hit the *precise* timbre and inflections of the President's voice—and that, in this context, it must have been unsettling to hear.

They stared at each other for a few seconds, uncomfortably, and then, she drank a full mouthful, shivering from the aftershock of— heat? Fumes? *Some*thing. When the sensation faded, it seemed very cold in the room, and she gulped another mouthful.

"I'd take it easy," he said.

"*You'd* take it easy," she said. "Then, how come the bottle's half empty?"

He didn't answer, drinking.

Thinking about reasons why he might feel like he had to get drunk was scary, and she focused down on her glass. "Half full, I mean," she said quietly.

He paused, his glass halfway to his mouth. "What?"

"Half full," she said. "The bottle is half *full*." She nodded to punctuate that, then took a sip of her scotch. His feet were propped up on the side of the bed frame, and she looked down at the heavy leather high-tops, deciding not to think about the fact that he had used them to kick her knee to shreds. "So. You and the boys going to play some ball later?"

He grinned, but didn't say anything.

"How'd the Red Sox do tonight?" she asked.

"Couldn't tell you," he said.

"Bullshit." She drank more scotch. "You just don't *want* to."

"You're a chatty drunk, aren't you," he said.

Oh, yeah, like she'd ever been drunk in her life. She shrugged. "How the hell would I know?"

"Dream Teen," he said, his voice more than a little vicious.

Bastard. "What am I supposed to do—stumble around drunk, then have it show up all over the Internet and everything?" She shook her head. "Christ."

"They would've covered it up," he said.

"Are you serious? The tabloids always print stuff like that *anyway*." She finished off her drink. "All I need's for it to be true."

"And it's always lies?" He leaned over, pouring more into her glass. "On account of you being perfect and all?"

She frowned at the liquid. "Are you trying to make me drunk?"

"Does your leg still hurt?" he asked.

Yes. She nodded.

"Okay, then." He refilled his own glass, too.

"I don't know." She kept frowning. "Are you trying to be nice, or mean?"

"Hey, I'm not pouring it down your throat," he said.

True. She took a careful sip, in case it was going to make her drunk soon. "Do you drink a lot? In your life, I mean?"

"I'm not an alcoholic," he said, "if that's what you mean."

"No, I—" What *did* she mean? "My parents drink a lot." That wasn't what she meant. "Well, not a lot, I just—I mean, before, they only—well, it was just sometimes. Now, like, they almost always have a drink."

"They share it?" he said, his mouth in the half-smile.

"No, I—" Was he stupid? She squinted at him. "Before dinner, I mean. You know, like a drink."

"So, they're alcoholics," he said.

"No." Actually, her mother almost never had a drink without *also* having a couple of shots of espresso, too—presumably to balance it out. "I just meant—" Could she really be getting drunk already? Nothing was making sense. "The White House made things different, that's all. They worry more."

"Bet they're drinking up a storm right now," he said.

"*Coffee*, maybe." During crises, they always drank coffee. Most people probably did. She glanced over. "Um, are you getting drunk for a *reason*?"

"I'm not drunk," he said, his voice belligerent enough to be a contradiction.

He was up to something. He had to be. "Are you—" She stopped, not wanting to give him any ideas.

"What?" he asked.

She shook her head.

"*What*?" he asked, less patiently.

She took a swallow of scotch. "I just—are you going to do anything—bad—to me?"

His face relaxed. "What do you mean, 'bad'?"

"Well, I mean—*you* know," she said. "Bad."

"Oh." He grinned. "You mean, just for example, yanking teeth out of your head wasn't—'bad'?"

She shook her head, kicking herself for having brought it up.

His grin widened. "And mangling your leg wasn't—"

"Look. I just want to know, okay? I mean, if you're going to—" She couldn't actually say it. "I mean—"

"Oh," he said. "*That*."

She nodded, suddenly exhausted, her knee hurting worse than ever.

He smiled, leaning closer. "Do you want me to?"

"I just want to be *out* of here," she said, "okay?"

"I'll bet you do." He got up and sat on the bed—which was definitely not a positive sign. "The thought *does* keep crossing my mind."

She didn't say anything, her good leg pulled up, trying to protect her chest with her right arm.

"Feelings might be a problem," he said.

Yeah, right. "You're worried about *my* feelings?" she asked.

"Hardly," he said.

"Oh." She moved her jaw, which hurt. What *didn't* hurt? "You mean, raping *me* would hurt *your* feelings."

"Some sort of feelings would be inevitable," he said, patting her hip in a distracted sort of way.

She frowned. "I don't get it."

"Let's say, for instance, I start hating you." His hand trailed down her thigh, squeezing lightly, then moved back up to her hip. "If I *do*, I lose perspective. And if I do *that*, I stop thinking about my job, and—" He shrugged, raising his drink with his free hand. "Well, it's not a good idea."

She didn't respond, edging away so that he wouldn't be able to touch her as easily.

"Then again, worst scenario, I start *liking* you," he said. "And liking you makes it a hell of a lot harder to do the things I have to do to you."

"*Have* to do to me," she said, almost under her breath. Then, she thought about that. "Wait a minute. You don't like me at *all?*"

He shook his head.

"Even with me being such a—you know, under the circumstances—good sport?" she asked.

He laughed. "Afraid not."

If she hadn't been handcuffed, she would have put her hands on her hips. Or, at the very least, folded her arms. "Well, for Christ's sakes," she said.

He laughed again, moving back to his chair.

She scowled at him. "Yeah, well—fuck you."

"Such conviction," he said.

"*Fuck you*," she said.

He nodded. "Keep trying. You'll get it right."

Damn him. She looked down at her hand, wrapped around the glass. "Would it make a difference?" she asked, ashamed by the question.

He cocked his head. "What?"

She kept her eyes down, feeling herself blushing. "Me making you like me."

A slow grin spread across his face. "In exchange for not killing you?"

She nodded, incredibly ashamed.

"Probably not," he said, then paused. "Would you do it?"

"Probably not," she said.

"Just curious?" he asked.

She nodded, her face hot with embarrassment.

He looked her over, in a calculating sort of way. "It's not the *worst* idea I ever heard."

"Yeah, it is," she said stiffly.

"Oh, I don't know." He rested his hand on her stomach. "You might *enjoy* it."

She shook her head, moving away from the hand.

"You might be"—he shifted his hips slightly—"surprised."

She looked right back at him. "You know what they say about people who carry *guns* around."

He grinned, taking the gun out, holding it between his first two fingers. "What, *this* little thing?"

He was so god-damn arrogant that she found herself grinning back. "Yeah, right."

"*Well*," he said, and put the gun back.

What a—she couldn't even think of a word—but, it was somewhere between jerk and psychopath.

"What?" he asked.

"I don't know." She shook her head. "You must listen to a lot of Screamin' Jay Hawkins."

He nodded. "My man, Screamin' Jay."

"You really do?" she asked, surprised.

"Well—not recently," he said.

The fact that he even knew what she was talking about was—weird. Too weird. She slugged down some of her scotch. "You're not anything like a terrorist."

"Ah," he said. "You know a lot of terrorists, do you?"

"No, I—" Something new occurred to her, and she stopped drinking. "Was it like, an inside job? I mean, do you work for the government?"

He made a face. "Oh, right. Definitely."

"Well, I still don't get how you pulled it off," she said.

He shrugged.

Her mind felt so damn sluggish that it was frustrating, and if there were a table or anything nearby, she would have put her drink down, once and for all. "They should have been able to stop it. I mean, I don't care about Dennis, or how smart you are—"

"They *could* have," he said. "A little quicker with the flashbangs and the rest of the NLWs, and they *would* have."

Which didn't make much sense. Christ, was she drunk? "Flash—" She shook her head. "I don't—"

He grinned wryly. "You have a lot more back-up than you think you do."

"You mean—" Jesus. "You paid off *all* of them?" she said.

He snorted.

"Then—" She must be drunk— "I don't—"

"Took a gamble," he said. "Figured it out as much as I could, and then it depended on how far they were willing to go."

Why couldn't she follow any of this? "I don't understand," she said.

"It's simple," he said impatiently. "Either they were going to blow away everything in sight, *or* they would decide your life wasn't expendable and try to arrest the situation at a different point."

She frowned, her brain still feeling fuzzy. "You thought they would *kill* me?"

He shrugged. "Tough call. Me pulling it off makes the government look pretty stupid."

"Yeah, but—they wouldn't've *killed* me," she said. Would they? Jesus.

"It would've stopped it," he said.

Well—yeah. It probably would have, at that. But—Jesus. "So—" There had been so much shooting. "They didn't fire back?" she asked.

He shook his head. "Not where you were. Didn't even seem like they had the nerve to try a thermobaric, or any of their other little toys."

She had no idea what he was talking about—and wasn't sure

she *wanted* to know. "If they'd killed me, you *definitely* would have been killed."

He nodded.

Jesus. What kind of person was he? Not normal, that was for sure. "That's kind of a chance to take," she said.

His shrug was entirely disinterested as he poured more scotch into his glass.

How did someone make a comprehensive, ambitious plan, knowing that it might well result in his being killed? It couldn't have just been because of the money—no matter *how* much it was. Had he, at some level, been trying to commit suicide-by-cop, or—

"What," he said, as she kept looking at him.

"I can't tell if you're crazy or not," she said.

"Oh, really?" He filled his glass one more time, and put the bottle down.

"Well—you just seem regular. I mean, like you went to a good school, and could be doing all sorts of things. So, I can't see why—" She paused. "Are you a veteran, maybe? And washed out or got stop-lossed, or something, so you're all bitter towards the government and stuff?"

He rolled his eyes.

Okay, but it had to be something along those lines. "Maybe," she said, "you're like, a mercenary? Going around to the Middle East and Africa and all?"

He didn't answer, but made it clear that he thought she was tiresome—and also, not very bright.

"I don't know," she said defensively. "I just—I can't figure you out."

He shrugged, drinking.

She watched him, trying to make some sense out of this. He was just—a guy. A guy in Levi's, basketball sneakers, and—today—a blue flannel shirt. An expensive one. Well cut.

"*What*," he said, letting out an irritated breath.

"I just—" She looked at him uncertainly. "You *really* don't like me?"

"No," he said. "I really don't."

# — 10 —

IT WAS VERY, very quiet. So quiet, that none of this seemed real. Then again, the world—the *actual* world, where she would be hanging out in the solarium or someplace, reading or holding her cat or watching movies with her brothers—that didn't seem real, either.

But, *this* situation, so oddly civilized and violent, was even more mind-bendingly strange. Bizarre. *Impossible.*

Exhausting.

"You were going to kill me this morning," she said, breaking the silence.

He nodded. "Probably should have."

She sipped some of her drink, hunching her shoulders for warmth. If *only* her leg would stop hurting. "H-how come you didn't?"

"I don't know." He looked at his own glass. "I'd rather do it as planned, not because I lose my temper."

As planned. "You mean," she had to swallow, "you're still going to?"

He nodded, expressionless.

Oh. "You don't have to," she said, trying very hard not to sound panicky. "I mean—"

"Don't beg," he said, "okay?"

Jesus, had it sounded that way? "I wasn't, I just—" Seeing utter contempt come into his eyes, she stopped. "I just wondered," she said quietly.

Neither of them spoke for a while, the guy staring straight ahead, Meg just sitting there.

"What about—" He could, at least, answer *this*. She took a deep breath. "Did you kill him?"

He smiled faintly. "Who, your *boy*friend?"

Even her heart muscle felt tense with fear, and she clenched her hand around the glass. "My friend, yes."

It was quiet again.

"I don't know," he said finally. "I think I saw him out there, though."

"On the *ground*?" she asked.

He looked at her, not answering.

"Oh, come on," she said. "You're doing all this bad stuff to me, can't you just—*please?*"

He sighed. "He has glasses, right? Was wearing a red cap?"

Jesus. He *had* been outside, then. She nodded, her muscles even tighter.

"We were already leaving. He—" The guy moved his jaw. "He wasn't involved."

"You're *sure?*" she said.

He nodded, and she felt her shoulders relax a little for the first time since all of this had happened.

"You really wouldn't lie to me?" she asked. "I mean, *this* time?"

"He was fine," he said. "Don't piss me off, okay?"

She nodded, blinking away tears of relief. "Thank you," she said, almost whispering.

He shrugged, lifting his glass.

Again, they didn't talk for a while, Meg struggling not to burst into thankful tears. He was telling the truth. She was almost *sure* he was telling the truth.

Then, immediately embarrassed by the thought, she realized that the alcohol was having at least *some* effect.

"What," he said.

"I, uh," she didn't look at him, "I need to use the bathroom."

He looked annoyed. "Christ."

"I really do," she said.

He sighed heavily, and fumbled in his pocket for the handcuff keys. "Got any bright ideas of how you're going to get out there?"

She shook her head, feeling—whether she should or not—very ashamed. He didn't make any move to cuff her hands together once he'd freed the left one, so, carefully, she eased her bad leg towards the edge of the mattress. It dangled horribly, hurting so much—even through the haze of scotch—that she had to groan, new tears coming out of her eyes. She brought her right leg over to the edge, too, and tried to use it to stand up, fingernails pressed into her palms. It hurt too much and she had to cry in earnest, covering her face with her hands.

"Can't get up?" he asked.

She shook her head, even more ashamed.

"Christ." He put his glass down on the floor, then moved next to her, bending to lift her.

"I can do it!" she said, trying to pull away.

"Shhh." He cupped her cheek with one hand. "I'll try not to hurt you."

Oh, yeah. Definitely.

He picked her up, one hand around her back, the other under her legs. She had to gasp in pain, and he moved his arm further away from her bad knee. Being carried was humiliating, and she put her hand over her eyes, leaning away from him as much as she could.

"Be easier if you put your arm around my neck," he said.

That was about the *last* thing she wanted to do, but then she remembered the gun in the waistband of his jeans. If she put her arm around his shoulder, maybe she could reach down, grab the gun, and—

"If you go for that gun," he said, "I'll break every bone in your body."

She took her hand off his back, so frustrated that she wanted to hit him. "The hammer, the anvil, and the *stirrup?*"

He didn't answer, banging her leg into the doorjamb, instead, and she gasped, having to grab his shoulder for support. Horrified, even through the pain, that she'd *touched* him—voluntarily—she yanked her hand away, covering her face with it.

They were at the bathroom door now, and he pushed it open, then set her down, Meg grabbing onto the knob to keep from falling. With her hands free, though, it was easier to get around, and she maneuvered herself into the little room, closing the door.

The whole operation was excruciatingly painful, and after she'd lurched over to the sink to wash, she collapsed onto the floor, gripping just above the knee with both hands, rocking in an attempt to ease the pain. He opened the door, but she was in too much agony to look up, the leg throbbing and jerking in what had to be muscle spasms.

"Oh, Christ." He crouched down next to her, trying to ease her hands off. "Come on, take it easy now."

"Don't make like a coach when you're the one who hurt me!" she said, trying to protect herself. The leg really seemed to be jerking now, hot scary spasms, hurting so much that she couldn't seem to breathe. And it was going to get worse and worse, and he was going to kill her, and, and—

"Planning on having hysterics?" he asked, his voice breaking through the blur of terror.

"You'll be the first to know," she said weakly, and he laughed.

His hands were soothing the muscles, unexpectedly gentle, and she watched him do it, some of the panic—and a little bit of the pain—fading.

"Trust me not to, all of a sudden, twist it?" he asked.

She stiffened, just in case. "I don't have much choice."

"No," he said. "You don't."

The muscle spasms had pretty much stopped now and he picked her up, still surprisingly gentle. There was something scarily intimate about being carried, and she was so exhausted and afraid that she wanted to rest her head on his—*anyone's*—shoulder. To have him promise that it was going to be okay, that he wasn't going to hurt her anymore, that she was safe. That everything was going to—she held herself rigidly in his arms, pretending that she had fallen on the tennis court or something, and was being taken to the hospital, and—he was lowering her onto the bed, which hurt, but not as much as it could have.

Slowly, he recuffed her to the frame, then sat on the edge of the mattress. Feeling his hand touch her cheek, she opened her eyes all the way, startled by the strange look on his face.

"You would, no doubt, have grown into a spec*ta*cular woman," he said.

"You'd better watch it," she said, just as quietly. "You're going to lose your edge."

Abruptly, he got up. He stood there, looking at her, his expression unreadable, and then suddenly smashed his fist into the wall above her head, Meg cringing. He must have been even drunker than she thought, because even though he'd dented the plaster, his expression never changed. He picked up the scotch bottle with his other hand and turned to go, not speaking to her. The door slammed behind him, and she was alone in the dark, trembling, not sure where the scotch left off, and the *real* fear and confusion began.

IF NOTHING ELSE, she slept *heavily*. Dead, dreamless sleep, waking up with a pounding headache—to go along with all of the other pain—and an unbelievably dry mouth. She licked her lips, trying to moisten them, wishing he would hurry up and come in, so she could get a drink of water from the bathroom.

But, he didn't. Not for a long time, anyway. She lay on the bed, just being in pain, her eyes so heavy that it hurt to keep them open, too tired to worry, or be afraid—or even to think. She was also too tired to sleep, so she rested her head against the wall, holding her aching jaw. Sometimes, the warmth from her hand made it feel better. Her leg and nose hurt too much to touch at *all*.

When the door finally opened, she shook herself out of her doze with some difficulty. He didn't look that great, either—wearing the same shirt, unshaven, shadows beneath his eyes.

"Need to use the bathroom?" he asked, not looking at her.

She nodded, although if he didn't carry her again, she wouldn't be able to make it. "How's your hand?" she asked, *not* kindly, seeing that it was swollen.

He glanced down, a little self-consciously. "I'll live," he said, with extra irony.

They didn't look at each other.

"Yeah, well," he said, and came over to uncuff her.

As he reached for the keys, there was an urgent knock and instantly, he had his gun out. He moved to the door, opening it partway. One of the men said something to him in a low voice, and she heard him say, "*Shit,*" before he answered, his voice just as low.

Then, without any explanation, he was gone, and the other man had posted himself inside the room, machine gun ready, staring straight ahead through his mask.

"Wh-what's going on?" she asked.

The man didn't even look at her, giving no indication that he had heard.

"Is something wrong?" she asked, although from the sounds of quick movement and muffled orders in the hall, the answer was obvious.

The man never spoke, and when the regular guy—Jesus Christ, she didn't even know his *name*—came back with another stocking-masked man, she knew. The way they came in—very quiet, very professional, emotionless. She stiffened even before she saw the syringe in his hand and then, felt bile come up into her throat.

They were going to kill her. Jesus Christ. Right now, without any warning, or preparation, or—she drew her good knee up, moving defensively into the corner.

"What's going on?" she asked, voice shaking.

None of them said a word, which was scarier than an answer. She edged further into the corner, making her body as small as it could be, hampered by the handcuffs.

"At least tell me what's going on," she said, looking at the regular one, trying to find some sign of the man who had seemed almost—fond—of her last night.

He avoided her eyes, turning to one of the other men. "Hold her down," he said, which was when she panicked, forgetting about the handcuffs, trying to dive past them.

The man in the stocking mask caught her easily, pushing her back down on the mattress, keeping her there. She fought as hard as she could, twisting and turning, never taking her eyes off the syringe—or the man holding it. He was going to kill her. Without even—she struggled harder, adrenaline bursting into her in uneven jerks.

He just waited, letting the man in the stocking mask do all of the work. "Come on," he said, sounding very tired—and maybe even a little sad. "Don't fight."

When she didn't stop, looking directly at him as she flailed at the other man with her free arm, fighting with more strength than she thought she had left, he sighed and pressed his hand into her left knee. The combination of that—and the other man's weight and fists—worked, and she found herself pinned, breathing hard, trying not to cry, her left arm forced out at an unbearable angle along the bed frame.

She watched him come towards her arm with the syringe, and as their eyes locked, a weight even heavier than the other man seemed to press into her whole body. She had to do something to stop him, *say* something, something to make him change his mind—*anything* to—it was almost over, the whole thing was almost—she had to *think*, had to—

"Nurse *R*atched, I presume?" she said, and managed, just as the needle went in, a very weak laugh.

# ~ 11 ~

SHE WAS AWARE of pain first. Darkness second. And—dirt. She was lying somewhere, with her face in the dirt. There was some in her mouth and she tried to spit it out, her throat so dry that she couldn't. She was too dizzy and sick to lift her head, and everything else hurt so much that she let her eyes close again. She wasn't ready to deal with this yet.

The next time she woke up, it wasn't as dark. She lay there for a long time, not trying to move. After a while, she turned her head, lifting it just enough to see where she was. Light. Not much—coming in through boards or something. The air smelled mildewed, but there was also a draft. A cold one. Jesus Christ, was she in a *cave*?

Okay, okay, it wouldn't make sense to freak out. Yet. The first thing to do, was to try and turn over. See what was going on. Assess the situation calmly. For all she knew, she was just in a different *room,* not in a whole new—a room with a dirt floor? But, maybe they'd just stashed her outside whatever building she had been in before, and that wasn't as scary as—except, wait, *that* would be pretty god-damn scary, too.

Okay, she needed to get up, and figure out what was going on. Using both hands, she tried to push herself to a sitting position, her arms weak and trembly. There was a heavy cuff of some kind on her right wrist and she pulled experimentally, discovering that it was attached to a chain. A *short* chain. Jesus Christ.

She didn't seem to be strong enough to sit up, but she managed, groaning, to turn over onto her back. She stayed there, exhausted by the tiny achievement, letting her eyes—one of which wouldn't open—get more accustomed to the darkness.

Oh, God, she hurt. *Everything* hurt. Pain she didn't remember from before. Something must have happened to—oh, Christ, was she *alone*? Or was he sitting there, watching her? All of them, watching her. Or—it was so dark.

But, she didn't see anyone. In fact, she didn't see *anything*. Just a tunnel or something. She reached out, tentatively, to feel the wall with her left hand. Rock. Cold, dry, fairly smooth rock. Which established—what, exactly? If she was in a tunnel carved out of rock—well, that sounded a hell of a lot like a cave. She could be near the end, or it could go back for miles—it was too dark to tell.

She made herself listen for a few seconds, still trying to figure out if she was by herself. Wind. What might be a bird. Maybe some creaking, over where the light was. Sunlight? Maybe. Daylight, anyway.

Okay, okay, it was time to find out how badly injured she was— starting with her legs. She flexed each foot, cautiously; moved her ankles, bent her right knee. Small, dull pains; some old, mostly new. Bruises, probably—no reason to panic. Her left knee felt as bad as it had before, and she didn't try moving it.

One hip hurt a lot, the other one was just stiff. It was her ribs, where the serious new pain started, the slightest breath or movement causing twinges sharp enough to make her gasp. Vaguely, she could remember being punched—repeatedly, by a very large man—before the other man jabbed the syringe into her. Had they kept hitting her *after* she went unconscious? Had they tried anything *else* while she was—no. She couldn't feel anything to indicate that they had done something—awful—and the drawstring—she checked, and double-checked—to her sweatpants was still tightly knotted.

She tried moving her head. Her neck. Her arms. Just bruises. And stiffness from lying in cold dirt for God only knew how many hours. Either she had been battered around during the transfer to this place—she could smell and feel a smear of motor oil across her clothes—or they had intentionally hurt her, tried to beat her to death, maybe.

Jesus.

She touched the cuff on her wrist, then followed the chain with her fingers to a metal stake driven deep into the rock wall. She yanked on it, neither finding—nor expecting—any weak points. Christ. Her working eye was starting to be able to see better, and she looked around, seeing man-made, but very rough, rock walls, and a thick wooden beam here and there, supporting the ceiling. Was this place a *mine shaft*, maybe? It obviously went further back—and down?—but, she couldn't tell *how* far.

Only a little bit of light was coming in through the boards, and she realized that it wasn't a door. No, someone had put them across the entrance, and—apparently—*nailed* her inside. Nailed her in with dirt, and rocks, and—nothing else. No food. No water. No blanket.

No water. She swallowed, her mouth and throat so dry that it was difficult. No water. He and the others might be out there somewhere—but, she doubted it. He'd left her here, nailed in, chained, without any water.

Left her here.

Panicking, she yanked on the chain with both hands, trying to pull free. It wouldn't budge, but she had to try, struggling with it until she was out of breath and crying, and too weak from pain to continue. She collapsed into the dirt, trying not to pant because it made her ribs hurt so much.

Help. She should call for help. So, she turned her head towards the light.

"Hey!" she said, her voice rasping out. "In here!"

Talking made her throat feel as if it were rupturing and she tried to swallow again, not able to come up with much saliva.

"Hey, help!" she shouted. "In here!"

There was no answer. No sound at all, except for maybe the damned wind.

She felt in the dirt until she found a rock, and then threw it at the boards to try and break them. It fell harmlessly inside, about ten feet away, and she threw another, with the same result. For the hell of it, she threw one towards the back of the cave, hearing it go at least twenty feet. So, she threw a whole handful of small rocks, listening as they hit dirt, other rocks, and maybe some more boards. No comforting splash to indicate that there was a pool of water, or something, back there.

No water.

No god-damn water. The inside of her mouth tasted terrible—blood and dirt, mostly—and she swallowed yet again, the muscles in her throat noisy in protest. Damn it, she had to *think*. Maybe she could *dig* for water. Maybe—she fumbled around until she found a fairly sharp rock, and began using it to scratch a hole in the dirt, her fingers cramping with the effort. She would dig as long as she could stay awake—which wasn't going to be long—and then, when she woke up, maybe water would have seeped into the bottom of the hole, and she could drink it.

Yeah, chalk up another one for Nature Girl.

The ground was hard and rocky, but she was so relieved to be *doing* something that she kept digging. One inch. Another. The dirt felt very cold. Damp? Maybe. But, definitely cold.

Energy ebbing, she dug another half inch, then was too exhausted to continue and let the rock drop out of her hand. She tried leaning her head against the wall, but it was too uncomfortable, so she curled up in the dirt, trying to find the least painful position, using her right arm as a pillow.

Too tired and afraid to think, she closed her eyes.

"MEG, ARE YOU all right?" she heard someone saying.

A nice voice. She was safe! The whole thing had been a—she smiled, opening her eyes—except, she couldn't see anything. Oh,

God, she was blind. She raised her hand in front of her face, trying to see it. She *was* blind! She couldn't—

"Where are you?" she asked, her voice barely working. "I can't see you!" She didn't hear anything. She didn't *see* anything. "Talk to me! Where are you?"

As she tried to sit up, she heard the chain clank—and both the relief, and fear, went away, as she realized where she was. That there was no one there. Unless he *was* in here, unless he was trying to—

"Where are you?" she asked, trying to look in every single direction at once. "Are you in here? Are you trying to scare me?"

*Trying?* Yeah, right. Succeeding, and *then* some. Except, she didn't hear anyone. She didn't hear anything at *all*. The wind again, maybe.

She rubbed her hand across her face, feeling dirt, and a thick crust below her nose and lips that could only be dried blood. Her nose was stuffed up—also with blood?—and she was having to breathe through her mouth, which was even drier than it had been before. She licked her lips, feeling more than one crack. Oh, boy. This was getting more and more serious with every—the hole! She felt for the hole in the darkness—so black that she couldn't see her hand moving—but, finally found it.

An empty hole. A *dry* hole.

Serious, serious trouble. And her mind just felt numb. Blank. *Stupid*. She eased herself back against the wall, gripping her ribs with her free arm, and focusing in the direction of the boards. The only thing she could think of to do was wait for morning.

DAYLIGHT ONLY MADE things seem worse. More hopeless. All she knew for sure was that she couldn't just sit here and wait for something to happen. She had to *do* something. To think of a way out of this place.

The only possible solution was to break the chain, somehow.

How, being the operative word. She didn't have much energy, so she had to choose. She could chip away at the stake, and the rock wall, trying to loosen it, or she could choose a weakest link, hammering on it until the chain broke. She pulled on the stake, then pulled on the chain. The chain. It wasn't as thick. She felt for a rock, then pounded at the place where the chain and stake met. Double her odds, that way.

Hammer, hammer, hammer, rest. Hammer some more. And some more. As many times as not, she would miss, scraping her knuckles against the rock wall. When her left hand hurt too much to continue, she switched to her right, hammering and hammering, not sure if ten minutes—or ten hours—were passing.

Her sweatshirt was damp, and her arms were so heavy that it felt as if her strength was draining out, along with the perspiration. But, she kept hitting the chain, trying not to perspire, to lose liquid. Each time she lifted her arm, she wasn't sure if she could do it again, but she kept going, on the theory that it was keeping her sane. Oh, yeah, terribly. Although there was nothing in there to vomit, her stomach was upset and she wished she could swallow more easily. More often.

Hammer. Hammer. Hammer again. What time was it? What *day* was it? It had been dark—twice? More times? She'd slept so much that it was hard to tell.

Her hair seemed like a great weight, and she pushed it off her neck and shoulders. It felt disgusting—dirty and sticky, hanging in damp clumps. Talk about gross.

"I'm going to get out of here," she said, needing to hear a voice. Even a voice that pathetic and hoarse. "I swear to God I'm going to get out." Which seemed kind of melodramatic. "I'll *never* go hungry *again*," she said, being Scarlett O'Hara. She laughed weakly. Might as well make jokes. Nothing else to do.

Her hands were numb from hitting the wall by accident so many times, and she dropped the rock, giving up for a while. She should probably sleep. If she was going to have to die, she'd prefer to have it happen as soon as possible. Survival was too god-damn tiring.

Maybe she was cracking up. Then again, the last few days had been pretty rough—she was entitled.

"Miss Powers, I'm sorry," she said. "You're going to have to be put to sleep."

Sleep. Good idea. She fell forward into the dirt, with barely enough energy to turn her face out of it. She wanted to cry, but couldn't get any tears out. Jesus, she must be *really* dehydrated. If she was longing for death, maybe she was getting her wish.

She should sit up. Go out fighting. Try and *make* herself keep going, no matter how awful she felt.

"'You've got to have heart,'" she sang, and laughed. Could she possibly be getting a little—*punchy?* Just *maybe?*

With more effort than it was probably worth, she managed to sit up, but then couldn't figure out what to do next. She puzzled over that for a minute, then decided to finish the song. It couldn't *hurt*. Other than her throat. Which already hurt, so what the hell.

Singing the song cheered her up, so she went into "I Whistle a Happy Tune" from *The King and I.* "Tomorrow," from *Annie,* was probably a little obvious—but, hey. She sang it with enthusiasm. With gusto, even.

Andrea McArdle's reputation was safe.

Before going on, she suddenly imagined some poor hiker going by, hearing a squeaky little croaking of "*Tomorrow*"—and being absolutely terrified by the sound. Then, she thought of Bill Murray in *Ghostbusters* saying, "What a *lovely* singing voice you must have," and laughed again.

Not that she had *ever* been able to sing. She was always threatening to sing for people, but she never did. Except for Vanessa, who would yawn—if, in fact, she woke up, in the first place.

In junior high, she had once cut through what she *thought* was a vacant lot near the school, singing "I Have Confidence" at the top of her lungs, when she came upon a group of the very coolest kids in her grade, all of whom were standing around, ineptly smoking cigarettes. They looked at her; she looked at them. She considered her options—die from mortification, or shrug self-deprecatingly and continue on her way, and with her song. To maintain her last vestige of cool, she chose the latter, escaping with the tatters of her dignity. "If you'd been singing 'The Seven Deadly Virtues,' you might have pulled it off," Beth had said later, after laughing for about twenty minutes. "Mmm," Meg had said, less amused.

But, she would sing it now. What the hell. In fact, since *The Sound of Music* was her favorite movie in life, she sang several songs from it. Did her imitation of the Mother Superior singing "Climb Every Mountain," even. The trick, was the quaver.

Gosh, time flew when you were having fun. She looked at the boards, seeing very little light left. Another day over. Christ, was this *ever* going to end?

"Yes, sports fans," she said through her teeth, speaking to an imaginary audience. "It's . . . Your Musical Journey to Hell. And coming up next, we have—" what?—"that old, that unforgettable favorite, 'Tea for Two.'" She sang it very sweetly, remembering being on vacation when she was about eleven—*her* family, on *vacation? Un*believable—and seeing *No, No, Nanette* in summer stock up in Vermont somewhere. Her father had sung "Call of the Sea" for about the next *year.* When Meg suggested to her mother that this was very embarrassing, her mother reminded her of the year he'd spent singing "Bewitched, Bothered and Bewildered." "Next year, we'll find a production of *My Fair Lady* somewhere," she said, "I promise. We could live with *that,* right?"

The next year, naturally, had been an election year. Translation: no vacations.

Okay, okay, there wasn't much point in getting angry. None of this was her mother's fault. It was just—bad luck. If she'd had any idea that this could happen, she never would have—why did she think Meg and her brothers had Secret Service protection, for Christ's sakes? Decoration? If she really cared about them, she—no. Damn it. That wasn't going to help.

It'd be interesting to know if the country thought she was a selfish, bad parent, or if they thought it was such a terrible thing that they felt sorry for her.

Tough call.

Angrier every second, she picked up the rock she'd been using, taking advantage of the energy to hammer at the chain. And hammer and hammer and hammer. It was almost completely dark now, and she missed practically every time, hammering until her hands were so numb and bruised that she had to stop, loosening her fingers from around the rock with some difficulty.

Her face felt wet and she touched her forehead. More perspiration. Terrific. How much time was that going to cut off her life? Minutes? Hours? She felt new, furious energy and yanked at the chain, using all of her weight, bracing her good leg against the wall. If her stupid hand were smaller, she could pull it through the cuff and—but, it wasn't. She fought the chain until her muscles wouldn't work anymore, making no progress, then slumped into the dirt to try and catch her breath, her ribs damn near on fire from the effort.

All she had accomplished was more perspiration. Swell.

She lay in the dark for a long time, too exhausted to think about being angry, or scared—or anything.

Except that death was sounding better and better.

# ～ 12 ～

SHE FELT COLD—or hot—it was hard to tell. Cold, mostly. She curled up in the dirt, arms wrapped around her body, hugging the thin sweatshirt closer.

Water. What she wouldn't give for a glass of ice-cold water. She licked her lips, her tongue feeling almost as dry. Coke, lemonade, iced tea, milk, orange juice—*liquid*. A Slushie. Oh, Lord, her *kingdom* for a Slushie. The water left over from a can of green beans, prune juice, *anything*.

It was dark, and scary, and she tightened her arms around herself, the chain heavy across her body. Christ, if she could just *sleep*, and not have to lie here and—footsteps. Hundreds of footsteps. She sat up in instant terror—pain suspended—shrinking back against the rock wall. An army of them, coming to get her. To hurt her.

It took almost a minute for her to realize that the sound was only rain.

Rain. She was dying of thirst, and water was only about fifteen feet away. Jesus Christ. She stared at the boarded-up entrance, hearing blessed, noisy rain. Christ, how was she going to get to it?

She had to think, god-damn it. She crawled as far as the chain would allow, dragging her bad leg, but was still a good ten or twelve feet short. Damn it, damn it, damn it. She tried to think, tears of frustration starting. Ten feet would save her life. Damn it to hell.

The hole. Maybe water would soak into the ground, end up in the hole she'd dug, and—she felt for it in the darkness, scraping her hands on small jagged rocks in the process. Finally, she found it—as cold and dry as it had been before. She dug some more, using both hands until she was too tired to keep on, but the hole stayed dry.

She leaned against the wall, still crying, listening to the rain. Would water condense on the rock, maybe? Moisture she could lick off? Eagerly, she felt the wall. Cold, dirty rock. *Dry* rock. But, it would take a while, right? Okay, so she'd wait.

Like she really had any other options.

She slumped there, using her arm as a headrest, trying to think. Ten feet. Ten god-damn feet. If she had a rope, she could tie some cloth to the end, throw it out there, let it get soaked, and—wait, could she *make* a rope? Maybe, if she—what, and throw it through those damned boards? She'd spent enough time staring at them to know that there were only a few chinks where light came in. And she was going to throw her wad of cloth—in the pitch dark—through one of them? Yeah, right.

Not that *trying* would kill her. She felt for a rock and tossed it at the boards, hearing it bounce back towards her. Only, what if she used a bigger rock? Maybe, if she threw hard enough, she could knock a couple of the boards off.

She threw rock after rock, trying to tell by the sound of each what had happened. Nothing, apparently. And the bigger ones she found didn't even seem to go as far as the boards. Terrifying to be so frail that she couldn't even throw a rock ten feet.

After a while, she gave up, slouching down to think. Maybe she should go ahead with the rope-making plan. Then, once it was light out, she would be able to see the best place to throw it, and—what if it stopped raining? What if—making a rope would give her something to *do*, at least.

The drawstring in her sweatpants was the logical place to start, but they were way too big, and would fall down if—not that she was going anywhere.

Apples. When she was little, Trudy had taught her how to peel an apple, starting at the top and slowly working her way down. Trudy had always taken a great deal of pride in completing the job with one long, impressive strip, instead of lots of smaller pieces.

Meg hadn't been very good at it, but if she could rip her sweatshirt sleeves off, and then carefully tear them in a slow, circular pattern, she might end up with a decent rope, after all.

"Oh, good plan," she said aloud, rather pleased by her ingenuity. Less pleased by the sad little rasp of a voice.

She felt for a sharp rock, trying to use it as an awl or something, to separate her left sleeve from the sweatshirt at her shoulder. The whole operation would have been a lot easier if she took the sweatshirt *off*, but—what if someone came, and—what if *he* showed up, and saw her, and—besides, it was cold. And the chain would prevent her from getting it off completely, *anyway*. And—Jesus, her life must have really gotten out of control if she could be chained up inside some godforsaken mine shaft in the middle of nowhere, and *still* not feel alone. *Safely* alone.

It was a pretty cheap sweatshirt, and she was able to rip the sleeve off without much trouble. Starting at the ragged end, she tore it once around, careful to keep the strip at least an inch or two wide, working very slowly and patiently. After all, she had all night. In fact, if one chose to look at it that way, she had the rest of her *life*. She chose not to.

The rain seemed to be stopping, but doggedly, she kept ripping. Nothing *better* to do. She ended up with a piece of cloth about five feet long, the cuff dangling at one end. Hanging on to the other end, she threw the cuff towards the boards, hearing it land about halfway over. Not bad. If she weren't nailed in, the damned idea would actually have worked. Although the rain sounded more like a sporadic drizzle at this point.

"Damn," she said aloud.

With much less enthusiasm this time, she started ripping at her right sleeve.

IT WAS LIGHT again. Big fucking deal. A nice, bright sunny day. At least, as far as she could tell through the cracks. No fucking way could she have thrown her rope through one of those tiny openings. So now, not only did she have a dumb cloth rope she didn't need, but without sleeves, she was that much colder.

What a stupid waste of effort that had been. Taking her time—why not?—she wrapped the cloth rope around her neck. *Now,* she had a very long and ugly scarf. Swell.

She stared at the widest crack, at the beauty of the sunlight, then down at the chain on her wrist. Christ. She gave it a half-hearted yank, a couple of tears rolling out.

God, she was tired. Unbelievably fucking tired. Every bone in her body hurt from being on the hard, rocky ground for so long and she shifted, trying to find a comfortable position. Or, at least, a less agonizing one.

She hadn't felt hungry for what seemed like years—sometimes, her stomach hurt; mostly, it was upset—but maybe she was losing weight, and that's why her bones ached so much. That is, the ones that weren't already *broken.* She touched her hips, surprised by how sharp they felt. And her ribs. And her collarbones, and—well, if she got out of this, she'd be able to *eat* any damned thing she wanted. As much as she wanted. When*ever* she wanted.

If she got out of this.

SHE TOOK SLOW deep breaths, trying to stay very calm. Panic would come from nowhere—jarring, paralyzing panic—and she'd hear her heart against her eardrums and feel her fingernails cutting into her palms. But, she had to stay rational and logical and—what if her throat closed? Everything felt so dry and swollen that she could barely swallow at all anymore, and—what if it just sealed up? Then, she wouldn't be able to breathe, or—oh, Christ, what a horrible way to—tracheotomy. She could do a god-damn tracheotomy with—with what? The end of her shoelace. Which there was a word for, not that she could remember the stupid thing. But it was plastic-encased, pretty solid, and if she had to, she could jab it right into her windpipe. Okay. Yeah. She relaxed.

One worry down.

"With millions rising up to take its place," she said, her voice not quite working.

What time was it? What *day* was it? *Was* it day? She squinted at the boards. Yeah, there was some light out there. Christ, even her *eyes* hurt when she tried to move them, her eyelids scratchy and dry.

Good thing she didn't wear contacts.

Oh, yes, indeedy, things could be worse.

She should think about something good. Something nice. Something *not* fatal.

Awards shows. God, she loved awards shows. From the Teddy Awards on *Mary Tyler Moore*, right on up to the Academy Awards. The Emmys were her second favorite, although the Golden Globes were a goof, too.

"And," she said aloud, "for Best Actress in a Television Drama—" She fumbled with the flap on her pretend envelope. "They really *are* hard to open," she said to the audience—who chuckled warmly. She opened it, pulling the card free. "And the winner is—I'm sorry, I mean, *the Emmy goes to* . . . Meghan Winslow Powers."

*Tremendous* applause.

She allowed herself to smile shyly, modestly, on her way up to the stage. "Love your work," she said politely to the presenters, then lifted her Emmy. "They really *are* heavy," she said to the audience, receiving terribly warm chuckles in return. She gazed at her nice shiny trophy. "I didn't prepare a speech, I—" She paused for demure reflection. If she was gracious, maybe they'd give her one *every* year. "It was such an honor just to be nominated." Which was probably enough groveling, since—obviously—she *deserved* every single bit of the attention, acclaim, affection, and admiration her peers had decided to bestow upon her. "I'd like to thank the Academy, of course."

Oh, to be able to say that, and *not* be addressing the faculty at Exeter or someplace. *There*, she'd be saying something like, "I'd like to thank the Academy in general, and Mr. Jarvis, in particular, for his splendid array of jam tarts." To which, her audience would respond with kindly smiles and delighted chortles, of course.

She had been—family legend had it—the kind of child you could put in an empty room, and it would sit there for hours, laughing wildly at nothing. "Meg is very imaginative," her mother would say tactfully. Meg was a bloody simpleton, more likely. Give that child a shoebox, or a piece of string, and she'd be amused for hours. Kind of like Dudley Moore in *Arthur* shrieking with laughter, and then saying, "Sometimes I just *think* funny things."

"Like I said—" How colloquial—and non-elitist of her—"I didn't prepare a speech, but—" She pulled out a thick sheaf of papers, greatly amusing the crowd. "There are one or two people I'd like to thank." She paused to examine the pages. "My agent. My broker. My sponsor. My parole officer." The audience, of course, went off into gales of laughter. "Working with Brad was—well, unforgettable. And let me assure you that the rumors were—just that." Sympathetic, respectful nods from the audience. Her millions, upon millions, of fans. "I'd also like to thank my family, and—"

Family.

Suddenly, this game didn't seem quite so funny.

SHE HAD TO get *out* of here. *Now*. If she didn't, she was going to die, and—any second now, she was going to—she had to get out of here.

She yanked at the chain, crazily, with both hands, pulling so hard that it felt like the muscles were ripping right off the bones in her arms. It wouldn't move. Oh, Jesus *God*, she had to get out of here. Why wouldn't the god-damned thing break, or—she *hated* him. Fucking coward. How could he have left her here, and—how could *any* human being do that to someone else? Let her sit here for hours, and days, slowly, slowly feeling herself dying. A new symptom every hour—less movement in her hands, her tongue so swollen that it seemed to fill her whole mouth, dizziness—that god-damned son of a bitch.

She toppled over into the dirt, trying to cry, but her throat was so dehydrated that she couldn't even *whimper*, and breathing hard and making self-pity noises somewhere inside was all she could manage. Then, she lay there, drained, not sure if she was going to be able to sit up again. *Ever* again.

This was it. This was abso-fucking-lutely it. And now, she just wanted it to hurry up and happen already. It wasn't scary anymore, or something to fight, or—she was ready. It was too soon—in life—but, there wasn't anything she could do to change that, so she was ready. It was going to be *over*.

"I'm sorry," she said, not sure who she was talking to. Her parents, probably. Josh, maybe. If her tear glands were still working, she would have cried. "I'm really sorry." She hadn't ever *done* anything, she hadn't *helped* anyone, she had wasted her whole pathetic life. Seventeen years of—coasting. Drifting along like she had all the time in the world. No direction, no conviction—just a complete and total *squander*.

And she didn't even give a damn. Just wanted it to end. The sun would come up, her family would go on, her class would graduate—and her being there, or not, wouldn't make much of a difference. People would be sad, for a while, but they'd get over it. Everyone would. Every*thing* would.

It was going to be peaceful. At least, it'd damned well better be. She would let her eyes close gently and—there'd probably be warm light, and music, and—she opened her eyes. Music. With her luck, she'd get English madrigals or something. Gregorian chants. Rap. *The Best of Bread*. Seventeen years of listening to good rowdy rock and roll and—if she had to listen to stuff like "Bridge Over Troubled

Water" and "Amazing Grace," death definitely wasn't going to be her kind of place.

Motown'd be okay. Or the Doors, or the Stones, or—"I Love Rock and Roll" was probably asking for too much. So was Rodgers & Hammerstein. Sadly, that would probably be reserved for a much higher caliber of dead person. But, maybe she could get—hey, wasn't she supposed to be *dying* right about now? Christ, instead of chess, she and the Grim Reaper were going to be fighting over the jukebox.

"Put it this way, pal," she said. "You play me any folk or country, and you will *never* work on the East Coast again. On *either* coast."

That'd be telling him. Was Death a him? Oh, no doubt. But, her Death wouldn't look like Darth Vader—no, not a chance. She'd get stuck with a little, fat, effete one. A Republican. If her Death was a woman, it would be a Disneyland tour guide. With Tupperware. And make-up samples.

If she went to hell—always a possibility—there would be a lot of standing around, holding hands and singing "Don't Worry, Be Happy"—or, maybe, "My Heart Will Go On." *Over* and *over.* Indiscriminate hugging. Waiting in an endless Wal-Mart line, while some grating, yet cheery, voice kept shouting, "Attention, shoppers!"

Hmmm. For someone who was about to die, her mind seemed to be clicking again.

"Death Scene, Take Two," she said aloud.

Except this time, she was going to change the ending.

# ~ 13 ~

THERE *HAD* TO be a way out of here. The chain wasn't going to break, or fall off, or unlock, or anything. But, there had to be some way—like, if she could cut her damn arm *off,* or—wait a minute. Maybe—that might be it.

Heart beating faster, she looked at her hand, not sure if she was overjoyed or nauseated. She could *cut her hand off.* That's how poor little animals got out of traps, right? She'd be free, she could run away, and—blood. All that blood. And what was she going to cut it off *with*—that nice, straight orthodonture? Or one of the rocks? Yeah, right.

If only there was some metal around. On television and everything, they always seemed to have an ax or a saw or something conveniently nearby. And usually even a tourniquet. And sometimes, afterwards, they said, "Ow!"

Lucky sons of bitches.

Maybe she could find an old can lid buried in the dirt, or—Jesus, what a thought. But, that was the only possible—the Idea hit with such force that she actually flinched. A way out. She had actually thought of a—she yanked at the cuff, the base of her thumb keeping her hand from going any further. She'd lost weight—her hand was a little slimmer, maybe—all she had to do was *break* it. Break a few of the bones, so her hand would be able to slip right through. It would work. It would actually—she pulled the cuff, studying her hand. Figuring out what to break, so excited she could barely breathe.

And, it wouldn't be so hard. Just a question of the right rock. With a solid edge, but not too sharp—she didn't want to slice herself open. And it couldn't be too blunt, because she needed to shatter the bones at the right spots. Oh, what a wonderful, wonderful plan.

Scrabbling through the dirt, trying to find a good rock, she actually found herself grinning. She *loved* this plan.

And, she'd found the rock. Fist-sized, with a slightly flattened edge, maybe an inch wide. Perfect. She rubbed it across her leg, wiping the dirt off. The edge even came to sort of a rounded point at one end. Absolutely perfect. She kept cleaning it on the only slightly cleaner sweatpants, getting ready.

If her hand was resting on the ground, the dirt would absorb most of the blow—so, she'd have to flatten it against the rock wall. Hand pressed down, fingers spread apart, so she could see the bones.

She clenched her fist, testing it once again at the cuff. It was the joint at the base of her thumb—the bottom knuckle—and the bone leading from there into her wrist that were causing the problem. The knuckles at the bases of her forefingers and pinky might be trouble, too. Mainly, though, it was her thumb. If there was some way to cut *that* off, she'd be in business. However. With luck, pulverizing all of those bones would work almost as well.

Hard enough. She had to be damned sure to do it hard enough. If she just bruised, or cracked, the bones, her hand would swell horribly—and she'd also probably never have the courage to smash herself again. Hard. Very god-damned hard. And fast. Any time she'd broken a bone in her life—including recently—it had swollen up instantly, almost before she felt the pain. Big tight swelling, not flexible stuff she could yank through the cuff. So, she would need to move very, very quickly.

Okay, okay. She had to get ready. Had to do this before the light faded. She flexed her right thumb, wondering—with a sudden twist of nausea—if this were going to be the last time she'd move her hand like that in her life. Maybe she'd maim herself permanently, have a crippled—for Christ's sakes, better crippled than dead.

Calmer, she leaned back, moving her thumb back and forth, watching the bones' and muscles' responses. Okay, okay. A couple of deep breaths, and she'd be ready to go. This was the *only possible* way out. A way he obviously hadn't anticipated. The *only* thing he hadn't anticipated.

Bastard.

*Now,* she was ready.

She pressed her hand against the cold rock, trying to decide where her other hand would have the most striking power. The best angle. Eye level, maybe. No, slightly below eye level would be better. Then, she hefted the rock, adjusting its position in her hand until it felt just right.

Okay, okay. One shot. Well, actually, two—to break both places. One quick break, then another. She couldn't take time to think, or—*slam!* She heard some kind of yelp come out of herself as the rock crunched into her hand, but was already swinging harder, smashing the rock into the other place. She pulled against the cuff as hard as she could, feeling a scream rip out. But her *hand* didn't come out. Oh, God, it didn't come out. Oh, God, oh, God, oh, God. She smashed the rock down again, panicking, and again, and again, and *again,* wrenching at the cuff with all of her weight, suddenly finding herself lying flat on her back, a convulsion of pain jerking through her hand, and then her entire upper body.

She was out. Dear God, she was out. Her hand was twitching and jerking, the pain so hot and horrible that she was whimpering, but she was out. Out!

She had to hurry. To get *out* of this place! He might come back, to see if she was dead yet. What if he came back? What if he was on his way right now, and—she had to hurry. And half of her body was useless, and—it was time to *go,* damn it!

Pulling with her left hand, pushing with her right leg, she dragged herself to the boards, the fear giving her energy. Heart thumping with excitement, she peered out through them. There might be a house right out there, or—woods. Forest and mountains, darkening fast.

Okay, okay. She twisted around, her broken hand resting limply on her stomach, and gave the boards a kick with her good leg. They were rotten. Thank God for *that*. She kicked a couple of them free, then crawled out.

Outside. Jesus, she was *outside.*

She couldn't waste time; she had to get away. But, first, she had to put the boards back, so he would think she was still in there. *Then,* she had to escape. *Fast.*

Except, she was in the middle of the damned woods. Where was she supposed to—who cared *where*? She just had to *go*. She crawled towards the thickest part of the woods, feeling too panicked and exposed to think about anything except finding a place to hide. Someplace safe.

Push with the right leg, pull with the left arm. Push, pull, a few inches at a time. She made it about fifty feet—well into the woods—before collapsing completely. But, she couldn't stop, she had to—except, even breathing seemed like too much of an effort. Okay, she was going to have to rest for a minute—and think. Think *hard.*

It was dark now, and very quiet. A few birds, trees in the wind, rushing. None of which she could really hear over her heartbeat and breathing. Her hand and knee were throbbing, agonizingly, but she was too exhausted to focus on that. The ground felt prickly, even through her clothes, and she realized that she was lying on pine needles. Chilly, sharp, scratchy needles. So what. She stayed there for a long time, somewhere between sleep and passing out, still unable to catch her breath.

Rushing. The rushing sound was loud, and fast, and—water! She opened her eyes. Where was it? Somewhere nearby, somewhere—it was all around her, rushing louder, almost deafening. She raised her head, turning it to try and find the right direction. It was coming from her left, or—no, behind her. It sounded like it was coming from behind her. She dragged herself in that direction, new adrenaline pumping in.

Every few feet, the underbrush got thicker and she had to struggle through it, but the ground seemed spongier. Then, moss, damp ground, mud, rocks. Lots of rocks. Louder and louder rushing. Closer and—there it was. A fast-moving stream, barely visible in the early moonlight. She stared at the water, so happy that she would have cried if there had been anything left in her tear ducts.

She was going to let herself fall right in, but had enough control to remember that water wasn't always safe to drink, and—for Christ's sakes, she was damn near dead *anyway*. It wasn't like she could take the time to crawl around and find *different* water. And this stream had a pretty decent current, which—she was almost sure—was a good sign.

Carefully, she touched the water with her left hand. It was cold. Wonderfully cold. She splashed some across her face, and that felt so good that she splashed more. Across her face, her neck, her chest. She touched a palmful to her lips—cold—fresh—then sipped some, waiting to see what happened.

*Nothing* happened. And it *tasted* okay. She drank more, then put her whole face in the stream, her skin seeming to soak it up, expand. Okay, okay, she shouldn't go crazy with this. After not having any for so long, drinking too *much* water probably wouldn't be too intelligent.

But, Christ, it was tempting.

She lifted her face out of the stream and lay in the mud by the edge, trailing her left hand in the water, and washing her face again and again. The water was numbingly cold, and she lifted her right forearm, slowly lowering her hand and wrist into it. There was one hard jolt of pain, then icy relief. She let her hand float until the current made everything hurt too much, then lifted it out.

Safe. Saf*er*, anyway. Lost God only knew where in the

wilderness—maybe not even in *America*—but, safe. And alive. And a hell of a lot better off than she'd been an hour ago. It was dark, and shiveringly cold, and she hurt—badly, but it didn't matter. Right now, it didn't matter at all.

SHE MUST HAVE either fallen asleep or fainted, because suddenly, it was light out. The brightness hurt her eyes and for a minute, she couldn't figure out where she was, except that her teeth were chattering, and she was covered with mud—and in pain. A *lot* of—she started remembering—and remembering and remembering and *remembering.*

"Jesus," she said aloud, her voice cracking from disuse.

Which reminded her that she was probably supposed to be overjoyed. Eternally grateful and all. Sing a song, maybe.

She slid her left hand into the water, then wiped it across her face, the coldness waking her up even more. Then, she drank a couple of palmfuls, almost able to *feel* her mind clearing. And definitely feeling the pains sharpening. *All* of the pains, her right hand now the dominant one.

She looked down at it, the shape so swollen and deformed that she came close to throwing up. If she could find anything inside *to* throw up. Her stomach—empty for, Jesus, *days* now—felt shriveled. It hurt. And her knee hurt, and her jaw, and her nose, and *Christ,* her ribs—okay, okay. She couldn't just lie here and feel sorry for herself. If he came back to the mine shaft and found her gone—she had to get out of here. Move as fast, and far away, as possible.

What a tiring thought.

Using a nearby boulder, she hauled herself to a sitting position—not bothering to fight the requisite groans, and leaned against it, looking around.

Yep, she was in the woods, all right. And, judging from the pitch of the land, mountain woods. *American* woods? Pine trees, other trees, bushes, and stuff. Who the hell knew? She'd never exactly been one to sit around watching PBS nature specials. The only thing she could be pretty damn *sure* of was that this wasn't the Amazon. Probably not the Nile, either.

It would be nice to sleep some more. Block out all of the pain. But, he really might show up here any second now and—all that work breaking her hand, just to have him—she needed to get away from here.

She closed her eyes, trying to concentrate. To make her mind work. There had to be a road nearby, because they wouldn't have carried her *miles*. For one thing, she'd be heavy; for another, the odds of their being seen went up that way. So, all she had to do was crawl back to the mine shaft, look for their footprints, and—oh, yeah, *right*. Follow the prints to wherever the road was, and have them find *her*. No, she couldn't take that chance. Unless this was the stupid *Yukon* or something, she had to be relatively near civilization. And the nights hadn't been cold enough to indicate that she was way far north like that.

The only slightly logical thing was to go downhill. And stay near the water. It had to go somewhere, right? So, she could just pull herself along, and—what if she went *in* the water? If she could swim—or float—she could maybe move a little more quickly, *and* not leave any tracks for them to follow.

"Good plan, good plan," she said. Nothing like a little pep talk.

She looked at the stream. It couldn't be all that deep, and she would just stay near the edge. Only, what if there were fish and gross things in there? Of course, if there were *fish*, she could catch them, and—she had to laugh. Even if she could catch one somehow, was she really going to sit down and eat something *raw* like that? Something that had been alive? Even fish sticks made her sick.

In the meantime, he could be on his way here. So, she took a deep breath, and eased herself into the water, yelping from the shock of the cold. She supported her bad hand on her chest, trying to protect it, gritting her teeth against the pain in her knee. *Damn*, it was cold.

But, in another way, it was a tremendous relief, making her feel more awake than she had in days. And she might actually get *clean*.

"*That'd* be something new," she said. Not that anyone was around to appreciate her irony.

Not that, in all honesty, anyone had *ever* particularly appreciated her sense of irony.

She ducked her head under the water, scrubbing her hair with her good hand. Some soap would be swell right about now. Of course, if she were Nature Girl, she would probably be able to *make* herself some soap out of special leaves or something. She had read all of the *Little House on the Prairie* books—she should really be able to come up with some fun facts. But, for some reason, all she could remember was Jack, the brindle bulldog. And Almanzo, eating those incredibly delicious meals. Cracklin' bread, and fried apples and onions, and—thinking about food would not be a good idea. Although she would damn near kill for a bag of Cool Ranch Doritos.

Hell, she'd kill for a little plate of *okra*.

Pretty much used to the water temperature—cold as it was— she let her body float along the edge, controlling her progress with her good arm, touching—and sometimes, slamming into—algae-slick rocks. Luckily, the current wasn't very fast, but she still banged into many more rocks than she avoided, her progress much slower than she'd hoped. Sometimes, trees and bushes grew so low over the water, that branches would smack her in the face, and she lost count of how many times her bad leg banged against yet another rock.

She floated along for what seemed like hours, getting more and more tired. It was so *quiet* out here. Peaceful. Had she ever been in the woods before? Once, in New Hampshire, she and her family had gone on like, an Audubon trail, but they'd had a tape recorder to tell them what they were seeing, and exactly where to walk, and—it wasn't *wilderness.* So—quiet. So *big.*

The water didn't even seem cold anymore, just sort of relaxing, and soft, and—she didn't realize she was falling asleep until her head was already underwater. She fought her way back up to the surface, broken bones forgotten, choking on a lungful of water. Oh, Christ, oh, Christ, she was sinking, she couldn't get—she thrashed around wildly, trying to keep her head above water, gasping for air.

The bank. She had to get over to the bank. Grabbing rocks wherever she could find them, she managed to pull herself onto the mud, half in and half out of the water. She couldn't get air, she couldn't get any—she coughed up what had to be half the god-damn river, and when the bout was finally over, let her face slump into the mud.

Jesus. She lay in the same spot for a long time, too tired to drag herself the rest of the way out. Christ, that'd really be stupid—to drown out of plain old exhaustion, after everything else she'd managed to do. It might be faster to use the water, but if she could fall asleep in the iciest damn stuff she'd ever been in, then she couldn't take chances.

*Christ,* she was tired.

WHEN SHE WOKE up again, it was dark. Scary. There was a tree a few feet away, and she made her way over to it, hunching against the trunk. Except, there might be animals. Bears, and wolves, and—*snakes.* What if there were snakes? There might even be *poisonous* snakes. Her skin felt crawly, and—bugs! What if she was covered with—she slapped at her back and shoulders with her good hand, in complete revulsion, not feeling anything moving, but—*Jesus.* What if something crawled on her? She would die. She would just flat-out, on the spot, die.

There were rustling noises all around her—animals? wind?—and she felt the nearby ground until she found a stick. A heavy stick. She backed up right against the tree so no one could get her from behind and clenched the stick tightly in her good hand, ready to defend herself.

It was so dark—darker than anything she'd ever imagined—and there seemed to be eyes everywhere. Looking at her, watching her. *Haunting* her. Maybe there weren't just animals—and terrorists—out here. Maybe there were spirits and, and supernatural things, and—they were all going to get her, and—somewhere up above, there was a bird noise, and she almost screamed.

A bird. Okay, it was just some stupid bird, no reason to panic. But, maybe sometimes, birds attacked people, and—Hitchcock! Swarms of birds flying down to—not *even* birds, swarms of *everything*, all coming to—oh, Christ, why couldn't that son-of-a-bitch have just killed her?

She was too afraid to sleep. Too afraid to lie down, even. She couldn't look around, because she kept seeing shiny eyes and movement, and—but, if she *closed* her eyes, she wouldn't be able to see them coming. Even now, he was probably following her and laughing. Hiding somewhere, waiting for her to think she'd gotten away, then he would jump out and—she had to get away from here. But, lots of animals were nocturnal, and if she moved, she might see some.

More to the point, snakes and things might see *her*. Kill her.

There was rustling everywhere, and she couldn't tell if they were getting closer. Whatever they were. And it was *cold*. Ripping off her damn sleeves had certainly been a stupid idea. Instead of using the cloth as a scarf, should she wrap it around her arms? No, too much work. But, could it get so cold that she would *die*? It was, after all, May—or maybe June? So, unless she was way far north—could she be in like, *Canada?* No, she wouldn't have survived *last* night, if she was someplace like that.

There was a loud crackling sound off to her right, and she stiffened, turning to face it, her stick ready. It *was* an animal, because she heard the noise again, going away from her. Away. Thank God.

If she was lucky, maybe little animals and things would be as afraid of her as she was of them. Rabies! What if something bit her, and she—by the time rabies symptoms showed up, she'd be long gone, anyway. It'd be more sensible to worry about freezing, and starving, and the ribs that hurt so much that they—if they were broken—might puncture holes in her lungs, and—what would be sensible, would be to sleep.

Only, it was so dark that she couldn't. Even at home, she had been known to leave the bathroom light on, and the door open a crack, "just in case she had to get up in the night and might trip on something." Yeah, right. Just in case scary things came to get her, more likely. Which, since there were supposed to be all kinds of ghosts in the White House, was a reasonable fear. One time, when Beth came to visit, she had insisted upon sleeping in the Lincoln Bedroom, and then been full of tales about the many spectres she'd seen. Beth, however, was prone to putting people on.

What did Beth think about all of this? Did she know about it, or was there really a blackout? But, the blackout would have started *after* her mother's speech, and—what about Josh? One of the times, the man had to have been lying, and maybe Josh really was—she didn't want to think about that. She hadn't actually *seen* him—just the door opening through the smoke—but, who else could it have been?

Actually, it could have been someone else she knew, or a teacher, or—it wasn't going to help to think about that. Or Josh, or what had probably happened to Chet—who was one of the swellest agents she had ever had, or about *anything*. She shouldn't think, or move—or even breathe loudly.

All she should do was stay very, very still—and wait for morning.

# ~ 14 ~

SHE LOOKED UP, seeing stars above the trees. The most she had ever seen. Really *bright* stars. The same stars she had seen in Chestnut Hill. The same stars she had looked at from Pennsylvania Avenue. Not that she was the kind of person who gazed longingly at the dark night sky and wanted to travel to other worlds. She had liked *E. T.* and all, but in general, space could not have held *less* fascination for her. People were supposed to feel small and insignificant and all that, when they looked at the stars, but—well, she just thought they were pretty.

She remembered lying out on the White House lawn one summer night with her brothers, all of them staring up at the sky. If they looked behind them, they could see the White House; if they looked ahead, they saw the Washington Monument, lit up against the blueish-black darkness. If they looked *around*, they saw a lot of hovering Secret Service agents. Mostly, though, they just looked up at the stars and tried to figure out which one was the North Star. Her father was the only one in the family who ever spent time admiring Nature's Beauty, so the Big Dipper was the only thing they could locate with any certainty, but it was nice, lying there on the perfectly groomed grass, admiring the sky and thinking summer thoughts. Finally, Neal decided he was hungry, and the three of them went scuffling inside.

In Chestnut Hill, it was always lawn chairs. Lying on lawn chairs in the backyard, smelling of mosquito repellent, eating whatever brownies or cookies Trudy had most recently baked for them. If her mother was home—August, with Congress in recess, was the best bet—her parents would be sitting on the patio, and lying out in the yard, Meg would hear ice against their glasses, low voices, and the ever-present New England sound of the Red Sox on the radio, or maybe on one of the televisions inside. "Hi again, everybody, and welcome to Fenway Park in Boston. It's a *beautiful* night for a ball game, and—" If she and her brothers took Kirby for a walk around the neighborhood, they would hear the Red Sox game coming through the open windows of almost every house.

She missed that house. Missed their lives. Missed having no one know, or care, who the hell she was, and what she did with herself. What she *wore*, while she was doing it. Her mother was still a hot-shot, a "rising star in the Party," but she *was* only a Senator, and there were ninety-nine others. Many of them men and women—mostly men, of course—who had been there longer than she had, and made more headlines. Congress was even better—there were over *four hundred* of them. Of course, they all wanted to be President, but very few of them *made* it. Most of them never even tried.

Meg gritted her teeth—where she still *had* teeth. Life would have been a hell of a lot nicer, if her mother hadn't had to try.

MORNING AGAIN. SHE had finally fallen asleep, all crunched up against the tree, and when she opened her eyes, she was stiffer and colder than she thought it was possible to be. And the birds were very damn loud. She looked around, the woods still seeming almost as scary and forbidding as they had all night long. But somehow, she would have to stay awake today. Another night of not being able to fall asleep and staring at utter blackness—being awake was worse than the nightmares she had when she *wasn't*.

Also, tonight, she would have to try and find some kind of shel-ter. A fallen tree, maybe. Boughs she could burrow into for warmth. And here she was, with these worthless cloth strings, and—a splint. Maybe she could use them to make a splint. If she could walk—at *all*—she might actually get out of this. She could tie a couple of sticks in place, and use another stick as a cane—it just might work.

Energized by this unexpected—and, in retrospect, obvious—idea, she looked around for some straight, sturdy sticks.

One of the few good things about being in the forest was that there were sticks all *over* the place.

She dragged herself around the clearing until she found two nice straight ones, which she broke to approximately the right size by propping them against a rotting log and kicking down hard with her right foot.

That accomplished, she moved her bad leg out as straight as it would go, feeling reaction shudders from the pain go all over her body. There were two tree roots growing closely together, and on an impulse, she stuck her ankle between them, then used the weight of her body to pull her leg out straight. Then, she tried to ease her kneecap back into place with her left hand, not afraid—since she *was* alone; she hoped—to make every pain-moan and groan she knew how to make. Should she try a rock, maybe? Pound it into—no, *enough* with the rocks already.

How about her *foot*? She thought about that, then grabbed onto a tree with the crook of her arm, using her right foot to push on the kneecap. The pain got worse and worse, until she was damn near shouting with it, the swollen muscles fighting the pressure every millimeter of the way. Just when she thought she couldn't stand it for another second, something in her leg jerked—and then, it felt better. Not a lot better, but better. Noticeably so.

She sat up, not moving her right foot away so that the kneecap wouldn't slip right back out again. Frowning, she pulled her sweat-pant leg tight, seeing what looked like an almost normal knee. Still deformed, but not unrecognizable.

Hunh.

"Good work," she said aloud.

She reached for the two sticks, set them on either side of her leg, then unwound the sleeve ropes from her neck. First, stomach muscles straining, she leaned forward far enough to slip one of the sweatshirt cuffs onto her foot and then pulled it over her ankle, and up around the two sticks to hold them in place. It was hard as hell to do it with only one hand, but she wrapped the cloth tightly around her leg again and again, then tied several awkward knots.

Finished, she sat back, testing to see if the splint was secure. It appeared to be, without cutting off her circulation, and she couldn't help being pleased with herself. Not that it was like, some miracle cure—but, it was an improvement, no question.

The only problem, was that *now* she was too trashed to move. If she was *really* clever, she would have made herself a sling, and—to hell with it. She'd used up all of the cloth, anyway.

She stayed on the ground for a while, resting. When she felt a little stronger, she crawled over to the stream to drink. Then, she sat up, looking around for another stick to use as a cane. Once she'd found one, she pulled in a deep breath, aware of how much her knee still hurt. But, if it was going to hurt *anyway*, she might as well walk on it. It'd be faster than trying to drag herself along, and safer than trying to swim. After all, the worst that could happen was that she would fall down. Like, big deal.

Using a tree, she hoisted herself up onto her right foot, groaning from the various knifing pains, so dizzy that she had to lean there for a few minutes. When was the last time she'd stood up, anyway? It seemed like years. And the combination of starvation and exhaustion wasn't exactly a strengthening one.

When the worst of the dizziness and spots in front of her eyes ebbed away, she let her left foot touch the ground. It hurt, but not as badly as it might have. She sucked in a deep breath, reached out with her stick, and then hopped over to it on her right foot. One step. Jouncing her hand hurt like crazy, the dizziness was back— and worse, her good leg was trembling almost too much to hold her up. Still, it was a step.

"A step in the right direction," she said, to amuse herself.

If, in fact, it *was* the right direction.

Lean, hop. Lean, hop. She made it five steps, then had to rest, sagging against a tree. Then, she tried three steps—and rested. And two more, her breath ragged, her ribs hurting so much that they felt as though they might actually burst right through her skin.

Lean, hop. Lean, hop. She fell—more than once, the splint jarring loose each time. But she would just fix it, rub away as many tears as she could, and force herself to get back up again.

Tonight, at least, sleeping wasn't going to be a problem.

IT WAS DARK, it was light. Dark, light. Lean, hop. Lean, hop. Stagger, fall, crawl. Cry, sleep. What a fucking nightmare.

Her right leg really wasn't strong enough to do all the work anymore and she drank some water, then pulled herself into a pine-needle clearing, checking first for snakes. She had actually seen a few in the last day or two—mottled brown or black, slithering in the reddish dirt—and had had to quiver in disgust—and fear, holding her stick as a weapon.

Luckily, they didn't seem to want to have much to do with *her*, either. None of the animals did—she kept *hearing* things, but other than a couple of deer, she almost never saw them.

Every sound, no matter how tiny, was terrifying—it might be him, coming after her—but, they were usually very small sounds. Scuttling. Fluttering. Rustling. Probably squirrels and rabbits and stuff. When she was moving, she would use her stick to poke the underbrush ahead, hoping to scare out whatever might be in there. So far, as a strategy, it seemed to be working pretty well.

She knew she was supposed to be hungry, and sometimes, she sort of was, but mostly, she was dizzy and sick, the ground seeming to move up and down in front of her eyes, trees dipping away from her.

People had gone through worse. She had to keep remembering that. People had gone through things that were much, much worse. People *survived* worse things than this.

Stronger people. And—*braver* people.

It seemed like she had been in these stupid woods for years. Not that the seasons had changed or anything. So far. She leaned over, lifted her filthy sweatpant cuff—the dirt *was* kind of reddish; was she in the South, maybe? Did it matter?—just enough to look at her leg. Hair. Actual *hair* on her legs. How gross.

She always shaved her legs. Almost every day. Skiing and tennis were the main reasons. It would just figure that the *one* day she forgot, she would break her leg, and have to go to the hospital, and everyone would look at it in disgust. Hell, *she* was pretty god-damn disgusted.

There could be people looking at her right now. Or animals, or—when it was dark, she saw eyes. Eyes, everywhere. Looking at her, laughing—no! If she didn't *look*, she wouldn't have to see them.

Jesus, she really couldn't take another night. Especially if it rained again. She'd spent last night pressed into a rock hollow, soaking wet from the storm, trembling with fear and cold, too afraid to close her eyes, but even more afraid to look out at the forest—and *see* things, so she spent hours staring down at her good hand, clenched weakly around a rock.

People had gone through worse. Much worse. Somehow, she had to keep—it would be dark again soon. Christ. If she had to spend another endless—it was so much easier, when she passed out.

Unfortunately, she couldn't count on it.

NOTHING MADE SENSE anymore. She was in the woods, and it was morning, or afternoon, or—her hand hurt. Her hand hurt a lot. And her knee. And her face—she stumbled against a tree, more pain jarring through her.

"God-damn it," she said weakly. "God-damn *you*."

She took one more step—and fell, landing heavily on the ground. She stayed there, groaning, the sound like a creaky door. An *old* creaky door.

Finally—ten minutes? ten hours?—she rolled onto her back. It was getting dark. Again. How many nights had she been out here? Four? Five? More? It was too hard to keep track.

She let her head fall to the right and looked around. Dirt. Rocks. Bushes. Brambly stuff with weird berries. Pine needles. Trees. Scary leaf growths, climbing up all over things, like philodendrons gone wild or something. Creepy-looking.

Anything she tried to eat—like the berries—would probably poison her. Not that she was hungry. Exactly. But, she was so damned tired. Ten steps was a good hour's work. Pretty soon, she was going to be too weak to move at all.

She rolled her neck enough to look at the sky. Stupid, darkening sky. Stupid stars. Stupid everything.

"Find me!" she yelled, hurting her throat. "Jerks!"

*Who* did she want to find her? The guy? The god-damn incompetent FBI? *Anyone.* Just so she could see a person, hear a voice. Even a *cruel* voice. It didn't matter what the person did to her—good or bad—just as long as it was a person.

It was dark now, and the animal noises were starting. She felt something crawl over her and shuddered, knocking it off. A beetle or something. What if there were more? She moved, painfully, to a safer place, not seeing anything except trees, and rocks, and—lights. She saw lights. Oh, God, she was saved. Thank God.

She limped towards them, barely using her stick, forgetting about the pain. Lights. She was actually safe. Actually, finally safe. She limped as fast as she could, branches slapping her across the face, stumbling over uneven ground. Then, suddenly, the lights disappeared. She stopped, horrified, trying to find them. Where the hell had they gone? She turned in all directions, squinting at black empty woods, not seeing anything.

"Come back, damn you!" she shouted. "Come back!"

But, it was dark—everywhere—and she fell down, bursting into weak tears.

She was still crying when she heard running. Crashing, racing footsteps. People coming to save her, or hurt her, or—she sat up, trying to see who it was.

"Hey, over here!" she said. "I'm over here!"

But now, the footsteps seemed to be fading.

"Don't leave me!" she said. "I'm over here!"

The woods were silent.

"Oh, God." She slumped down, holding her ribcage with her good hand. Yelling hurt.

She was losing it. She was very definitely losing it. Sometimes, she was sure people were talking to her; other times, she heard music. Loud, pounding music. She hated to look up at all anymore, because she knew that she was going to see things. Flowers. Lots of flowers. People, or houses, or—mostly, it was people. *Specific* people. Him. Her family. Josh. Once, it was a bunch of doctors and nurses wearing scrubs, and she would have believed it, but they looked like people she had watched on television. And even if it was them, they wouldn't be out in the woods; they lived in a *city*. Besides, she was pretty sure that they were actors, that they weren't even real.

*Nothing* seemed real.

IN THE MORNING, she was too weak to stand up, so she just crawled. She would reach out with her left hand, pull, then push with her right leg. Rest. Cry. Then, reach, pull, push. Sometimes, she made it a couple of feet; more often, just inches. Christ, how long was she going to be able to go on?

Reach, pull, push. Each time, it was harder—knowing how much it was going to hurt, and how tired it was going to make her. Exhaustion and pain. She couldn't even remember the mine shaft anymore. Just these god-damn woods. Being covered with dirt and sticky perspiration, crying whether she wanted to or not. She felt so—confused. Like her mind was completely gone. Reach, pull, push, the trees above her swirling around. Swirling, and spinning, and—she came upon the backyard so suddenly that it was almost an anticlimax.

There was a man, with his back to her, chopping wood. With an ax. Terrific. What if, after all this, she had found her way back to the kidnappers' house, and—maybe she should—he must have sensed something, because he turned, and she saw that it was a boy, not a man, probably about fifteen.

His eyes widened, and he took a step back, hanging onto the ax, looking as scared as she felt.

Automatically, she lifted her hand to straighten her hair. Or, rather, the thick tangled clumps that had once *been* her hair. She did her best to smile at him, not sure if she remembered how.

"I—" Her throat felt as if it were full of crushed glass. "Is that your house?" she asked, managing a feeble point from her position on the ground.

He nodded, his eyes huge.

"Are your parents home?" she asked.

He shook his head.

Naturally. "I, uh—" God, she was tired. So tired, she couldn't think. "Do you have a telephone?"

"Well—yeah," he said, looking at her uneasily.

"Good." She rubbed her forehead, her brain feeling as heavy and exhausted as the rest of her. "That's—good."

"W-were y'lost or something?" the boy asked, still keeping his distance. He had an accent. A Southern accent.

Or something. She nodded. "Can you do me a favor and call the police? Tell them—" Tell them what? "I don't know. Tell them someone got shot, and to send every car they can."

"Someone *shot* you?" the boy said.

Okay, more like fourteen. "That's to make them come fast," she said, hearing the same patient tone she used when her brothers were being particularly dense. "Ask them to send an ambulance, too."

He nodded, not moving.

"Go on now," she said, "okay?"

He hesitated. "Shouldn't I help you—"

"I'll catch up," she said.

He turned to go to the house, his eyes still wide.

"Don't run with an ax in your hand," she said automatically.

He nodded, put the ax down, and ran to the house.

Fifty or sixty feet. She could make it fifty or sixty feet, even if it was uphill. Stick or no stick, she could damn well *hop* it. Under the circumstances.

Using a log, she pushed herself up onto her right foot, arms and legs shaking. Safe. She was actually—she wasn't safe *yet*. Now, when she thought about it, was the exact kind of moment when he would step out of the woods, give her that scary half-grin, and—she limped over to the house, scrambling up the back steps, afraid to look behind her in case he and the others were there. Close to absolute panic, she banged on the screen door with her fist, tumbling inside as the boy opened it.

"Please lock it," she said, out of breath. "Lock it!"

He did so, looking scared.

"Are the police coming?" she asked, her heart jumping around, closer to hysteria than she had been during this entire nightmare.

He nodded, clutching a phone. "I-is someone after you?"

Thirteen. "I think so, yeah." She shivered, crouching down so no one would be able to see her from the yard. "I mean—I don't know. I don't—I mean, I think—" If they were that close, they would have gotten her already, not waited for her to go inside a house. Maybe she was safe. She might actually be—she had to call her parents. And Josh. And—but, she needed a couple of seconds to think, first. To remember what she—"Where are we?" she asked.

"Well—" He looked at her uncertainly. "This, um, is the kitchen."

Maybe he was a very tall and well-built *twelve* year old. Who had an accent. "Are we someplace in the South?" she asked.

He nodded, apparently too unnerved by all of this to speak.

Jesus. She reached up to grab the edge of a marble counter, trying to pull herself to her feet. But, even her good leg didn't want to work so she sank back down to the floor, very tempted to put her head on her arms, and either sob—or sleep. "*Where* in the South? What state?"

"Uh, Georgia," he said.

Georgia. Okay. She had been to Georgia before, and—it was comforting to have been to Georgia. To know where it was. It also explained why she hadn't frozen to death. And the reddish dirt. "What day is it?" she asked.

"Tuesday," he said, sounding very uneasy.

Tuesday. That didn't help much. Was it May? June? Did she even care? She leaned her head back against a wooden cupboard door and looked around, seeing that she was, indeed, in a kitchen. With a stove, and a refrigerator with children's drawings stuck to it, and nice clean linoleum, and—a normal, everyday kitchen.

Jesus. A kitchen. In someone's honest-to-God *house*.

"Is it okay if I use your phone?" she asked.

He nodded, holding it out, and she reached up to take it from him, shocked to see how filthy her hand was, the skin covered with deep scratches and scrapes, a couple of the nails actually *torn off*. "I, um—" She stared at the grime, and blood, then shook her head and focused on the keypad, trying to remember her number—and how to dial. It took her several attempts—her fingers were clumsy, and then, she realized that she was trying to call the house in *Massachusetts*—which wasn't going to help much.

But, she finally managed to punch the right numbers in, and when the phone rang on the other end, and the switchboard answered, "White House," she knew that everything really *was* going to be all right.

# 15

SHERIFFS, POLICE OFFICERS, National Guard soldiers. Cars and SUVs everywhere. The boy, standing awkwardly in the kitchen, giving her a glass of water, shifting his weight from one foot to the other. The boy's *mother*—and a little sister—rushing into the house from the grocery store, alarmed by all of the cars, maybe even more startled by the reason that they were there. And Meg, feeling a strange combination of exhaustion and self-consciousness, was too shy to answer questions with more than small yes's or no's, just waiting for the ambulance and hanging on to the open line to the White House, as Preston—with God knew how many people listening in—said calming, comforting things to her—including telling her that her brothers and Josh were safe. Her parents had left immediately, on their way to meet her somewhere, Meg too tired to pursue the logistics.

When the ambulance came, she was bundled onto a gurney and taken outside, surrounded by one of the tightest cordons of security she had ever seen. At least the press didn't seem to have shown up yet, although she wasn't completely sure, because it was so crowded. There seemed to be both doctors, and men with guns, inside the ambulance, and being surrounded by a group of strange men in a speeding vehicle was so much like actually being kidnapped, that she couldn't help being afraid. They were all talking at once, and she knew one of them had told her where they were going, but she couldn't remember what he had said. Either way, she kept a small, vague smile on, so she wouldn't have to say anything.

Someone put something into her arm—a needle?—which hurt, but she was too tired to protest, too tired to answer all the voices and questions, too tired to watch the IV being set up, or the lights flashing in her eyes. They were doing something to her leg, an air splint ballooning around it, and she woke herself up to watch.

"Did they wreck it up for skiing?" she asked, her voice sounding pathetic even to her. Small, weak. Lethargic. "My knee, I mean."

"You're going to be fine," one of the men said, his voice a little bit too soothing.

She nodded, too shy to ask where they were going again, letting her eyes close. Then, they did something to her hand which hurt so much that she had to cry, trying to turn her face away, so they wouldn't see. Voices apologized, and she felt a hand on her forehead, brushing her hair back. She managed another little smile, acutely embarrassed by all of this.

She happened to meet eyes with a soldier to her right—a *young* man, not much older than she was—and he smiled the same sort of scared smile at her. She smiled back, relieved to see that someone else was feeling almost as shaky and nervous as she was.

"I—I look so terrible," she said.

"You look *great*," he said, everyone else seeming to agree with him.

Nice to be humored. She had a pretty good idea of how disgusting she looked. How filthy. "So, what do you think?" she said to the same man. "Am I going to get out of finals?"

He nodded, very seriously, but she heard a couple of the other men laugh. Making a joke, however minor, was exhausting, and she blinked a few times, trying to stay awake. It would be too vulnerable to fall asleep in front of all of them. All these men. But, it would be nice to—she felt her sweatshirt being lifted, a hand touching her stomach, and had to fight off a scream, doing her best to sit up.

The hand had already left her stomach. "I'm sorry," one of the doctors said. "I was just—"

135

"Well, you can't!" She shoved the sweatshirt down, clamping her left forearm across it.

"I'm sorry," he said. "I just wanted to take a look at your ribs. I'm worried about the way you're breathing."

She looked at him suspiciously, tightening her arm. "I'm fine."

He nodded, lifting his hands as though showing her that he wasn't going to do anything, and she eased the pressure of her arm slightly—since it was killing her ribs, but still kept her eyes on him.

"Do you think you can answer some questions?" he asked.

She nodded—carefully, watching him.

"Where are you having the most pain?" he asked.

"I don't know, I—" Her tongue felt thick, and she looked at the IV again, afraid. "Are you giving me drugs?"

"That's glucose," he said. "And we've given you a mild tranquilizer."

She frowned, not sure if she should believe him. "I don't want to fall asleep."

"It's just to help you with the pain," he said.

She looked around at the other men, checking to see where they were. What they were doing. Theoretically, these were the good guys, and they weren't going to hurt her—but, then again, how could she be *sure*? She looked back at the doctor. "I don't mean to be rude to you," she said. "I just—I don't know you."

He nodded. "I'm Doctor Amesley. I live up here in Gilmer County."

Which meant absolutely nothing to her. She studied his face. He *looked* nice enough. Normal enough. Not that *that* meant anything. "I don't remember where you're taking me," she said, very quietly, so that the others might not hear.

"To a helicopter," he said, without hesitating. "Which will transport you to an Army base, where you'll meet your parents."

She tried, her mind sluggish, to think of military bases in this part of the country. "Bragg?"

136

He nodded.

Since there wasn't much she could do *but* trust him, she forced herself to relax. Somewhat.

"Is your hand the worst?" he asked.

Tough call, but—she nodded.

"What about your head?" he asked.

Her *head*? She looked at him blankly. "You mean, my nose?"

He frowned. "Is that all that hurts?"

"Well—where they got the teeth, too." She shifted a little, not sure why he looked so worried. "Do you think it's broken? My nose?"

The men all seemed to exchange glances, which made her nervous.

"Yes," Dr. Amesley said. "I think it's broken." He started to raise his hands, then hesitated. "I'm just going to feel your skull for other injuries, okay?"

She nodded.

His hands went right to the side of her forehead where—Christ, it seemed like *centuries* ago—the man in the van had hit her with the gun. Then his hands, very gently, moved around to the back of her head.

"Phrenology," she said, and blinked. Where the hell had *that* come from?

The doctor blinked, too. "I guess your memory isn't impaired," he said, sounding less worried.

"I guess not." But, there had been some word she'd been trying to think of recently. In the cave? Her shoelace. The stupid thing on the end of her shoelace. It was—zygote. Or, no—*argot*. Except— that wasn't it, either. What the hell was it? "*Aglet*," she said aloud, remembering suddenly.

They were all looking at her.

"On your shoelace," she said, too tired to elaborate.

The doctor kept examining her, asking permission before he

did anything, Meg only scared when he felt her ribs, his hands up under her sweatshirt.

"Do you think they're broken?" she asked, struggling not to panic again.

"It's hard to say." He took his hands and the stethoscope out. "From the way you're breathing, I'd guess that a couple are at least cracked."

*All* of her bones felt cracked. She nodded, feeling a great wave of sleepiness, fighting it off.

"When did you eat last?" he asked.

"Breakfast," she said, more and more tired, rubbing her face with her shoulder.

He stared at her. "You had *breakfast* today?"

She shook her head, the motion of the ambulance making her even sleepier. "Before school."

"The day you were kidnapped?" he asked.

She nodded, hearing more than one gasp, someone saying, "Jesus *Christ*" in a low voice. The doctor was asking another question, but she couldn't keep her eyes open anymore, falling into a confused sort of daze.

It seemed as if they drove for hours, and as if they drove for seconds, because then, she was being carried out of the ambulance, into what had to be the helicopter. People were talking at her, but she was too tired to pay attention, feeling the helicopter lift off the ground. She hated helicopters.

After a long time, the motion stopped and, hearing many more voices, she forced her eyes open. It was bright outside, and there were soldiers everywhere. She heard the word "President" and tried to get off the gurney, so eager that she forgot how much everything hurt.

Then, her parents were there, and she was hugging them with her good arm, trying not to cry. But they were, so maybe it was okay.

"I'm sorry," she said weakly. "I'm really sorry."

They were both talking, which was too confusing to follow, and she felt her eyes closing, letting herself slump against them. They wouldn't mind if she—just for a minute—if she—she was aware of being moved—into another helicopter? Air Force One? Aware of new voices, and questions, and her parents hugging her, but mostly, she just slept, feeling safe, and protected, and *extremely* happy.

SHE WOKE UP to feel the gurney moving again and opened her eyes, seeing fluorescent lights overhead. A hospital. Maybe they were at the hospital. Her parents were right next to her, holding on to her good hand, and she tried to smile at them. They were saying nice, soft things to her, their faces pale and worried.

"Are Neal and Steven okay?" she asked, and saw them nodding. "Are we at the hospital?"

They seemed to be saying yes, and she nodded, too, about to close her eyes again. Josh. Preston had said—"Is Josh going to be here?" she asked.

"I'll have someone get him," her mother said, motioning behind them.

There was a lot of dirt all over the front of her mother's dress—which was really strange to see, and Meg was going to say something about it, but instead, let her head fall back on the pillow, seeing a blur of people standing against the walls as they passed. Blue and olive drab uniforms, mostly. Grey suits, too. Then, they were in a very bright room, and the people were wearing white coats, or surgical scrubs.

"I'm pretty drugged out, hunh?" she said, her voice feeling distorted. She closed her eyes, too tired to wait for a response.

The doctors were doing stuff to her, poking and probing, and flashing more lights at her eyes.

"—going to hurt a little," a voice was saying.

She opened her eyes. If they were *warning* her, it was going to be something bad.

"I'm just going to numb your arm, so it won't hurt when we take the X-rays," a man said.

She nodded dully, then recognized him. Dr. Brooks, the White House physician. "Oh. Hi."

"Hi." He smiled at her. "I'm very glad that you're here."

She smiled back, sleepily, and let her eyes close again. The needle *did* hurt, and she gripped her mother's hand, her father's hand squeezing her shoulder.

"Okay?" Dr. Brooks asked.

She nodded, although it hurt *a lot*. Much worse than novocaine.

"Okay, all finished," he said. "In a few minutes, it'll be numb, and then we're going to take you down to radiology."

She laughed a little. "What are you doing to do—a full body shot?"

He smiled, and touched the split in her eyebrow. "How did this happen?"

"I don't know." She tried to remember, and shook her head. It was hard to remember *anything*.

There was a small sound, like a gasp, and she saw Josh standing by the bed, tears running down his cheeks. Seeing him there, looking the way he always did, she had to cry, too, so happy to see him safe that she was close to losing the little bit of control she had left.

"He told me they killed you," she said weakly. "He told me—I thought—"

He was bending over the bed, kissing her cheek, and she got her arm around his neck, hugging him as hard as she could.

"I," she hugged more tightly, "I'm sorry I look so ugly, I—"

"You look *beautiful*, Meg," he said, and she could hear his voice shake. "I-I can't believe you're here."

She hung on to him, her eyes closed, the last major worry leaving, now that she had actually *seen* him.

There was a low voice—Dr. Brooks?—and Josh bent closer. "They want me to go now."

She nodded, not wanting to let go of him. "I'll, uh—" She didn't want to cry again, either. "See you in school tomorrow?"

"S-school?" he said.

She laughed, which hurt her ribs. "Got you."

"Yeah." He kissed her cheek. "I'll be here if you need me. The hospital, I mean."

She nodded, the fatigue seeping back, feeling her parents take her hand again as he moved away. The doctors were doing something excruciating to her knee—and then, Dr. Brooks crouched down very close to her face.

"Meg," he sounded both awkward and gentle, "is there anything you need to tell me? Anything they might have—done to you?"

Rape. She felt her parents tense, and shook her head.

"You're *sure*," he said.

She nodded.

"Okay." He straightened up. "We're going to take you down now."

She nodded, her eyes already half closed. "Is it okay if I sleep?"

"It's *fine* if you sleep," he said.

# 16

SOMETHING—SOMEONE?—LOOMED over her and she slid hard to the right, trying to protect herself, only her left arm responding. Hands fastened around her wrist and elbow, yet another hand touching her face, and she struggled away from them, realizing that she was surrounded. That three, or maybe even more of them, had come in to—to—her mother. One of them was her mother. She stayed very still, waiting to see what was going to happen.

Her mother—it *was* her mother—was saying something, and Meg frowned, trying to focus.

"—safe," her mother said, then something about a hospital.

Hospital. She began to remember the night before—and the night before that, and—Jesus.

"Wh—" She swallowed, her mouth so dry that her voice didn't want to work. She licked her lips. "Wh—"

A straw came into her mouth and she choked, spilling water down her front. Water. They must have thought—which was funny, and she laughed, moving away from the straw. "No, I—" She choked again, spilling more water. "What *time* is it, not—" She laughed some more.

Her mother was holding her hand now. "It's three o'clock in the afternoon," she said, gently sponging the water away.

Afternoon? Meg frowned. "Today? Or—" She shook her head, confused. "I'm sorry, I don't—"

"Shhh," her mother was saying, and she saw that her father was there, too.

"I *am* sorry," she said. "I didn't mean to—I mean—I'm really sorry."

They were saying things that blurred somewhere inside her head and she realized, embarrassed, that there were a number of other people in the room.

"I can't remember where we are," she whispered.

"Bethesda Naval Hospital," her father said.

"Oh." She gulped, feeling tears for some reason. "I thought we'd be right near home."

Her parents said more soothing things to her and she tried to smile at them. She looked down, saw that she was wearing a hospital gown—and froze, not wanting to think about *another* group of people taking her clothes off, and looking at her. The way all of those men must have—"What happened to my—?" She swallowed. "I'm not—"

"Your mother and the nurses did it," her father said. "To make things easier."

"Only women," her mother said quickly.

"Oh." She still didn't like it, but she made herself relax a little, starting to wake up enough to feel pain. *Lots* of pain. Her hand was still the worst, encased in plaster and metal and wires, pushed up at an agonizing angle. There were bandages on her face, and her leg was trussed up in some kind of weird splint and pulley. She took an experimental breath, to see how her ribs were, and felt tight, mediciney-smelling tape. "Am I going to be all right?"

They both nodded, some of the tears in her mother's eyes spilling over.

"It—" She stopped before saying that it hurt, not wanting to sound whiny. But they must have figured it out, because a military nurse was already by the bed, injecting something into her IV. She was going to ask what it was, but decided that it was easier to close her eyes, let sleep take over again.

She would wake up for a few seconds at a time, see—blurrily— one or both parents, feel pain, and fall back asleep. At first, it was dead, black sleep, but then, nightmares began. Being punched, the school and all of the shooting, the mine shaft. Drowning, burning, *falling*. She would wake up, muscles rigid, crying, and warm hands—her parents?—would calm her back to sleep.

One of the nightmares was worse than the others—she was chained, unable to move, and rats were crawling over her. Crawling, and biting, and—this time, she woke up screaming, fighting to get away. A lot of hands were holding her down, and she lay on her back, trembling, tears rolling down her cheeks and soaking the pillow.

"It's all right," her mother said. "You're safe. We're here with you."

"They were—" It wasn't just her parents; there were other people. "I mean—" She closed her eyes, embarrassed.

She heard her father's voice, then people withdrawing.

"It's all right," her mother said. "We're the only ones here."

Meg saw that they were, and let the tears fall—slow, tired tears. "I thought rats were on me," she said, and shuddered. Which hurt, and she had to cry some more, ashamed and embarrassed.

Her parents were telling her not to be afraid, that she was safe, that everything was all right, and she did her best to stop crying, working to find a smile.

"I—" She swallowed, her throat hurting. "What time is it?"

Her father checked his watch. "Just past midnight."

That meant that she'd been safe for at least a day. A whole day.

"Here." Her mother was holding a plastic glass with a bent straw. "Sip some of this."

Obediently, Meg sipped, but then started crying again, hating herself for obeying that meekly. Even her parents. Oh, Christ, if only she'd been tougher. She shouldn't have—

"It's all right," her mother said, touching her cheek. "It's really all right."

"I'm sorry," Meg said, still crying. "I really tried. I didn't mean to—I'm sorry."

"Listen to me." Her father bent much closer. "You did *everything right*. *More* than everything. I have *never* been more proud of you."

She looked up at him, wanting to believe it. Also wanting to fall apart; cry the loud, scared tears—the *emotion* tears—she'd been holding back, but she was afraid to start, afraid that she'd never be able to get control again. She pulled in a deep breath, wincing from the instant jab in her side, aware of pain. *Very* aware. She wanted to ask questions—like, would her hand ever work again, was her knee ruined—but was afraid of the answers. Tomorrow, maybe, she'd ask questions.

The thing to do now, was sleep. It was the only way to get through this.

THE NEXT TIME she woke up, it was still dark. The room went in and out of focus, then she saw her father, slouched in a chair by the bed.

"How do you feel?" he asked, straightening up and taking her hand.

"I don't know. Tired." She wanted to yawn, but it seemed like too much work. "What time is it?"

He squinted at his watch. "Five-thirty."

"Wow." She looked around the dark, quiet room, seeing a nurse sitting in the far corner, discreetly ignoring them. "Where's Mom?"

"She has an early staff meeting, but she went down to check on the boys, first," he said.

Her brothers. "Can I see them?" she asked.

He nodded. "In the morning."

She grinned a little. "*Later* in the morning."

"Yeah," he said.

It was nice to be quiet, and she looked at him, seeing for the first time how exhausted he was—unshaven, his face greyish and thin. And his hand, although it felt strong holding hers, was shaking a little.

"How long have you been up, Dad?" she asked.

"Two weeks," he said, with the same edge of hysteria she could hear in her own voice. In damn near *everyone's* voice.

Jesus. "How bad was it?" she asked.

"Pretty bad." He laughed a little, and wiped his free hand across his eyes. "Pretty god-damned bad."

Looking at him, she realized that she couldn't imagine it, any more than they could *really* imagine what it had been like for her. Feeling tired again, she pulled his hand closer, leaning her head against it.

"How's the pain?" he asked.

Pretty god-damned bad. She tried to smile.

"I'll get Brooks in here," her father said, starting to stand up. "He can—"

Meg shook her head. "I'd rather be quiet for a while. Just, you know, sit here."

Her father looked worried, but glanced at the nurse, and sat back down.

"Is it true there was a news blackout?" she asked.

"Well—" He hesitated. "They haven't been getting anything from *us*, if that's what you mean."

That wasn't what she meant. "I guess they're all over the place here?" she asked.

"Don't worry," her father said. "They won't be able to get anywhere near you."

Remembering, suddenly, the time her mother had had a post-shooting, and general, checkup, and had to spend the night in the hospital, and the way the media had actually trained *searchlights* up on her window, Meg looked uneasily at the window in the far corner. The shade was down, and it *seemed* dark. "Are they like, filming my room?"

Her father shook his head. "They're not sure where you are."

This room *did* look different from the Presidential Suite. More—ordinary. Sterile. "Are Steven and Neal in the Suite?" she asked.

He nodded.

With luck, the lights weren't shining on *them*.

She still had a bunch of questions, but also wanted to go back to sleep. "Did she run the country, or transfer to Mr. Kruger?" she asked. Mr. Kruger was the Vice President.

Her father sighed, not answering right away. "She didn't really have a choice, Meg."

Which didn't quite answer her question. Meg frowned. "It would have been like, a concession? Taking the 25th?" Which was the Amendment governing the transfer—temporary or otherwise—of Presidential power.

He nodded.

There was no need, then, to ask whether it was true that she hadn't negotiated. Besides, staying awake was hard work. "I might sleep again," she said. "Is that okay?"

"I just want you to get better," her father said. "I just—that's all I want."

WHEN SHE WOKE up again, Dr. Brooks was there, checking her pulse.

He smiled at her, and it was comforting to see his nice, grandfatherly face. "Good morning."

"Hi." She blinked to focus. "Where are my parents?"

He indicated the door. "Just outside. How do you feel?"

How *did* she feel? "Tired," she said.

He nodded. "Well, your system's had a pretty rough couple of weeks."

To put it mildly.

"How else do you feel?" he asked, lowering her wrist.

"I don't know," she said. "Confused, mostly. And—everything hurts. I mean—" She stopped. "I don't want to be whiny."

"I think you've earned the right," he said.

She glanced at the door to make sure her parents hadn't come back in. "How hurt *am* I? I mean, am I going to be all right?"

"You're going to be *fine*, Meg," he said. "Do you have any appetite yet?"

Did she? "I don't know," she said. "Not really."

"Well, what we'll do is bring you some broth and crackers, see how you do." He smiled, but his eyes were very sad. "You have a lot of weight to gain back."

There were worse problems to have in life. She waited for him to go on.

"You did a pretty fair job of *re*hydrating out there, but," he glanced at her, "you must have been in pretty bad shape at some point."

She nodded. *That* was for damn sure.

"We've run tests, in case you'll need certain medications for anything you might have picked up from the water," he said.

What a thought. She shuddered.

"Don't worry, there's no sign of that so far. The main thing," he indicated the IVs, "is that we want to get you built back up. Repair the electrolyte imbalance, that sort of thing."

She nodded, *basically* understanding what he was talking about. Sort of.

"We took a few stitches inside your mouth to help the healing process, and the antibiotics will take care of the infection. A couple of your other teeth were loosened, but you're not going to lose them." He studied her face, looking more unhappy than he'd probably intended. "We had to, essentially, rebreak your nose to set it."

Meg automatically lifted her left hand in the direction of her face, but didn't touch it. There was a big splint there, anyway. "How bad does it look?"

"Not bad at all," he said quickly. "But, if you're not happy with it, cosmetic surgery is always an option later on." He gestured towards the rest of her face. "There weren't any other fractures, but we had to put some stitches up past your eyebrow. There's evidence of a mild concussion, but you obviously came through it all right. Actually," he looked uncomfortable, "considering the extent of the beating you sustained, your face is healing very nicely."

"What about here?" She pointed at the tape, and what seemed to be a huge Ace bandage, around her ribcage. Tape that smelled like a veterinarian's office.

"You broke two and cracked one on the left side, and cracked two more on the right side," he said.

Only *cracked*? She looked down. "It feels a lot worse."

He nodded. "Ribs are bad. You have a lot of bruising in the rib area, as well as the stomach and kidneys, but there doesn't seem to have been any internal bleeding to worry about."

Save the worst for last. "What about my hand?" she asked.

He suddenly seemed very concerned about the positioning of the stethoscope draped around his neck.

Great.

"Well, that and your knee are the most serious injuries," he said finally. "The knee was severely dislocated."

She had to swallow, feeling very nauseated. "I tried to fix it."

He nodded. "That was our impression. You have some major ligament damage, and the entire meniscus was—well—"

"Will I be able to ski?" she asked.

He hesitated. "With surgery, and intensive physical therapy—" He stopped. "Right now, I'm afraid we have some serious concerns about—what I'm going to do, is have the orthopedic people come in here to discuss it with you and your parents."

Not exactly encouraging. "What about tennis?" she asked, mentally feeling a good portion of her life come crashing down.

"I don't know," he said. "Lateral movement is going to be—I'm not—we'll have to talk to the orthopedic people about that."

She nodded, unhappily. "Now, my hand."

"With microsurgery, they were able to set the bones pretty well, but—" He didn't quite look at her. "There's a fair chance you'll get fifty percent mobility and functionality back, and depending on surgery and therapy, we'll hope for—again, we'll have to spend some time talking all of this over with the surgical team."

Fifty percent. *Maybe.* But, it was better than being dead. She put on what she hoped was a cheerful smile. "Sounds like I'm going to be spending a lot of time in hospitals, hunh?"

"Most of it will be out-patient," he said. "And we'll work directly through WHMU"—which was the White House Medical Unit—"as much as possible."

She nodded, the prospect of this endless—and possibly fruitless—recuperation exhausting.

"It—" He coughed. "It was a very unusual break pattern."

"I used a rock," she said.

He looked startled. "*You* used a rock?"

Strange to realize that she hadn't actually told anyone much of what had happened. But, then again, she hadn't been *awake* much, either. Odds were, the FBI and everyone had been pacing up and down for hours now, waiting to pounce on her. Another tiring thought. "He, uh, he left me in this—I don't know—cave or something, and the chain wouldn't break, so—" She shrugged.

"Oh, Meg," Dr. Brooks said.

He looked so upset that she knew she had to make a joke. She shrugged. "Well, it seemed like a good idea at the time."

"You were extremely courageous," he said.

She shook her head, shyly. "Not really." In fact, barely *at all.* Then, she changed the subject. "How soon can I go home?"

"Well—it may be a few weeks," he said.

She stared at him. "*Weeks?*"

"We'll play it by ear," he said. "The important thing is for you to get your strength back."

Then, she would sure as hell cooperate. "Okay," she said. "How about some broth?"

# 17

BEEF BROTH. SALTINES. A glass of milk. Mmmm-hmmm. Her bed had been propped up and a sliding table pulled over to hold the tray. The spoon was heavier than she would have imagined, but she was too embarrassed to have anyone—even her mother—feed her, so she lifted it, her whole arm seeming to tremble with the effort.

Her mother was instantly right next to her. "Meg, let me—"

Meg shook her head. "I can do it." She spilled more than actually stayed in the spoon, but managed to get four spoonfuls down before she had to rest.

"How about some of the milk?" her mother asked.

Too much work. Meg shook her head.

Her mother started to say something, then just nodded, stepping back with her arms nervously across her chest. Seeing her in the light—like seeing her father the night before—had been a shock. She was pale and shaky, her eyes so deeply shadowed that it looked like *she* was the one who had been getting punched. And—at least when no one else was looking—they seemed to be filled with tears most of the time, too. She was also—jumpy. Skittish, really. *Different.*

Meg sighed. "The FBI must want to talk to me."

Her mother's expression darkened. "They can wait."

"Yeah, but—" It would be nice to wait. "I want them to catch him," Meg said. "I mean—catch all of them." Him, in particular.

"Well," her mother sounded very reluctant, "if you're feeling stronger later, maybe—"

"If I put it off, I have to worry about it," Meg said.

Her mother nodded. "All right, I'll take care of it."

Good. "Thanks." Meg closed her eyes, amazed by how exhausted she was—even though she'd slept so much. She heard people coming into the room, and forced her eyes back open.

Her brothers, with her father behind them.

"Hi, guys," she said, trying to make her voice sound normal. Like it always did. *Had*.

Neal hung back against their father. "Hi, Meggie," he said, almost whispering.

Steven was scowling, which—if she hadn't known that he did that when he was trying not to cry, especially in hospitals—would have hurt her feelings. "Hi," he said briefly, hands stuffed in his pockets.

Meg glanced at her mother for help.

"Neal," her mother said, "come give your sister a hug."

Meg winced. "Oh, please—I *already* feel sick."

That won her a little snicker from Neal, and something like a smile from Steven.

"How do you feel?" her father asked.

"Well," Meg indicated her tray, "I get to have this delicious soup." She had always hated clear soup. In fact, she hated most soups, but at least minestrone was interesting to look at.

Her family was standing there with the same uncomfortable expressions she remembered from when her mother had come home from the hospital after being shot, no one seeming to know what to do, or say—and, in retrospect, she realized that it wasn't fair that the one who was actually *hurt* had to do all the work. Set the tone.

"So," she said aloud. "How'd those crazy Red Sox do while I was gone?"

They all looked at each other, either not knowing, or not wanting to *admit* that they knew.

"What do you think we did," Steven said, sounding hostile, "sit around and watch games?"

"You didn't even check any damn *scores*?" she asked, irritated by his tone, even if she *did* understand it. Her head hurt, and she rubbed at it with her good hand.

"As far as I know, they're holding their own," her father said smoothly. "Would you like some ice cream, maybe? Instead of the soup?"

She wanted to sleep, that's what she wanted. She shook her head. Neal's staring was also getting annoying, and she frowned at him. "You're not at the damn zoo, okay, Neal?"

He looked very hurt, like he might cry even, and she saw her parents exchange quick glances. Then, her father put his hand on Neal's shoulder, steering him towards the door.

"We're going to let you get some rest, kiddo," he said to her. "Come visit you later."

Oh, Christ, now everyone was all offended. "Look, I didn't mean—" The three of them were gone, and she let out an angry breath. Great, now she was in trouble. She looked down at her bowl of broth, fighting the urge to slam it to the floor. "I didn't mean to hurt his feelings."

"He knows that," her mother said, sounding very soothing.

*Now,* she was being humored. "Yeah, well, I didn't mean to." Christ, her hand hurt. Her hand hurt worse than ever. She clenched her good hand, wishing that she could, at least, smash one of the stupid packets of crackers. "Steven could have said he was happy to see me."

Her mother sighed, reaching over to brush some hair out of her eyes. "You know how he is."

Yeah, she knew how he was. She didn't have to *like* it. Her knee was throbbing horribly, and she rubbed her eyes, not wanting to cry.

Her mother moved closer. "Meg—"

"Are they *ever* going to untie my god-damn leg?" she asked.

"After the next operation," her mother said, visibly uncomfortable. "They want to—"

"Great, the next fucking operation." Terrific. Now she'd gone and said "fuck" in front of her mother. She covered her eyes with her arm, tenting her elbow over her heavily-bandaged nose, feeling very close to exploding. If she could only get, Christ, even ten *seconds* of privacy, maybe—she raised her arm slightly. "Do you think you could get me a Coke?"

Her mother turned to motion to the nurse, stopped, looked at Meg, then moved to get it herself.

"Thank you." Meg re-covered her eyes, taking the deepest breaths she could manage without making her ribs worse. She'd slept like that more than once in the forest, her arm over her eyes to make day seem like night. As opposed to *actual* nights, with the noises, and darkness, and—feeling scared, she wanted to move her arm, but decided in favor of preserving the illusion of privacy. Pretending she was home, maybe. Wherever the hell *that* was.

When she smelled perfume, she knew her mother was back, and took a last few seconds alone before lowering her arm.

Her mother set a glass of iced Coke on the bedside table. "Is there anything else you want?"

To be *alone*. Meg shook her head.

Her mother studied her for a minute. "Maybe some time by yourself?"

Meg opened her eyes all the way. "Am I allowed?"

"You're allowed," her mother said, and guided her left hand over to a little hanging box with a white button on it. "If you want anything, or need anyone, just press that."

Meg nodded, eager for the privacy to start. "It can be for a while? I mean, as long as I want?"

"If *hours* pass," her mother said, "we may begin to worry about you."

A joke. About *time* someone made one. Meg grinned. "How many hours?"

"Six," her mother said. "Eight."

Ten. Twelve. "What time is it now?" Meg asked.

Her mother glanced at her watch. "Just past noon."

All right, then. "Can you get the FBI to come at like, one-thirty?" Meg asked.

Her mother looked worried. "If you're sure—"

"I'm sure," Meg said.

When she was finally alone—even the nurse left, she lay there, looking up at the ceiling. It was very clean. The whole room was, which was probably a good idea, seeing as it was a hospital and all. For the first time, she noticed that there were a lot of flowers around. Very pretty flowers. There were also a few stacks of envelopes, as well as some stuffed animals which had to be from political leaders and people like that who didn't know her. Kind of funny. She looked at everything for a while, especially all of the roses, then closed her eyes. Except that it would be a shame to waste her privacy on sleep, so she opened them again and picked up her Coke, sipping some. Pretty great to know that she could have something to drink whenever she wanted, as *much* as she wanted.

Before stepping out, the nurse had given her some pills, and even the pain in her hand was better. Fuzzier. She sipped more Coke, absolutely loving the taste. Nice and sweet, with so much crushed ice that it was almost like a slush. She drank the whole thing, taking her time, enjoying every second of it. Enjoying the *ice*. Enjoying the silence in the room. If her cat were here, on the bed, this moment would be damn near perfect.

IT WAS HARD to tell the story in order. It was hard to remember details. It was hard to stay *awake*. Her parents had insisted upon staying in the room, although the agents seemed uncomfortable about the idea, either self-conscious about asking difficult questions in front of them—or afraid that she would hedge away from the answers. A psychologist had come along, too, which would have worried her, if she hadn't known that that was fairly standard in debriefings like this. He hadn't actually introduced himself as such, but she had picked him out right away—agency people, whether they were from three-letter agencies, or Secret Service, or whatever, were always very distinctive. The same haircut or something. Kind of like—astronauts.

"And then what happened?" one of the agents was asking.

She woke herself up. "I'm sorry, I don't—when?"

"After you came to the conclusion that you had been abandoned in there," he said.

There. The mine shaft? Christ, if that's where they were, she had a long way to go yet. She sighed, picking up the fresh Coke one of the nurses had brought in.

"Do you remember?" he asked.

What did he think, that she was stupid? Of *course* she bloody remembered. Her hand was shaking, and she had to be very careful setting the Coke down so she wouldn't spill it. "I—" Was she going to be tired like this for the rest of her damn life? She sighed. "I mean, I—"

"I think we ought to finish the rest of this later," her father said, frowning at the agents.

Who promptly glanced at her mother for confirmation.

"I think that would be an excellent idea," her mother said, her voice very even, and calm—and *ice* cold.

One of the agents, the leader guy, reached out to shake Meg's hand, and she vaguely remembered him having introduced himself as Special Agent Morehouse. Morgan? Something like that. "Thank you, Meg," he said. "You did very well."

She shrugged, not sure if he meant it, or was just being patronizing. "You think you're going to catch them?" *Him?*

The agent nodded. "Maybe not right away, but—it's only a matter of time."

Maybe. She nodded back, to be cooperative, hearing her father mutter something that sounded suspiciously like "Keystone Kops" as they left the room.

Her mother must have heard, too, because she touched his back. "They will *certainly* come up with something," she said, in the "*heads* will roll" voice Meg rarely heard her use.

Her father didn't exactly shake her hand off—but, in either case, he moved away from her. "Well." He picked up his coffee cup from the sliding table. "Would you like something to eat, Meg? Or, to rest? Or—"

Decisions. "I don't know," she said. She was tired, but—she was getting *tired* of being tired. "Who sent all the flowers?"

Her parents looked at each other.

"We just thought we'd have a few small arrangements put in here," her mother said. "Because—well, there's been quite an outpouring."

She wasn't quite sure why such a bland question had made her parents look so strained, but it definitely had. She frowned. "Are you worried that it isn't, you know, *secure* to have stuff like that around?"

Judging from her father's expression, he hadn't been terribly anxious about that before—but he was *now*.

Her mother shook her head. "No, of course not. It's just—well, the response has been overwhelming."

Oh, whoa, now she got it. "You mean, they're leaving stuff at the House, like when you got"—since none of them ever said the actual word "shot," she wasn't going to, either—"um, hurt?" When it had happened, though, hundreds—and maybe even *thousands*—of people had come and left flowers and cards and all in front of the White House fence. It had been sweet, and thoughtful—and sort of unsettling.

Her mother nodded. "Very much like that, but a great deal more extensive."

Jesus. Because the piles of tributes left for her mother had been *huge*.

"Anyway," her mother said, "all of these are from people we know."

"Okay." She didn't have the energy to read, or even ask to see, the cards. "Those, um, animals are going to look nice in my bedroom."

Her parents actually grinned.

"It was my first thought," her father said.

Which was pretty funny. Vanessa, who was occasionally on the destructive side, would probably like nothing better than the chance to batter those bunnies around. Then, she thought of something. "Do people like Beth know I'm here? That I'm all right, I mean?"

Her mother nodded. "Would you like to call her? WHCA"— the White House Communications Agency—"has everything all set—"

Meg shook her head. "I'm too tired. Later, maybe."

"Would you like to sleep some more?" her father asked.

*Yes.*

# 18

WHEN SHE WOKE up, instead of her parents, she saw Preston sitting in the chair by the bed.

He smiled at her. "Hey."

She smiled back, very happy to see him. "Hi."

He got up, gave her a kiss on the forehead, then sat down again. "How you doing?"

"Okay." Sort of. She noticed another large bouquet of roses. "Where did those come from?"

"I don't know," he said. "Maybe it was the Flower Fairy."

Meg smiled shyly. "They're really pretty."

Neither of them said anything for a minute, then Preston grinned.

"Phrenology?" he said.

She relaxed, feeling a little sheepish. "They told you that?"

"They told *everyone*," he said.

Which was embarrassing, so she studied what he was wearing for a minute. A slouchy grey suit—the jacket unconstructed, a pale yellow shirt, and a grey-and-yellow paisley tie. His pocket handkerchief was a brighter yellow.

"Armani?" she said.

He shook his head. "Ah, would that it were. Versace."

Which was still pretty damn good. She checked his shoes and felt her grin widening. "Are you wearing little *boots*?"

He stretched his legs out, and she caught a glimpse of grey socks—a shade lighter than his shoes, but darker than his suit—above the ankle-high boots. "Indeed I am," he said.

For some reason, she found that hilarious—even more so than

the black-and-white zoot suit shoes he sometimes showed up to work in—and it took a great effort not to laugh. "You know what would have been one of the worst things about getting killed?"

"I don't know, Meg," he said, sounding much more serious.

She gestured to indicate his entire ensemble. "Not seeing any more of your outfits. I mean, your outfits are usually the high point of my day."

He laughed.

"I'm serious," she said.

"Well, maybe we should work on making your days a little more stimulating," he said.

She laughed, too, feeling an immediate, nearly gasp-inducing twinge in her ribs.

"How you feeling?" he asked.

To lie, or not to lie. "I don't know," she said. "Kind of terrible."

He nodded. "At least you look better than you did the last time I saw you."

She frowned, trying to remember. "I saw you?"

"In the emergency room," he said. "I brought your brothers to see that you really *were* all right."

She frowned more, not remembering any of that. "My brothers were there, too?"

"You were pretty much out of it," he said.

Jesus, she *must* have been. "Was I talking to you?" she asked.

He shook his head.

"I talked to you on the phone," she said, suddenly remembering *that* much, at least.

He nodded.

"Did I make any sense?" she asked.

"You weren't really saying anything at *all*, kid," he said. "I was pretty worried."

"I was so tired." She sighed. "I'm *still* so tired."

He started to get up. "You want me to—?"

"No, I'd rather talk to you," she said. "Or, you know, have you stay here."

He nodded, and reached over to pick up her hand, Meg noticing—again—how strange and nice it was to feel safe.

"Where are my parents?" she asked.

"Thought they looked pretty tired themselves," he said.

She hadn't seen either of them sleep so far, so they definitely must be. "You mean, they're resting?"

"I think your father might be," he said. "Your mother's in a meeting."

The latter, not being at all surprising. "She worked the whole time I was gone," Meg said, "right?"

Preston nodded.

Because not negotiating would mean much less, if the government noticeably stopped functioning. And she wondered what the country thought about that—but didn't *really* want to know. Aware that Preston was looking at her intently, she let out her breath. "My father thinks the FBI's stupid."

"It's been a pretty frustrating time," he said.

Preston was a master at non-answers. Although he was usually pretty straight with *her*. "I guess if they don't come up with something, heads'll roll?" she asked.

"Heads have *already* rolled," he said. "Believe me."

A phrase which, taken literally, was terrifying.

"What?" Preston asked.

She shivered, not sure if she wanted to let go of his hand—or hang on more tightly. But, she didn't want to fall apart in front of him—or anyone else—so, she forced the image out of her mind. "I can ask you stuff, right? And you'll tell me?"

He nodded.

"I asked those FBI guys and everything, but they wouldn't really—" She swallowed. "What happened at the school?"

Preston hesitated—which was an answer in itself.

"I saw them both go down," she said.

He nodded.

"I wish—" Now, on top of everything else, she was about to cry, too. "I really liked Chet. I liked him a lot."

His other hand came over so that he was holding her hand between both of his. "The thing you have to remember, Meg, is that *none* of it was your fault. It's terrible, but it wasn't your fault."

She blinked, some of the tears spilling over. "I stopped walking. I *know* I'm not supposed to—"

"You were told to stop," Preston said. "Anyone would have."

Meg looked up. "They heard that?" Her back-ups—in some form or other.

He nodded. "Took a second for them to realize that it wasn't just a reflex on his part."

It had seemed so—benign. As though he was looking out for her. "The guy said they almost made it with the stun grenades and stuff," she said.

Preston nodded again.

It was *way* too soon to be thinking about any of this. Ideally, she didn't *ever* want to think about it. "Shouldn't Dennis have *figured* they'd kill him?" she asked. "For knowing too much?"

"He talked a little," Preston said, and she was glad he left off the "before he died" part. "I guess he thought they were just going to wound him."

Christ, there must have been an *unbelievable* amount of money involved, from start to finish. "And then later, they would have like, retired him, because of the stress of it all?" she asked, a few more pieces of the whole thing falling into place.

Preston shrugged. "I don't know, maybe. No point in thinking about it *now*, though."

Well, he was definitely right about that. In fact, there were a lot of details she'd just as soon never know. Which didn't make it any less her fault. "I *knew* I didn't like him," she said. "I knew there was something—"

Preston shook his head. "If anything, Meg, you thought he was *over*protective."

Which was true, but—"I know," she said. "But if I'd told you, or maybe my father, or—"

"Yeah, your buddy Josh was all worried about that, too. Says he knew you weren't going to tell anyone, so he should have," Preston said. "But—initially, at least—the reality is that he probably would have just gotten a warning to back off a little. Give you some space."

It was nice of him to try and let her down easily, but that didn't make it true. "He *probably* would have been taken off the detail," Meg said.

"Maybe," Preston said. "Not necessarily."

She disagreed—but, okay. What she wanted to do, was stop asking questions, but there was still so much that she didn't know. "Were other people—" She *really* didn't want to know the truth about this one. "I mean, people in my class, or teachers, or—"

Preston shook his head. "No. There were some minor injuries from glass fragments, and the ricochets, and so forth, but—well, thank God you warned them all to get out of the way."

What? She frowned at him. "I didn't do that."

He nodded.

Well, she was the one who had been there—and she was damned sure that that hadn't happened. "What about, you know, the terrorists?" she asked.

"Your back-ups brought down three of them," he said.

Jesus. "Were they—?" she asked.

"Two of them," Preston said, nodding. "The other one's in a prison hospital, for now."

She didn't want to know whether extraordinary rendition, or anything like that, was in his future. "Is he like, plea-bargaining?" she asked.

164

"I don't think he *knows* much. Whoever planned the thing was—" He stopped.

"Pretty god-damned brilliant," Meg said. And then some.

"Well, no one's *that* smart," Preston said. "They'll get him."

Not bloody likely. She shook her head.

"The Agency's reputation was pretty tarnished by this one," he said. "*All* of the security agencies, actually. I think they'll do everything it takes."

Yeah, right. Meg narrowed her eyes at him—which pulled at her stitches. "You sound like a *press* secretary."

"Wonder why," he said, and grinned at her.

Well, yeah. But, even so. "You *know* they're not going to get him," she said.

He shrugged. "They got the damn group that *funded* the thing."

She perked up. "Really? When?"

"I don't know," he said. "I guess it was the third or fourth day."

Third or fourth day. It was the third or fourth day when they had panicked—or whatever it was that had happened, and—"Did it leak?" she asked.

Preston nodded. "Hit the Internet first, and then most of the networks started running with it."

Great. It was impossible to keep the Internet in check, but, because of some television networks grubbing for extra ratings—and, she assumed, advertising dollars, she'd ended up chained in a mine shaft in the middle of nowhere. "That was *stupid*," she said. "They almost got me killed."

"I don't think your mother's going to forget it anytime soon, either," he said.

Big deal. Meg shrugged. "Well, it's not like she can do anything. I mean—"

"Would *you* want to be a major news organization the President had a grudge against?" he asked.

No. Meg looked at him uneasily. "All she can really do is restrict access, or—"

"That's a lot, Meg," he said.

But not *enough*, considering the way it had played out. Feeling very thirsty, she reached for the glass of water on the bedside table. "She can't actually come right out, and—"

"They'll get the message," he said.

A person didn't get to be the President without learning how to handle enemies somewhere along the line. "My father's even less forgiving than she is," she said.

Preston nodded, pouring some fresh ice water into her glass. "Especially where his family's concerned."

Yeah. "Who were they?" she asked. "The terrorists, I mean."

Preston scowled, and she was surprised to see his right fist tighten. "Some new damned Islamofascist splinter group."

Swell. "Are they in jail?" she asked.

"Some were detained; others were deported," he said. Cryptically.

Foreign policy was always scary, and she wasn't sure if she wanted to know any more details. "Was it—" She hesitated. "State-supported?" Christ, a *war* could be started over this.

He shook his head. "Doesn't look that way."

"Thank God for *that*," she said.

The tension in Preston's face eased slightly. "Yeah, I'd say so."

"Do you think she would have—" Meg stopped, since saying "blown them off the map" lacked a certain—"I mean—"

"Your mother is a very prudent woman. I like to think—" He grinned. "Well, you know me, kid, I'm big on economic sanctions."

None of this was funny, but she laughed anyway. "Can you imagine my father's reaction if that's all she did?"

Preston laughed, too. "I'd rather *not* imagine it."

Picturing her father signing on with the Delta Force or HRT

or something was kind of amusing, but everything was starting to hurt again, so she closed her eyes.

"You okay, Meg?" Preston asked, sounding worried.

"I'm just tired." She opened them. "What time is it?"

He looked at his watch. "Almost six."

She nodded. Not that it really made any difference.

"Feel up for some dinner?" he asked.

"I guess," she said, without enthusiasm.

"Couldn't hurt," he said.

She shrugged, and looked in the direction of the door. "Does everyone think I'm going to be psycho from this?"

He shook his head. "I think people are probably just going to be afraid of saying the wrong thing."

Hell, she didn't even know what the wrong thing *was*.

"My feeling," he said, "is that you should probably just worry about getting better, then worry about how you feel about things."

Right now, all she felt was tired. In lieu of yawning, she sipped some water. "An Army psychologist was here, when the FBI was." At *least* one.

"I really wouldn't worry. I mean—" he glanced at her—"later on, you may want to talk to someone, but—"

"*You* think I'm going to be psycho?" she asked.

"No," he said. "Just don't rule it out—it might be something you'll want to do."

"Thomas Eagleton," Meg said grimly.

He laughed. "I think we've come pretty far past that—but, I dig your sense of history."

Well, yeah—*decades* had passed. She smiled a little.

He reached over, touching her cheek. "I'm just going to give you one piece of advice. Do whatever the hell *you* feel comfortable doing, okay? Don't put on an act, don't be a sport, don't do *anything* that isn't the way you really feel."

Must be nice, to live in whatever galaxy he was apparently

167

from. "That's not exactly *realistic* advice, Preston," she said, sort of amused. "I mean—well, Christ."

He nodded. "Yeah, I know. Just thought I'd throw it out there."

Even though it had fallen quite flat. "Can I be straight around *you?*" she asked. "If no one else is around, I mean?"

"Absolutely," he said.

# ~ 19 ~

VEGETABLE SOUP, CUSTARD, milk. None of which she really liked, but she was too shy to say so.

"Is there anything else you want, Meg?" her father asked. "Anything you'd like better?"

She couldn't really think—even about something that basic, so she shook her head, lifting the spoon. Her hand trembled, the same way it had at lunch, and she glanced around to see if anyone—her whole family was in the room; although her mother kept going out to the hall to take phone calls and have conferences with people— had noticed. Since they were all carefully not paying attention, she knew that they had. So, she took as deep a breath as her ribs would allow, and tried again, getting a small spoonful down.

"I'm in the mood for a milkshake," her mother said, unexpectedly. She looked at Meg. "Anyone else? Boys?"

"Okay," Neal said in a very small voice, and Steven shrugged.

"Okay," Meg said. "I mean, please."

Neal looked guilty. "Please," he said, his voice even smaller.

Her mother glanced at Meg's father, who shook his head. "All right, then." She got up, Meg unnerved by how—fluttery—she was. "I'll be right back."

The room seemed very quiet as she left, and Meg focused on her brothers. "So," she said. "How was school?"

They looked at her father uneasily before shrugging.

Oh. Right. It was—sometime in June, and their school must have already let out for the year. Then, something else occurred to her, and she looked at Steven. "Wait, did you go to your graduation?"

169

He checked their father's expression before answering. "What, like eighth grade's some big deal?"

Aw, hell. "What about Kings Dominion?" she asked. Which was the end-of-year class trip he'd been looking forward to for *months*.

Steven just shrugged.

Great. She hadn't been hungry, anyway, but what little appetite she'd had was now completely gone.

"Well, we'll figure out something," their father said smoothly, "later this summer, maybe." He stood up. "Meg, would you like some more soup?"

She shook her head, and it was very quiet for a minute. Depressingly so.

Neal gestured, tentatively, towards the television. "Can we, um, maybe—?"

"If your sister's feeling well enough," their father said.

"Sure," Meg said. "I mean, yeah, that would be good. Are the Red Sox on?"

It developed that they were, playing Cleveland at Fenway, and the tension eased a little in the room, once they could just sit there, and watch something so very familiar and comforting.

Meg started to pick up her soup spoon again, then realized that what she should probably do, tired or not, was call Josh. Say hello, at least. She lowered the spoon, having to concentrate to come up with his number, wishing she had a pencil so she could write it down.

*Boy*, was she tired.

"What is it?" her father asked, looking worried.

"I should call Josh," she said, glancing around to see if there was a telephone anywhere—locating it on the bedside table.

"I think he's here, actually," her father said.

What? Meg frowned. "Did I know that?"

He shook his head. "Probably not. Tonight's the first time you've seemed well enough for visitors."

Weird to think of Josh as a *visitor.* "Can I see him?" she asked. "I mean, you know, say hi?"

Her father nodded, picking up the phone and asking whoever it was who answered—the nurses' station? the Secret Service?—to send Josh up, Meg feeling anxious in spite of herself. Shy.

Her mother, a nurse with a tray of milkshakes, and Josh all arrived at just about the same time. Josh stopped to let them go first, giving Meg a chance to get a good look at him. An upsetting look. He was as shaky and tired as her family and Preston seemed, his hair parted strangely, with a cowlick she'd never even known he had. His shirt was rumpled underneath his sweater, and he seemed unsteady on his feet, like they had just woken him up. Which, for all she knew, they *had.*

Seeing her, he smiled. Nervously. "Hi."

"Hi," she said. "I didn't know you were here. I mean, they just told me."

"Well, I thought—I mean, it seemed like you might—" He blinked a few times. "I mean, um—" he handed her a small package—"here."

"Thank you." It was too hard to open it with one hand, but she could tell by the feel that it was a bag of orange marshmallow circus peanuts. She grinned. "My favorite."

"Yeah," he said. "H-how do you feel?"

Instead of saying anything negative, she shrugged. "Did they wake you up or something? You look tired."

"Well, I—" He flushed slightly. "I guess I kind of just dozed off."

"But, my God, son," she indicated the television, "the night is young." Surprisingly, she heard Steven laugh, and winked at him before looking back at Josh.

"I don't—" He was shifting his weight from one foot to the other—"should I—?"

"Pull a chair over," she said.

171

"Oh." He looked around. "Yeah."

As he carried one over, she watched her mother jittering around with the milkshakes and handing the one she'd no doubt ordered for herself to Josh, who held it uncertainly. Then, very obviously ill-at-ease, she found a chair for herself, Neal immediately moving over to sit on her lap.

Meg couldn't think of anything to say, and Josh couldn't seem to, either, so she looked up at the baseball game. The Red Sox were losing, 5–1, in the third. Christ. *Last* week at this time, she'd been dragging herself through mud and thorns and pine needles, dizzy and confused, and—Jesus. Last week, the thought of being in a room with her family and Josh would have seemed—it *was* unbelievable.

It was hard to follow the game, and she let the sounds drift in and out of her ears as she sipped a little of her milkshake. Vanilla, pretty thick. Then, she pulled on Josh's arm.

"What?" he asked, instantly attentive.

"When's graduation?" she asked. "Did it already happen?"

He shook his head. "No, it's tomorrow night."

Which meant that today must be—she had to think—Thursday. "You're going, right?" she asked.

"Probably not," he said.

Oh. She glanced in her mother's direction, then lowered her voice. "Who's speaking?"

Josh shrugged. "I don't know. Jon's father, I guess."

Which made sense. Her knee was really hurting, and she tried to slide into a more comfortable position, only finding *worse* ones. She must have groaned because, suddenly, they were all looking at her.

"Are you all right?" her father asked, already on his feet.

"I'm fine," she said.

They were still looking at her.

"I'm *fine*," she said, and saw her parents exchange glances. "I'm sorry," she said, more calmly. "Can we please just watch the game?"

Slowly, they all refocused on the television.

Jesus, it was unnerving to be the focus of attention. And to think that there had been times in her life—*many* times, in all honesty—when she'd felt that her parents—well, one parent in particular—didn't pay enough attention to her. Now, she'd give just about anything to be back to those days. Back to when everything hadn't hurt so much, too. But, she had pretty much just taken a pain pill, so whining about it wasn't going to accomplish a whole lot. Only, why the hell, now that she supposed to be safe and everything in the hospital, did her knee seem to hurting *more*?

"Meg," Josh said, looking as though he might be about to leave the room.

"I'm *fine*," she said, again. "Let's just watch the Red Sox."

WHO—IT WAS only fitting, probably—lost by a final score of 9 to 8. Her mother took Neal off to get ready for bed, Steven—atypically—trailing after them.

Meg's father got up, too. "I'm going to go find Brooks, see what he can do for you."

Her knee was throbbing so much that Meg didn't protest—at all.

Hesitantly, Josh stood up. "I should probably—"

"You don't have to leave," Meg said. Her knee wasn't *his* fault—she could try being polite to him. "I mean—please don't."

He sat back down, avoiding her eyes.

Christ, did she look *that* bad? "I, uh—" She touched her hair self-consciously. "I must look pretty awful."

"You look *hurt*," he said.

"Well—" She couldn't think of a response to that. "Well, you know."

It was quiet. *Silent*, really.

"I, um, I hope you weren't here too long," she said. "I mean, no one told me."

He shook his head. "Just during visiting hours."

Which was pretty long. She moved, trying to find a better angle for her leg, biting her lip against the instant flash of pain. She glanced over, hoping that he hadn't noticed, but, of course, he had.

He started to stand up again. "Should I get—?"

"No," she said. "Thank you."

The room got quiet again.

"I still can't believe you're here," he said. "It's—I'm *really* glad."

"I can't believe *you're* here. He kept telling me that you were— I thought—" She stopped, not wanting to think about it. About any of it.

"I ducked," Josh said, so softly that she almost didn't hear him. "When you said to."

Which she still had no memory whatsoever of doing. She frowned, not sure why he looked so upset. "Well—that's good, isn't it?"

He shook his head. "I should have *done* something. I should have—"

Yeah, right. "Against *machine* guns?" she said. "They just would have killed you."

He shivered, instead of answering, and remembering the whole scene, she did, too.

"I'm sorry," she said. "I almost got you—it's all my fault."

"It's *my* fault," Josh said. "I *knew* you didn't like him, and I knew you weren't going to—"

"I knew I had Secret Service for a reason—I never should have—" She sighed. "I'm sorry." Like, big deal. Her *mother* was probably sorry, too. For all the good it was going to do any of them.

"You're the last person whose fault it was," he said. "You're the brave one who had to go *through* all of it."

Oh, yeah, real brave. Like, just for example, when she'd offered to sleep with the guy, so he wouldn't—"I wasn't all that brave," she said stiffly.

"Yeah, you were." He shivered again. "They're shooting, and grabbing you up off the ground, and you're yelling for *me* to get down."

"I was afraid they—" This conversation was upsetting, and her knee was hurting so badly that it was hard not to cry. Impossible, in fact. She turned her head, hoping that he wouldn't be able to tell. "Did you, um, drive here?"

"Yeah," he said. "I—"

"It's kind of a long way back, at night," she said, trying to keep her voice steady. "Maybe you should—"

He was already standing. "Is it okay if I come to see you tomorrow?"

The thought of spending time with anyone—even him; maybe even *especially* him—was too hard. "I think I—" She didn't want to hurt his feelings. "I need some time alone, I think."

"Okay," he said, looking unhappy.

"I'll call you," she said. "When I'm ready."

He nodded.

"Can you make sure no one from school calls me or anything?" she asked. "I mean, you know, if they were going to?" If they could get *through*, even.

He nodded.

"Thanks." There seemed to be tears all over her face, and she wiped at them clumsily with her good hand. "I *will* call you. I just—maybe not right away."

She could tell he was upset, but he just nodded. "Okay. Whenever you're ready. Um, feel better."

"Yeah," she said. "I mean, thanks."

He bent down, gave her an awkward kiss on the forehead, and walked quickly towards the door.

"I think you should go to graduation," she said.

He shook his head, firmly. "No, I—"

"You really liked that school," she said.

"*Liked*," he said grimly.

He had a point there. She nodded. "Yeah, but I still think you should go."

He looked guilty. "It wouldn't feel—"

"I wasn't even there for two years," she said. "It's not the same for me, anyway."

"I don't know," he said. "I'll think about it."

Maybe.

When he was gone, she sank down into the pillows, not worrying about letting the tears fall, crying mostly about her knee, but also just in general. She was going to press the little white button for the nurse, to see if they could bring her some stronger pain medication, but she didn't want them to come in and see her crying.

They were doing a bunch of post-game analysis—like it *mattered*, when they lost—and she fumbled for the remote control, turning the television off. Then, she cried harder, feeling both alone and surrounded. Trapped. As a precaution, she covered her eyes with her arm, then let herself *really* cry, feeling the bed shake underneath her. Oh, God, her knee hurt. Her knee hurt nightmarishly badly. Maybe there was something wrong. Something new. Maybe she should call—but, not while she was crying like this. Christ, how could it hurt so much? How could *anything* hurt so much?

"—just *sit* there, and watch my child—" She heard her father's low voice going past her door. That meant that any minute now, they were going to come back in and—she tried to stop crying, dragging in a slow, rib-stabbing breath, and then, another.

By the time there was a small knock on the door, and her parents and Dr. Brooks came in, she was almost under control. Almost, being the operative word, and she lowered her arm only partway.

"Do you think you can sit up enough to take this?" Dr. Brooks asked, holding a small paper cup of water and another cup with some pills in it.

She nodded, as he pushed the control to raise the bed, keeping her head down so that while they might see that she had been crying, they wouldn't be able to tell how *much*.

"Wh-what are they?" she asked, looking at the pills. Not that a tearful little *voice* wasn't a dead giveaway.

"Those should help you get some sleep," he pointed, "and that one should take care of the pain you're having."

She nodded, tipping the contents of the little cup into her mouth, then gulping the water, her hand trembling.

"It's your knee, mostly?" Dr. Brooks asked.

She nodded, tensing in case he was going to have to examine it.

"All right." His hand touched her hand very gently. "I'm just going to check your pulse for a minute, okay?"

She nodded, surprised when he took it down at her left *ankle*, his fingers resting so lightly on her skin that it didn't hurt. Much.

"Dr. Steiner is on his way up," he said, "and we're going to see what we can do to help you feel better."

"I don't—" She swallowed. "Do I know him?"

"Your father and I have met him," her mother said. "He's one of the orthopedic specialists."

"Is he going to move it around?" she asked, already scared. Hurt her *more*?

"He's just going to have a look," Dr. Brooks said, pumping up a blood pressure cuff on her arm. "Ask you a few questions, maybe."

Meg nodded, still scared. But, the pills took effect quickly, and by the time Dr. Steiner came in—tall, with glasses and bushy brown hair—she could barely keep her eyes open. He *did* poke around a lot, but the pain seemed faraway, and the questions he asked—when the pain had started getting worse, where, and that sort of thing—took all of her concentration to answer.

177

They all seemed to be talking somewhere above her—to her, maybe?—and she tried to pay attention, but it was too hard.

"I'm going to—I mean, is it okay if I—" It was too much work to stay awake anymore, and she let her eyes close.

# 20

YET ANOTHER WAKENING in darkness, not sure where she was at first, then not sure what time it was. But she saw her mother, blurrily, by the bed, her father asleep in the chair by the window.

"Okay?" her mother whispered, seeing her open her eyes.

Meg nodded, relieved that her mother understood she was too tired to talk.

"I'm sorry," her mother said softly. "I'm sorry about *everything*."

Meg nodded, sleepily.

"How's the pain?" her mother asked.

Terrible. More awake now, Meg looked down at the bulky contraption holding her knee in the air. "Is there something bad—wrong with—?"

"Well—" Her mother was choosing her words. "Apparently, there's some pressure building up in there, and one of the nerves is—they've elected to do a surgical intervention tomorrow, and see if they can address some of that."

Which sounded absolutely terrifying, and Meg stared at her.

"It's going to be fine," her mother said. "Your father and I are very impressed by the team Bob's been putting together."

It still seemed really scary. "Do I have to be unconscious?" Meg asked.

Her mother shook her head. "No, right now they're planning to use an epidural."

Meg swallowed uneasily. "Will it hurt?"

Her mother shook her head again.

"Can you and Dad be in there with me?" Meg asked.

"We've made it very clear that we would prefer it that way, yes," her mother said, although her hands tightened nervously. Her mother was almost as bad as Steven about All Things Medical. Except, in Steven's case, sports injuries. He was the only person she had ever known who actually *did* things like rotator cuff exercises.

"Will the blood and all bother you?" Meg asked.

"Of course not," her mother said. Rather heartily.

Unh-hunh. Almost completely awake now, Meg moved her pillows—her mother helping her—so she could sit up a little. "What exactly are they going to do to me?"

"Well." Her mother's hands clenched again. "I think primarily they're going to evaluate the ligaments, and the meniscus and, um, your neurovascular—one of the surgeons has worked extensively with the U.S. Ski Team."

Meg felt a flash of great hope and excitement. "You mean, I *will* be able to ski again? And play tennis and all?"

"He's supposed to be the best in the country," her mother said. The President, neatly sidestepping a direct answer.

She was beginning to get a pretty bad feeling about all of this, but decided not to think about it. Was too *afraid* to think about it.

"It was good to see Josh tonight?" her mother asked.

Not really. Meg shook her head.

"Well," her mother said, after a pause, "maybe we can have Beth—"

Meg shook her head more firmly. "I don't *want* to see people." Didn't want to have them see *her*. "Um, where are Steven and Neal?"

"Asleep down in the Suite," her mother said.

Which she should have been able to remember. Christ, had something happened to her *brain?* From the concussion, maybe? She looked over at her father, who was still slouched in his chair, asleep, his face haggard. "Thank God it wasn't Neal," she said, keeping her voice low.

Her mother shuddered, but didn't say anything.

"I mean, Steven would have been bad, too, but—" Worrying about concussion complications had made her head start hurting, and she pressed her palm against it, her mother's hand covering hers, very warm and soothing. "Besides, with me—he *wanted* everyone to be thinking about rape."

Her mother's hand stiffened. "Everyone was."

"Yeah." Seeing the genuine fear in her mother's eyes, she managed a very small smile. "I swear he didn't. I mean—" she felt the smile get tighter—"it was *discussed*, but—"

Her mother nodded, letting out her breath, her hand stroking Meg's forehead.

It seemed cold, and she wished she were strong enough to sit up for a hug. "I don't think I'm going to make it through this," she said. "I *really* don't."

Her mother's hand came over to squeeze her shoulder. "You will," she said. "We all will."

Again, just a shade too hearty. "I don't know," Meg said, and pulled her blanket up higher.

"Would you like another?" her mother asked, tucking it around her.

Meg shook her head.

Her mother readjusted her pillows for her. "Why don't you try to get some sleep?"

Meg nodded, her eyes already feeling heavy. Her knee was throbbing, though, and she knew she wasn't going to have much luck. Strange to think about what tonight *would* have been like. Should have been. Her last night as a high school senior. She'd only been waiting for—well, since about *third* grade. Someone at school was probably having a big party, and—well, not that she'd ever been totally into school or anything, but it *would* have been a big deal. An important step.

Which also, damn it, was true for Steven, and—she sighed.

"Your knee?" her mother asked, sounding worried.

Meg shook her head. Not primarily, anyway. This was more—general—misery. She glanced up at her mother, whose expression *looked* the way hers felt. "I wish—" She stopped. Wished *what*? Something real helpful, like that none of this had ever happened? That her mother had lost the election, that they were still in Massachusetts, that—*pointless* wishes? "I wish you were still speaking," she said finally. "At graduation." That everything was *normal*.

Her mother picked up her hand. "I'm sorry, I know how—"

"It's not like I *loved* school," Meg said. "It's just—I don't know."

Her mother nodded. "I'm sorry. I *really* am."

"Steven didn't get to go to Kings Dominion," Meg said.

Her mother looked unhappy. "I know. Unfortunately, it wasn't—well."

"Is he mad at me?" Meg asked.

"Mad at *you*?" her mother said. "No. Of course not."

Maybe. She suspected otherwise, though.

The room was so quiet that she could hear her father breathing.

"What does the country know?" she asked.

"That you're safe," her mother said. "That you escaped."

"They don't really know details, though," Meg said.

Her mother shook her head.

"So, there's like, *conjecture*," Meg said.

Her mother shrugged, but her expression looked very tense.

She was much too tired to get into all of this, but—"Do you think they think there's a cover-up?"

Her mother shrugged again. "Let them."

The President, indifferent to public opinion? Kind of funny. Especially since she and Steven had occasionally mumbled the word "cover-up"—even out of context—*just* to watch her mother's blood pressure go up. The word "corruption" was a good one, too. However. "Have you spoken to the press at *all*?" she asked.

Except for the "can not, have not, and *will* not" negotiate speech, of course.

"Well—there have been other matters to address," her mother said carefully. "But, insofar as you're concerned, no, I've only released statements. I'd anticipated a press conference in a day or so."

Meg frowned. "From *here*?"

"Downstairs, somewhere," her mother said. "I'll just have Linda"—who was her press secretary—"prepare something—"

"If you do it from here," Meg said, "won't it look—I mean, people'll think—"

Her mother sighed. "I *can't* speak at the graduation, Meg. It would be—well, 'circus' is putting it mildly."

Which was true. Her mother's being there would turn it into an epic media event, and ruin the ceremony for everyone else. Christ, this was making her head hurt. "Yeah," Meg said, "but if you do it from the hospital, won't it look like I'm lying around all traumatized, and—you know, that *all* of us are."

Her mother's glance around the room was more than a little ironic. "Which, Lord knows, isn't the case."

Meg had to grin. "Yeah, but I don't want them *thinking* that."

Her mother nodded. "Would you like me to have it back at the House? Just a standard press conference?"

"Yeah," Meg said. "I think that would be good. Um, can you do it tomorrow night, maybe?"

"Well—" her mother glanced at Meg's knee—"wouldn't it be better to wait until—?"

Meg shook her head. Vehemently.

"Okay, then," her mother said. "I'll have Linda set it up."

"And you won't just talk about me, right?" Meg asked. "Or release a picture, or anything?" Not that her mother, obviously, could *ignore* the situation. "I mean, you'll talk about normal stuff, too?" Little things like—foreign policy, say.

Her mother nodded, bending down to kiss her cheek. "I'll do whatever you want, Meg. I promise."

Meg lifted her shoulders off the bed enough so that her mother could hug her. "I just want to be safe," she said. "I want *all* of us to be safe."

THE OPERATION WAS at nine o'clock. The doctors, Dr. Steiner among them, had all introduced themselves earlier, before the anesthesiologist had given her the epidural—which *was* scary—and now, they were behind the green operating cloth hiding her lower body from sight. Her parents and Dr. Brooks were on her side of the cloth, her parents clasping her left hand between theirs. They were wearing full green surgical outfits, right down to the masks and booties, which under different circumstances, would have been hilarious.

She hung on to them, terrified that it was going to hurt, even though she couldn't really feel *anything* below her waist. A nurse was injecting something into her IV, and she felt almost immediately calmer. Her parents were telling her not to worry, that she was safe, that everything was going to be fine, but she could hear the surgeons' quiet voices and—sounds. Suction, and—she clutched at her parents with her good hand, trying not to panic.

"I can hear them *cutting*," she whispered.

Her father moved so that he was holding her hand and her mother's hand between both of his. "We're going to talk to you," he said calmly. "You won't hear anything."

She looked up at him, watching his face as he talked about the day she was born—night, actually; *late* night—and how happy he had been, how fat and wrinkled she was, and how they brought her home to her mother's old yellow baby crib, and how they—even the dog, Trevor—would just sit and look at her, and he and her mother

184

would talk about how lucky they were, and how beautiful she was, and how smart they *knew* she was going to be—sometimes, Meg would hear a scary soft sound behind the operating cloth, but she concentrated on keeping her eyes on her father's, listening to him.

He talked about the little red cloche hat she had had, and her first lacy Easter dress, and the white-and-yellow bonnet she wore to go with *that*, and how she was always so good and happy, and *loved* to have her picture taken. And how he would sit her up on his lap, and she would eat Uneeda biscuits, and drink grape juice, and laugh and laugh.

Sometimes, she would fall asleep for a few seconds or minutes, but when she woke up, her father would still be talking. About how she used to put flour in one half of her hair and walk around singing "Cruella De Vil." About the red plaid dress with a Peter Pan collar she wore on her first day of kindergarten. About the big dishes of mashed potatoes and creamed corn she was always eating. And root beer. She had loved root beer. About how disapproving she was when Steven was born, especially because he had too much hair. About how the Speaker of the House would let her stand up in the front, after the session was over, and bang his gavel, and how funny she thought that was. About how damned stubborn she had been, *literally* trying to put the square block in the round hole, and when he'd suggested that she try the round green one, she'd said—scornfully—"*Babies* can do that." About how much trouble she had pronouncing Garciaparra. Presumably, Yastrzemski would have been entirely beyond her.

When the table moved, she woke up completely, afraid that the doctors' scalpels would slip, then realized that the operation was over, and she was being wheeled back to a recovery room or something.

"Am I all right?" she asked. She couldn't quite understand what the doctors said to her, but was pretty sure she heard the word "encouraging" in there. Which would have to be a positive sign.

A lot of people were fussing over her—taking her temperature, pumping up a blood pressure cuff, sponging off her face—and she watched from what seemed like way inside her head, too tired to do more than nod or shake her head when they asked questions.

When she woke up again, the first thing she felt was pain. Her leg was propped up, in some kind of strap-on surgical brace, and she groaned before she could stop herself. There was a flurry of activity around the bed, people trying to make her more comfortable, and she put on the best smile she could come up with, wanting to be a good sport. A good scout. A good *soldier*.

Her mother was holding out a glass of water with a bent straw, and Meg gratefully sipped some.

"What time is it?" she asked, her tongue less than responsive.

More than one person answered, and she gathered that it was after five. The press conference was at eight, and she looked at her mother. "You're still going," she said, "right?"

Her mother nodded.

"Good." She drank some more water, trying to wake up, then recognized one of the surgeons and moved her head to get his attention. "Is it going to be okay?" she asked, indicating her leg.

"Well, I'm afraid we're looking at a multifaceted and protracted process, but we're encouraged by the degree to which you're maintaining vascular sufficiency and the fact that the peroneal was not fully transected," he said.

Maybe that was her cue to go back to sleep for a while.

"Perhaps you could clarify that," her mother said, frowning.

The surgeon looked uncomfortable. "Yes. Of course, Madam President." He focused on Meg. "I guess what I meant to say is that, if the current situation holds, and the surgical grafts we do later are successful, there's a chance that, down the road, you'll be able to walk unaided."

Meg blinked. "*Walk* unaided?" She shot a look at Dr. Brooks, who didn't quite meet her eyes. Okay, he was a nice primary care doctor; of *course* he wouldn't have wanted to tell her anything that grim. But, still—it was *her* god-damn leg. They bloody well could have—Jesus, the whole thing was such a nightmare that it was almost starting to be funny. She looked back at the surgeon. "My leg won't have—un*sight*ly scars, now will it?"

"Well," he said, hesitantly.

"I believe my daughter's kidding," her father said, and Meg laughed. A little.

Except that she was going to be a whole god-damned *bundle* of scars. Scars, and crippled things, and *general* unsightliness. She covered her eyes with her arm, her fist clenched, wishing that everyone would go away and leave her the hell alone. They *did* back off a little, although there was a big production about moving her down to her room to rest still *more* comfortably.

She kept her arm over her eyes, afraid that she might be going to cry—or yell at someone—or both. Once she was in bed, and everyone but her parents had cleared out, she lowered her arm, just to make *sure* that they were alone.

"Meg," her father said, looking unhappy.

"I'm really tired," she said. "I need to sleep for a while." She covered her eyes again, her teeth pressed together almost as tightly as her fist.

*Walk* unaided. Christ.

# ～ 21 ～

BY THE TIME she heard her mother moving around, getting ready to leave, she felt under enough control to lower her arm.

"I'm sorry," her mother said. "I didn't meant to wake you up."

"I wasn't asleep." She rubbed her hand across her eyes. "Can you say hi to Vanessa for me? I mean, you know, pat her and all?"

Her mother nodded. "Of course. Is there anything you'd like me to bring back?"

*Vanessa.* Meg shook her head.

"Maybe some books," her mother said, "or—?"

"No, thank you," Meg said. Like she would ever be awake long enough to *read* them? "I mean—good luck."

"I'll be back soon." Her mother bent down to kiss her good-bye, then straightened up, giving her hand a gentle squeeze.

"We'll look for you," her father said, gesturing towards the television and sounding so vague that Meg almost smiled.

"Okay," her mother said, smiling briefly, too.

After she had left, Meg glanced at her father. "She looks nervous."

"She's worried about *you*," her father said. "We both—"

Meg interrupted, before he could go on. "I might be getting hungry soon. Where are Steven and Neal?"

He studied her for a second, then nodded. "They're down in the guest rooms. I'll check about getting you some dinner, too. Is there something special you'd like?"

"No, thank you," she said, and put her arm over her eyes.

He had only been gone for a minute when there was a light

knock on the door, and she glanced up long enough to see Preston. Preston. The *one* person who'd promised to be straight with her.

"Okay if I come in?" he asked, holding a large cardboard box.

She folded her good arm across her chest, not looking at him.

"Okay, no problem." He put the box down on the floor, out of the way. "Unless you need anything, I can give you a hello later."

"You said you'd be *straight* with me," she said, as he turned to go.

He stopped, turning back. "I'm not sure what you—"

"*Walk* unaided?" she said.

He sighed.

God-damn it. "You son of a bitch," she said. "You *did* know."

He sighed again. "If you could see what your eyes looked like, *you* wouldn't tell you unnecessarily upsetting things, either."

"Not tell me that I'm going to be *crippled*?" Saying the word made her so angry that she clenched her fist to try and keep from losing control.

"I don't know, Meg." He sat down in one of the many chairs, running his hand over his hair. "I guess the logic was, if you didn't know, you'd be up and walking around that much faster."

Yeah, *right*. "The logic *was*, 'Let's play God.'" She gritted her teeth—the ones she had *left*—wanting to smash her fist through something. *Anything*.

"Meg—" he started.

"I mean, it's *my* god-damn leg," she said. "What's the deal with my *hand*—they going to cut it off or something? Maybe tell me a week later? *Maybe*?"

Preston looked very tired.

"I shouldn't ask *you*, anyway," she said. "It's not like you're going to tell me the truth." What was going to happen, was that she was going to cry. Cry, and swear, and—she held her hand against her eyes, fighting not to fall apart.

"Meg," he said, "I—"

She shook her head. "Don't say *anything*. I don't trust you."

"Meg." He let out his breath. "I would *never* do anything to hurt you. I mean, you know that, right?"

She moved her hand enough to look at him. "Omission can be just as much of a lie."

He nodded.

"It's just like being a prisoner," she said. "People telling you *what* they want, *when* they want."

He nodded.

"I—" She swallowed, having to look away from him. "I don't want you to remind me of him." The thought made her shiver, and she looked at him again. "I mean, *you*, particularly."

He sat back, looking almost—stricken. An expression she had never seen on his face. "I would never want to," he said quietly.

Jesus Christ, this was *Preston*. One of the very few people in the world who she absolutely, one hundred percent trusted and loved. Being angry at him was too—if he got angry at *her*, it would be—

"Meg, I would *die* before I let anyone hurt you," he said.

She nodded, the thought too scary to imagine. But, she could tell that he meant it. "I'm not mad at you," she said—almost whispered. "I'm just—mad."

He nodded. "You have every right to be, Meg."

"About everything, not just—" She looked down at her leg, exhausted now that the energy of being furious was gone. "How bad *is* it?"

"I don't know," he said, sounding worn out, too. "Until they reconstruct the ligaments, and get you into physical therapy, I don't think *they* really know. From what I gather, right now, they're mainly relieved that your popliteal artery didn't rupture."

If her leg hadn't been all strapped up, she might have grabbed at it, protectively. "That could have *happened*?" she said.

He nodded.

Jesus. If it had, maybe she would have—"When are they going to do the ligaments?" she asked.

"Within a week or so," he said. "They're waiting for as much of the swelling to subside as possible."

Well, at least *that* was pretty specific. She slumped back into her pillow, staring up at the ceiling. "Will I be completely crippled? In a wheelchair and all?"

He shook his head. "A brace and a cane, probably."

Great. "Permanently?" she asked, her stomach hurting.

"I don't know, Meg," he said. "I honestly don't."

Honestly. She smiled a little. "*Honestly?*"

He nodded, very serious.

"What about my hand?" she asked. "The same basic deal?"

He nodded again.

Swell. Just swell. The only *good* thing was that she was too drained to think about it very much.

"I can't tell you how sorry I am," he said. "About this whole damn thing."

She nodded.

"I'll do anything I can to help you," he said.

Odds were, she was going to *need* it.

They sat without speaking for a few minutes, Preston looking almost as lost and sad as she felt.

Finally, she rubbed her hand across her eyes, then looked over at the cardboard box on the floor. "What's that?"

"Well, I don't know. It must be a gift." He got up, whipping off the cover with some theatricality, revealing a fancy DVD/DVR recorder and two stacks of movies. "Thought you might be too tired for reading," he said, and handed her a remote control.

He was definitely right about that. "Thanks," she said.

"*And,*" he said, "we have some lovely films for you."

She grinned wryly. "POW dramas?"

"Well, let's see." He lifted each small case in turn, pretending to examine it at length. "*The Sound of Music. The Music Man. Oklahoma.* And—what's this?—*Mary Poppins!*" He widened his eyes at her, and she smiled back.

"Are they all musicals?" she asked.

He nodded. "*Many* lovely things," he said, and held up a thick pile of unmarked disks. "Know what we have here?"

Hmmm. "*It's a Wonderful Life,*" she said.

"No, but that's a good idea—I'll have them bring it over." He winked at her. "*Un*colorized."

She flushed, since he had been forced—more than once—to listen to her speech about the evils of colorization.

"Anyway," he said, "*these* are all the Red Sox games you missed."

Whoa. She sat up partway. "Really?"

"Would I lie to you?" he asked, looking a little sheepish.

"So, wait," she said, missing that, "in the middle of everything, you were like, recording the Red Sox every night?"

"Except for that first night," he said, not smiling anymore.

"But—like, what if I hadn't—" She stopped, not wanting to get into that, but still curious. "What would you have done with all of them?"

"I don't know," he said, quietly. "It was a sort of good-luck charm, sort of—I don't know."

Which was really—sweet. Feeling tears in her eyes, she blinked so he wouldn't see them. "My father always likes to sit in the same chair when he watches them," she said. And drink from the same beer glass, and—almost always—wear his lucky hat.

"I know. And this was probably equally effective." Then, he actually looked embarrassed. "Burned you a few E! specials, too."

Meg laughed, feeling out of practice. "Particularly *scandalous* ones?" Especially when they involved child stars who had come to unsavory ends.

He nodded. "Yeah. I know they're your favorites."

Meg laughed again, aiming the remote control around the room, pretending to be surprised when nothing came on or off. "Do my parents know about this?"

"Well—good-luck charms should be private," he said.

Pretty funny.

"I have to warn you, though," he said, taking the machine out of the box. "They dropped both ends of a double-header one of the days."

Oh, nifty. *That* was going to be a treat to watch. "Naturally," she said.

He nodded. "Yeah, that's what I thought."

"Do you think her press conference'll go okay tonight?" she asked.

"Well—" he looked around for a good place to put the player/recorder down—"she'll certainly have a receptive audience."

"People don't—blame her?" Meg asked. "I mean, you know, the country."

"I think people *empathize*," he said, starting to set the machine up. "They know how much all of you have gone through." He paused. "Do *you* blame her?"

"I don't know," she said. "I haven't decided."

He nodded.

*Did* she? Probably. Or not. "I don't know," she said, again. "It'd be kind of like blaming her for getting *shot*. Maybe it's just—I don't know. Bad luck."

He nodded, bending down to plug the machine in.

"*Real* bad luck," she said.

"I'll buy that one," he said, straightening up.

"Is her speaking tonight going to be a big deal?" she asked, pretty sure she already knew the answer.

He just looked at her.

193

Okay, that had been a dumb question. "Am I going to look—pathetic?" she asked.

He shook his head. "Are you kidding? Whether you know it or not, you've hit folk-hero time."

Meg blushed. "It's not like I—"

"Trust me on this one," he said, double-checking the connections. "People want to grow up and *be* you."

Oh, *right*. "I'd advise *against* that, myself," she said.

"Well, just don't worry about anyone thinking you're pathetic." He held up one of the plastic cases. "Want me to put in *The Sound of Music*?"

Sort of—but, maybe she should save that. "How about one of the E! specials," she said.

He smiled. "Sure. Sounds great."

They were watching a behind-the-scenes exposé of an old ensemble drama, when her father and brothers came in with dinner.

"Figures," Steven said when he saw the television, then looked guilty.

Meg, however, was amused. "Hey, you know me, I like to be on the cutting edge." Of all of the latest gossip, anyway.

Her father set up a tray of dinner on her sliding table: scrambled eggs, toast, butterscotch pudding, milk.

"Um, thank you," she said, as he handed her a fork.

Her brothers, sitting on either side of a small table, were eating the exact same meal, obviously self-conscious. She took a small bite of the eggs, feeling pretty self-conscious herself.

"What are we looking at here?" her father asked, indicating the television.

Meg hesitated. "I was sort of thinking of watching *The Sound of Music* in a little while."

He nodded, checking his watch so subtly that she almost didn't see him do it. Almost.

The press conference. "Dad, I—" Was he going to be mad at her? "I really don't want to," she said. "I just—I'd rather not."

"Whatever you're comfortable with," he said. "That's what's important."

"I'm *comfortable* with the Von Trapps," Meg said.

Her father smiled. A small smile, but unmistakable.

Preston got up. "Tell you what. How about I go check it out, and report back?"

"You can go, too, Dad. I mean, you know—" Meg gestured towards her brothers—"the three of us can just like, hang out."

Her father looked at them, then nodded. "We'll be right down the hall," he said, and kissed the top of her head. "Call me if you need me."

When they were gone, she couldn't think of a single thing to say, and it didn't seem as though her brothers could, either.

"Do you want anything, Meggie?" Neal asked, extra-polite.

"No, I—" The fork was shaking in her hand again, and she put it down. "Um, no, thanks."

Neal looked concerned. "You should eat."

"Yeah." She tried sipping some of her milk.

"Does your leg feel better?" he asked.

She nodded, although it felt pretty much the same. Worse, even.

Then, Neal looked at the door. "We're not supposed to ask you questions." He jumped, and she could tell that Steven—who was just eating his dinner and not looking at either of them—had kicked him under the table.

Meg glanced over at the door, too, to make sure they were alone. "I won't tell them you asked any."

"Why don't we just watch the stupid *Sound of Music*," Steven said, eating.

"I don't care if he asks me stuff," Meg said.

Steven ignored her, scowling across the table at Neal. "Just shut up and eat."

Meg scowled at *him*. "He can ask me whatever he wants."

"I don't want to," Neal said quickly.

Meg sighed. "Well, *obviously*, you do, or you wouldn't—" But, she shouldn't yell at him. If she was going to yell at someone, it should be Steven. "Look," she said, more calmly. "I don't mind if you ask me stuff. I would kind of prefer it, if you want to know the truth."

Neal shook his head.

"I would *prefer* it," she said. Less calmly.

He checked the door. "Was it scary?"

If they weren't supposed to ask questions, then she probably wasn't supposed to answer them. Or, anyway, she shouldn't tell the truth. "I was alone, mostly," she said.

Steven held out his dish of pudding. "You want this, Neal, or what?"

"I'm talking, Steven, okay?" Meg said, irritated.

Steven slapped the dish down. "Yeah, well, he's not supposed to bother you."

Meg frowned at him. "You're *supposed* to make me feel like you're glad I'm back."

"I'm glad you're back," he said, "okay?"

This time, Neal kicked *him*.

"Yeah, well, *act* like it," Meg said, "okay?"

"*Okay*," Steven said.

"Good," Meg said, and it was such a typical way for them to argue, that she had to grin. "Look, can't you just pretend like I was in a car accident or something, and you're waiting for me to get better is all?"

Steven actually cracked a smile, too. "Yo, Meg, you talk *excellent*."

They both laughed, Neal joining in a little late.

"Neal, do me a favor," she said. "Go out there and ask someone to get us some Doritos and Coke and Twinkies and all."

He looked uneasy. "Are we—"

"We're allowed," she said. "Hurry it up, so we can watch the movie."

Neal stopped by the door. "Fritos, too?"

"Yeah, sure, whatever you want," Meg said. Expansively. "Also, if they sell hats there, can you ask them if they can get me like—a little cap or something? I hate my hair being like this."

Neal looked anxious, but nodded, leaving the room.

Since they were all in a good mood now, Meg decided not to start trouble. Even though there were probably things Steven knew that he could—

"I wish it had been me," he said, his voice startling her.

"No, you don't." Meg shook her head. "Believe me, you don't."

His expression was somewhat offended, and even more uneasy.

"I don't mean that you wouldn't be—" She sighed. "It was terrible. I mean, *really* terrible."

He glanced at her leg, then quickly away. "Because of stuff they did to you?"

"Oh, hell, I looked *forward* to him coming in," she said, without thinking. "I mean—" She stopped, realizing how that sounded. "I don't mean I wanted them to—at least then, I had someone to talk to."

Steven turned to make sure the door was still closed. "Did they *look* scary?"

Her parents were right; she *didn't* want to answer questions. "He looked regular," she said. "I mean—he could have been anyone." Anyone at all. Someone they *knew*, even.

"Did they speak English?" he asked.

"Very well." She grinned slightly. The man had been a goddamn *grammarian*. "Exceedingly well."

"Were they—" Steven started.

Neal came back in, smiling happily. "They said they'd buy everything!"

"You know I'm going to get my way for about the next hundred years," Meg said to Steven, who made a sound that was close to a laugh.

"That mean we have to watch this damn thing?" he asked, getting up to put the movie in.

"We'll have to watch it *repeatedly*," Meg said, Neal laughing. "Hey, fatso," she said to him. "You want to sit up here with me?"

Neal hung back. "We're not—"

"I know you're not supposed to," she said. "You want to do it, anyway?"

He didn't move.

"Come on, already," she said, impatiently, indicating the left side of the bed.

He stayed where he was. "Will I hurt your leg?"

She shook her head, and he climbed over the railing—which, yeah, hurt—but, it was nice to have someone sitting with her. Less like being in the zoo.

"We ready?" Steven asked, holding the remote.

Meg nodded. "Play it, Sam."

"If she can stand it, *I* can," Steven said to Neal, and turned on the movie.

Maria was just running into the Abbey when Dr. Brooks, a nurse, and a corpsman arrived with the food. Seeing them, Meg felt guilty.

"Am I allowed to eat this stuff?" she asked.

"I'm just happy to see you have an appetite," Dr. Brooks said, as the corpsman unpacked a grocery bag full of junk food and the nurse gave each of them a plate, some napkins, and a glass full of ice, pouring them some soda as they nodded polite thank-yous.

Dr. Brooks smiled, taking a cap out of the bag and handing it to her. "Oh, your—hat."

An Orioles cap. Yuck. Meg grinned sheepishly, and put it on. "Thank you."

"It was all they could find," he said.

"It's great," Meg said. Having it on—whether it looked stupid or not—was a tremendous relief.

The nurse and the corpsman left, and Dr. Brooks folded the empty bag, sticking it under his arm. Then, he ruffled Neal's hair. "Watching the movie with your sister?"

Neal nodded, starting to get off the bed.

"No, it's all right. Just be careful." Dr. Brooks gestured towards Meg's knee. "Much pain?"

"It's okay," she said. Which was a lie.

He looked at his watch. "Well, I'll come back in about an hour, see how you are."

She nodded. Nothing like having life revolve around the next pain pill.

"What do you want first, Meggie?" Neal asked, as Dr. Brooks headed towards the hall.

"Twinkies," Steven said, already eating one.

Meg grinned. "Doritos," she said. "Definitely Doritos."

# 22

THEY ATE A lot. Enough so that by the time the Von Trapps were singing at the Salzburg Festival, Meg was having trouble staying awake. Of course, she'd been up for—gosh—five or six whole hours now. And the Demerol or Vicodin or whatever the hell it was that they were giving her, wasn't helping matters any.

"You want to watch another?" Steven asked.

Meg jerked awake. "What?" She must have missed the ending. "I mean, yeah, I guess." Neal was asleep, too, leaning against her, and she maneuvered her arm enough to put it around him. "*Mary Poppins?*"

Steven groaned, but got up to put it in.

As the movie started—a dark London skyline, with the familiar soundtrack, Meg smiled. Musicals were so—sweet. So *swell*.

She looked around, waking up a little more. "Wasn't Dad in here?"

"Before, yeah," Steven said.

"Where'd he go?" she asked, noticing that it was dark, except for the small light over near where the nurses usually sat.

Steven shrugged. "To wait for Mom, I think."

"Oh." She looked up at the movie, at Bert singing and dancing in the park. "Did we talk about the press conference?"

Steven shook his head. "You were sleepy."

She was *still* sleepy. But, now that she thought about it, Bert must have been one of her very first crushes. Her grandfather—it would have been a couple of years before he died—had even given her a little striped blazer, a straw hat, and a cane, so she could do the Bert Dance. Steven was a baby, so he had only gotten a hat. Once, she had taken some ashes from the fireplace to do a chimney sweep dance, but her parents' reaction—to say nothing of Trudy—had been less than enthusiastic.

"How come Trudy isn't here?" she asked.

"Because Jimmy's still in the hospital," Steven said. "I think she's coming on Sunday. Neal was on the phone with her for like, a really long time today."

Jimmy was her son, and—oh, wait, he had had a *kidney transplant*. "Was his surgery okay?" she asked.

Steven pulled over the mostly-empty Fritos bag and ate a few. "Dad says yeah."

Okay, that was good. He had been on dialysis for a long time.

"Can't believe I like, know all these words," Steven said, as Mrs. Banks sang the "Suffragette's Song."

Meg nodded. "Mom used to sing this."

"Yo, no way," he said.

Yep. "English accent, and everything," she said. "She was always singing musicals' stuff."

Steven frowned. "I totally don't remember."

"Yeah, well, it was a long time ago," Meg said stiffly.

Steven started to say something, then just looked at the television.

By the time her parents came in, Steven had fallen asleep, too, and Meg was, foggily, watching Julie Andrews sing "Feed the Birds." Her father gently picked Neal up, carrying him out of the room, while her mother bent down to kiss her.

"How do you feel?" she whispered.

Meg shrugged, half-asleep.

"Do you want to keep watching the movie?" her mother asked.

Meg shook her head. "I'm pretty tired."

Her mother clicked off the machine, pausing to kiss Steven, too, before returning to the side of the bed.

"How'd it go?" Meg asked.

"A lot of people care about you," her mother said. "Even more than you know."

Whatever *that* meant. Meg let her eyes close partway. "What time is it?"

"Past midnight," her mother said.

Her father came back in, taking Steven out of the room.

"Do you guys sleep down there, too?" Meg asked. Although mostly, they seemed to do all of their sleeping sitting up in chairs.

Her mother nodded.

"When can we go home?" Meg asked.

Her mother paused, before answering. "Soon, I hope."

In other words, *not* any time soon.

"I know," her mother said. "I'm sorry."

She was curious about the press conference, but she also felt like going back to sleep. She wasn't exactly tired, but the pills made her feel—funny. Slow.

Her mother seemed to be saying something, and Meg looked up.

"I was just wondering if you wanted anything," her mother said.

Philosophically, an ironic question. Meg shook her head, noticing that her mother didn't look like *she* was in very good shape, either. "You guys don't have to, you know, stay up with me."

Her mother, about to sit in the chair by the bed, stopped. "Do you want privacy?"

Did she? "I just meant you should maybe get some *normal* sleep, and not—" She indicated the chair.

"Your father and I feel better being in here," her mother said, and sat down.

Since it was their decision, Meg wasn't about to argue. "What time did you say it was?"

Her mother turned her wrist to look at her watch. "A little after twelve-thirty."

"Oh." Meg glanced at the telephone. Twelve-thirty was pretty late.

"Would you like to call Josh?" her mother asked. "Or—"

"I kind of thought I'd call Beth," Meg said. Which she hadn't realized she'd been thinking until she heard herself say it. "Only, I guess it's too—"

"I think you should," her mother said. "You'll both feel better."

Meg tilted her head curiously. "You mean, you've talked to her?"

Her mother shook her head. "Your father did, at one point. I assume Preston has, too."

"Oh." Weird. "That was nice of them." She looked, uneasily, at the phone. "I can't call this late—you know how her stepfather is."

Her mother shrugged. "We'll have someone place the call *for* you."

Which might make things even worse, given her stepfather's tendency towards conservatism. "No," Meg said. "I mean, I don't want it to be a big deal, I just—"

Her mother moved the telephone onto the bed. "Why don't you just go ahead and call."

Meg reached for it, then pulled back. "Will the FBI or someone be listening in?"

"*No,*" her mother said. "They very definitely will not." She got up. "If you need anything, we'll be outside."

"Oh." Meg looked at the window in pretended confusion. "Do I like, open that and yell out?"

"What?" Her mother looked *genuinely* confused, then smiled. "Right," she said, and gave Meg's hand a squeeze before leaving the room.

Once she was alone, Meg put down the handset, and looked at it some more. It *was* pretty late. Only, if she sat around, it was going to be even *later.* She picked up the receiver again, flinching when she heard a voice say, "How may I help you?" A White House operator, or someone.

"Were you on there before?" Meg asked. "Did I like, hang up on you?"

"Of course not," the man said, sounding as overly kind as *everyone* was being to her. Not that White House switchboard people were *ever* rude. "Would you like me to ring a number for you?"

"Uh—" She had to make a decision here. "Yeah, I mean—please." Meg gave him the number, the call going through damn near *instantly*. *Extra*-special fiber optics, presumably. She probably should have called her cell, instead of calling the house directly—but didn't want to go to voice-mail, which was likely, after midnight.

Naturally, Beth's stepfather answered. Sounding cranky.

Meg swallowed. "Um, may I please speak to Beth?"

"Who is this?" he asked. "Do you know what the hell time it is?"

"Um, yes, sir. I'm sorry, I—" She could hear a voice in the background—Beth's mother, probably—and her stepfather came back on.

"Just a minute," he said.

Meg started counting, getting ready to hang up when she got to ten, but she was only on seven when Beth came on. And, once she heard her voice, Meg couldn't think of anything to say.

"Hello," Beth said again.

"I'm sorry, I—" Not knowing what to say made her feel panicky, and she gripped the phone tightly. "I mean, did I wake you up?"

"Meg?" Beth sounded almost stunned. "I mean, hi. I mean—Jesus, I don't—Jesus Christ."

"I, um—" Meg shifted slightly on the bed—which sent a serious jolt of pain through her leg. "I just—hadn't talked to you yet, so I thought—I know it's late and all—"

"Where are you?" Beth asked. "I mean, no, that's stupid. Are you—I'm *really* glad you called."

Her friend's voice sounded so strange that Meg felt even more uncomfortable. "You're not like, going to cry, are you?" she asked. Beth *never* cried. About anything.

"No." Beth laughed shakily. "I mean, yeah—what do you expect?"

Beth *absolutely* never cried. Never had. "Well," Meg said uneasily, "do I call you back, or—"

"Just relax, okay?" Beth took a deep breath, then laughed a normal laugh. "You know how emotional my people are."

Her people. Meg had to laugh, too. "What, and my people aren't?"

"Oh, yeah," Beth said. "Famous for it."

There was another silence, but this one wasn't as strained.

"How, um, are you feeling?" Beth asked.

Meg sighed. "I don't know. I guess I'm going to be here for a while."

There was more silence, Beth apparently finding this conversation as difficult as she was.

"They don't even seem to know if I'm ever going to be able to walk right," Meg said, when the dead air made her too nervous. "Only, I don't know if that means a brace, or crutches, or what."

"Maybe they're just being cautious," Beth said.

"I don't know. No one gives me straight answers." She tightened her fist around the receiver. "Well. I guess it doesn't matter. It's not like I don't have plenty of other things to worry about, right?" This whole situation really, *royally*—"Did you watch the press conference?"

"Yeah," Beth said, sounding a little hesitant. "I thought it was great."

"What did she say?" Meg asked.

"Oh. Well, she——" Beth stopped. "She was pretty angry."

As well she should have been.

"I just meant, she didn't *sound* the way she looked," Beth said.

Well, how likely would *that* have been? "What was she *supposed* to do," Meg said, "sound all defeated? Jesus, Beth!"

"I guess I thought she'd be more——frazzled," Beth said.

Yeah, right. "Not hardly," Meg said. "Not in *public*."

To her surprise, Beth laughed. "I was impressed, okay? Take it easy."

Yeah, she should probably dial it down a couple of notches. Being tense wasn't a good enough reason to start barking and snapping. "What did the pundits think?" Meg asked.

Beth laughed again. "They agreed with me."

Meg was too tired to be amused. "What were you, a guest commentator?"

"Yeah," Beth said. "You should have watched. I was very articulate. C-Span says they're going to ask me back."

Knowing the media, they actually *could* have tried to get Beth to come on. Best friend of First Family victim, and all. "You weren't——were you?" Meg asked.

"Yeah," Beth said. "In fact, I did a whole bunch of satellite hook-ups with different news shows."

Which had to be a joke. Although, even under the best of circumstances, she couldn't always tell when Beth was kidding. It was usually safe to assume that she *was*.

"Sorry I missed it," she said. Grumpily.

"She *was* good, Meg. Tough as anything. Saying things like '*beneath* contempt,' and 'reprehensible,' and all." Beth paused. "And even the reporters said nice things about *you*."

Not something Meg really wanted to pursue. She looked at the television, wondering if she should turn it on, and try to catch some of the late coverage. "They talked about other things, too, right? I mean, other issues?" Christ, was *she* an issue now? What a thought.

"Oh, yeah," Beth said. "She read a statement, and said she'd take a few questions on it, and then she talked about, you know, health care and stuff. Like everything was—normal again."

Precisely what Meg had *hoped* she would accomplish, so that was good. And she should have probably watched—but, it would have been too weird. Creepy, even.

"You still there?" Beth asked, sounding tentative.

Meg nodded. "Yeah. Sorry."

"Are you, um, allowed to have visitors?" Beth asked.

"I don't want to," Meg said. Which sounded really callous. *Too* callous. "I don't want people seeing me like this."

"Does that mean me, too?" Beth asked.

"Yeah." Which was way too harsh. "I mean, I think so. I mean—" Meg let out her breath. "I haven't washed my hair in three weeks."

"So what?" Beth asked.

"I *hate* it. I hate—I'm not ready. It's too much pressure," Meg said, suddenly feeling so panicky that she was afraid she would have to hang up.

"It was just an idea," Beth said. "You know, if you wanted me to come down."

Meg shook her head. "I *can't*. I'm supposed to know what to say, and I don't, and—no one else does either, and—I fucking *hate* it. I hate all of it."

Beth took her time answering. "Okay. Maybe when you get home, I can—"

"Yeah," Meg said quickly. "Maybe then."

There was a long silence.

"I wasn't trying to hurt your feelings," Meg said. "I'm just—" Fucked up.

"You didn't," Beth said. "Don't worry."

Either way, it was too late now. "Well, I didn't mean to." Meg slumped down into her pillows, having trouble keeping her eyes open—yet again. "I'm sorry, I'm really tired. I shouldn't have called."

"I'm glad you did. I'm glad you're—" Beth stopped. "I'm glad," she said, her voice sounding strange again.

"Me, too," Meg said quietly.

# 23

SHE SPENT MOST of the next few weeks watching movies and baseball games with still-heavy eyes. Various members of her family were almost always with her, although once Trudy had come up, her brothers had started going home and sleeping in their own beds at night again. Since they didn't have any living grandparents, she and her brothers had always thought of Trudy that way—and during the day, *she* was at the hospital a lot, crocheting by the window. Preston was usually around, too.

Mostly, she was still too exhausted to talk much, and it was a relief when no one made her try. A couple of times—more out of guilt than anything else—she called Beth and Josh, but there never seemed to be much to say, and the conversations wouldn't last long.

Investigators from various agencies showed up, more than once, and she tried to answer their questions and work on composite sketches and everything, unnerved by how often she got confused. She had also had surgery twice—putting more pins in her hand, and doing ligament grafts and a peroneal augmentation or something in her knee—and various specialists and physical therapists—and psychologists, and counselors—seemed to come in and out of her room constantly, and she did her best to cooperate with them. Or, at least, stay awake.

Which was even harder than it had been before, because her knee had been hooked up to a continuous passive motion machine, and she not only had to stay in the same, uncomfortable position on her back, but the non-stop motion really got on her nerves, and she was having a terrible time getting more than short bursts of sleep, no matter *how* much medication they gave her. And if she *did* fall asleep, someone would show up and haul her off for another arteriogram or some damn thing.

In the afternoon, she usually got pushed up and down the hall in a wheelchair for a while, although most of the time, she would lean her head against her good hand and wait for it to be over. Her ribs were getting better, though, so it was easier to sit up without needing to hunch over. Every now and then, they wheeled her into this stupid sun-room, like it was going to be a magical cure or something—although looking outside was the *last* thing she felt like doing. And riding up and down the hall was scary, because there was so much security—agents, soldiers, check-in stations, bulletproof glass.

Everyone was very nice, and would talk to her, and she was always polite, but tried to keep the Orioles cap down low on her forehead as much as possible, so they would know to leave her alone. The hat was especially good if she started crying—which would happen unexpectedly—because that way, no one could see her face.

Waking up from yet another nightmare, so terrified that she couldn't catch her breath, she saw Trudy hurrying over from her chair.

"Are you all right, dear?" she asked, helping her back down onto the pillows.

Meg stared at her—at the familiar blue knit dress, the pearls, and the pair of half-glasses swinging from a chain around her neck—then realized where she was. "I—" She tried to calm down. "I thought he was in here. Dressed like a doctor." She shuddered, picturing it again—her, lying alone in the dark room, not afraid when she saw a doctor come over, until he looked up and she saw the crooked grin.

Trudy was moistening and squeezing out a small washcloth, then sponging Meg's face. "It was just a dream, everything's all right."

Meg was going to tell her the rest—about how he kept grinning at her, then pulled out the gun, pressing it into her forehead, getting ready to—she shivered. "Do you think there are more blankets somewhere?"

"Of course." Trudy bent down, opening a little cabinet below the bedside table and taking out a smooth pale green one, spreading it over her.

The blanket smelled of antiseptic, but Meg yanked it closer. "Where is everyone?"

"I'm not sure where your mother is," Trudy said, "but your father took the boys home for a while. They'll be back later this afternoon."

Meg nodded. It would probably be good for her brothers not to come back at all today, and just *relax*, for once.

"Are you hungry?" Trudy asked. "Would you like anything?"

Meg shook her head, still trying to get rid of the dream. She stiffened, seeing a man with short dark hair at the door, then recognized the Army psychologist guy.

"May I come in?" he asked.

Meg shrugged, not at all interested in the idea. *So* uninterested, in fact, that she had never bothered getting his name straight.

He came in, nodding at Trudy, stopping near the bottom of the bed. "Just thought I'd see how you're feeling today."

She nodded. Politely. "Fine. Thank you."

"I hear you may be going home by the weekend," he said.

That was the rumor. She nodded.

"You must be looking forward to that," he said.

She nodded.

He looked at her thoughtfully. "I'm from New Hampshire, you know. Durham."

So, what, they were going to bond over New England? "It's very nice up there," she said.

Trudy looked as though she was going to leave the room, and Meg shook her head, as subtly as she could.

"We used to drive down to the city all the time," he said. "Go to Celtics games."

She had never liked basketball much, but she nodded. "That must have been nice."

He examined one of her many—still-arriving—baskets of flowers. "Have you been sleeping well?"

"Yes, thank you." Except, maybe that was a way to make him leave. She pretended to cover up a yawn. "I'm still very tired, though."

He took the hint. "Well, I'll let you get some rest, then. Maybe I'll look in on you tomorrow."

She nodded.

When he was gone, Trudy spoke first.

"He seems like a nice man," she said.

Meg shrugged. "I don't like his looks." Not that men in their thirties with dark hair and strong cheekbones were *ever* likely to appeal to her again.

"Would you like a brownie?" Trudy held out the tin she'd brought from the White House the day before.

Meg took one, even though she wasn't hungry. "Thank you." If the psychologist guy had come, that meant the room was going to turn into Union Station soon, with physical therapists and nurses and everyone.

The worst, was when they touched her. And almost all of them did. Giving her sponge baths, changing the bed, taking her temperature, helping with the bedpan, moving the two fingers on her right hand that still worked, carefully flexing and extending her left leg and foot, hooking her other arm and leg onto little pulleys and weights and things, so she could exercise them without having to get out of bed. They even did these sorts of massages, which she hated more than anything else. All of the ones who actually touched her were women, thank God—but, they were still strangers.

She saw that Trudy was watching her with a worried expression. "Um, this looks good," she said, and took a bite of the brownie. It *was* good, but her stomach was so tight that she had to force it down.

"If you don't like him, they could send someone else by," Trudy said.

"Yeah, they had a woman psychologist in here yesterday." Meg put what was left of the brownie neatly onto her bedside table. "Guess they really think I've gone around the bend."

"They just want to help you," Trudy said.

"Yeah, well—" Meg picked up the remote control. "Think there's anything good on?"

"If not, we can watch one of your movies," Trudy said.

They had run through just about every musical or Disney movie ever produced, so now she was watching things like dumb teenage high school movies and *Mary Tyler Moore* episodes. She was sick of looking at the television, but at least it made the time pass a little faster.

Not that she *needed* time to zip along, since it wasn't like she had anything to look forward to.

"Meg?" Trudy asked.

"Um, yeah." Meg handed her the remote control. "Let's watch a movie."

THE DOCTORS ESTABLISHED that, indeed, Saturday would be a good day for her to go home. Her mother had arranged to have Camp David set up as a recuperation site, but—despite its privacy—the idea of being in, or near, the woods was so terrifying that Meg had asked her to do *anything* else. Even the hospital would be better than *that*.

So, they were just going to go back to the White House. And Meg had asked to be put in her room, not upstairs in the solarium, or something. Sadly enough, her mother's own convalescence was re-cent enough so that the staff probably wouldn't have much trouble getting everything ready.

The therapists were letting—making?—her do more, and with the motorized wheelchair, she was starting to be able to deal with the bathroom by herself. The—at her request—mirrorless bath-room. Things like brushing her teeth were so demanding that she would have to rest afterwards—sometimes for several hours—but, it was a relief to finally be able to have a *little* privacy. She wasn't al-lowed to do anything weight-bearing yet, so they wouldn't let her even *try* to walk, but sometimes, they had her stand up and lean on a railing or something, to try and get her equilibrium back. Her right hand wasn't going to work anytime soon—if ever—but once her knee was stronger, the therapists seemed confident that she would be able to get around, for very short distances, on one crutch. Around a *room,* at least. Meg figured they were being overly optimistic, but she just did whatever they told her to do, even when she felt so weak and unsteady that she practically had to bite through her lip to keep from crying.

Everyone was very happy and excited the night before she was supposed to go home, and Meg manufactured as much enthusiasm as she could, eating takeout Chinese food and watching *Tootsie.* Then, Trudy left with Steven and Neal, and Preston grinned and said, "Catch you in the morning," and the room was quiet again.

Alone with her parents, Meg let herself stop smiling. Stop fak-ing it. Her parents had moved to chairs on either side of the bed, and none of them spoke right away.

"I think that cat of yours is going to be pretty happy to see you," her father said.

Meg nodded—although she'd had a dream a couple of nights earlier where Vanessa didn't recognize her—and was hostile about it. "I'm going to be pretty happy to see *her.*"

It was quiet again.

"Are we really going to be able to get out of here without—well, you know. Being surrounded?" Meg asked.

Her mother nodded. "We've indicated that you'll be leaving mid-afternoon."

Meg couldn't help grinning. "You like, outright lied?"

"Well—yes," her mother said, and blinked a couple of times.

Originally, they had been going to take Marine One back, but it would have been cumbersome to get her on and off safely, with the surgical brace and all, and she *really* didn't like the idea of being carried up and down the steps in front of what would inevitably be countless cameras. She was pretty sure Dr. Brooks would have preferred that she ride back in an ambulance—but, she was damned if she was willing to look *that* injured. So, they were going to go in a standard motorcade, and a wheelchair would be waiting for her on the South Drive, to help her get inside the White House.

Of course, motorcades weren't exactly *stealthy*.

"Word'll get out though, right?" she said. "Before we get home, I mean."

Her parents nodded reluctantly.

Meaning that there was probably no way of avoiding a crowd of media—and maybe even an *actual* crowd. Apparently, there had been a huge one when she came to the hospital, but she couldn't remember any of that. This time, she wasn't going to have the luxury of sleeping through the whole thing.

"We're going to get you right inside," her father said. "You don't have anything to worry about."

The Szechuan shredded beef and Yu-Hsiang chicken were suddenly feeling pretty lousy inside her stomach. "Do I have to say anything?" she asked. "Like, a statement?"

Her father frowned at her mother, who immediately shook her head.

"Of course not," she said. "Linda or Preston, or maybe Natalie"—who was the Deputy Press Secretary—"will brief them after we're inside."

"What if there are signs?" Meg asked, getting more and more nervous. "Or, if they clap or something?" Which they had done when her *mother* came home from the hospital.

Her mother reached over to take her hand. "We're going to get there, and go right inside to the elevator. The staff is under *very* strict instructions."

Meg swallowed. "And we'll go right to my room, and I won't have to deal with anyone? Won't it look rude?"

"I don't bloody care *how* it looks," her father said, her mother giving him a warning glance.

Okay, okay, maybe she wasn't the only one who was a little on edge here. Meg took a deep breath. "*I* care how it looks, Dad. I mean—" She needed another breath. "*I'm* the one they're going to be looking at tomorrow, not you guys." The eyes of half the damned free *world*, probably. Most of the news networks might even—what she needed, although it was going to hurt his feelings, was to talk to her mother for a minute. Alone. "Um, Dad?" She didn't quite look at him. "Would you mind getting me a Coke?"

He barely hesitated. "Sure," he said, and got up.

When he was gone, she looked at her mother. "What's *really* going to happen?"

"Precisely what we just told you," her mother said. "You honestly don't have to—"

"Is it going to be *safe*?" Meg asked.

Her mother nodded. "The security is extremely—"

"I don't mean just tomorrow," Meg said.

Her mother nodded, not answering right away, her hands tight in her lap.

"Should I take that as a no?" Meg asked stiffly.

Her mother shook her head. "No, I just think we should take it one step at a time."

"Explore our options?" Meg asked, even more stiff.

Her mother gestured towards the door. "Explore *their* limitations." They, meaning the Secret Service. "But, it's not something you should be worrying about tonight. We'll talk about it later. As a family."

"Oh, yeah," Meg said. "Neal's going to enjoy *that* conversation a lot."

Her mother sighed. "Please don't worry about it, Meg. I *promise* that we'll be able to arrange something that we're all comfortable with. I promise."

Yeah, that sounded *real* promising. Meg moved her jaw, the room so quiet that she could hear a phone ringing somewhere far down the hall. "You should have told me about the teeth," she said.

Her mother hunched down, looking visibly smaller. "I'm sorry," she said, her voice so low that Meg almost couldn't hear her.

Meg touched the side of her face, remembering the terror of unknown metal objects being forced into her mouth. "It was—a surprise."

Her mother kept hunching, not looking at her. "I'm sorry, Meg. I *never*—that is, your father and I—"

"Yeah, no precedent," Meg said, still holding her jaw. Of course, what it *really* came down to was "can not, have not, and *will* not negotiate"— "You kind of sold me out," she said, her voice even lower than her mother's had been.

Her mother nodded, looking less like the President than Meg had ever seen her. "I know."

Meg nodded, too. "Yeah."

The silence was more awkward than any of the others, her mother rubbing her hand across her eyes.

"I wouldn't accuse you of wanting to do it," Meg said. "And— well, I'm here, right?"

Her mother folded her arms tightly around herself. "I expect you to hate me for it."

Which was more than a little annoying. "I'm a better person than that, don't you think?" Meg said.

For the first time, her mother looked at her. "Yes. Actually, I do."

Meg nodded. "That's not the part I'm mad at you for. It's the only thing you *could* have done, really. I mean, like, it's already too late at that point."

"Last fall," her mother said. "It would have been better if— things—had worked out differently last fall."

If she'd been *killed*? Meg scowled at her. "That's like saying you wish the three of us had never been *born*."

"I know, I'm sorry." Her mother looked at her, her eyes very bright. "I really *am* sorry. If I'd ever *dreamed* that—I never would have—"

"What about what happened to *you*?" Meg asked. "Would you still have run, if you'd known that was going to happen?"

Her mother considered that, then shook her head. "I don't know. Probably. But, *not* any of you. Not *ever*."

Jesus. So, her mother considered *herself* an acceptable loss? Then, Meg thought of something that had never really occurred to her before. "You didn't think you'd win, did you? I mean, you *really*—you thought you were like, paving the way."

Her mother took a long time answering. "I don't know," she said finally. "I've spent a lot of hours wondering."

Meg nodded. It probably wasn't a question that had an answer. Particularly not in retrospect. "I wish you hadn't run for Senate. *That's* where it started."

Her mother nodded, too. "I think you're probably right."

There was a quiet knock on the door.

"Um." Meg glanced at her mother, then raised her voice. "Just a minute, please." She didn't want to keep hurting her father's feelings, but she still had to—"How bad do I look? For the cameras?"

"You look beautiful," her mother said without hesitating.

Which wasn't very helpful. "I'm serious." Meg touched her hair self-consciously. The nurses had managed to keep it pretty clean lately, but—well, it wasn't exactly *bouncy*. "I don't want to look—beaten."

"You don't," her mother said. "You're just—very pale."

Meg lifted her hand towards her nose, but didn't touch it. "How bad is my nose? I mean, is it *different*? Is it terrible?"

Her mother started to stand up. "Let me get you a mirror. You'll feel much—"

Meg shook her head. *That*, was something she was going to do in private. And not any time soon.

"Mainly, you look exhausted," her mother said.

Which she was. Too exhausted to continue. Her mother was already tucking her blankets in and, increasingly sleepy, Meg didn't protest.

"I don't want them all to pity me," she said, as her mother turned her pillow, the fresh side nice and cool.

"Hero-worship is going to be more like it," her mother said.

Oh, yeah. *Definitely*.

"You'd be amazed by how many people care about you," her mother said. "How many people *admire* you."

"Not hardly. I mean—" She shook her head, trying to stay awake.

Her mother spread the extra blanket over her. "I think you should get some sleep."

No argument there. Meg nodded. "Can you have Dad come in and say good-night to me?"

"I'll go get him." Her mother leaned down to kiss her cheek, not straightening up right away. "I love you, Meg."

Meg held herself stiffly, then couldn't *not* return the hug, her good arm tight around her mother's shoulder and neck. "I love you, too," she whispered.

When her mother finally let go, Meg had just enough time to wipe the unexpected tears off her face before her father came in, looking a little tentative.

"Are you comfortable?" he asked, picking up her hand. "Everything okay?"

She nodded, the extra blankets feeling nice and warm.

"This'll be right here, if you get thirsty." He put a glass on her bedside table, and she remembered, faintly, having asked him for a Coke. Then, he sat in the chair next to the bed. "You okay for to-morrow?"

She nodded, more and more sleepy.

"Is it all right if I stay in here for a while?" he asked. "Keep an eye on you?"

She smiled, seeing that her mother was already in the chair by the window. "Yeah. That'd be nice."

# 24

LEAVING THE HOSPITAL was pretty James Bond-ish. Wearing clothes—her own clothes—felt strange. Not having been able to shave her good leg and all, she *really* hadn't wanted to wear a skirt, and she didn't want to ruin any of her jeans by cutting them to make the brace fit better, so she ended up in blue sweatpants, a tennis shirt she'd always loved—and one sneaker. Since she couldn't take the surgical brace on and off by herself, Dr. Steiner had carefully strapped it on over her sweatpants, and she assumed he or Dr. Brooks or one of the WHMU nurses would help her take it on and off, when she got home.

After spending all that time in that one awful pair of sweatpants, she felt brave for wearing *this* pair. Falling off the horse and getting right back on, and all. Wearing a bra felt *really* strange. Comforting, and uncomfortable. And embarrassing, since she'd had to have her mother help her put it on.

It felt rude not to be able to say thank you to all of the hospital people, but once everything was ready to go, the Secret Service didn't waste any time, whisking them right onto a large, private elevator, the corridors crowded with agents and Marines and people from the White House advance team.

She sat very straight in the wheelchair, too scared to try and make conversation, her parents and Dr. Brooks hovering around. The elevator was taking them to a sub-basement or something, so that they could secretly meet the motorcade. Preston, who was lounging against the side, grinned at her and she tried to smile back.

"Are you, um, riding with us?" she asked.

He shrugged. "Whatever you all want me to do."

Meg looked up at her mother, who nodded.

The doors slid open, and they were in a parking garage, the motorcade ready and waiting for them. There were men—and a few women—with guns everywhere, and she suddenly thought about bombs. Terrorists, with bombs, throwing one in front of the car, and they would all be—her father and Dr. Brooks had lifted her gently inside, her mother and Preston right behind them. The door closed, and the car started moving almost before she was buckled into her seat, her leg propped up on a special cushion.

She could see light ahead—the outside—and held her breath, terrified. Her parents were on either side of her, her father holding her hand, her mother with her arm around her. They might have been talking to her—probably were, in fact—but her heart was thumping so loudly that she couldn't hear them. Couldn't hear *anything*.

They were outside now. Targets. Who *else* could be in a large motorcade speeding away from the National Naval Medical Center? Even though the windows were tinted, she could see *out*, and the sunlight made her dizzy. Afraid that she was going to cry—or maybe even scream, she dug her teeth into the inside of her cheek, feeling a couple of tears spill out, anyway. She turned her head towards her mother's shoulder, hoping that none of them had seen.

"Hey, kid," Preston said.

She looked up. Barely.

"Forgot to give you your gift." He put a small, brightly-wrapped package in her lap. Green and white checked paper, with a green bow. "Meant to give it to you inside."

Opening it with one hand was hard, but she shook her head when her father offered to help her, preferring the difficulty. She managed to rip one end open, then slide the paper down the rest of the way. Inside, was a glasses case. Sunglasses. Ray-Bans. Black.

"Better try them on," he said, "or I'll think you don't like them."

Cooperatively, she put them on, blinking to focus.

"Very nice," he said. "Very Hollywood."

She looked at her parents, to see if they agreed.

"Very cool," her father said.

"Greta Garbo," her mother said.

She looked back at Preston. "Um, thank you. Thank you very much." Ray-Bans were expensive, he shouldn't have—

He shrugged. "You don't look right to me without them."

She felt a little safer behind the glasses, safe enough to peer past her father and out the window for a second. Road. Trees. Buildings. The speed at which they were passing was scary, so she stared down at her leg, instead.

"Any pain?" Dr. Brooks asked.

Yes, and no. "It feels kind of dead." Numb. She wasn't supposed to, without therapists supervising her, but she tried moving her foot—which *did* hurt. A lot. But, her ribs were okay—as long as she didn't cough, moving her head didn't make her dizzy anymore, and her nose and mouth felt pretty normal. Odds were, they didn't *look* so great.

The main thing, still, was fatigue. In fact, it was a long enough ride—oh, gosh, forty whole minutes—so that a nap wasn't altogether out of the question. The dark glasses were making her sleepy, too.

"Are you tired?" her mother asked. "Do you want to rest?"

Yes. "No, I'm all right." She sat up, adjusting her sling, and looked around some more.

Her parents' faces were tired and nervous—and quite pale. Her mother was wearing a yellow linen dress—nice and crisp and perky, and her father had on his standard summer blue blazer and light khakis ensemble, with a blue-striped tie. Dr. Brooks had on the same sort of outfit, except that his coat was white, and rumpled.

She saved Preston for last—he had on a purple-and-white striped shirt with a skinny mauve tie, and beautifully creased cream-colored cotton pants. His shoes were Italian leather slip-ons; his belt was leather, too.

Preston smiled at her. "Well?"

"No jacket?" she asked.

"I left it at the house," he said.

"Well—all right," she said, making her voice sound disapproving. Her mother's arm felt very tense around her shoulders, and she felt very stupid for not remembering that it was *her* bad one. "Mom—" she leaned forward—"why don't you rest your arm a little."

"Excellent idea, Madam President," Dr. Brooks said, and her mother nodded, removing it with almost-disguised relief.

Nothing like a family of the Walking Wounded. Meg was going to crack a joke to that effect, but decided that it would just make things more tense.

"Trudy's mashing you a batch of potatoes," her father said.

Meg grinned, picturing the scene. Trudy was *nothing* if not a tyrant, when it came to people underfoot in the kitchen. "Is she creaming me some corn, too?"

"I expect she is," her mother said.

Meg had always been big on mashed potatoes with creamed corn. Odds were, Trudy had cooked up—she always made it from scratch—a batch of butterscotch pudding, too. And maybe some tacos. And she would make *all* of them drink milk. Sometimes even her parents.

When she saw the first landmark she recognized in downtown Washington, she began to get scared again, the two swallows of juice she'd had for breakfast jumping around her stomach. She could feel herself trembling and struggled not to, not wanting her parents to worry.

"L-looks pretty much the same," she said. Who the hell did she think she was—Ulysses? It hadn't been *that* long. She couldn't repress one especially hard shake, and her father's arm came around her.

"It's going to be fine," he said.

She nodded, but still couldn't stop the trembling. "I wish I could *walk* in, not look all—" She gestured to indicate the wheelchair, which was in one of the cars behind them.

"We're going to get you right into the elevator," her mother said. "Preston'll stay outside to give a statement."

Meg nodded, the streets more and more familiar. More and more threatening. She could see tourists—and even Washingtonians—stopping to stare as the motorcade sped by. At least they weren't going to be driving anywhere near the school. She had no intention of *ever* going near *there* again.

Then, they were approaching the Southwest Gate. She could see people—Jesus, *a lot* of people—gathered out in the street to watch, many of them holding cameras—and *flowers*. Lots and lots of flowers. And, yeah, stuffed animals. There were police officers and uniformed Secret Service agents all over the place—but, it was still scary.

There were cameras and reporters stationed behind a rope-line, near the South Entrance, and she pressed her left hand into a nervous fist. A large sign, red and blue on white, was hanging from the Truman Balcony, reading: "Welcome Home, Meghan, and God Bless You."

She nudged her father. "Is that on account of us being so religious and all?" she asked, amused in spite of herself.

He actually grinned. "No doubt."

When the car doors opened, her wheelchair was already set up, and she was helped into it, aware of voices and lights. Possibly—probably *not*—some applause; she was too nervous to look up all the way. There were faces everywhere, mostly male, mostly unfamiliar. Or, maybe some of them *were* familiar, and she was just having trouble focusing.

Her mother was on the left side of her wheelchair, while her father pushed it, and she fought the urge to grab on to them.

"—you feeling?" one of the louder voices yelled.

"Um, fine." Her voice was weak, and she tried to make it stronger. "Fine, thank you."

"—feel about—"

"—home?"

"—courage in—"

"—your leg?"

Not that she had heard the whole question, but she decided to answer that one, anyway, turning in her chair to face the direction from which it had come. The television lights and camera flashes were blindingly bright, and she was very glad to have the sunglasses on.

"I'm a little worried," she said, startled by the way the crowd instantly quieted down. She gestured towards her brace. "This could add thirty, maybe forty, seconds to my mile."

More than a few people laughed.

"Mr. Fielding will be happy to answer questions for you," her mother said, indicating Preston, and suddenly, they were inside, on their way to the Ground Floor Corridor, and then, the First Family elevator.

Meg took off her sunglasses and let out her breath, hearing her parents do the same thing.

"I-I guess word traveled fast," she said.

Her mother hugged her. "You handled them *perfectly*."

Meg closed her eyes. "I can't wait to sleep."

The elevator doors opened and she saw Trudy and her brothers, and quite a few members of the Residence staff, including the Chief Usher, waiting in the Center Hall.

"Hi," she said to her brothers.

"Hi," Neal said.

"Yeah," Steven said.

"Well, aren't you three silly." Trudy came over to give her a hug. "Come on, boys, show your sister how happy you are to see her."

Meg heard claws on polished wood and happy panting, turning to see Kirby, his tail wagging wildly as he tried to climb into the wheelchair.

"Down, Kirby." Her father grabbed his collar. "*Down*."

"I want to see him, Dad." She patted him, Kirby whining with excitement. "Where's Vanessa?"

"She ran away," Neal said.

Meg stared at him. "She *what*?"

"He means she ran down the *hall*," Steven said, and punched him—hard—in the arm. "Stupid."

If she hadn't seen how upset Neal looked, she probably would have punched him, too. "Where'd she go—upstairs?" Vanessa loved the light in the solarium.

"It's 'cause I was hitting her," Steven said. "I was just hitting her, and hitting her, and she—"

"*Steven*," their father said, in the same voice he had used with Kirby.

"I know he's kidding, Dad," Meg said. Somehow, no one ever thought she and Steven were as funny as they did themselves. "Can you like, go find her, Steven?"

Dr. Brooks was pushing her wheelchair down towards her room, and the Chief Usher approached, looking solemn.

"Welcome home, Miss Powers," he said, in his very deep voice. "It's so good to see you."

She was too embarrassed about the way she looked to meet his eyes, but smiled at him—and the rest of the staff, in general. "Um, thank you. I mean, me, too."

For a second, as her father opened her bedroom door, she was afraid. Afraid that it would be different. That it would seem—not that it hadn't *always* been stiff and formal. But, except for the vases of flowers everywhere, it looked pretty much the same. Same four-poster bed, same fireplace, same desk, same bureau, same bookcases. Same rug, same rocking chair, same computer, same tall window. The only scary thing was how *neat* it was. Sterile. Not a room anyone *lived* in. She gripped the arm of her wheelchair, almost sure that she was going to cry.

"Meg," her mother was saying, "would you like—"

"I'd like to be alone," she said, knowing that her voice was too loud. "For—" As long as possible. "A while, please."

"Would you like some help—" Dr. Brooks started.

"No! I mean, no problem," she said, more calmly.

Someone—her father?—touched her shoulder, but she didn't look up until she heard the door close and was sure she was alone.

Alone. In her room. A place she'd never expected she would be again. The last time she'd been in here—getting ready for school that day. In, as she recalled, a hell of a good mood.

Christ, she was sick of crying. That, and sleep, were all she did anymore. She was closest to her bureau, and without bothering to wipe her eyes, she aimed the chair over there, even though she wasn't exactly great at steering the damn thing.

She opened one of the drawers, the socks and underwear folded so neatly that it looked almost military. Jesus, had they been going through her clothes or something? *Bugging* everything? She reached her hand in, messing the rows up. Then, she opened the next drawer—razor-creased t-shirts and polo shirts—and yanked a few out, throwing them in the direction of her bed and desk. That made things a *little* better, at least.

It was kind of hard to reach the top of the bureau from her chair, but she shifted the arrangement of perfume bottles—she *was* mighty fond of perfume—and hairbrushes, too. She pulled the nearest bottle down—Chanel—and sprayed some on. Maybe now, she wouldn't smell quite so much like a veterinarian's office.

As she was putting the bottle back, she remembered that there was a mirror up there. A mirror. She thought about it, then pulled herself up onto her right foot to look.

It was a mistake. The stitches had only been out for about a week, and there was a red shiny scar going right through her eyebrow and up her forehead. Her eyes were even more red—probably from crying all the time—and her nose was—Jesus. Her nose was actually *crooked*. Hooked, almost. It was *more* than obvious that a fist had been there.

And her face actually looked *gaunt*. Like she'd been in a prison camp or something. A prison camp without any sunshine. And her *hair*—Jesus.

All of which was so upsetting that she sat down. Quickly. She was going to cry some more, but—it could have been worse. Much worse. As long as she remembered that, maybe she could—what she needed, was Vanessa. But, it was too soon not to have privacy. There had to be something else she could—music. To her surprise, she felt herself smile. Yeah, music.

She pushed the little control button on her wheelchair, motored over to her desk, and turned on her computer. Of course, this being the White House, there wasn't a speck of dust *anywhere*. Had they even dusted in here when she was missing, or just while she was at the hospital? Not that it mattered, really.

She waited until all of the software loaded, and then clicked on her music folder. It would be too weird to put on the same playlist she'd been listening to the day—everything happened—but then again, "I Love Rock and Roll" *was* her favorite song in life, so she had it at the beginning of every single one of her playlists.

So, she picked one at random, made sure the volume was set at its highest level, and then clicked on the song.

Hearing it burst out of the speakers made her grin. An honest-to-God happy grin.

Being home suddenly felt a hell of a lot better.

# 25

AFTER LISTENING TO about ten of her favorite songs, she was in a pretty good mood. Songs like "Teenage Lobotomy" by the Ramones, "Hello, I Love You," by the Doors, and—of course—"Jumpin' Jack Flash." "We Are the Champions" was playing when she finally opened her door and wheeled herself into the small corridor, seeing her parents and Trudy out in the Center Hall, sitting on the Sheraton settee and chair set. They were all drinking coffee and when they saw her, her parents got up.

"I was just—" She grinned as a small grey-and-white head peeked out from over Trudy's lap. "Hey, there."

Vanessa's head stretched out further, her ears pricked forward.

"Yeah, it's me." Meg snapped her fingers. "Come on."

Vanessa scampered over, stopped just out of reach, and began to wash. Very delicately.

"*Vanessa*," Meg said. Her cat had never liked to be hurried.

"Wait." Her father came over to pick her up. "I'll—"

Meg shook her head. "I don't want to force her." She frowned at her cat, who was now rubbing up against an American Federal end table, still just out of reach.

"The minute we get you into bed, she'll show up," her mother said.

Meg nodded, grumpy now. "I just wish she—"

Kirby came barking down the hall and Vanessa skittered towards the East Sitting Hall and out of sight. Kirby ignored her, greeting Meg all over again, his front paws up on her lap, her mother guiding him away from her surgical brace.

Meg patted him. "At least *someone's* glad to see me," she said.

"Animals, I mean," she added, before everyone got their feelings hurt. But, Kirby's enthusiasm made her tired, and she was kind of glad when her father hauled him away.

As they all went into her room, her mother bent reflexively to pick up one of the t-shirts from the floor, hesitated, and left it there.

"I, uh—" Meg sighed. Vanessa's not being happy to see her was depressing. "I'd like to go in and get cleaned up."

Her mother handed her an impeccably folded Lanz nightgown, then pushed the wheelchair into the bathroom.

"Do you need help?" she asked, turning on the light. *Bright* light.

Meg shook her head, carefully not looking at the mirror over the sink. Once had been more than enough.

"Well." Her mother took a step backwards. "Well, then, I'll—" She moved forward, giving her a hug that was almost fierce. "It's *very* good to have you here."

Meg shook her head, not hugging back. "It doesn't feel right."

"It will," her mother said. "You just have to get used to things again."

Maybe.

Her mother hung on to her for what seemed like a long time, then straightened up. "Well," she said, her eyes wet.

Meg coughed. "I'm just going to get cleaned up now."

"Right." Her mother stepped away. "If you need—"

"Yeah," Meg said.

After her mother was gone, she realized that she *did* need help—but, Christ, she didn't want to spend the rest of her life having people take her clothes on and off. She would just put the nightgown on over her sweatpants, and not worry about trying to take off the god-damn surgical brace.

When she finally opened the door, her whole family, Trudy, and Dr. Brooks were all standing around the room.

"Uh, hi," she said.

Her father pushed the wheelchair over to the bed, then lifted her into it.

"How about your sweatpants?" her mother asked.

"I'm a little chilly," Meg said.

Her mother nodded, pulling up the sheet and blankets.

"Are you hungry, Meg?" Trudy asked.

She smiled shyly. "I heard a little rumor about mashed potatoes."

Trudy smiled back, and bustled out of the room.

"Stupid's here," Steven said, jerking his head towards the window.

Meg looked away from Dr. Brooks and the blood pressure cuff he'd already managed to get around her arm to see Vanessa sitting on the low windowsill. Washing. Just as she was about to give in and ask someone to bring her over, Vanessa jumped down and onto the bed, walking right up her bad leg.

Dr. Brooks frowned. "Oh, my."

"Yeah." Meg grinned, pulling her already-purring cat over for a very close cuddle. "She's kind of a jerk." She gave her a kiss, then patted her some more, Vanessa trying to climb into her sling, her head and front paws disappearing from view. Meg glanced up at Dr. Brooks, who she knew was not particularly fond of cats. "Pretty cute, hunh?"

"Mmmm," he said, and checked her pulse.

By the time he had finished examining her, Trudy was already coming in with a tray, and she arranged it across Meg's lap, moving Vanessa aside. It was nice to see familiar—if overly ornate—china, and the arrangement on the tray was just about a work of art: a crystal vase with a small yellow rose, matching crystal salt and pepper shakers, a flat bowl mounded with mashed potatoes and creamed corn, a matching bowl of salad—Boston lettuce, tomato roses, and carrot curls—with, no doubt, Trudy's special honey vinaigrette, a dish of butterscotch pudding with whipped cream, and a glass of milk.

"Does she make tomato roses faster than anyone you know, or *what?*" Meg said to no one in particular.

"She made them before," Neal said, helpfully.

"*Oh,*" Meg said, as though that explained everything, and then picked up her fork.

"Would you like anything else, dear?" Trudy asked.

"No, thank you—this is great." It was embarrassing to have them all watching her, but everything looked so good that Meg started eating, anyway. "You all don't like, have to *stand* there or anything," she said, tasting the salad. Yup, honey vinaigrette. "I mean, I'm home now, right? You might as well pretend like I'm normal."

"*Pretend,*" Steven said quietly.

At least *he* was acting regular. "Do you want to watch the game with me later?" she asked.

He looked at their father guiltily. "Um, game?"

So much for acting normal. Meg drank some milk. "Yeah. You know, the thing we watch about 162 times every year."

He looked at their father again, then shrugged. "No big deal if I don't see it."

Oh, for Christ's sakes. "Okay, but *I'm* going to watch," Meg said. "I just thought you might want to watch it *with* me."

"Me, too?" Neal asked.

"Sure." Meg tried the mashed potatoes, which were delicious, then looked at her father. "Are you going to watch with us?"

"I'd love to," he said.

"Uh, you guys can, too," she said to her mother and Trudy. "I just—don't feel like you *have* to."

"Wouldn't miss it for the world," her mother said.

ALONG ABOUT THE seventh inning, with the Red Sox down 8–2, Meg figured they were all maybe sort of regretting tuning in. The atmosphere in the room probably would have been more than a little cranky, but Preston had shown up during the fourth, and kept saying jolly things. Even when the Red Sox rallied for five runs, then had the bases loaded in the bottom of the ninth, before someone popped up for the third out.

There was a long, and rather deadly, silence in the room.

"Never a dull moment," Preston said, and Meg's father and Steven scowled at him. Anyone *else*, they would have smacked.

"They never give up," her mother said. "They're to be admired for that."

Her father and Steven didn't say anything.

Since he wasn't about to yell at *her*, Meg looked at her father. "Maybe it's because you weren't in your lucky chair."

He shrugged. Pleasantly. "It's only a game."

Next to him, Steven pretended to commit hara-kiri, then fell to the floor. Meg—at least—was amused. Maybe things were different now, but "it's only a game" was something people in her family occasionally *said,* but never meant. Not deep down inside. Particularly, of course, when the Red Sox were involved.

"Well, this has been very nice," her mother said, "but I'm afraid I'm going to have to—" The phone next to Meg's bed rang and she answered it, then looked at Meg. "They have Beth on the line for you."

Meg thought about that, then nodded. If she got tired and had to hang up, Beth would understand. As she took the phone, she saw everyone in the room tactfully leaving. Who would ever have thought that having people be constantly, completely considerate would be sort of tiresome?

"Hello?" she said into the phone.

"Thirty seconds to your mile?" Beth said.

Meg felt herself blushing. "What was I supposed to say?"

"It was pretty funny," Beth said. "You in your sunglasses and all."

"Preston gave them to me," Meg said defensively.

Beth laughed. "The man has taste."

"Yeah." Still embarrassed, Meg shifted her position. Vanessa, who had been *very* comfortably asleep on her lap, flounced away to the bottom of the bed and curled up again. "Was it a special report, or just like, on the news?"

"What an ego," Beth said.

Yeah, yeah, yeah.

Beth sighed a very deep sigh. "They interrupted regularly scheduled programming."

"Pretty weird," Meg said.

Neither of them spoke for a minute.

"So. How are you doing?" Beth asked. "Is it okay being home?"

"Yeah, I guess," Meg said. "We just watched the game."

"Did they win?" Beth asked.

Meg shook her head. "No."

"Was Steven mad?" Beth asked.

"Yeah," Meg said. "Not as much as my father, but—yeah."

"Was Vanessa glad to see you?" Beth asked.

Meg looked down at the bottom of the bed, where Vanessa was already deep in sleep. "Not really."

"Well—she's like that," Beth said.

Yeah.

There was another long silence.

"Well," Beth said. "I just, you know, wanted to see how you were doing."

Meg nodded. "Yeah. I mean, thanks."

"People up here said to say hello to you," Beth said. "I mean, the next time I talked to you."

Not that it really mattered, but it was thoughtful, at least. Meg looked at the glass of water on the bedside table. It would have been nice to drink some, but she couldn't do that and hold on to the phone at the same time. Since she no longer had two hands. "Um, my father says I got cards and stuff from a lot of them," she said.

"The Greater Boston area?" Beth asked.

"Yeah, kind of." She was definitely thirsty—but, okay, it could wait. For another minute, maybe. According to her father, she'd received a card or letter or something from almost every teacher she'd ever had—even the ones who hadn't liked her, and from people who had gone to school with her, and practically every neighbor they'd ever met—as well as something from almost everyone her *parents* had known in Boston. Hell, in the *world*.

Plus, thousands and thousands—and *thousands*—of strangers. Weird.

"Have you seen Josh or anyone?" Beth asked.

Meg sighed. "No."

"Oh," Beth said, sounding a little embarrassed. "Sorry, I— maybe it'll be easier, now that you're home."

Maybe. Meg frowned at the glass of water, noticing that the ice was starting to melt. "Um, look, I'm getting sort of tired, and—"

"Yeah, I just called to see how you were," Beth said, and paused. "You, uh, you looked good on television, Meg. Really confident."

Now, Meg frowned at the phone, instead. "You don't have to humor me."

"Oh, yeah," Beth said. "I *constantly* humor people."

Which was valid—Beth was, as a rule, quite blunt. "Did you see where my nose used to be?" Meg asked.

"I thought it looked pretty much the same," Beth said.

It was quiet again—for what seemed like about an hour.

"Well," Beth said. "I guess you're pretty tired and all."

Christ, *that* was for sure.

After hanging up, the phone seemed too heavy to lift over to the bedside table, so Meg let it stay on top of the quilt, adjusting her pillows so she could lie down. It was *definitely* naptime.

THEY HAD TACOS for dinner. Which were hard to eat one-handed. But, everyone was relaxed enough now, so that Steven and Neal

236

laughed when two of her tacos in a row broke in half and fell all over her plate. Laughed *at* her. Meg thought it was funny, but her parents frowned at her brothers.

"Would you like to watch television," her father said after dinner, when her mother had long since gone down to the West Wing to work some more, "or—"

Meg shook her head. "I think I just want to read a book."

"Anything special?" he asked.

Meg shrugged. "Just not a mystery." Blood and guts and guns weren't anything she wanted to deal with. Ever again.

He went off to gather up a stack of novels—some of which she had been given in the hospital, but been too tired to bother opening—and carried them in. At the hospital, even *People* had seemed like strenuous literature.

"Do you want anything else?" her father asked.

"No, thank you." She looked at Trudy, who had been hovering. "Um, dinner was delicious."

Everyone pretty much cleared out, and she examined the books, selecting *Digging to America* by Anne Tyler.

Her father kept coming in to check on her—or maybe just *look* at her, it seemed like, and every so often, Trudy would bring her something to eat or drink. Cookies, hot chocolate, orange juice, homemade applesauce with extra cinnamon. But mostly, it was very quiet and peaceful, and she just read her book. Kind of strange to have reading seem like such a special treat. A couple of times, she dozed a little, and that was peaceful, too.

It was past ten, and there was a knock on the door. Trudy with more treats, probably.

Meg lowered her book. "Come in."

The door opened and she saw Neal, wearing sweatpants and a New England Patriots t-shirt that was way too big for him.

"Hi," she said.

He nodded, hanging back.

"What's going on?" she asked.

He stayed by the door. "Do you want anything? Dad said to ask."

"No, thanks," she said, then sighed. "Come on, don't stand there on the threshold—you know I hate that."

Quickly, he stepped inside. "I'm sorry."

"What's going on?" she asked, again.

He shifted from one foot to the other, not looking at her, one hand behind his back. "Don't be mad."

What, because he stood in the hall for a few seconds, instead of coming in? "What do you mean?" she asked.

"I took something," he said.

Judging from his expression, it must have been half of Fort Knox. "Okay," she said, cautiously.

"Something of *yours*," he said.

She shrugged. "Okay, no problem."

He hesitated, then brought his hand out, dropping a rock on the bed. More than a little confused, Meg picked it up. It was the rock she used as a paperweight on her desk, mostly quartz, with bits of mica or something, too. She'd never really retained Mo's Table of rock categories or anything like that.

"You took my rock?" she said, not sure why he was so worried.

He nodded. "I'm sorry."

She was about to say, "It's just a *rock*," but considering how upset he seemed to be, that would have been tactless. "Um, like I said, no big deal." She held the rock up to the light, studying it. She'd found it about five summers before when they'd rented a house on a lake in New Hampshire for a couple of weeks. One of those quiet lakes, where motorboats were forbidden and all. "Remember when I found it?"

He nodded.

The house had had a rickety little dock, and—not that they were the world's greatest swimmers or anything—they would dive off it and see if they could find things on the lake bottom. This rock had looked particularly pretty, and she and Steven had spent almost an entire afternoon trying to dive down far enough to get it.

"Funny how they always looked prettier when they were in the water," she said.

Neal nodded.

"If you like it so much, why didn't you just *ask* me for it?" she asked.

"You weren't here," he said, not looking at her.

Oh. She shook her head. "I don't mean *recently*. If you liked it, why didn't you ask me like, *years* ago?"

"It's yours," he said.

"Yeah, but—" Somehow, she could sense that this was going to be a losing conversation. "Can I give it to you?"

He shook his head.

"Take it," she said. "It'll make me happy."

After a moment, he picked it up, holding it almost reverently. "Remember how me and Steven couldn't hardly dive at all?"

"Well, you were just a little guy." Meg grinned. "And Steven was a klutz." One of the days they were there, Steven had even managed to hit his head on the dock, and her parents had had to rush him to the emergency room with a mild concussion.

"I knew *you* could get it," Neal said. "I *knew* you would."

Yeah, it had only taken her about six hours. She smiled at him. "You were that sure, hunh?"

He nodded.

Funny to think of him wanting it all those years, and never saying a word.

"Remember how you always used to bring me stuff?" he asked.

She could *sort of* remember, but not really. "Yeah," she said.

"Like," he said, "when I was too little to go, and you'd bring me movie candy?"

*That*, actually, she remembered. He'd always been wild about Junior Mints. She, personally, despised them, but had always had a couple to be polite.

"And that funny pioneer soap?" he said. "From the field trip?"

She remembered that, too. Sturbridge Village. "What about the three-colored pen? That I got downtown?" In Boston, one of the first times she and Beth had been allowed to take the T into the city by themselves. "I could never figure out why you liked that pen so much." He seemed awfully quiet, and she looked up, startled to see him crying. "Neal? You okay?" She motioned for him to sit on the bed. "Come on, sit up here."

"I'm not supposed to," he said, crying.

Jesus. Exactly how many rules were her parents *giving* her brothers? "Just come on," she said.

He got up next to her, and she put her arm around him.

"I didn't mean to hit you," he said.

What? She blinked. "When?"

"Ever," he said. "I didn't know how bad it was."

"It's not like you ever *hurt* me. I mean—" She shook her head. "When *we* fight, it's different."

"Steven isn't going to hit people anymore, either," he said.

Oh, yeah, *that'd* be the day. "Well, that's good." She tightened her arm around him. "Please don't cry, okay? I mean—I'm home, right?"

He looked up at her. Actually, he was getting tall—his head barely had to tilt up anymore. "I was crying a lot when you were gone."

She smiled a little. "So was I."

"I saw Steven," Neal said, "but he got mad."

Meg refrained from asking if Steven had hit him. "Well, it was a hard time for everyone." Be nice if that were past tense.

"I was really scared," he said.

She nodded. "You and me both, cowboy." She let out her breath. "You and me both."

# 26

THE NEXT DAY, Josh called and, feeling guilty, she said that yeah, sure, he could come over for a while, no problem. She regretted it almost before the words were out of her mouth, but by then, it was too late.

So, she got dressed, allowing Trudy to cut the left leg off one of her pairs of jeans, and having Steven "borrow" for her an old Radcliffe sweatshirt of her mother's that she'd always coveted.

When Josh arrived, she and her father and her brothers were up in the solarium, watching the end of the Red Sox game. In *this* one, they had been ahead 6–0, gotten behind 10–6, and finally won 11–10—just as Josh came in, carrying a box of chocolates.

"Yo, *candy*," Steven said cheerfully. "*Ex*cellent." As long as the Red Sox won, *how* they did it never seemed to matter to him. No matter how tortuous it was.

"Uh, yeah," Josh said, giving the box to her, then putting his hands in his pockets. He coughed. "Did they win?"

"Of course," Steven said. "They're too *excellent* not to always win."

Talk about selective memory. "Thank you," Meg said to Josh. "They look delicious."

"You don't know that," Steven said. "You haven't opened them yet."

Their father smiled. "Come on, guys, let's go out and throw the ball around."

"Yeah!" Neal said, jumping up.

Her father touched her shoulder. "Anything you need, kiddo?"

Meg shook her head.

"Well, if you do, I'll be right outside." He put his hand out to shake Josh's. "Good to see you, Josh. Come on, boys."

Steven sat down on the couch, linking his arm through Meg's. "I must stay with my sister," he said solemnly. "My sister *needs* me."

Their father sighed. "Steven."

"I *must*," he said.

Meg looked over at him, amused. "Go away."

"But, Sister dear," he said.

She grinned at him. "*Go away.*"

He laughed and went after Neal and their father.

"He seems pretty chipper," Josh said.

And *then* some. Meg nodded.

"So, uh—" He cleared his throat. "So."

"Sit down," she said.

"Right. Yeah. Sorry." He sat in the chair next to the couch.

It had been a pretty long time since they'd seen each other, and it *felt* even longer. Meg made herself smile at him—what she hoped was a relaxed smile. "So."

"You, you look good," he said.

Time for him to get that glasses prescription changed, maybe. She reached for the box of candy. "Thank you for these. Should we open them?"

He shrugged. "Sure."

Instead of struggling one-handed, she gave the box to him. "Beth says hi."

He unwrapped the plastic. "When's she coming down here?"

"I don't know. No time soon." She turned off the television, which made the room seem so quiet that she turned it back on.

"You want to watch something?" he asked.

"Not really." She clicked it off again. "I mean, unless you do."

He shook his head, and held out the open box of chocolates.

She took one. "Thank you." Vanilla cream. "How are Nathan and everyone?"

"Okay," he said, selecting a piece for himself. "I mean, you know, fine."

"Um, tell them I said hi," she said.

He nodded.

"Thanks." A sudden wave of fatigue hit her, and she closed her eyes, trying to will the feeling away.

"Would you like to rest?" he asked.

Yes. "It's not that," she said. "It's just—I'm sorry."

He shrugged. "You don't have anything to be sorry about."

As far as she could see, she didn't have too many things *not* to be sorry about. But, it was probably time to change the subject. "So, um, graduation was good," she said. "You went, I mean."

He nodded.

"Well—that's good," she said. "Are you working at the golf course?" Which was his regular summer job.

"Some, yeah," he said.

"Getting any good tips?" she asked.

"Stay out of coffee futures," he said.

Okay, that was funny. She smiled, and he smiled back.

"You making any *money* over there?" she asked.

He shrugged. "Some, yeah. Not enough."

Money for school. It wouldn't be much longer before he would be leaving. Before *everyone* her age would be going away to school. Or doing whatever adult thing they were going to do. "Well, that's good," she said aloud. "You'll be able to use it, when you're away."

He looked uncomfortable. "I don't know, yeah."

Unable to think of anything else to say, she reached for the box of chocolates and, left arm across her body, offered it to him. He shook his head and, not hungry herself, she put the box back on the coffee table.

"How's your leg?" he asked. "And your hand?"

"I don't know." She looked down at the brace and splint. "Pretty much the same."

"Oh," he said. "I mean, I was hoping they were better."

"A little, maybe," she said. Jesus, as conversations went, this had to be one of their worst of all time. "You're getting a pretty good tan."

He glanced at his arms, very brown against his white t-shirt. "Yeah, kind of." He looked towards the door leading to the Promenade. "It's still pretty sunny. You want to go outside for a while?"

*No.* She shook her head. "I'm kind of tired."

"Just for a minute," he said. "I could—"

Jesus! "I *don't want to*," she said. "Okay?"

He nodded. "I'm sorry. I didn't mean to—"

"You didn't," she said. "I just—" Christ, this was too much work. "You want to watch something on television?" Television was easy; television was safe.

"Sure," he said, and reached for the remote control, not quite looking at her. "Whatever you want."

HE DIDN'T STAY for dinner. She knew she was supposed to ask him, but all she really wanted to do was be taken back to her room, close the door, and spend the rest of the night alone. Trudy, as always, prepared her a wonderful tray, but she felt too numb to do much more than rearrange the food with her fork. After assuring her family that she was fine, that she just needed to rest, and could they please make sure no calls were put through to her room, they left her alone. It was too scary to sleep in the dark, so she had her father turn on the bathroom light on his way out.

She slept, waking up on and off—when they came in to make sure she was okay, when Vanessa got restless, when the blankets felt too hot. Even when she was awake, she didn't bother turning on the light, too tired to do more than watch the red numbers on her clock change. At one point, when her mother was in to check on her, they managed to scare the hell out of each other—her mother not expecting her to be awake, Meg not expecting to see her standing by the bed.

Her mother recovered first. "I'm sorry, I didn't mean to startle you."

"You didn't," Meg said, trying to sit up. She looked at the clock, which read 2:53. "Pretty late."

"Well, I just wanted to be sure you were sleeping all right," her mother said.

Like a contented, angst-and-despair-free baby.

"It was hard having Josh here today?" her mother both said and asked.

*There* was an understatement. Meg nodded.

Her mother frowned. "Well, what if we had Beth get on a plane, and—"

"I really don't want to see anyone," Meg said. "I'm just—I'm not ready."

Her mother nodded.

"I'm kind of tired." Meg tried to turn her pillow, her mother moving closer to do it for her.

"Do you need anything?" she asked.

Meg shook her head, lying down.

"Well—I'll see you in the morning," her mother said. "Sleep well."

Meg nodded. "You, too."

THE WORK-OUT ROOM on the third floor had been set up with some "injury-specific" equipment, and she had to resume serious physical therapy the next day—which was awful. Exhausting. The primary therapist was a nice woman named Edith, whom she remembered from the hospital, but Meg didn't talk to her—or the WHMU nurse who had come upstairs to supervise—any more than she absolutely had to, to be polite. She just concentrated on

245

finishing the terrible exercises and the electro-stimulus stuff—
which was supposed to promote healing, so she could get back to
bed. The tub in her bathroom had been modified, with an arm and
a leg rest, as well as a small plastic shower bench, but she still needed
help—which was embarrassing, even though it was only Trudy,
usually with a nurse sitting outside the door, just in case.

"Well, dear," Trudy said, tucking her into bed, after she got
washed up. "Would you like anything?"

Meg shook her head.

"Would you like me to keep you company?" Trudy asked.

Meg shook her head harder. "No, thank you. I just want to
rest."

Trudy looked worried, but nodded, giving the blankets one last
tuck before leaving the room.

So, mostly, she slept. Dr. Brooks came by to check on her, her
family was in and out, and in the middle of the afternoon, she
woke up long enough to eat half a grilled cheese sandwich and a
cup of mushroom soup. Other than that, she slept.

She managed another small meal—chicken, part of a baked potato, some salad—for dinner, then let Steven watch, while she half-
watched, the baseball game. Other than that, she went back to
sleep.

The scary part, was how fast the happy novelty of being home
was evaporating. Replaced by, for the most part, paralyzing fear.
She wasn't even sure what she was afraid *of*—some combination of
the past, present, and future—or *lack* of a future—but, she knew
that she was afraid. She didn't want her family to know how bad it
was, so she was careful to seem calm and cheerful in front of them.
On the mend.

She stayed with her pattern of almost-constant sleep, because it
was the only way she could function. It wasn't even so much that
she was *tired*, but sleeping meant that she didn't have to be scared.
Didn't have to pretend that everything was fine, no problem, not to

worry—and other such platitudes. Obviously, her family wasn't stupid enough to believe that she had been magically cured, but no one pressured her, either.

She was lying in bed after a physical therapy session, looking at a glass of lemonade she was too tired to drink, when Preston came in. He had popped in and out a lot lately, too.

"Hey," he said cheerfully, putting a new hardcover on her bedside table. "How you doing?"

"Fine, thank you," she said.

"Yeah." He sat down, his look penetrating. "PT going okay?"

She nodded.

"Good," he said. "Word is, they're going to let you try some weight-bearing soon."

Whatever. She shrugged.

"That'll be good," he said. "You'll be able to get around better."

Maybe. Not that it mattered much, either way.

"Well." He indicated his outfit. "What do you think?"

"It's nice," she said, not really looking. Pants, a shirt, a tie. That sort of thing.

He sat back, folding his arms across his chest. "You know, could be just me, but it seems like you're maybe beginning to internalize a little."

"I'm just tired," she said.

"How about a change of scene?" he asked. "We'll go sit on the Truman Balcony."

The balcony any psycho with a good pair of binoculars—and a sniper's scope—could see onto? She shook her head.

"Think some fresh air'd do you some good," he said.

"No, thank you," she said, politely.

"It's nice and sunny out," he said.

She nodded, wishing he would drop it already.

"Hate to see you looking so pale," he said.

247

She glared at him. "Back off, okay, Preston?"

He nodded. "Sure. I just hate to see you going *down*hill, you know?"

"I'm just tired," she said.

"Okay." He tilted his chair back, looking up at her chandelier. "Given any thought to sitting down with Gary Crowell?"

The Army psychologist guy. "*No,*" she said.

He shrugged. "He knows his stuff, Meg. He's worked with a lot of the embassy people, after—"

"I don't like him," she said.

He nodded. "Okay. What about someone who's been through the same sort of thing? A hijacking, or—"

"I don't even want to talk to people I *know,*" she said, "forget people I *don't* know."

"Sometimes it's easier when you don't know the person," he said. "Nothing to hide that way."

Since she wasn't capable of responding politely to that, she didn't say anything at all.

"Okay." He sighed. "Just can't stand seeing you turn yourself into a little time-bomb."

Why he thought it *mattered* was beyond her. "I'm just tired. *Really* tired," she said, hoping that he would take the hint and leave.

"I know you are." He folded his hands behind his head, still looking up at the ceiling. "You know, at some point, you've got to let yourself start thinking about it."

"About what?" she asked.

"I don't know," he said. "The future, primarily."

*What* future did he think she had, exactly?

"Come on, Meg, talk to me," he said. "Give yourself a break."

She scowled at him. "I don't *have* a future. In case you didn't notice."

He turned his head enough to look at her. "Mention this to your parents yet?"

"No." She managed a weak smile. "I don't want them to worry."

He nodded. "Why spoil their tranquility."

"Oh, yeah, right," she said. "Tell them I'm not even glad to be back?" Which sounded terrible. "I mean, I'm glad, but—" But what? "It's sort of like I didn't come back *to* anything."

"How do you mean?" he asked.

Wasn't he listening? She frowned. "You don't understand?"

"I want to be *sure* I understand," he said.

Was he being intentionally dense, or was he tired, too? "I'm not going to have a life," she said. "Even if I was *allowed* to go anywhere, I can't—I mean, even if they *could* protect me, I wouldn't be able to—what are they going to do, come here and tutor me *college*?"

He shrugged. "It's not the best scenario, but—"

She stiffened, remembering the guy. "Don't say 'scenario.'" "*Worst* scenario," he'd said, "I start liking you," and—she shivered.

"Sorry," Preston said. "Can't help falling into press secretary talk sometimes."

She shrugged, unable to bring herself to look at him.

"Funny word to give you bad associations," he said, thoughtfully.

She felt herself shiver again. "I'm going to sleep now, okay?"

"Meg—" he said.

"I'm *going* to," she said, covering her eyes with her arm. "*Okay?*"

He sighed, standing up. "Okay."

# 27

SHE WAS CAREFUL to hide it, but over the next week, she could feel the pressure building. Even sleep wasn't working as a cure, because the nightmares were back, worse than ever. Most of them were about the guy—or even just his grin, like some deranged Cheshire Cat—but falling, seeing people she knew get killed, and being trapped in places were regular themes, too.

Her appetite was pretty much gone and every day, the therapy seemed harder and harder. She tried to keep a constant "don't worry, I'm fine" smile pasted on, but knew she wasn't really fooling people. And she still wasn't taking phone calls. From *anyone*.

Preston was around a lot, but she avoided being alone with him, because she knew he could—*would*—make her talk. Upset her. Whenever Dr. Brooks came in, he would look very serious and worried, but he didn't push her. Her family was being quiet and careful, too. Thank God.

It was very late—she wasn't sure what night it was—when she had the worst nightmare so far. She was chained to the iron bed frame, the room smaller and darker than she remembered, and he was coming at her—more crazed than he had been with the gun that time—apparently planning to kill her with his bare hands. He was breathing hard, like an animal, and when she saw his eyes, she screamed, because they *weren't* eyes, they were fire. Not *even* fire— more like red light. Burning red light. She screamed again, as he started laughing, his hands around her throat.

"Who did you *think* I was?" he asked.

"Y-you don't exist," she said, some awake, sane part of her

brain aware that this wasn't happening, that it couldn't be—"This isn't real."

"I *do* exist," he said, and as she watched his eyes, his face reddened and lengthened, turning into the honest-to-God devil, his laugh more and more high-pitched.

"You'll never get away from me," he said, wrapping the rope around her neck. "You'll be with me *forever*."

She tried to get free, but the rope was already too tight, cutting off her air.

He laughed some more, laughed wildly. "You know who I am? Do you? Do you know who I am? That's who I am!"

She screamed again, was still screaming when she realized that the room was much brighter. That she was in *her* room, and her parents were there, holding her.

"It's all right, Meg," her mother was saying. "Wake up, Meg, it's all right."

Maybe it wasn't her room, maybe it was a trick, maybe—

"*Wake up*, Meg," her mother said gently.

She looked at her parents, at her room, at Steven standing near the door, his eyes huge. Normal eyes. She looked at her parents, who also had normal eyes. Normal eyes. She tried to get her breath, her heart pounding so hard that the force seemed strong enough to knock her off the bed.

"I-I think I'm having a heart attack," she gasped.

"Shhh—" her mother was holding her close—"you're all right. It was just a dream."

Jesus, didn't her mother understand how much danger they were in? That they were going to get *killed*? "He's coming to get me!" Meg said. "He can get in *anywhere*!"

"You're safe," her father said. "I promise."

Meg shook her head. "You don't know him!"

"I *promise*," her father said.

She trusted her father. Her father never lied to her. She looked at him, wondering with a sudden terrified quiver if *his* eyes were going to change, if all of them were going to turn into— "Are you *sure*?" she asked.

"I'm sure," he said.

She let herself relax a little, the dream beginning to fade. "You're *sure*?"

He nodded, and she sank down into the pillow, pulling in slow, deep breaths. They were all looking at her with such concern that she managed a small laugh.

"You're not going to believe this," she said, "but I think I just had an evangelical dream."

"A what?" her mother asked, as her father said, "I don't understand." Steven didn't say *anything*.

Meg just shook her head, too spent to try and explain.

"Would you like—" her mother started.

"Yeah," Meg said, gesturing weakly towards the television. "Could you put on *The Sound of Music*?"

"Of course," her mother said. "Whatever you want."

"Good," Meg said, watching her father search through the pile of movies on her desk, as she tried to stop trembling. "Because I think I need to see some nuns."

HER PARENTS stayed up with her for a long time. They all sat there as the movie played, not talking much, the memory of the dream slowly disappearing as Meg stared at the screen. By the time Maria was singing "My Favorite Things," she was calm enough to let her eyes close.

"Feel better?" her father asked.

Meg grinned sheepishly. "Yeah."

"Good," he said, and clicked the television off.

It was quiet for a minute, her parents looking almost as exhausted as she felt.

"How would you feel about going home to Chestnut Hill for a while?" her mother asked. "You could see your old friends, and—"

Oh, yeah, like they'd be safe *there*. At least the White House was a god-damn *fortress*. Meg shook her head. "It was only a bad dream. I'm going to be *fine*."

Her mother nodded. "I know. We just thought you might feel better if—"

"I don't want to go anywhere," Meg said. "I'm not going to ruin everything."

Her father patted her good hand. "Your mother and I just want to make things easier for you. We thought going home for a while might—"

"I'm *trying* to get better," Meg said defensively. "I can't help—"

"We want to make it easier," her father said. "That's all."

They didn't seem to get that things weren't *ever* going to be easy again. Meg sighed. "I don't want everything messed up because of me. I don't want to go home, and—I mean, we live *here* now. I just—I want things to be *normal*. Anything else means they got what they wanted, you know? That they—I don't know—changed the order of things."

Her parents nodded.

"Besides," Meg said. "If we're not safe here, we're not going to be safe anywhere else. I mean, you *know* we're not."

They nodded.

"I want things to be normal." She looked at her mother. "You, especially. Work, I mean."

Her mother frowned, but then nodded again.

"I just—I don't know." Except that talking was too hard. She wiped her sleeve across her eyes. "I'm sorry, I'm really tired."

Her mother started rearranging her pillows, and fixing her quilt, while her father turned the lamp off.

"Can you make sure the bathroom light stays on?" Meg asked. "So I can sleep?"

Her father nodded, flipping on the switch and leaving the door ajar about a foot.

"Thank you," she said, and closed her eyes.

SHE DID HER best to feel better. To eat normal meals. To smile. To *function*. She had to go back to the hospital that week—in a helicopter this time—to have a bunch of MRIs and another arteriogram and other things done, and they sent her home with a tall metal crutch, which her physical therapists would be teaching her how to use. The doctors still seemed to be divided about whether "walking unaided" was even a remote possibility, and she found it demoralizing when a couple of them debated the dim prospect right in front of her. Well, okay, they were down the hall, but she could hear the entire depressing conversation.

She was also taken to a dentist, who did the preliminary work for the implants they were going to try and put in to replace her teeth on the left side, although if that didn't work, she was going to be stuck with a permanent bridge. Either way, it sucked. The whole trip was very grueling—and scary—and she resorted to the sunglasses-on/slight-friendly-wave strategy when she and her father finally got back to the White House that evening.

"Long day," he said, once she was in her room, with a small dinner tray that she was too worn out to eat.

And then some. Meg nodded. Most of the time that they had been outside, transferring to and from the helicopter, she had been so afraid that she had had to keep her eyes closed behind the sunglasses, her good hand clamped tightly around the arm of the wheelchair.

"Anything else you want?" her father asked.

Mostly, she just wanted this day to be *over*. Meg shook her head, and very slowly picked up her fork.

ALTHOUGH SHE WAS utterly exhausted from having Edith teach her how to try and use the crutch, she went up to the solarium the next afternoon for her "change of scene." The Red Sox were playing the national game of the week, and since they won, handily, Steven was very cheerful.

"You want some chow?" he asked, happily watching the recap of the game—a solid shut-out victory.

Meg shook her head. "No, thanks. I mean, go ahead."

"Should I like—" he looked at her wheelchair—"take you downstairs?"

"No, I'm too tired," she said. "I'm just going to hang out here for a while." Once the game had seemed to be pretty well in hand—or, at any rate, with the closer on his way in from the bullpen, her father had taken Kirby, and Neal, out for a walk on the lawn. Her mother was in a meeting or something.

"Well—okay. You can like, call—" he motioned towards the phone—"if you, you know, want anything or anything."

"And you think *I* talk excellent?" she said.

He laughed, did a pretend pitcher's warm-up toss at her, then headed for the door.

When he was gone, the silence made her nervous, and she picked up the remote control, turning channels until she found another baseball game. This one was National League and therefore, inherently not as interesting, but she left it on, anyway.

Slouching down to watch, she felt the usual wave of depression starting. She was *never* going to feel better, or be able to do anything normal. *Weeks* were passing, and she still—hearing someone at the door, she prepared a game little "don't worry about *me*" smile, then looked up to see Beth. A somewhat tentative Beth, holding a small blue gift box.

No *wonder* her parents had kind of been making themselves scarce all afternoon.

Feeling even more tired, she sighed. "They went behind my back, didn't they?"

Beth grinned and came into the room, wearing jeans, pink

Chuck Taylors, and a very pink bowling shirt. "Is that anything like 'Hello, how nice to see you, what a pretty outfit!'"

God, she was tired. "I *told* you I didn't feel well enough to see people," Meg said.

Beth shrugged, gave her a shy hug, then sat down in an easy chair. "Hey, the President calls and tells you to do something, you *do* it."

"Beth to the Rescue," Meg said grimly.

"*There's* a hell of a chapter title." Beth leaned across the coffee table to hand her the present. "Here."

"Thank you." Meg turned the box over in her hand, but didn't open it. "She shouldn't have gone behind my back like that."

"Who knows," Beth said, "maybe she was trying to help you."

"Maybe." Then, Meg frowned at her. "You don't wear a *hat* to come see me, even?"

Beth looked grave. "It's with all of my luggage, of course."

"What, are you moving in?" Meg asked.

"Yes," Beth said. "I'm taking over the Department of Housing and Urban Development."

Well, stranger things had happened.

"*Now,* you have to ask me something nice," Beth said.

Meg sighed, trying to think. "How was your flight?"

"Just the swellest," Beth said cheerfully. "How are *you*?"

Meg shrugged.

"If you don't mind my saying so, you don't look so good," Beth said.

Meg frowned at her again. "I mind your saying so."

"Are you eating?" Beth asked.

Oh, yeah, this was *just* what she needed.

"Do you *ever* see sunshine?" Beth asked.

"I got to go to the hospital the other day." Meg put the present down, unopened. "Look, just so I'll know. What did my mother say to you?"

"That you maybe needed some cheering up." Beth grinned. "*Ob*viously, she was mistaken."

"Yeah." She didn't—really—want to be rude, so she tried to smile back. "You, uh, you want anything to eat, or drink? I can call downstairs."

"No, thanks." Beth looked at her. "If you don't want me here, just say so."

Like it wasn't already obvious? "It's not that," Meg said. Well, okay, it *was* that. "I just—anyway. How's your family?"

Beth shrugged. "Fine. How's yours?"

"You should know—you *talk* to them all the time," Meg said, before she could stop herself.

"Just looking for your perspective," Beth said, very cheerful.

Meg stared at her. "You mean, you *do* talk to them all the time?"

Beth laughed. "Jesus, Meg. Relax, why don't you?"

No, she wasn't going to get off that easily. "How often have you talked to them?" Meg asked.

"Twice, Lieutenant," Beth said. "Your father called from the hospital to let me know you were all right, and your mother called me yesterday." She paused. "You want transcripts?"

"Do you talk to Josh, too?" Meg asked. "And Preston?"

"Yeah, it's kind of a nightmare, having people care about you." Beth indicated the television. "Big Padres fan now?"

"It's something to *do*," Meg said.

Beth looked at her for a minute. "If you really don't want me here, the shuttle leaves every hour."

The truth was, she had no idea what she wanted anymore. "I'm not much fun to be around," Meg said.

Beth shrugged. "Were you *ever*?"

To her horror, Meg felt her eyes filling with tears, and had to look away.

"I'm sorry," Beth said quickly. "I was just kidding."

Meg nodded, mortified to feel the tears start coming out.

"Oh, Jesus, I'm sorry." Beth moved over to sit next to her on the couch. "Meg, I really—" She touched her shoulder hesitantly. "I thought if I—I didn't mean to upset you."

"I'm *terminally* upset," Meg said.

Beth nodded, leaving her hand on Meg's shoulder.

"So, I feel better being alone," Meg said. "Okay?"

"Can I hang out and be upset *with* you?" Beth asked.

"Oh, yeah, sounds fun," Meg said.

"This—" Beth pointed to herself—"is a girl who knows how to have fun."

Meg had to grin. "Right."

They looked at each other.

"So, what do you want to do?" Beth asked.

"I want to watch the game," Meg said.

Beth leaned back, swinging her feet onto the coffee table. "Then, let's watch the game."

# 28

HER FAMILY AND Trudy were in and out during the next couple of hours. Her father and brothers to watch some of the game—National League, or not; Trudy, to bring them fudge-marshmallow bars and milk—and some pain medication; her mother, "just to say hello." When she came in, Meg didn't look at her, answering questions in monosyllables, and her mother left the room relatively quickly.

"For Christ's sakes," Beth said, frowning over at her. "She was trying to make you happy."

"She just likes to call all the shots," Meg said, and gritted her remaining teeth. "She always has."

Beth shook her head. "Oh, come on, Meg."

"You wouldn't be mad at *your* mother?" Meg asked.

Beth smiled sheepishly. "I'm *generally* mad at my mother."

Which was true—Beth and her mother had started clashing around the time Beth was ten, and had never really slacked off since. Meg shrugged. "At least *your* mother has never almost gotten you killed."

Beth looked tired. "Meg, come on. It's not like she—"

"I don't want to talk about it," Meg said. "Okay? Please just stay out of it."

"At the moment, I seem to be in the *middle* of it," Beth said.

"*I* didn't put you there." The silence was deadly enough so that Meg felt guilty. "I *told* you I shouldn't be around people," she said.

Beth nodded. "You weren't kidding."

They both stared at the television.

"Seems like you keep feeling worse, instead of better," Beth said.

Meg sighed. "Yeah. Looks that way."

"Well," Beth said, "is there anything—?"

Meg shook her head. "I don't think there's anything anyone can do."

"You can't just quit," Beth said.

It wasn't the *worst* option, among her very limited choices. Meg shrugged. "I don't have any better ideas."

Beth considered that, then looked down at her watch. "When's dinner?"

"Is that supposed to be a better idea?" Meg asked.

"It's a start," Beth said. "Come on, let's head downstairs, see if it's ready yet."

Meg shook her head. "I have trays."

Beth looked suspicious. "Always?"

Meg nodded, picking up the remote control to switch to ESPN.

"Wait a minute," Beth said. "You *always* have trays?"

Meg flipped past ESPN to see what might be on E!. "In case you haven't noticed, I'm having a hard time."

"So, let's try eating at the table," Beth said. "You might feel better."

She probably meant well, but *Christ,* this was annoying. Meg shook her head. "I'm too tired."

"Do you *eat* your trays?" Beth asked.

Meg sighed, and dropped the remote. "They're made of metal, usually."

"My God." Beth clapped her hands to her chest. "She made a joke."

Meg reached for the phone. "Look, if you're hungry, I'll just—"

Beth took the receiver away from her, then stood up. "Let's go downstairs. I haven't seen your family for a long time."

Christ. Meg sighed again. "Are you going to pressure me the whole time you're here?"

"Is this pressure?" Beth asked.

Meg nodded.

"Then, yeah," Beth said. "I probably am." She handed Meg her crutch. "Come on."

She'd already *done* physical therapy today; she didn't need to do any more. "You don't understand how tired I am," Meg said.

"You're right, I probably don't." Beth put her hand out to help her up. "Come on."

Since she knew Beth wouldn't stop bugging her until she gave in, Meg let Beth pull her up to her feet. For a few seconds, she was dizzy, and had to hang on to her friend's arm for support. Then, she shifted her weight to the crutch, the thought of making her way to the door too awesome to face right away.

"You all right?" Beth asked.

"I'm not faking," Meg said defensively.

"I know you're not, buddy." Beth rested her hand on her back. "Think you can get to the elevator?"

*No.* Meg scowled at her. "You're not going to make me do the *stairs*?"

"That would be sadistic," Beth said.

Meg nodded, taking it one slow step at a time, resting every so often—which felt too god-damn much like being in the woods with her stick and her ragged splint. Her wheelchair was right by the door, and she paused to look at it.

"Don't want to get used to the damned thing," Beth said.

"I *need* the damned thing," Meg said.

Beth just shook her head.

The little hall leaving the solarium sloped down to the Third Floor Central Sitting Hall—*very* convenient for wheelchairs—and rather hard going with one crutch. "You're an M.D. now?" Meg said, out of breath.

Beth nodded. "Yes. My stepfather was very pleased."

Meg didn't have enough energy to respond to that, leaning against the wall, the elevator seeming very far away.

"You want to sit down?" Beth asked.

Meg shook her head, pulling in a deep breath and grimly crutching her way across the hall and down to the alcove where the First Family private elevator and staircase were.

Beth pushed the elevator button. "You're tougher than you look."

Meg glanced up, breathing hard from what had felt like monumental exertion. "If I had a free hand, I'd slug you."

"Then, I'm lucky you don't have a free hand." Beth stepped aside, as the elevator door opened. "After you."

Meg limped in, then sank against the wall, carefully *not* looking at any of the mirrors hanging inside.

Beth pressed the button for the second floor, which was good, because normally she would have goofed around and pressed the Basement Mezzanine or something. "Home-stretch, now."

Meg didn't answer her, resting.

When they got off the elevator, she caught a glimpse of herself in the mirror right across the hall, by mistake—and if she hadn't known quite well who it was, she might not have recognized the frail, white-faced person leaning unsteadily on a crutch.

Beth gestured towards a closed door to their right: the White House Cosmetology Room. "Want to stop off and get a quick blow-out?"

Meg shook her head.

"Come on, that was funny," Beth said.

"Hilarious," Meg said, painfully crutching her way towards the West Sitting Hall.

Her father, who was sitting on the couch reading, glanced up, looking startled to see her.

"Anything wrong?" he asked.

Meg shook her head, sitting heavily—damn near *collapsing*—at the round mahogany table they used for breakfast, or late night snacks, sometimes. "Beth was wondering when dinner was."

"Oh." He was maybe going to say more, but didn't. "Any time now, I think. Let me go find your mother and the boys."

As he left, Meg leaned her head on her arm, very tempted to fall asleep. Her mother came down the hall from the Treaty Room, holding her reading glasses in one hand and some papers in the other, as a group of various advisors and aides clustered around near the stair landing.

"I *thought* I heard your voice," she said, looking surprised.

"Excuse me." Beth got up from the table, heading towards Meg's room. "I'm going to wash up for dinner."

Her mother hesitated, then sat down in the chair Beth had vacated. "I'm sorry," she said. "I know you don't really feel ready for visitors."

Meg looked down towards the advisors, mostly men in grey suits, with a few women in business-dress sprinkled in. "Hey, *you're* the President. It's your show."

Her mother ignored that. "I thought you needed to see her."

"Thank you," Meg said. "I'm not able to make these decisions for myself."

Her mother sighed. "Meg, I'm just—"

"Trying to help," Meg said. "Yeah."

"Yeah." Her mother stood up. "Have your father let me know when supper's ready."

BETH WAS HER usual self at dinner—fairly hyper, quite glib, and rather entertaining. Which was good, because everyone else was pretty quiet.

"So, there we are," Beth said, nodding thank-you as a butler served her some salad, "in Tunisia, right? And Meg, of course, has *no* money. So, we go to this bar. A—men's bar, really. And—" She paused, looking at Meg. "Would you like to tell the rest?"

"I wasn't listening," Meg said, eating a piece of ham. With her hand and all, her father or someone always had to cut the meat *for* her.

Not that it made her feel pathetic, or anything.

"Oh," Beth said, and grinned. "Then, maybe we should speak of other things." She looked across the table at Steven. "Think they're going to win the pennant?"

He shook his head. "No."

"They're *good* now, Steven," Beth said. "You're allowed to enjoy it."

"Doesn't mean they're going to win," he said.

Beth nodded. "Now, *that* is what I call dogged optimism. It's—it's inspirational."

He helped himself to some more baked beans. When Trudy was around on a Saturday night, they *always* had baked beans. "Still don't think they're going to."

"Well, that's that Puritan heritage of yours," Beth said sadly. "You really can't help yourself."

Meg shook her head, starting to be amused by this. "What a jerk."

Beth gave her a stern look. "Being a Puritan doesn't make him a jerk. Be more tolerant."

"Yeah," Meg said. "America is a melting pot."

"It certainly is," Beth said. "What a clever observation."

Meg laughed. "Jesus." Her parents were, reluctantly, used to them swearing, but she looked guiltily at Trudy. "Excuse me."

Her father smiled. "What kind of summer have they been having up there?" he asked Beth.

"Well." She gave that some thought. "It's been endless fun and happiness. I'd have to say."

264

Meg nodded. "Kind of like here."

"Well, not *quite* as fun," Beth said. "But then, I don't have your sunny disposition."

Meg grinned, motioning for Neal to pass her the brown bread.

"Graduation was pretty fun, too," Beth said. "I came in first," she paused, "*and* second in the class, so I was pretty busy, but—" She shrugged, indicating helplessness in the face of her own success.

"Your family must have been very proud," Meg's mother said, smiling.

"Well, they were a little disappointed," Beth said. "They were hoping I'd come in *third*, too."

"Ba-dum," Steven said, and pointed at Neal, who made a cymbals sound, a little late.

Meg couldn't not grin, passing her plate to her father for some more ham. Beth was, undeniably, a girl who knew how to have fun.

"So," Beth said, sitting back and plucking significantly at her sleeve, where the name "Louie" was embroidered. "What are we going to do after dinner?"

Meg, having just picked up her fork, put it back down. "You're not going to make me *bowl*, are you?"

Beth looked down at her shirt, the pocket of which read: Clover Lane Bowling Championships, 1972. Duckpins, apparently. "You didn't notice my shirt?"

A shirt so pink that it almost certainly glowed in the dark. "Are you kidding?" Meg said. "Every ship within fifty miles changed course."

"Oh, now, don't exaggerate," Beth said. "Four miles. *Maybe* five."

There was, in fact, a bowling alley in the basement, and whenever Beth visited, she *always* insisted upon playing a few frames. Every once in a while, Meg and her brothers played for the hell of it, and once, Meg had had the rare privilege, and unforgettable pleasure, of seeing her parents play with the very patrician Senate

Minority Leader—who was a close friend of her mother's—and his wife. One of those evenings when she would have damn near sold her soul to have a camera handy.

"I feel that it's *imperative* for us play," Beth said. "Right after dinner."

"Me, too?" Neal asked.

"Of course," Beth said, and glanced at Meg's crutch. "If you *want*, you can sit in your damn chair." She looked at Trudy. "Excuse me."

"Oh, yeah, sounds great," Meg said, passing her plate to Steven for another helping of baked beans, nodding when Trudy put some coleslaw on there, too. As she took her plate back, she saw her parents exchange happy glances, and she flushed. Her mother, as a rule, had too much dignity to say, "I told you so," but maybe it *hadn't* been such a terrible idea for Beth to come down and visit.

BY THE TIME dinner was over, Meg was so exhausted that it was an effort to sit up in her chair. And her knee hurt. Her knee hurt *a lot*.

"Would you like some more cake?" Trudy asked. "Some ice cream?"

She shook her head. "No, thank you." Which made her even *more* tired, and she held back a yawn, resting her chin on her propped hand.

"You want to maybe skip bowling tonight?" Beth asked. "Watch some television?"

"I, uh—" She didn't want to be rude. "I'm sorry, I'm really tired." *So* tired, that sitting here at the dinner table was beginning to make her feel panicky. "I kind of—I think I need—"

Her mother shot a glance at one of the butlers, who instantly brought over her wheelchair, Meg nodding gratefully. The idea of moving was more than she could handle, but her father was already up and helping her into the chair.

Feeling guilty—and ashamed, she looked at Beth. "I'm sorry, I—I just can't—I'm really sorry."

Beth shrugged, but was obviously a little unnerved. "No problem. I'll see you later."

Meg nodded, wishing desperately that she was already in bed, relieved when her parents took her down the hall, her mother helping her into her nightgown, then under the covers. As her father turned out her lamp—the bathroom light already on—she was so glad to be in the safety of her bed that she almost started crying. Then, when her mother bent to kiss her good-night, she *did* cry.

"This is why I can't have visitors," she said. "It's too hard."

"It's all right," her mother said. "Beth understands."

*No one* understood. Meg pulled a Kleenex from the box by her pillow—a concept depressing in and of itself—and wiped at her eyes. "I don't want her to be mad at me. I just—I *can't*."

"Beth will be fine," her father said. "Don't worry about a thing."

Don't *worry*? Jesus, was he from another *planet*? "All right," she said, trying to keep her voice steady. "I just have to sleep."

"Okay." Her father leaned over to kiss her, too. "We'll see you in the morning."

"*Please* don't let anyone come in here," Meg said, fighting back what felt like an *explosion* of tears inside. "I just want to sleep."

Her parents nodded, then quietly left the room.

# 29

WHEN SHE WAS sure she was alone, she let the tears come, turning her head away from the door, praying that no one would hear. She cried until she was so exhausted that she couldn't do anything *but* sleep, her arm over her eyes in case someone came in. For some reason, Vanessa wasn't on the bed—or even in the room, which made her feel even worse.

If nothing else, she slept *soundly*, not waking up—or maybe even moving—until Trudy knocked on her door the next morning and came in with her breakfast.

"Good morning, dear," Trudy said, putting the tray down on her desk, then moving the curtains to let in some light. "How do you feel?"

*Awful.* Meg sat up with some difficulty, hoping that her eyes weren't as red as they *felt*—and wondering where Vanessa was. "I-I'm all right. I mean, good morning."

After helping her into the wheelchair so she "could go into the bathroom, Trudy set up the tray for her—orange juice, broccoli and mushroom quiche, toast triangles, and a dish of strawberries and cream.

"I, uh—" Meg picked up her juice glass, her hand so shaky that she almost dropped it. "Is Beth still here?"

Trudy nodded. "Would you like her to come in?"

"Well, I—" The room seemed very bright—painfully so—and she wished Trudy would pull the shade back down. "I don't really—I guess so." She looked at her clock. Ten-fifteen. That meant that she would have to do the god-damned physical therapy in—Jesus, there was *no* way she could face that today. "I, uh, I don't feel very good. Can you tell them I'm going to stay in bed today? That I can't—I *really* don't feel good."

Trudy looked at her clock, too. "Maybe after you—"

"Can you *please* tell them?" Meg asked. "I *need* to stay in bed today."

Trudy nodded, her eyes so sad that Meg couldn't look at her, focusing down on her tray.

"Thank you," Meg said. "For breakfast, too."

After Trudy had been gone for a few minutes, there was a small knock on the door.

Her parents, to *make* her do her therapy, probably. Meg pressed her teeth together. "Who is it?"

"Me," Beth said.

Christ. "Okay," Meg said, humiliated by the idea that she was going to be caught lying in bed with a god-damn tray.

Beth came in, wearing jeans and her old—but, Meg knew, beloved—maroon Sunnydale High t-shirt. "Hi," she said, her hands awkward in her pockets. "How do you feel?"

Meg shrugged, not looking at her, ashamed of how red her eyes—she knew, from her trip to the bathroom—were. "You, uh, you get breakfast and everything?"

Beth nodded. "Trudy went all out."

Meg nodded, too, although she hadn't touched hers yet. "Uh, sorry about last night."

Beth shrugged. "Your brothers and I did some bowling."

"Oh. I mean, that's good," Meg said. "I guess they're not having much fun lately."

"Not really," Beth said.

Yeah.

Neither of them spoke for a minute.

"You should at least eat the strawberries," Beth said. "They were really good."

Meg nodded, and moved the dish closer, but didn't pick up her spoon.

"Look, I—" Beth stopped. "I don't know what I should do."

*Go home.* Meg shrugged, looking at her breakfast.

"Meg—" Beth let out her breath. "I don't know. You're a lot worse than I thought you'd be."

Meg looked up, furious. "It's not my fault!"

"I meant *feeling* worse, not *being* worse," Beth said.

Oh. Meg scowled, her good hand clenched around the side of her tray.

"Look, just tell me what to do," Beth said. "I'll do whatever you want."

"I kind of —" she *really* didn't want to hurt Beth's feelings—"I want you to—" Oh, hell.

"I *know* you're not ready to see people yet," Beth said, her voice very quiet. "And Christ, the last thing I want to do is—" She stopped, her voice getting even quieter. "Did it ever occur to you that maybe *I* sort of needed to see *you?*"

Beth, whose goal in *life* was to be ever cool and invulnerable? Beth, who—at the moment—looked rather small, and upset. "I don't know," Meg said.

"Well, think about it," Beth said.

Meg thought about it. About how she would feel if something terrible happened to *Beth.* Thought about how much she would want to see her, be sure she was all right. "I'm sorry," she said, looking down. "It's just so hard."

"Dragging yourself through the fucking *woods* was hard," Beth said. "Hanging out with *me* is easy."

Meg smiled a little. "Oh, yeah?"

"I promise not to pressure you," Beth said. "You just tell me what you can't do, and we'll go from there."

"What I *can't* do?" The question was so all-encompassing that Meg smiled a little more. "How much time do you have?"

Beth grinned, sitting down in the rocking chair. "This girl has nothing *but* time."

THEY DIDN'T DO much. In fact, about the most Meg could manage was to—watch *The Brady Bunch*. She and her brothers owned the entire series, courtesy of their aunt, and loved every single episode in which Cousin Oliver *didn't* appear.

They started at the beginning—and kept going.

"I think I may be lapsing into a coma," Beth said, as they watched the episode where Cindy got to be the fairy princess in her school play, but was only given *one* ticket—and couldn't decide which parent to invite. "Slide over."

Meg nodded, and carefully eased herself to one side, so that Beth could stretch out on the bed next to her.

They were watching the one where Jan seemed to be allergic to Tiger, but was, in the end, only allergic to his new flea powder, when her father and Trudy brought in lunch—chicken soup, BLTs, and—of all things; Trudy winking at her—Cokes.

Her father looked at the television. "Maybe we should have just brought you two some Jell-O."

"There's *always* room for Jell-O," Beth said, to no one in particular.

Meg's father smiled, then looked at Meg. "Bob is going to come by in a while? Say hello to you?"

Meg nodded, drinking her Coke.

They watched *The Brady Bunch* for a very long time. *Hours,* to be precise. Dr. Brooks came in, checked her over, and said jovially that a nice day of rest might be "just the ticket." Steven and Neal showed up more than once, and each time, they looked at the television, then one of them would say, "*Still?*", and they would shake their heads and leave. Her mother called from the West Wing, "to say hi," although when she asked what they were doing, Meg just said, "Oh, you know, hanging out."

"We're getting stupid, Meg," Beth said, as they watched the one where Alice hurt her ankle—and was in danger of not being able to attend the Meatcutters' Ball with Sam the Butcher. "I can *feel* it happening."

Meg nodded. She was, indeed, feeling pretty stupid. "You want to call it quits?"

"What, are you kidding?" Beth said. "The one where Marcia gets braces is next."

Oh, yay. Meg grinned. "*Perfect,*" she said.

WHEN NEAL CAME in to tell them it was almost dinnertime, Beth looked over at her.

"Well? What do you think?" she asked.

Meg sighed. "Okay, but that's *it* for tonight."

"Fair enough," Beth said.

So, Meg put on sweatpants, and *her*—not quite *beloved*, but certainly well-*liked*—Sunnydale High t-shirt, and they went down to the Presidential Dining Room. They compromised, Meg riding the wheelchair down there, but crutching into the room itself.

She was too tired to participate in the dinner conversation, but luckily, Steven and Neal had spent the afternoon playing basketball with Preston and off-duty Secret Service agents, and were all charged up, agreeably yapping away throughout the meal. Beth was pretty quiet, too, suffering—almost certainly—from a severe situation comedy overdose.

"Steven and me played *excellent*," Neal said, his mouth full of scalloped potatoes. "We—"

"Try some chewing and swallowing," their father said from the end of the table, sounding much less annoyed than he ordinarily would have. *Before*, anyway.

Neal chewed, and then swallowed. "They couldn't stop us at *all*, practically."

Steven laughed. "Yeah, you should have seen Baby Skyhook here. He's a wild man."

Which was all too easy to picture. Steven had been coordinated before *birth*, but Neal was—to put it nicely—kind of a late bloomer.

"So, hey." Steven jabbed his fork in her direction. "We watching the game tonight?"

Meg shook her head. "I sort of think I'm sleeping tonight."

"Yo, you traitor," he said, and pointed his fork at Beth. "*You* watching?"

"Sorry," Beth said, and shook her head, too.

"Traitors," he said grimly. "I'm *totally* surrounded by traitors."

Meg grinned, finishing up her last piece of asparagus. Steven was pretty funny when he wanted to be.

"I bet those girls are going to watch the *Yankees,*" he was saying to Neal. "I bet they're going to watch the Yankees, and *clap*."

Beth laughed. "You know it. And the Mets are on the coast tonight, so we can watch *both* games."

Steven collapsed in his chair, pretending to faint. "Smelling salts," he said weakly to Trudy, who was sitting to his left. "Where are my smelling salts?"

"You just sit up and eat your dinner," she said, rapping sharply on the table with her fork. "Don't be so silly."

Meg found *that* amusing, too. Trudy had always been one to crack the whip of authority, especially during meals. Felix paused by her seat to offer her more salad, and she shook her head, her eating energy depleted. But, she sat through the rest of the meal, smiling at the right times, and nodding or shaking her head, if anyone asked her a question.

Her mother spent half of the meal out in the West Sitting Hall, conferring with Glen, who was her Chief of Staff, the Secretary of State, and the National Security Advisor, and various aides about— Meg assumed—the latest wave of turmoil in Pakistan, although it was sometimes hard to keep track of the rapidly changing problems her mother juggled on a daily basis. Anyway, when she finally came back in, Meg caught her checking her plate to see how much she had eaten, and then glancing at Trudy for confirmation.

Although Meg didn't think she had a right to be critical—since she'd barely touched her *own* dinner.

However, the butlers were now *used* to working for a President who forgot to eat on a regular basis, and as they served dessert, Felix brought out some fresh yogurt and fruit, as well as a small chef's salad and some matzoh crackers for her. It seemed to take her mother a minute to remember that she was—ever so briefly—back to being a regular human being again, and start eating the salad.

In the meantime, her father and brothers were digging into dessert, and Beth—because she was just too god-damn cool for her own good—opted for black coffee, to which she added quite a lot of sugar.

"Are you sure you don't want some, dear?" Trudy asked, after giving Neal a second serving.

Butterscotch pie, no doubt delicious. Meg shook her head. "No, thank you, I'm full."

"You look like you've just about had it," her mother said.

Very much so. Meg nodded, reaching for her crutch. "Yes. In fact, I kind of think—"

"You're right," Beth said, getting up. "The Yankees game starts in about five minutes."

Shaking her head when her father moved to help her, Meg eased herself up onto her good foot while Beth went out to the hall to get her wheelchair.

"We'll be down to say good-night?" her mother said.

Meg nodded, crutching her way to the hall.

THE NEXT MORNING, bright and early—if eleven o'clock was bright and early—Edith, the physical therapist, arrived. She was very pleasant, in her thirties, with blonde hair and glasses, but Meg sure as hell hated the sessions. Hated every single minute of them. Each time, she had to fight the urge to throw a Presidential-progeny tantrum and intimidate Edith into not ever coming back.

However, the odds of Dr. Brooks letting her skip two days in a row were slim.

Beth came upstairs to the work-out room to watch, and Meg let herself be strapped into the Cybex weight machine, which was apparently used a lot for sports rehabilitation. Oh, yeah, like *she* was going to be playing sports again.

"Okay," Edith said, once she had set the resistance on the machine. "Can you do three sets of ten?"

No. Meg set her jaw, and forced the weight up with her right leg. Her supposedly *good* leg. Ten times. Then, ten more. Slowly, she started the final set, already perspiring, her leg shaking in protest. The weight was incredibly heavy, and even though she had seven repetitions to go, she had to stop.

"Come on," Edith said, very kind and encouraging. "You can do it."

Meg shook her head, breathing with some difficulty. "I'm sorry. It's too hard."

Beth was sitting on the recumbent bicycle in the corner, her ankles propped up on the wheel, reading *Dispatches* by Michael Herr. As a concession to Meg's having to exercise, she had put on a pair of sweatpants, too. Bright red. "Come on, keep going," she said, not even looking up. "You want to ski, or not?"

Meg forced the weight up again, scowling over at her. "Can't you at least pedal that thing?"

Beth turned a page. "*I* don't want to ski."

Still scowling, Meg pushed the weight up again. Five more to go.

"That's it," Beth said, as she managed another, and then another. "Keep it up."

"Easy—" Meg forced the weight up, out of breath—"for *you* to say."

"Three months, Meg," Beth said. "Three months, and it'll be snowing out West."

Meg glared at her, but finished the set of ten.

"Very good," Edith said, smiling. "Good job." She had a bit of a Romper Room quality, but she *was* nice.

Beth turned another page. "Do ten more."

"*You* do ten more," Meg said, accepting the white towel Edith gave her, and wiping her face.

"Thanksgiving," Beth said. "Mountains all over the country will be open by Thanksgiving."

Meg ground her teeth together, but started another set, keeping a hard, constant rhythm.

"Ski," Beth said conversationally to Edith, who looked a little nonplussed. "'Ski' is the magic word. Say 'ski,' and she'll do just about anything."

Seven, eight—Meg glared at her—nine, *ten*. Then, she let her leg fall, too out of breath to say anything.

"What does she do now?" Beth asked. "Pull the weight *down*?"

"Well—" Edith blinked a few times—"yes."

"Good." Beth nodded her approval, then focused on her book. "Sounds good."

Meg watched as Edith set the machine for the opposite work-out, her glasses slipping down. "You know, that damn shuttle still leaves every hour."

Beth nodded. "So you hear."

The machine was ready, and Edith checked to make sure the Velcro strap was fastened tightly around Meg's ankle, then stepped back.

"Three sets of ten?" Meg said.

Edith nodded.

Fine. Meg pressed her teeth into her lip, and began.

When the first half of the session was finally over, and Edith had strapped ice packs to the arm and leg Meg had exercised—which was the regular routine—she left the room with a fluttery "I'll just see if Admiral Brooks—I'll be right back." Meg looked over at Beth, who was still reading.

"What happened to not pressuring me?" she asked.

"That wasn't pressure," Beth said. "That was *inspiration.*"

Yeah. Right. "You made her nervous," Meg said, gesturing towards the door with her hand splint.

Beth shrugged. "She'll get used to me."

"You're staying that long?" Meg asked.

Beth laughed.

"Having fun?" Meg asked, tired enough from the exercises to feel good and cranky.

Beth took a bookmark out of her red terry-cloth headband, and closed the book. "It looked pretty hard."

That was because it *was.* "We haven't even done the part where I exercise the things I *hurt* yet," Meg said. None of which involved weights, because her bad hand and knee still weren't strong enough to handle anything more than *very* thin elastic bands—and so far, even that seemed to be pushing it.

Beth nodded.

"And I'm not ever going to *walk* right," Meg said, "forget ski."

"You're *already* walking," Beth said.

Meg gestured towards the crutch. "You call that walking?"

"Better than nothing," Beth said.

Yeah. But, still. Meg slouched down, pressing the towel against her face, feeling heavy with fatigue. "You really don't understand how hard it is."

"It's going to be a long time before you do *anything* that isn't hard," Beth said.

Meg lowered the towel. "That's cheering."

"Want me to humor you?" Beth asked.

Christ, no. Meg shook her head.

"So," Beth said. "What happens next?"

"I try to move my fingers for like, *half an hour straight*, and cry part of the time, then try to flex and extend my leg," Meg said. During which, she also sometimes had to cry. "And *then,* she shoots electricity into me."

"Where?" Beth asked uneasily.

Meg sighed, very tired. "I put one hand in water, and the other in the socket."

Beth laughed. "Sounds exciting."

Hair-raising, even. "They shoot it into my knee, mostly," she said, gesturing towards a little machine with wires and suction cups, "and my hand a little, too. It's supposed to stimulate healing."

"Oh." Beth looked at the machine dubiously. "Does it hurt?"

Yes. "Stings, sort of," Meg said.

"Oh." Now, she looked at Meg. "This really isn't much fun, is it?"

"Not much fun at all," Meg said.

# 30

THAT NIGHT, PURSUING the list of things Meg could and could not do, they went up to the solarium and watched *Mean Girls*—which Meg had always loved—and ate popcorn, upon which Steven put altogether too much Parmesan cheese. Neal went a little heavy with the seasoned salt, too.

After the movie, Meg crutched her way to the third floor elevator, then switched to the wheelchair for the ride downstairs, holding her crutch.

"So," Beth said, pushing her in the wheelchair once they were on the second floor. "You tired?"

"I don't know." She'd had a *very* long nap that afternoon. "A little."

"You want to go downstairs?" Beth asked. "Look at the East Room and all?"

Meg tensed in her chair. "If I go down there, I have to have agents." Since they were only free of said albatrosses up in the Family Quarters.

"Oh." Beth considered that. "Well, you want to go outside?"

Was there a comprehension problem? Meg frowned at her. "I told you, if I—"

"I meant, the balcony," Beth said, indicating the Yellow Oval Room.

Meg shook her head.

Beth sat down on one of the settees in the Center Hall—obviously a girl with nothing *but* time. "It's okay if you can't. I'm just wondering why."

Christ, was she stupid? "They can *see* me," Meg said.

"What, from the street?" Beth asked.

Meg nodded, the thought so terrifying that, even in the windowless Center Hall, she felt exposed. Afraid.

"We always sit out there when I come," Beth said. "And we *never* see anyone."

Meg hunched a little in the wheelchair. "We see people walking."

"We see little tiny shapes far away," Beth said. "Besides, I thought that's why your parents have the lights kept low out there."

Meg shook her head. "That's to save energy."

"And here *I* was, thinking it was for privacy," Beth said.

Which was, of course, exactly what it was for. Meg sighed.

Beth got up from the settee. "If you don't like it, we can come right back in."

"This is pressure," Meg said.

"Yeah, but just barely." Beth guided her wheelchair into the Yellow Oval Room and over to the combination window-and-door which led to the balcony. As she opened the door, fresh summer air blew into the room, feeling warm and clean. "Hey, it's nice out."

Less humidity than usual, for Washington. Meg nodded, hoisting herself onto her crutch, concentrating on not being afraid. Or, at least, not letting Beth *see* that she was afraid.

"Need help?" Beth asked.

Meg shook her head, tremblingly making her way outside. *Outside.* She lowered herself onto the white wrought-iron couch—which had thick green cushions to make it more comfortable.

Beth dragged over one of the smaller white chairs and set it in front of her. "Here."

Meg lifted her leg onto it. "Thanks." Also, if there was trouble, she could take—slight—cover behind it, which might have been Beth's strategy.

Or not.

"No problem," Beth said. "You want me to go get some soda or something?"

And leave her *alone* out here? "No," Meg said quickly.

Beth paused, halfway to the door. "I'd only be gone a minute."

"*Please* don't," Meg said, ready to panic.

"Okay." Beth sat down in a heavy wicker chair. "No problem."

Meg took a few deep breaths, trying to relax. To get the courage to look *up*.

"Maybe it's a little chilly out here," Beth said, very casual. "You want to go back inside?"

"I'm *fine*," Meg said, gripping the iron arm of the couch with her good hand. This was the White House; they were safe. No one could see them. They couldn't be much *safer* than where they were, even if—she opened her eyes. "I-I am kind of thirsty. Would you mind getting us something?"

Beth looked at her, then nodded. "Sure thing. Be right back."

Alone on the balcony—maybe safe, maybe not—Meg could feel herself shaking. Feel her heart beating. *Nothing* was going to happen. Not here, anyway. She forced herself to look up and out at the view: the West Wing and the OEOB to her right, and then, straight ahead, the bright fountain near the end of the South Lawn, the iron fence, where there were *still* piles of flowers and cards strangers kept leaving, the Ellipse, the Washington Monument, and the Jefferson Memorial beyond that. She couldn't see them, of course, but the Capitol was down the Mall to the left; the Lincoln and Vietnam Memorials, to the right. And off in the distance, obscured by the night sky, was the Tidal Basin, the Potomac beyond.

She took some deep breaths. *No one* could see her. Maybe no one was even *looking*. And if they tried, she had the chair back in front of her, and the big white columns, and some *huge* pots of geraniums. And there were security devices—most of which, she barely even *knew* about. Sensors and cameras and detectors and stuff. So, if anyone tried to—

"Hi," Beth said, her voice muffled by the bag of tortilla chips between her teeth. She put two glasses of lemonade and some napkins down on the glass end table. "Look good?"

Meg nodded, letting out her breath.

Beth moved her chair, so that they were perpendicular to each other—and could both reach the drinks and chips. "Nice out here."

Realizing that her hand was cramped from gripping the arm of the couch, Meg let go. "Yeah." She picked up her glass, and they sat there for a minute.

"You can talk or not," Beth said. "Whatever the hell you want."

"Not," Meg said.

Beth shrugged, opening the bag of chips. "Whatever you want."

They sat there for a long time, long enough to finish the lemonade and half of the chips.

"Neal's room is right there," Meg said, gesturing towards the window to their right.

"You know he can't hear us," Beth said. "Besides, he sleeps like a rock."

Which he did. Sometimes, even when Steven did obnoxious stuff like dump water on him, Neal didn't wake up.

"I can't talk to *anyone*," Meg said. "I mean, I told the FBI stuff, but—" But, nothing *personal*. "I mean, I didn't *lie* to them, but—I don't know."

" 'Just the facts ma'am,' " Beth said.

Meg nodded.

"What about your parents?" Beth asked.

Meg shook her head. "They're so upset that I don't want—I mean, my mother, especially."

"She must feel pretty guilty," Beth said.

Meg nodded.

Beth started to say something, then stopped.

282

"No," Meg said, anticipating the unspoken question. "I'm not all that mad at her. Just sometimes."

Beth nodded.

It was quiet, but she stiffened when she heard movement down in the grass, not relaxing until she saw that it was an agent patrolling the top of the South Lawn with a K-9 dog.

"I can't seem to talk to Josh, either," Meg said. "I mean, about *anything*."

Beth shrugged. "You guys were having trouble talking before this even happened."

True. Meg nodded.

"It's probably better that you'd already broken up," Beth said. "This would have *really* messed things up."

Meg nodded. "I still want to try and be friends with him, though. I mean, you know."

"So, we'll have him come over while I'm here," Beth said. "Maybe that'll make things easier."

Maybe. Meg nodded, looking up at the underside of the balcony ceiling—the edges of which kind of needed a fresh coat of white paint, frankly, and out at the dark night and the bright monuments. Then, she looked at Beth, who shrugged. Receptively.

"How much do you know?" she asked. "About what happened?"

"I don't know," Beth said, uncertainly. "I mean, you know, everything that was in the papers and *Newsweek* and on the Internet and all."

Meg frowned. "I haven't seen any of that." Although she was pretty sure that the White House would have released the simplest version possible. Just enough to be plausible. "Did my mother tell you stuff?"

"A little," Beth said, nodding. "Preston did, too."

She didn't like to think of people talking behind her back. "When was *that*?" she asked stiffly.

"He was with the car that picked me up at the airport," Beth said.

Oh. Well, okay, that made a certain amount of sense. But still. Meg frowned. "So, basically, you know what happened?"

Beth nodded.

Of course, she hadn't even told her *parents* everything. None of the more—personal—things. She checked to make sure that Neal's room was still dark—which it was—and then looked over at Beth, who shrugged again.

Oh, hell. "I got drunk with him," she said. Something *no one* knew.

"One of—them?" Beth asked.

"Just this one guy," Meg said. "He was the only one I ever really saw." Except for the faceless gunmen.

Beth nodded.

"It was after he ripped my knee up—I don't know how long." Meg stopped. Getting into this was a mistake. Maybe she should just go inside to bed, and—

"What happened then?" Beth asked.

Meg shook her head, looking out at the South Lawn.

"Come on, Meg," Beth said. "You have to tell *someone*."

The Truman Balcony—probably—wasn't bugged. She hoped. She took a deep breath, then released it. "I got drunk with him. He had this bottle of Laphroaig, and he wanted me to have some, too."

Beth nodded.

"My *parents* drink that," Meg said. Which had made it that much more disturbing. "I don't know what his motive was. I mean, maybe he thought I'd get sick, and he could laugh, or—I don't know."

"Pretty weird," Beth said.

Yeah. "I got *literally* drunk. I mean, I never have before." She looked over uneasily. "You think there's something wrong with me?"

"For not getting *drunk* before?" Beth asked.

Meg shook her head. "No, for—talking to him."

"Doesn't sound like you had much choice," Beth said.

"No, but—" Meg shivered. Thinking about this was— "I was *so sure* he was going to rape me."

Beth didn't say anything, but Meg saw her shoulders hunch up.

"Every time he came in, I thought—only then, I—" Meg stopped. "Don't tell anyone this."

"I won't," Beth said.

Not strong enough. "Don't tell *anyone,*" Meg said. "Not about *any* of this."

Beth reached out and started to touch her arm, pulled back—probably because of the splint, and patted her right knee reassuringly, instead. "You know I won't, Meg."

Which she *did* know. She and Beth never broke each other's secrets. Never had. "I kind of—" This was going to be humiliating, and Meg couldn't look at her. "I offered to—I asked him if my, you know, would keep him from—well—"

"Sounds *smart* to me," Beth said.

Meg shook her head, ashamed all over again.

"He was going to *kill* you," Beth said.

Which might have been preferable.

"What happened then?" Beth asked, after a pause.

Meg swallowed. "He, uh, said it wouldn't make any difference."

"That was honest of him," Beth said.

Meg looked up. "He *was* honest." Like about Josh? "I mean—I can't explain it." Beth didn't say anything, and she took a deep breath. "I *would* have done it. I mean, if I thought—" She met Beth's eyes. "Don't *ever* tell anyone. They'd think I—"

"I'm not going to," Beth said, "but everyone would understand. I mean, if something's going to save your *life,* you do it."

Meg nodded, automatically looking at her hand.

"Yeah," Beth said, following her gaze. "Like that."

Yeah. Meg looked away from the splint, and pins—and defor-mity. "I think that night saved my life. I mean, talking to him and all. I think he kind of—I think he *liked* me."

Beth nodded.

Meg looked around, even though she knew—hoped—they were alone. "Can I tell you something worse?"

"Sure," Beth said.

"I liked *him*." She felt herself blushing. "I don't mean I *liked* him"— yeah, she did—"but, he—he reminded me of Preston." Horribly enough.

Beth's eyebrows went up. "Of *Preston*?"

"Yeah." Despite the fact that it was *July*, Meg felt cold, and she folded her good arm around herself. "I mean, not *exactly*, but—" But what? "Like if he had an evil twin."

Beth laughed. "An *evil twin*?"

Meg didn't laugh. "I'm serious."

"Yeah, I know," Beth said. "I just—*Preston*?"

Meg tried to think of a way to describe it. "He was really smart. I mean, *really* smart. And really—calm. And—a little amused all the time, you know?"

Beth nodded.

"He got my jokes," Meg said.

Beth nodded again. "Ah. No *wonder* you liked him."

"I didn't like him, I—" That was a lie. "Yeah, I did. I—" She frowned, searching for a better comparison. It was too upsetting to associate him—in any way—with one of her favorite people in the world. "Like, if you had a *really* sadistic big brother, who you fol-lowed around *anyway*."

"Jesus," Beth said.

"I know I'm not explaining it right." Meg glanced over, trying to read her reaction. "He could have killed me. He *should* have."

"Yeah, but—" Beth shook her head. "He didn't exactly put you on a bus to Washington."

"No," Meg said slowly, "but—"

"Preston *would* have killed you," Beth said.

Meg stared at her, instantly afraid. "What?"

"I don't mean Preston would hurt you," Beth said. "Ever. I just—he wouldn't *leave* someone like that. Leave them to suffer."

"Yeah, but—" Meg blinked a few times, trying to digest that. "I got away."

"He didn't *plan* it that way," Beth said, looking very grim. "I mean—he chained you up. He *nailed* you in. I mean—*Jesus.*"

She hadn't really thought about it like that before—and it was awful. Stomach-turning. And sort of too much to absorb. "You mean, he *wanted* me to die like that?" Meg asked. "*Really* badly?"

"I don't know," Beth said. "But, I wouldn't be grateful to him for something *you* did yourself."

Meg thought about lying in the cold, hard dirt, the heavy chain clamped around her wrist, slowly, slowly feeling her life disappear. Hour by hour—minute by minute, even—she'd felt herself— "I guess it wasn't very—humane."

"I guess *not*," Beth said.

Thinking about the enormity of being able to sit out on the balcony, quiet and safe, her family a few rooms away, Meg shivered again. Hard. "I'm really not supposed to be here, am I?"

Beth seemed to shiver, too. "No."

There didn't seem to be much else to say, so Meg leaned back, looking at the very few stars she could see beyond all the lights. Strange to think how many, many more there were up there.

"You're looking pretty tired," Beth said.

So, what else was new? Meg laughed, a little.

"You want to call it a night?" Beth asked.

Meg nodded, reaching for her crutch.

# 31

BETH SAT IN on the physical therapy sessions for the next several days. Often, she gave slightly skewed sports advice; otherwise, she just read whatever book she was holding, while Meg ground her teeth together and lifted and pulled and pushed the various weights. Edith was very pleased. Dr. Brooks and the various orthopedic surgeons were, too.

After exercising, and sitting through the electro-stimulus therapy, Meg would take one of the uncomfortable showers on her bench, then get into bed with a very small lunch tray. Usually, as soon as she was finished, she would take a nap. Then, Beth would "convince" her to get up and have dinner with everyone, and later, they would watch a movie or a baseball game with her brothers. Generally, her father—or, sometimes, Preston—would sit up there with them, too. And, increasingly, Preston didn't remind her of anyone but himself. Thank God.

Things were getting enough back to normal so that Steven and Neal started having their friends over again. Steven's best friends were Vinnie and Jim, who were both punks. Cute punks, but still punks. Neal's closest friend was Ahmed, a nice little boy with thick glasses, who always wore a turtleneck. *Always.*

Her parents and Trudy were around, but not obtrusively so. Her mother clearly had a lot of catching up to do, because she was working even harder than usual—which was probably a good thing. But, Meg also sensed that she was spending quite a bit of time sequestered with FBI agents and the like. They hadn't made much progress so far, but they *had* done things like find the mineshaft. Which turned out to be—not that Meg really wanted any details—precisely that: an abandoned mine-shaft, way the hell in the middle of the wilderness, up in the mountains above a North Georgia town called Ellijay. And reporters were apparently annoying the hell out of the people who lived in the area, by tramping around constantly, looking for new angles and human interest stories, trying to goose a little more mileage out of the whole thing.

Regardless, although the summit meeting in Geneva had been postponed until October—and they weren't exactly having state dinners and things all over the place—at least, there were strong signals that the White House was back in business. So to speak.

Late at night, after Steven and Neal went to bed, she and Beth would sit in the solarium, or out on the patio on the Promenade, or down on the Truman Balcony, talking or not. Beth didn't push her, or press for details—so, Meg found herself telling her more than she might have otherwise. What had happened, how she felt, how afraid she had been. She never really talked about how afraid she still *was*, but Beth probably figured it out. Especially since she still refused to go down to the First Floor, even—forget outside.

On Sunday morning—Dr. Brooks had decided that it could be a day of rest—Meg was the last one to get up. By a long shot. Late enough, so that it was prudent to eat lunch, instead of breakfast. On, happily enough, a tray. Beth appeared in her room shortly after the tray did.

"What's on for today?" she asked, wearing shorts, a wild blue-and-yellow Hawaiian shirt, and black Converse All-Stars.

Meg shook her head. "You're too cool for me."

Beth grinned. "Well, *everyone* knows that." She sat on the bottom of the bed. "So. What are we going to do?"

Her preference would be to rest quietly—but, odds were, Beth wasn't going to let her get away with that. "I don't know." Meg made herself eat a bite of her Mexican omelet. "What do you want to do?"

"It's really nice out," Beth said. "Let's sit on the roof. Get some sun."

There was probably no point in arguing. Meg sighed. "Okay. Out on the Promenade, maybe?"

"Sure," Beth said. "Why don't we call Josh, too? See if he wants to come over."

Ah, the ulterior motive. But Meg nodded, and reached for the phone.

Josh, it turned out, had the day off from his job at the golf course, and so, the three of them ended up sitting out on the Promenade patio, on chaise longues, Meg feeling self-consciously pale in her shorts and t-shirt—and splint and brace.

"Thirty SPF," Beth said, handing her a tube of suntan lotion. "*Minimum*. Maybe even forty-five."

"Thank you, Doctor," Meg said, and put some on her face, neck, and exposed leg.

"Can you get your left arm okay?" Josh asked.

Probably not. She shook her head and gave the tube to him, Josh smoothing on the lotion very gently.

"Thank you," she said, and he nodded.

"We all have our shades?" Beth asked, already wearing a pair of large white cat-eyes.

Meg had decided to drape the pair Preston gave her rakishly from her collar, but put them on, instead.

Josh took the folded baseball cap out of the back pocket of his shorts and stuck it on his head. It was the same cap he'd been wearing the day everything happened, and looking at it made Meg sad. More sad than scared, because she knew he'd had that cap for years, and *loved* it. Once, she had offered to buy him a new, less battered one, but he had—a mistake, in her opinion—declined.

"Am I tan yet?" Beth asked, holding out her arms.

"Bronze," Meg said.

"Good." Beth lowered her arms. "So are you."

Unh-hunh. She glanced at Josh, who was putting on some of the suntan lotion himself. "I, uh, I'm glad you weren't working today."

He looked very happy. "Me, too."

That said, Meg lay back on the chaise longue, the sun feeling nice and warm. Hot, even. "You know," she said, "we're missing the Red Sox, being out here."

Beth didn't even lift her head. "Neal's going to come out every now and then, keep us up-to-date."

"Do you think of *everything*?" Meg asked.

"Yes," Beth said. "I do."

They had a low-key afternoon, talking a little, but mainly just lying in the sunshine. Neal, as advertised, appeared every half hour or so.

"Steven says to tell you the middle relief sucks!" he bellowed over to them on his third trip outside.

"What's the score?" Meg asked.

"They're up one run, but Detroit has the bases loaded," he said.

Great. The outcome of that state of affairs was somewhat predictable.

They lay in the sun some more, Meg feeling very comfortable, and a little sleepy.

"We need food," Beth said. "And something with *ice*."

Meg opened her eyes. "Just yell in to Steven and Neal. The refrigerator in there probably has—"

"No, I'll go downstairs." Beth got up. "Be right back."

She didn't really want to be alone with Josh—which was, almost certainly, why Beth had left. She glanced over, seeing that he looked anxious, too.

"You're feeling better?" he asked. "I mean, lately?"

In some ways, anyway. She nodded.

"You *look* better," he said.

"Thanks." She tried to think of something to say. "You do, too. I mean, you have a really good tan."

"Caddie tan," he said.

Which meant sock, sleeve, *and* shorts lines. Like the tennis tans she'd always had. Except that she didn't want to think about tennis—*or* tan lines she had once had, and that the guy had enjoyed—viewing.

"You haven't just been working lately, have you?" she asked. "I mean, you're having *some* fun, right?"

He shrugged. "They're giving me a lot of hours, and—I don't mind working extra days."

"But, you should have fun, too," Meg said. "I mean—Christ."

"I *miss* you," he said.

She nodded, flushing slightly.

"Is it okay if I say that?" he asked.

She had to smile. "Yeah."

"Is it, um, mutual?" he asked.

She looked at him, at his nice, kind face, then nodded. "Yeah. It is."

Hesitantly, he touched her arm, his hand feeling very warm. "I just want us to be friends. I mean, if that's all *you* want."

Here came the conversation she didn't want to have. She let out her breath. "That's all I can handle, Josh."

He nodded.

"I *do* miss you," she said. "It's just—everything's still kind of an effort."

He gave her arm a light squeeze, then let go.

"It doesn't mean I don't want to see you," she said. "I'm just—taking it slowly."

He nodded again, and then, the silence was awkward enough for her to wonder what in the hell was taking Beth so long.

"So, it'd be okay if I maybe gave you a call sometimes?" Josh asked. "On my day off, or whatever?"

Not necessarily. She felt her muscles tighten. "I can't go anywhere. I mean, not even *downstairs*. Or—"

"This is nice," he said, waving to include the entire Promenade. "Being in the sun and all."

She let some of the tension ebb away. "Yeah. This is fine."

"And," he said, "you *know* how much I like watching your family's favorite baseball team."

This, from the guy who not only wore his Nationals cap everywhere, but even had a vintage *Senators* shirt.

"They're *always* entertaining," he said. "I remember one time when I was watching them, they had this ten-run lead, and—"

"Josh, you are on *unbelievably* thin ice," she said, cutting him off. He grinned, and subsided.

"In fact," she said, "maybe you should—"

"Yankees suck," he said.

Those were, indeed, the magic words. She laughed. "Okay. You're forgiven."

"Hey, check it out," Beth said, carrying a full plate and some napkins, Felix behind her with a tray of sweet tea. "Fresh petits fours."

Meg loved petits fours.

"You know," Beth said, once she was settled back on her chaise longue, with her tea, "there really are worse places to live."

"Yeah, really," Josh said, eating petits fours.

They both had a point. Meg sighed. "Yeah," she said. "There probably are."

THAT NIGHT, ALTHOUGH clouds had rolled in and it was sort of misty and cool, she and Beth sat out on the Truman Balcony again, Meg drinking Coke, Beth drinking more of the notoriously popular White House sweet tea—to which she, increasingly, seemed to be addicted. The Washington Monument and Jefferson Memorial looked all the more impressive, but somewhat eerie, in the light fog.

"You and Josh looked like you were having an okay time today," Beth said.

Meg shrugged affirmatively.

"Did you talk?" Beth asked. "I mean, when I left?"

"I *knew* you left on purpose," Meg said.

"Well, hell," Beth said, and grinned. "So, you talked?"

Meg nodded. "A little, yeah."

The fog was thickening, raindrops beginning to fall.

"You going to be specific?" Beth asked.

Meg laughed, but didn't elaborate.

"I tell *you* the many details of *my* social life," Beth said.

Meg nodded. "Like the time you and Preston had your secret tryst in the Cayman Islands?"

"The *Canary* Islands," Beth said. "I have my bank account in the Cayman Islands."

Meg laughed, and drank some Coke.

It was raining harder, the sound quiet on the cement driveway and grass below them.

"Anyway," Beth said.

Meg shrugged. "He wants to be friends. Maybe come over, on his days off."

"That sounds okay," Beth said.

Yeah. As long as he didn't push her.

They watched the rain, and the trees bobbing slightly in the wind.

"He'll be going away pretty soon," Meg said.

Beth nodded.

"I mean, *everyone* will," Meg said. Everyone *else*.

"You want to talk about that?" Beth asked, her voice noticeably off-hand.

Did she? No. "Not really," Meg said, and sighed. "I'm not even ready to *think* about it."

Beth nodded, and they stared at the rain.

"Getting cold out here," Meg said.

Beth nodded, and handed her her crutch.

# — 32 —

BETH WAS GOING to leave on Thursday, and on Wednesday night, she suggested that they go outside. For real.

"Oh, come on," Meg said. "The balcony's fine."

"We'll just try it for a few minutes," Beth said. "And if you completely hate it, we'll come back in."

Where had she heard *that* one before? Meg sighed. "If we go down there, I have to have agents."

Beth handed her the phone. "Here. Let them know we're coming."

It was strange to be followed by agents again—except for going back and forth to the hospital, it had been a long time. And she wasn't sure if she felt guilty, because of poor Chet, or a little afraid of them.

Or both.

Six of them, one of whom was female, accompanied them outside, and Meg assumed that there were others lurking ahead of them in the darkness somewhere. Dogs, snipers, counter-terrorism people—the list probably went on endlessly.

All so that she could spend a few minutes in what was, technically, her own backyard.

"We aren't just going to sit in the Rose Garden or something?" Meg asked, as Beth pushed her wheelchair along the South Drive.

"Too boring," Beth said.

She had a sudden, sinking feeling that she knew where they were going. "You'd better not be taking me down to the tennis court."

"It's nice over there," Beth said. "Trees and all."

Meg slouched down. "God-damn it."

Beth stopped the wheelchair at the end of the stone path leading to the court, and the Lyndon B. Johnson Children's Garden, and Meg used the arm of the chair to push herself up. It wasn't exactly well-lit down there at night, and she hesitated.

"I don't want to fall down," she said.

"I won't let you," Beth said. "Don't worry."

The walkway was curved and uneven, and she tripped once on a loose piece of rock, but Beth caught her—just as Meg heard a noise which indicated that one of her agents had been about to intercede.

"Hmmm," Beth said. "Maybe this wasn't such a great idea, after all."

Too late now. Meg ignored her, making her way to the black chain link fence and—balancing cautiously on her right leg—opened the gate. At first, she didn't think she could bring herself to step onto the court—but, she wasn't about to chicken out, with so many damn agents around. So, she limped, very slowly, down towards the two round tables at the far end. Then, she eased herself into one of the thinly-padded metal chairs, so out of breath that she let her cane fall onto the cement with a clatter.

Jesus. Not too long ago, she had felt like she *owned* this damn court—that it was her absolute *domain*, if not her professional future—and now, just trying to stagger the length of it on her crutch was enough to exhaust her.

And *depress* her, horribly.

"You've got a lot of nerve dragging me down here," she said.

"You've got a lot of nerve *coming* down here," Beth said cheerfully.

Meg stared out at the dark, empty court, then down at her leg, feeling a surge of tremendous hatred for the son-of-a-bitch who had ruined all of this for her. Who had ruined her whole *life*.

"Nice weather we're having," Beth said.

Meg scowled at her, still having trouble catching her breath.

"Just an observation," Beth said.

They sat there, Meg feeling both furious and devastated, keeping her left fist clenched.

"So," Beth said, after a while.

Meg sighed. "I was going to be a tennis player."

Beth shook her head. "Oh, you were not."

Oh, yeah? "What the hell do you know about it?" Meg asked.

"*You* were going to be a tennis player, like *I'm* going to win an Academy Award," Beth said.

Meg frowned. "You don't even act."

"I know," Beth said, and looked sad. "That's why it's going to be even *harder* for me."

Meg kept frowning at her. "So, what's your point?"

"I just think you were destined for other things, that's all," Beth said.

As nearly as she could tell, she was no longer destined for much of *anything.* "Like what?" Meg asked.

Beth shrugged. "I don't know. I guess I wouldn't be surprised to turn around and see you be the House Majority Leader."

Oh, yeah, right. "Never," Meg said.

Beth grinned. "*Senate* Majority Leader?"

Which was only *slightly* more plausible. Very slightly.

"Okay," Beth said. "How about Assistant District Attorney somewhere?"

"*Assistant?*" Meg said.

Beth laughed. "Yes, my friends, she has an ego and a *half*."

"I do not," Meg said defensively.

Beth nodded, looking very amused.

Okay, she probably did. To some degree. "Even if I wanted something like that—which I don't," Meg said, "I'm not going to get to school *anyway,* so it's kind of a moot point."

Beth gestured around towards the unseen security shadows

around them. "They'll figure something out. I mean, Steven and Neal are getting to go places again."

Places like the *movies*. "Barely," Meg said.

"It's a start," Beth said.

Not much of one. "I guess so." Meg sighed. "Hell, even if they *would* let me, I couldn't do it."

"You're still scared?" Beth asked.

*There* was a stupid question. Meg frowned at her. "Wouldn't *you* be?"

Beth nodded.

Right. "Besides," Meg said, "it's less than a month away. I have to have more operations, and all kinds of therapy, and they *still* don't—"

"So, take a year off," Beth said. "Or, at least, a semester."

Meg stopped, very briefly, feeling sorry for herself. "You mean, go in January?"

Beth shrugged. "Why not? That's what people who get wait-listed do."

"Yeah, but—I'd be *behind*," Meg said.

"What," Beth said, "the world'll stop if you don't graduate in *precisely* four years?"

It might tilt on its axis, ever so slightly, but it probably wouldn't actually stop. So, Meg shook her head. "No, but—"

"What do you think the odds are that *I'm* going to finish in eight nice, neat semesters?" Beth asked.

Slim to none. Meg grinned. "Well, I'm kind of more—"

"Conventional," Beth said.

"Yeah," Meg said.

Beth nodded. "Well, you Puritans are like that."

"It's a work ethic thing," Meg said.

Beth grinned. "Yeah, I've heard about that."

Most New Englanders had. Of course, if she started college later than she should, she could always make up the lost semester—or two—during the summers, and—then, the obvious solution occurred to her. "Hey, I could go part-time," she said. "Here in the city." Especially since George Washington University was *literally* a few blocks away from the White House. Surely, her parents and the Secret Service could work something out. She looked across the table at Beth, feeling—almost—excited. "That might be—okay. Sort of."

"Well, don't be *too* enthusiastic," Beth said.

Then, Meg thought about the *reality* of the situation. The way people would stare at her—or maybe come *after* her, and how the press, and paparazzi would—

"What?" Beth asked, seeing her expression.

Meg looked around nervously, even though the tennis court was dark, and quiet, and secluded. "I don't think I can go out in public. I mean, even if they *could* keep me safe, everyone'll—I mean, I couldn't go anywhere *before* without people staring, and hanging around and all."

Beth frowned. "I guess it'll be a lot worse now."

"I guess," Meg said, wryly. And, nothing like having a crippled hand and leg to make herself even *more* conspicuous.

Beth was looking at her splint, too. "But you'll go nuts, if you don't get out of here at some point. I mean, even if you are— well—"

"A pariah," Meg said.

"Sort of, I guess, but—I don't think there's anything evil about it," Beth said. "I just think people are worried about you. They want to know you're okay and all."

Meg nodded. Judging from the stacks of mail that were still swamping the Correspondence Office, that was probably true. She hadn't had the energy to look at more than a couple of dozen of them—Preston generally had a few with him—but, she had still been startled by how genuinely heartfelt they were. Letters from people all over the country—and *other* countries, people she had never met, from places she had never been, who wrote about how hard they'd prayed, how happy they were that she was home again, and how they just wanted to let her know how they felt. Very nice, sweet, thoughtful letters.

"All these people wrote that they cried," she said. "You know, when they heard I was safe."

"I'm sure they did," Beth said quietly. "It was really something."

"Wait, you *saw* it?" Meg said. Jesus, there was still so much that they hadn't talked about yet. "I mean, you were watching television?"

Beth shook her head. "My stepfather was, and he called us right away." She grinned. "He *hugged* me, if you can believe it."

Barely. Meg grinned, too. "Who announced it—Linda?" Who was her mother's press secretary, blonde and aloof, and always *all* business.

Beth nodded. "Yeah, you should have seen it. She's got this big grin on, and the press room's clapping, and—everyone was pretty happy. I mean, it was sort of scary, because I guess the networks heard something was happening, because they cut to it *before* she came out, and you've got them saying that they knew the President was en route *somewhere*, and there would be an announcement any time now, and then, Linda comes out with this big—" She stopped, her eyes very bright. "Well," she said, and looked away, whisking her sleeve across her eyes.

"Pretty dramatic," Meg said.

"Pretty *amazing*," Beth said.

They sat there for a minute, Meg thinking about how strange it was that something so very personal could also be so very public.

"I have to face them," she said. "The press, I mean." The prospect of which was scary.

Beth nodded. "I think that's a good idea. Clear the air. Let people see for themselves that you're okay."

Depending upon how broadly one wanted to define the concept of being okay.

They sat there some more, looking out at the tennis court, Meg almost able to *hear* the sounds of sneakers, and balls striking racquets, and clanging up against the fence. Tennis, in all of its tactile, exhilarating glory.

She looked away from the court, and at Beth, instead. "I, uh—" She was never one to get emotional. If possible. "I'm glad you came. To see me and all. I mean—" She coughed uncomfortably. "Thank you."

Beth nodded. "Kind of a nightmare for you to say that?"

Yes.

"What I like," Beth said, "is that you're not uptight. It's refreshing."

No doubt.

"I'm glad I came, too. I mean—" now, *Beth* looked uncomfortable—"you know."

Meg nodded, and they both looked in different directions.

"I'm afraid," Meg said, after a while.

"I am, too," Beth said.

Meg turned to look at her again, not having expected that. "You are?"

"Well, yeah. I mean—" Beth ducked her head a little. "I don't want anything to happen to you."

Meg couldn't think of anything to say, and Beth couldn't seem to, either.

Finally, Meg broke the silence. "Well."

"Yeah." Beth stood up. "Let's go watch a movie."

She hadn't attempted to sit through anything with *any* kind of violence so far. No matter how minor. "Want to watch some *Buffy*?"

"Do you?" Beth asked.

"Yeah," Meg said. "Let's give it a try."

AFTER BETH WAS gone, the house seemed extremely quiet. Much more so than usual. They had watched three *Buffy the Vampire Slayer* episodes the night before, and after Beth left that morning, Meg spent the afternoon and evening watching more episodes—all from the second and third seasons, sometimes alone, sometimes not.

At about eleven, her mother came in, looking very tired.

"Working all this time?" Meg asked—since she had only been with them briefly at dinner, before hurrying back downstairs.

Her mother studied her before answering. "Things are busy."

Especially since the President hadn't exactly been working at full capacity recently.

"Did Beth get home all right?" her mother asked.

Meg nodded.

"It was good to have her here," her mother said.

Christ, yeah. Meg nodded again.

"Well." Her mother poured some fresh ice water into the glass on the bedside table. "Is there anything you—?"

"Thank you for calling her," Meg said. "I guess I *did* need to see her."

Despite the fact that she was a politician and spent most of her life putting on smiles, her mother's *happy* smile was always a special surprise. "I'm glad you feel better."

"Yeah," Meg said. "I think I do."

Her mother's smile was more like a *beam*. "I'm glad."

Since the water was right there, handy, Meg drank some, and after checking the clock, took a pain pill, too. "How's, um, everything going?" she asked. "With the country and all."

Her mother shrugged. "It looks like they're holding their own."

Which was probably about all a President could expect, most of the time. "Well, that's good. I mean—" Meg patted Vanessa, who was curled up next to her bad leg. "I like knowing who's in charge. It makes me feel—safe."

"I *do* think we're much safer now," her mother said. "They're working very hard."

Yeah. The Secret Service seemed to be nothing, if not driven in its current efforts to protect all of them. "Beth and I were talking about, you know, rising above," she said.

Her mother's nod was cautious.

"Like, that I've got to do something, and not just—I don't know." Meg tried to think of the right word. "*Languish*." Close enough.

Her mother sat down in the rocking chair, looking very attentive.

"I want to try and go away to school in January. Give them time to get things set up, and for me to—" She gestured towards her knee and hand.

"Okay," her mother said, her voice less than enthusiastic.

"I *want* to," Meg said. "I want to be normal."

Her mother nodded. "And I *want* you to be."

"Are Steven and Neal going to be able to do all their normal stuff again, too?" Meg asked.

"Your father and I have been spending a lot of time meeting with Thomas and his people, and planning how they're going to handle all of this," her mother said. Thomas was Mr. Gabler, the head of the PPD.

"Think he can arrange for some security at GW?" Meg asked. "So I can take a couple of classes this fall, maybe?"

"Another decision," her mother said.

"Yeah," Meg said, her voice purposely calm. Confident. More so than she felt—but, that was something she could keep to herself. "I don't want to get too far behind." Of course, there was also the little problem of her not being registered there. "Can you arrange to have them *admit* me, too?"

Her mother smiled. "Maybe I can pull a couple of strings."

Just maybe. Meg took a deep breath. "One more thing. I want—" *Did* she? "I think I want to have a press conference."

Her mother looked surprised. "You *do*?"

"Yeah," Meg said. "Try to get the story—or, you know, *a* story—out there, so after that, maybe they'll leave me the hell alone."

Her mother moved her jaw, considering that. "The idea has merit."

Meg nodded. "Yeah. I mean, I know they'll keep bugging me, but if I answer everything *once,* I don't have to again, if I don't want to." Ever.

"It makes sense," her mother said. "Your father and I can—"

"How about just Preston?" Meg said. "You know, so I can do it by myself."

"Okay." Her mother smiled. "Sure."

"Thanks," Meg said. And, hey, while her mother was in such a generous mood— "Can I have a car, too?" So what if she didn't drive. "And an apartment in New York, and—"

"How about apartments in Paris and London, too?" her mother said. "And—I don't know—maybe your own movie studio, while we're at it."

"Thanks." Meg grinned. "I'll let you know if there's anything else."

"You do that," her mother said.

# ~ 33 ~

PRESTON PROMISED TO set up the press conference for Tuesday morning, and most of the television news outlets were planning to carry it live. *Live*. Jesus. She hadn't thought that the whole thing would get so major, but when she called Beth to get her opinion, Beth said that she should go for it. Take a trip to the Cosmetology Room right before going on the air, even.

Josh came over on Monday afternoon—it was raining, so she knew he wouldn't be working—and helped her pick out an outfit. Actually, he didn't help much at all, saying things like, "*That's* pretty," and "Yeah, that's pretty, too." Preston made the final decision, choosing a dress that he thought would look especially nice against the background in the Briefing Room. And, he assured her, with a splash of color at her neck, she would "knock 'em silly."

That night, Meg watched part of the Red Sox game in the solarium with her father and brothers, but started feeling so nervous that she excused herself and went to her room to rest. Her father came down after her, tucking her in, bringing her a Coke, and being generally supportive.

"Big day tomorrow," he said.

Meg nodded, sipping Coke.

"Sure you don't want your mother and me in there with you?" he asked.

She nodded. "I want to do it myself."

"Okay," he said, and patted her shoulder. "But, don't be afraid to change your mind—even once it starts."

"What," she said, "get up in the middle of it?"

He shook his head. "We could have a code word."

Which struck her funny. "What," she grinned, "say, 'Gosh, it's *hot* in here,' and you guys'll come running in?"

He nodded seriously. "Something like that, sure."

The image was so funny—her parents bursting in—live—that it was hard not to laugh. "I think I'll pass, Dad," she said.

"Well, as long as you know the option is always there," he said.

She nodded, still wanting to laugh.

He sat down on the edge of the bed, and looked at her. "Been a pretty tough summer."

God, yeah. "It's been a pretty tough *year*," she said.

He nodded.

"Do you think things are going to be all right from now on?" she asked.

"It seems only fair," he said.

Well, they were all certainly *due* for a good spell.

"I really am proud of you," he said. "More than you'll ever know."

"Uh, thank you," Meg said, managing *not* to do her patented cough of embarrassment.

"If you want," he said, "maybe tomorrow night, we can sit down and look over the GW catalog. See what sort of classes you might want to take."

What a nice idea. She smiled at him. "I'd like that, Dad. I'd like that a lot."

THE SWITCHBOARD WOKE her up early the next morning, and after she hung up, she lay in bed without moving, feeling very tired, and a little sick to her stomach. She had had a few nightmares—none, luckily, that woke her up screaming—and this press conference idea was beginning to seem like a big mistake.

However.

"What do you think?" she asked Vanessa, who yawned a big yawn—a *squeaky* yawn—and stretched.

Well, *that* was a clear "no comment," if she'd ever heard one.

She sat up, stretching a little herself. Like the saying went, she was *already* on the damn merry-go-round, so she might as well try and enjoy the ride.

Then, she went into the bathroom and sat on her shower bench, doing her best to wash her hair, and shave her good leg, and all. Not that it would really matter—Preston was going to have a cloth-covered table set up so she could sit down the whole time, and her brace wouldn't show. She also had *no* intention of wearing her sling, or calling attention to her hand, in any way.

The dress was beautiful—a deep, rich red linen. A little Republican, but what the hell. The collar probably *would* look better with a scarf, but she was pretty sure she didn't have the nerve to wear one. Or the élan. Maybe she would just go the New England route, and settle for some discreet pearls. She *did* like her pearls, which she had gotten for her sixteenth birthday.

Finally dressed, and feeling very self-conscious, she crutched her way down to the Presidential Dining Room. The crutch, she suspected, spoiled the line of her dress, but there wasn't much she could do about that. She paused in the doorway, seeing her family and Trudy already in there—and they all looked up with the usual concern.

"Good morning, peasants," she said, magnanimously. *That* got their attention. "Yes. It is I. The Queen."

"You look beautiful," her father said.

Well, she looked *presentable*, at least. And—she hoped—somewhat dignified.

"You change parties or something?" Steven asked, eating some toast.

How nice to share a sense of humor with someone. "Yes," she

said. "In fact, I'll be announcing my candidacy today." She crutched—clumsily—into the room and sat down. "No, it's okay," she said, as Trudy started to get up. "I'm just going to have some cereal."

Neal came over with a box of Captain Crunch.

"Well, thank you, youngster," she said. "Will you pour it for me, please?"

He did, uncertainly.

"Thank you." She handed him her napkin ring. "Here's a prize." Her stomach felt much too uncertain for her to try eating anything, but she nodded as Trudy poured her a glass of orange juice. "Thank you."

"Would you like some toast?" her mother asked. "An English muffin?"

"What I *really* want is some clotted cream." She picked up her spoon, then decided that she didn't have any appetite at all, and tried some juice, instead.

"Would you like a different kind of cereal?" Trudy asked.

Meg shook her head. "Actually, um, the Queen doesn't have much appetite."

"That is so cool," Steven said. "Talking in the third person and all."

Meg grinned. "If you're lucky, maybe I'll teach you how."

"*Ex*cellent," he said, and bit into a Danish.

After finishing breakfast—well, half of her juice—she *did* make a little visit to the Cosmetology Room. Let them go crazy with mousse and such. When they were finished—television makeup tricks galore—she thanked them, and pretended to look in the mirror and admire their work. Actually, though, she would much rather *not* know how she looked.

It was getting late—the press conference was supposed to start at eleven—and Preston was out in the Center Hall, waiting for her. When he saw her, he pretended to faint.

"Is that good or bad?" she asked.

"It's *very* good." He brought over her wheelchair. "Come on, I'll give you a lift down there."

"I'm going to *walk* in," she said.

He nodded, and she sat down, holding her crutch across her lap.

Her family was in the West Sitting Hall; her parents looking tense, Neal curious, Steven bored.

"Aren't you supposed to be working?" Meg asked her mother.

"Later," her mother said.

Meg put on a very stern frown. "Well—*all right*."

"Break a leg," her father said, then winced.

Meg, however, was amused. "Wouldn't *that* be a disaster." Then, she looked at her family, feeling sort of like she was going on a very long—and difficult—journey. "Well. See you later."

Steven looked up from patting Kirby. "Yo, we'll watch the Cubs game this afternoon."

"Sounds good," Meg said.

When she and Preston were in the elevator, she let out her breath. "Think my parents are really going to stay up there?"

He grinned. "Maybe."

"No one'll know they came downstairs, though, right?" she asked.

He shook his head.

Good. She looked at him for a minute. "You *don't* remind me of him."

He smiled at her. "I'm glad."

Feeling very nervous, she decided to check out his outfit. A slim-cut, chalk-striped dark grey suit, a light pink shirt with a matching pocket handkerchief, and his tie—silk-foulard—was *magenta*.

"I know," he said, seeing her expression. "You think the tie's a little much."

"Well, Jesus, Preston," she said. "You don't want to be a *fop*."

He laughed.

"I hope your socks aren't pink," she said.

He lifted his pants leg and she saw that they were grey. And his shoes were conservative wingtips.

"Well, *good*," she said.

They were downstairs now, a small squad of agents joining them as Preston pushed her wheelchair through the Ground Floor Corridor, towards the Palm Room, and out to the West Colonnade, heading for the Press Briefing Room.

She looked at the agents, trying to think of something pleasant to say. A way to break the tension. "What do you think," she asked one of them, "is his tie over the top?"

The agent laughed, but didn't—she noticed—answer.

"That means yes," she said to Preston.

As they headed down along the Colonnade, Meg started to find it hard to get her breath. There were people everywhere—mostly press and communications aides and assistants, and the best she could do was try to smile when they spoke to her.

Linda came out to meet them, looking intense—and anxious. As ever.

"Good," she said, sounding unreasonably relieved. "You're here. Are you all set?" she asked, turning away before Meg had a chance to answer. "Good. Good luck. I'll go open it up, Preston." She disappeared into the Briefing Room.

Preston grinned, resting his hands on her shoulders. "You're going to knock them silly, Meg."

She swallowed, regretting ever getting into this. She had practically never even *been* in the Briefing Room before, let alone up in front of everybody. "How many people are going to be in there?"

"Not as many as it'll look like," he said.

Meaning *a lot*. The entire White House press corps, she assumed. "An FBI guy'll be there, right?" she asked. "In case there's something I'm not supposed to answer?"

Preston nodded.

She wanted to reach up and move some hair over the scar on her forehead—but she didn't want to screw up the make-up or anything. "Are you ever nervous before you go in there?"

"Almost always," he said. "But, you *look* beautiful."

The sounds of conversation in the room had abruptly ceased, indicating that Linda was behind the podium, speaking to the press. It seemed much brighter, too, which meant that the television cameras were rolling, their lights on.

Oh, boy.

Preston smiled at her, a nice, encouraging smile. "Ready to go?"

Meg took a deep breath, and lifted herself up onto her crutch. "Yeah," she said. "I'm ready to go."